*Book 6
of the
Cornish Chronicles*

Our Days in the Sun

Ann E Brockbank

Copyright © Our Days in the Sun

by Ann E Brockbank

First published in Great Britain as a paperback in 2022

Copyright © 2022 Ann E Brockbank

The moral right of Ann E Brockbank to be identified as the author of this work has been asserted in accordance with the Copyright, Designs and Patents Act 1988

All rights reserved. No part of this publication may be reproduced, stored in a retrieval system or transmitted in any form or by any means, (electronic, mechanical, photocopying, recording or otherwise) without the prior written permission of the publisher. Any person who does any unauthorised act in relation to the publication may be liable to criminal prosecution and civil claims for damages.

Our Days in the Sun is a work of fiction. All incidents and dialogue, and all characters with the exception of some well-known historical and public figures, are products of the authors imagination and are not to be construed as real. Where real-life historical or public figures appear, the situations, incidents, and dialogues concerning those persons are entirely fictional and are not intended to depict actual events or to change the entirely fictional nature of the work. In all other respects, any resemblance to persons living or dead, events or locales is entirely coincidental.

Front cover by © R W Floyd, from an original oil painting

All rights reserved.

ISBN: 9798359585422

To Kim

for your incredible support.

By Ann E Brockbank

Cornish Chronicles

1. A Gift from the Sea - 1901 - 1902
2. Waiting for the Harvest Moon - 1907-1908
3. My Song of the Sea - 1911 -1912
4. The Path We Take - 1912
5. The Glittering Sea - 1912 – 1919
6. Our Days in the Sun – 1919

Historical Novels

Mr de Sousa's Legacy – 1939 – 1960

Contemporary Novels

The Blue Bay Café
On a Distant Shore

ACKNOWLEDGMENTS

My grateful thanks go to all you lovely people who buy and read my books. I so appreciate your continual support. You are all wonderful I'm enormously privileged that you believe in me and chose my books to read.

As always, I couldn't have written this book without the editorial help and support of some very special people. My upmost thanks go to Angie, for her historical guidance, reining in my creative spelling and for improving this book no end. You have no idea how much I appreciate your generous time, friendship, and expertise. Also, to Hazel, who helped me to polish this manuscript.

To Kim, a friend who continually champions my books so that they reach a larger audience. This book is dedicated to you.

To my partner, Rob, for every single wonderful thing you do, your love and encouragement has kept me writing, and as always, your beautiful artwork adds a special quality to my novels.

To the amazing staff at Poldhu Café - Thank you for your continued support.

To my darling late husband, Peter, who encourage me to write, you are forever in my heart.

My heartfelt gratitude goes to Sarah and Martin Caton and their lovely family for allowing me to use their beautiful home Bochym Manor as a setting for my 'Cornish Chronicles' novels

If you enjoy this book, please can I ask a huge favour from you to leave a review on Amazon? You can do this even if you did not buy the book on Amazon! I cannot tell you how important reviews are to authors. If you loved this book, please spread the love, and tell your friends, hopefully they too will support me by buying the book.

ABOUT THE AUTHOR

Ann E Brockbank was born in Yorkshire but has lived in Cornwall for many years. Our Days in the Sun is Ann's ninth book and the sixth Cornish Chronicles book. Ann lives with her artist partner on the beautiful banks of the Helford River in Cornwall - an integral setting for all of her novels. Ann is currently writing her ninth novel. Ann loves to chat with her readers so please visit her Facebook Author page and follow her on Twitter and Instagram

Facebook: @AnnEBrockbank.Author
Twitter: @AnnEBrockbank1
Instagram: annebrockbank

Our Days in the Sun

1
Bochym Manor, Cury, Cornwall
Friday 11th July 1919

The gardens of Bochym Manor were shrouded in mist - though the sun was slowly beginning to burn it away. In a field adjoining the manicured front garden where the parterre led towards the flower borders, a lone female figure, dressed in black, walked quickly through the long grass - knee deep in wild flowers. The dew saturated her skirt and began to seep through her shoes to soak her black stockings - she knew the discomfort would be short lived. Reaching the wall which bordered the garden, her trembling fingers reached out to her favourite flower, the beautiful, but deadly foxglove. Bees loved these brightly coloured flowers as much as she did – their pink and purple tube-like flowers - dark spotted at the lip - were an important source of pollen for them and this morning they were incredibly important to her too. Casting her tear-filled eyes skywards, she whispered, 'I'm coming to you, Thomas,' as she pushed a handful of the bitter tasting flowers into her mouth.

*

The clock in the great corridor at Bochym Manor chimed half past five, the household staff were waking, so too was Ruby Devereux– a legacy from her days when she worked here as the housekeeper. After stretching languidly, Justin, her husband of almost seven years, reached out to pull her back under the covers, covering her face with soft, sleepy, morning kisses.

Theirs had been an unusual love story. Artist Justin Devereux had come to visit his sister Sarah Dunstan - Countess de Bochym and mistress of this fine manor - from his home in Italy. In his own words, he had been captivated from the moment he set eyes on Ruby, as she had been with him. It was a love story that crossed the barriers of social class, and one that proved to be as enduring as any great love story could be. After the initial shock of their relationship when it became known - they had married on New Year's Eve in 1912, with the love and approval of both the Earl and Countess de Bochym, the deep disapproval of Justin's father, but with the blessing of Justin's mother. Their married life thereafter was to have been spent in a villa in the small village of Pedona in the Tuscan hills - or so they thought. No one had envisaged that a war would rip through their lives.

Justin's breathing deepened as he fell back into sleep, his blond hair flopped over his face, and Ruby smiled with love for him - he was as handsome asleep as he was awake. Very gently she uncoupled herself from his embrace, got up, slipped on her housecoat, and stood at the window to watch the pale morning sun filter through the ribbons of mist across the gardens.

At the gates to the garden, she saw her brother-in-law, the Earl, Peter Dunstan, speaking with Mr Pearson the estate manager - possibly busy arranging to put the fields of the estate back to its pre-war status. While the rest of the estate had been turned over to grow food for the war effort, Ruby's sister-in-law Sarah had vehemently held onto her flower borders - insisting that flowers were a necessary therapy for the soldiers who had come to recuperate at the manor after being injured in the war. Ruby's curiosity was piqued as the men turned to greet another man – a stranger had come from the direction of the house and was now walking down the front path to meet with Peter. Peter must have known him as friendly banter was exchanged, then the man, who Ruby still could not recognise, shook hands with both Peter and the estate manager before heading down towards the front garden.

She watched as he walked slowly through the beautiful garden, now flooded with sunshine, and thought of her own small garden back at the villa in Italy. It was full of exotic plants that even Sarah would be unable to nurture. Ruby missed her life in Tuscany. Some thought she would not take to the heat and slower lifestyle out there, but Ruby had thrived. She and Justin lived and worked in pure harmony, eating warm bread and fresh food bursting with a flavour only hot sunshine could produce. In the evening, they would share a glass of wine, made from grapes grown from the vineyards that flanked the surrounding hillsides, and make love at night with the warm breeze billowing the sheer curtains into the room. The mosquitoes had been the only downside, but the surrounding hills grew an abundance of lemons from which citronella oil was made. This oil was burned continually during the night, and she massaged it regularly into her pale English skin. Her lifestyle saw her cast away dark clothes and her constricting under stays, her wardrobe of clothes in Italy were white linen, loose and flowing to keep cool in the intense heat. Her auburn hair, which had always been pinned into a tight bun whilst she had been in service, had then been worn loosely piled atop her head to keep her cool - strands of which hung down to frame her tanned, healthy face. Justin always loved to brush his fingers against her cheek and tuck the strands behind her ears before kissing her – he really was heaven sent.

As a budding artist herself, the first thing Justin did when they arrived at the villa was to bring in the builders to convert the run-down outhouse into a light and airy studio, ideal for her to produce the large canvases she was so itching to work on. Being a hugely successful artist himself, Justin had introduced her to some galleries in Italy and her work had just begun to sell when war broke out. Thankfully, at forty-two, Justin was considered too old to fight at first – not that he had any desire to, having just settled into married life there, but when Europe had begun to feel unstable, they very reluctantly returned to Bochym Manor in the summer of 1915.

Her Bochym family had welcomed them back with such warmth that this difficult transition had been bearable. Ruby's concern that the housekeeper, Molly

Johnson, who had taken over from her, would feel uncomfortable with her return, were unfounded as she too welcomed her, and they had become firm friends during the last four years. Molly had been particularly grateful for Ruby's organisational skills, especially when in 1916, part of the manor had been turned over for convalescing servicemen wounded in the war.

The war as it progressed began to take its toll on the male staff at Bochym. Thomas Ellis, the footman, had been ready and willing to join up immediately - as did many of the younger men working on the estate. Peter Dunstan had taken up his officer's commission as soon as war broke out, and to the relief of Lowenna Trevail, Sarah's lady's maid, Peter had not taken his valet, Theo, Lowenna's husband, with him to war. Lowenna had just had their second baby and Peter did not want to part them, but when conscription for married men aged 18 to 41 came into force in May 1916, everything changed.

Ruby's long-time friend and colleague, Joe Treen the butler at the manor, was torn from his wife Juliet, as was Theo from Lowenna. Both though returned within the year with wounds which saw the end of their war. Ruby would never forget the dismay she felt seeing the wounds on these gentle, kind men, with whom she had worked for so many years. Then the unthinkable happened. Justin, who thought himself too old, was called up in the latter months of the war. Ruby was not a religious woman, but she prayed to someone up high, and her prayers were answered, because thankfully Justin came back to her in one piece.

Ruby turned and smiled again at Justin, snoring gently in their bed. Now the war was over and the last of the rehabilitated soldiers had left them, they would soon return to Italy and their life there would resume, but she was painfully aware and saddened for those brave soldiers who did not get a chance to return home.

After washing and dressing in a serviceable plain, dark dress, she pinned her hair up, and by habit came down the stairs to see if she could help with anything. As she approached the kitchen, she met with Peter as he entered the side door.

'Morning, Ruby.' He kissed her on the cheek. 'I see you are up and about bright and early as always.'

Even now, seven years since her marriage to Justin, it still made Ruby smile when the Earl greeted his former housekeeper so affectionately. 'Yes, I see you are out and about early too.'

'Well, as you know we are going up to London this morning, so Pearson and I have been inspecting the hedges first thing. I am thinking of getting that master hedger here, Lyndon FitzSimmons - do you remember him?'

'I do - I seem to remember he made quite an impression on the younger maids when he was here last. Gosh that must be seven years ago!'

'Well, that should make the maids happy then.'

'Yes.' Ruby mused – *All but one, perhaps.*

'Matthew Bickford tells me Lyndon's normal work has dried up while he's been away fighting, so, I'd like to do something to help him find his feet again.'

'I am sure we shall all look forward to welcoming him back then.'

'Incidentally, we have also had a gentleman here, who very kindly came early today to assess the damage in the French drawing room. His name is Gabriel Trelease – a fine sculptor by all accounts - along with being a renowned restorer of fine plasterwork. He is normally based in London, but he is spending time down in Cornwall after being recently widowed.'

'Oh, dear, that is terrible. I'm sorry for him.'

Peter nodded sadly. 'I think it will do him good to be occupied.'

'Well, there is nowhere nicer to recuperate than here. When will he start work?'

'He is having a walk around the garden at the moment and then I've told him to come and make himself known to Treen, so that he can properly assess the work in the drawing room.'

A delicate waft of expensive perfume preceded Sarah as she descended the stairs ready for their departure. 'Good morning, Ruby,' she kissed her lightly on the cheek. 'Peter, darling, the chauffeur is waiting.'

'I am coming. I will tell Treen on the way out about Mr Trelease, Ruby. We must go now, or we'll miss the London train.'

'Of course. Have a good trip both of you,' Ruby smiled, 'I'll come to see you off.'

As the car drove off, and they closed the front door, Ruby and Joe were suddenly aware of a terrible kerfuffle going on in the kitchen.

'Mrs Blair, what on earth is the matter?' Joe frowned at the cook as he entered the kitchen.

'It's Mary, I still can't find the girl. She was nowhere to be found when I was making His Lord and Her Ladyships breakfast. It's not like her to shirk her duties, but Lucy here says she's gone out! I mean where could she have gone to when the rest of the breakfast needs preparing?'

Joe looked questioningly at the maid Lucy Hocking.

'I think she's gone to pick flowers, Mr Treen,' Lucy answered. 'She was going on and on last night about flowers being the answer.'

Joe tipped his head. 'To what?'

'I don't know, something has really upset her recently – I don't think she is coping very well - especially with what happened to Thomas.'

Joe's heart caught at the mention of Thomas – he had been in the trenches with him that day and had witnessed his death. It was hard for all of them to understand that that was how he had met his end. Thomas, who had been the first to join up, was as brave and fearless as any man Joe had ever known. He had fought many battles and should have come home with the rest of his mates but for that terrible incident that was to end his life so inappropriately. He shook the thoughts from his head. Poor Mary had taken his death extremely hard.

Joe cleared his throat. 'Was it any particular flowers Mary was looking for?' he asked for he was knowledgeable about most flowers.

'Foxgloves, I think.'

'Mrs Blair dropped the spoon she was stirring the porridge with and glanced ashen faced at Joe.'

At that very moment, the gentleman Ruby had seen earlier with the Earl, came running across the kitchen courtyard carrying someone. He burst through the open kitchen door, panting, and sweating profusely.

'I've just found this young woman in the meadow,' the man said frantically, 'she's dreadfully ill.'

Juliet, Joe's wife - the senior house maid - appeared from the housekeeper's room after collecting the rotas and stepped into the commotion of the kitchen. Seeing Joe rush to relieve the stranger of his burden, Juliet cleared the kitchen table with the sweep of her hand so they could lay Mary down.

'Oh, god, Mary! What have you done, you silly thing?' Joe panicked as he laid her limp body on the table. Her face was covered in pink vomit and her dress was soaked in dew and by the smell of it, urine.

The gentleman who had brought her in, raked his fingers through his blonde hair. 'I've lifted her eyelids, and her pupils are tiny, she also has a very slow pulse,' he said fearfully.

'Phone the doctor, Ruby, quick. Mrs Blair, fetch a jug of salt water please,' Joe ordered.

Molly Johnson the housekeeper, clasped her hands to her face. 'Surely she needs to go to hospital, Joe,' she said dropping all formality.

'No, no hospital!' Joe shouted, his eyes darting first towards the man who had brought Mary in and then to David the footman. 'David, help me upstairs with Mary. Juliet, come with me, bring a bowl and the salty water.'

Ruby returned to the kitchen after phoning the doctor to find the man still standing in the kitchen. She held out a hand for him to shake.

'Mr Trelease, I believe - you came to see the Earl earlier. I understand you will be working here.'

'I will yes,' he said shaking her hand.

'Well, thank you for what you did today. Can we…perhaps… get you some refreshments?' Ruby glanced at Mrs Blair to make tea but she could see the cook was ashen faced and too flustered.

Gabriel must have realised his presence in the kitchen was fast becoming unwelcome at this difficult time, because he answered, 'No, thank you. I shall not bother you further. I was meant to introduce myself to the butler, Mr Treen, but I can see that this is not a suitable time. Perhaps now you know who I am, may I be allowed to go back to the French drawing room to assess the work further?'

'Of course,' Ruby said,' follow me.'

After she took him to the room, Gabriel turned to Ruby. 'I hope the young lady pulls through.'

Ruby felt her bottom lip tremble as she nodded.

He smiled gently. 'I do understand what has happened here today, but you have my word that it will go no further.'

'Thank you, Mr Trelease,' Ruby said tremulously, 'we would appreciate that.'

2

When the doctor arrived at Bochym, Joe took him straight to Mary's room, where Molly was administering the salt water. Juliet was holding Mary's long, dark hair back while she vomited.

Downstairs Ruby was helping Mrs Blair make the breakfast for the staff.

'Will you and Mr Justin want breakfast in the library, Ruby,' Mrs Blair asked, holding aloft a wooden spoon with which she had been stirring the scrambled eggs.

'No thank you, I will make up a tray for us and we'll eat upstairs. It will save anyone the bother, and then after breakfast, I will take over from Molly and Juliet once the doctor has gone. I will suggest to Molly that Juliet helps you with the dinner.'

Mrs Blair gave her a grateful smile and returned to her cooking.

When the other members of staff filtered in for breakfast, they flopped down at the table - the incident with Mary had shocked everyone. Few of them had any appetite as they waited for news from upstairs, but as Ruby and Mrs Blair had made breakfast, they all felt obliged to eat something.

'What I can't understand, is why, why now, three years since Thomas died?' Joe said taking his place at the head of the table.

'Grief like this affects people in different ways,' Ruby suggested.

'No, it's more than that,' Lucy the maid interjected. 'I've been thinking about it, and her spirits have plummeted since she received that letter recently.'

'What letter is that?' Ruby and Joe said in unison.

'From the commemorative plaque committee. She wrote to them after seeing the list of men who were going to be commemorated on the plaque about to be erected in Cury. Thomas's name was missing from it.'

'Oh, dear!' Joe breathed. Everyone around the table knew why Thomas had been missed off. Joe cleared his throat. 'This is indeed a terrible day and I need to reiterate that not a single word of what has happened here today must pass from anyone's lips beyond these four walls. Do I make myself clear?'

'Yes, Mr Treen.'

'Attempted suicide is a criminal offence. Dr Martin is putting his reputation on the line to save Mary from jail, remember that!' he added gravely.

*

Ruby prepared a breakfast tray for herself and Justin and took it upstairs, but she found Justin, not in bed where she left him, but ensconced in the attic, packing things ready to be shipped over to Italy. They had both managed to produce canvases of work - in between reading to the convalescing service men unfortunate enough to be blinded, and giving painting lessons to the ones who still had limbs to hold a paintbrush.

'My goodness, Ruby but you were heaven sent the day I met you, 'Justin said, pinching a piece of toast from the tray. You seem to know exactly when my stomach begins to rumble.' He kissed her lovingly on the lips, took the tray from her and placed it on the table at the far end of the attic where the window overlooked the front garden. When they sat down, a frown creased his brow. 'Whatever is the matter, my love, you look pained.'

'Oh, Justin. The very worst thing has just happened,' and proceeded to tell him about Mary and the letter as they ate breakfast.

Justin was angered. 'That poor girl. I thought her heart was beginning to heal at last. My god, who are these people who pass judgment when they do not know the facts. From what I understand the commemorative plaque committee is made up of one elderly man and five women, none of whom who have ever experienced the filth and horror of being knee deep in mud and faeces.'

'Oh god, Justin, I just hope Mary pulls through.'

'Do Sarah and Peter know what happened?'

'No, they left for London shortly before Mary was brought in. Oh goodness. What are we going to do about Mary if she does pull through this? Is she going to try it again?'

'I suspect not,' Justin answered. 'More pressingly, will Sarah and Peter keep her on at the manor? If this gets out, there would be a terrible scandal.'

Ruby took a deep breath. 'Well, I for one will fight Mary's cause for her.'

Justin's eyes creased as he smiled. 'You two have always had a special relationship, haven't you?'

'Yes. Mary is the daughter I never had,' she said sadly.

Justin reached out to cup her hand in solidarity – they had hoped for children of their own but had not been blessed.

'Mary was so young when she came to the manor. Orphaned at ten years old and put into service - the same fate I had endured when I came here to work. The poor child arrived at the manor, wide eyed and trembling with fear, all I could do was wrap my arms around her and tell her she was safe now and everyone here was her family. It was wonderful to see her flourish in the kitchen with Mrs Blair. I feel sad that she didn't come to me when things so obviously had got on top of her.'

'Who did you say found Mary?' Justin asked, dabbing his mouth with his napkin.

'Gabriel Trelease. Peter has employed him to restore the damaged plasterwork in the French drawing room to its former glory. He's in there now assessing everything.'

Justin rubbed his chin thoughtfully. 'Gabriel Trelease - I know that name.'

Ruby nodded. 'I understand from Peter that Gabriel is also a sculptor.'

'Of course, that sculpture on the terrace at the villa was one of his – if it's still there,' he added. 'I might take my cup of coffee downstairs and introduce myself to him if you don't mind.'

'No, I'm probably needed in the kitchen, now Cook is without her assistant.'

'You're always busy, aren't you?' He grinned. 'How are you going to settle back into the slower life in Italy when we return,' he joked.

'I think I'll manage. Besides, we will be hosting guests in September when Matthew Bickford and his soon-to-be wife Hillary come to see us. I will have four years of dust to sweep out of the villa before they come. I must say, I am looking forward to their wedding at Trevarno – I've never attended a society wedding before.'

Justin grinned widely. 'I have no doubt that if Hillary Stanton has anything to do with it – it will be a lavish occasion. Now, one more kiss from my beautiful and very wonderful wife, and I will go and seek out Gabriel.'

Their kiss was warm and tender, and they laughed together, joyous that life after this dreadful war had slipped back into normality.

*

After the rushed assessment as to whether he could repair the damage in the drawing room before the Earl had set off to London, Gabriel Trelease was now taking his time to make a proper assessment of the once beautiful room. The constant moving of iron bedsteads while the room had housed the convalescing serviceman, had certainly taken its toll. It was nothing he could not put right though. He turned when Justin entered the room and recognised him immediately.

'Justin Devereux!' Gabriel extended his hand to him. 'I'm honoured to meet you. Not only am I working in a great house, but with great company now.'

'You flatter me.' Justin shook his hand.

'With good reason. I have three of your paintings hanging in my London residence.'

'Now, it is *I* who is honoured. Thank you. I too know of you, and would you believe I have one of your sculptures in my villa in Tuscany – well, I did have before the war – not sure if it will still be there now.'

'Happy to do another one for you, if need be.' Gabriel winked.

'So, I understand you are a restorer of plasterwork as well.'

'Yes. It is my other passion.'

'You have your work cut out here,' Justin said walking around the room.

'It is nothing I can't put right.'

'What brought you to Cornwall, I thought you had a studio in London?'

'I do. I was widowed last year and left with a six-year-old son to raise. Also, the Influenza, which took my darling wife from me last year, was rife in London, so we came down here to stay with my parents in March.'

'I'm so sorry for your loss, my friend,' Justin put his hand on Gabriel's shoulder. 'It must be very difficult for you.'

'It is, especially for my son, but we feel better being down here. Cornwall has a soothing calm about it, and my parents have been helping me.'

'Well, it is good to have you here, and nice to have another kindred spirit in the house. I shall leave you to your work. Ruby, my wife, will have instructed the kitchen that you are here, so feel free to go there should you need refreshments.'

*

Three miles away at Poldhu Cove, the Blackwell family were preparing for the day's work. Thatcher, Guy Blackthorn, and his co-workers - his daughter Agnes, Jake Treen and Ryan Penrose - were loading up their newly purchased motor vehicle and trailer, after Guy had finally succumbed to buying one. His trusty horse had been put out to grass, and if truth be known, and Guy would not admit this to anyone, the new motor vehicle had transformed their life. They could travel distances more quickly now, so could thatch further afield and still be home for teatime!

While Guy was preparing for his day, so too were his wife Ellie and her assistant, Betsy Penrose, in The Poldhu Tea Rooms. Before they opened, they were about to interview a young local woman, Marianne Enys for the position of waitress.

*

Marianne Enys walked along the coast road from Polurrian until Poldhu Cove came into sight. Standing at the foot of the magnificent Poldhu Hotel which held a prominent cliff top position above the cove, Marianne felt a real affinity to this place. She was a foundling baby, left here on 27th of September 1902, at the laundry door. Susan Enys had been a chamber maid at the hotel at that time and had discovered Marianne that morning wrapped in an exquisite and clearly expensive silk lace shawl. By the time the police and doctor arrived, the latter declaring that the child was only hours old, Susan, had formed a fierce bond with the baby she had been cradling. Susan and her husband Robert had not been blessed with a child of their own, so after an extensive and fruitless search for her birth mother, Susan and Robert were allowed to adopt Marianne - they called her their gift from God.

There was no doubt about it - Marianne had had a happy life with her adopted parents, and was undoubtedly loved, but the fact she had been found in the beautiful silk lace shawl, suggested to Marianne that her birth mother had been from a well-heeled family. She envisaged that her mother was the beautiful daughter of a Lord who had fallen foul of a young, handsome gentleman. Marianne surmised that her mother must have concealed her pregnancy, checked in to the magnificent Poldhu Hotel near her time, given birth and left her there for some kind soul to take her in. Marianne was seventeen now and extremely attractive. Standing five-foot-five in her stocking feet, she had large brown eyes and long, dark, glossy curls, which brought her many admirers. Convinced though that she had come from gentry, Marianne was secretly holding out for someone with a little more class than the local lads hereabouts.

Standing on the cliff, she looked down at The Poldhu Tea Room, a place she had visited many occasions on her days off from her previous employment. Marianne had no qualms about her ability to do the job – in fact, she was probably too qualified for it! She was good with numbers and people, and had excelled in school, well, as far as the teaching extended for girls. She had absorbed everything her teacher had taught her, and since leaving at fourteen, had managed to further her studies, having the good fortune to be employed as a companion to Lady Martha Jefferson - a fine lady who lived in a beautiful house in Mullion. Lady Martha had an extensive collection of books in her library and had encouraged Marianne to read to her as much as possible. Lady Martha had taught her French, in which she excelled, and allowed her to have lessons on the piano forte - in which she did not excel, still, she couldn't be brilliant at everything, could she? Unfortunately, Lady Martha had finally succumbed to the plates of sweetmeats she devoured every day and had suffered a heart-attack in May, dying instantly. The family no longer needed Marianne's services hence she needed another job.

There were worst places to work she supposed, and she would undoubtedly get the job. Occasionally she had cleared tables for Ellie and Betsy when times became busy, so she knew her way around the kitchen, which would stand her in good stead at the interview. It also helped that she knew the owner Ellie Blackthorn very well. Marianne's aunt, Helen Bray, had looked after Ellie and Guy's three children while they had been at school. Agnes was seventeen now though and had followed her father into the thatching business, and Zack, at sixteen, was an apprentice cabinet maker in Gweek. Helen still minded their youngest Sophie, along with Betsy and Ryan Penrose's first born, Josephine, or Josie as everyone called her.

It was Betsy's position Marianne was being interviewed for. Betsy was in her seventh month of pregnancy with her second baby and although fit and healthy, her husband wanted her to work less hours so as not to tire herself out. This meant it was only going to be a temporary job for Marianne, for she knew Betsy would return to work after the birth and had no doubt her Aunt Helen would be asked to take on this new baby as well. Betsy and Ryan, it seemed, had a modern type of marriage in Marianne's eyes - it certainly would not do for her! Marianne planned to marry well, travel and live the life of luxury. The books she had read whilst being in Lady Martha's employment made her want to see more of life now. They made her want to travel to the faraway places the stories took her too. One of her favourite authors was James Blackwell. She had heard that he too had recently died. He had travelled extensively and written stories about the places he had visited, and Marianne had the pleasure of meeting him once at the tearoom. She had approached him boldly to tell him how much she enjoyed his novels and he, ever courteous, had invited her to take a seat. They had spoken at length about the places he wrote about. When they finally parted that day, he had lifted her hand, kissed it gently and said to her, 'If you want something strong enough, you can make it happen.' His words resonated with her and that was what she was going to do. More than anything, she wanted to meet someone who could take her on these travels, and Poldhu Tea Rooms had their fair share of genteel clientele. Somewhere amongst those gentlemen would be her future husband. With a confident smile she set off down the coast path determined to make the best impression she could.

*

Half an hour later, Marianne Enys left the tearoom fizzing with elation! She had just secured a temporary position of waitress there. Everything was fitting nicely into place she thought, as she walked up the road to her home in Mullion. She would start work the next day – working alongside Betsy until she picked the job up - something she knew she would do very quickly. If she could prove herself to be a good worker, and make herself indispensable to Ellie, maybe she would be kept on part time after Betsy came back – well, certainly until she had found her future husband amongst the gentlemen customers!

*

Ellie and Betsy watched through the tearoom windows as Marianne skipped away over the dunes. They turned and smiled at each other.

'I think we've made someone's day today,' Ellie laughed.

Betsy stretched her aching back out. 'I think someone else will be very happy that you have employed her too.'

'Oh, who?'

'My Ryan says Jake Treen has completely lost his heart to Marianne, but she seems not have noticed him yet. Maybe we should do a little bit of matchmaking?'

Ellie beamed a smile. 'Maybe we should.'

3

The doctor had gone, only Ruby sat in vigil with Mary now, allowing Juliet and Molly to get on with their day's work. Normally anyone who had been accidently poisoned would have been taken to hospital where they could be treated, but this was no accident judging by the amount of foxgloves Mary had ingested. No one accidently eats something like that - so it was clear she had tried to take her own life. To take one's own life was a sin, and a crime, and Mary would be imprisoned if she pulled through and word got out. Fortunately, Dr Martin knew of Mary's predicament - he had attended her several times for bouts of morbid melancholia over the last three years – the household were confident that he would keep this a secret.

Ruby tipped her head, observing Mary with great sadness. Poor Mary, she had been in love with Thomas for years, but Thomas, teased and flirted with all the maids, but had never been in any hurry to marry any of them. When war broke out, he, like so many other men, saw the opportunity to do something exciting and joined up immediately and Mary had been naturally distraught. Undeterred by his reluctance to commit, Mary wrote to him every week telling stories of life back at Bochym and to everyone's surprise, no less than Mary's, he eventually wrote back to her with equal regularity. The Thomas who came home on leave in January 1916 was world-weary. The jack-the-lad attitude was no longer evident and the first thing he did, to Mary's delight, was to marry her. She found out, soon after he returned to the front that she was having his baby and though dreadfully worried about him, she bloomed with happiness. Six months later, he was dead, under the most shocking circumstances. Mary miscarried her baby, a little boy, two weeks later and had grieved for them both since.

Mary shifted uncomfortably as she curled herself into a ball. A low, raw, rasping noise reverberated from her throat which made Ruby grimace. The vomiting had ceased, but her body was wracked with a tremor so intense the bed shook. Ruby watched as Mary's stomach convulsed again, only to now bring up a foul-smelling belch. Periodically, Mary soiled and wet the large napkin she was wearing, and Ruby had to wash her down. Occasionally she would open her eyes to allow great fat tears to escape silently down her tragic face. The poor girl looked wretched and broken, and Ruby feared she was beyond repair. Holding her bony fingers, Ruby's eyes swept over Mary's emaciated body – the thin muslin nightdress unable to hide the protruding bones that her black uniform had so evidently done. Since Thomas's tragic demise, everyone had watched with despair, as she picked at her food and the flesh slowly fell from her once pretty face, leaving her cheeks hollow with grief. There was little anyone could do, although she valiantly continued to work as the cook's assistant, albeit in relative silence. Day by day though she plunged ever deeper into herself. There was no measure stick for grief – it takes as long as it takes – sometimes one never recovered - Queen Victoria for example had never got over the loss of Prince Albert.

Stroking her fevered brow, Ruby murmured quiet, calming sounds to settle her. 'Come on, Mary, come brave – we all love you,' she whispered.

*

There had been nobody at home for Marianne to tell her good news to, as her mother and father had been out at work, so at midday she caught the omnibus from Mullion to Cury Cross Roads. Her good friend Lucy Hocking – a maid at Bochym was due a Friday afternoon off today, so she decided to go and share her good news with her.

The Bochym kitchen door was open with the weather being so warm and when Marianne walked through the door, Mrs Blair was flicking her teacloth at the cat who had tried to steal food from the work tops.

'Oh, lordy me, we are all at sixes and sevens today, Marianne. Lucy won't be taking her afternoon off I am afraid.'

'Gracious, Mrs Blair, whatever has happened?'

'It's Mary …'

Marianne tipped her head waiting to hear more.

'Mary is very ill!' Molly Johnson the housekeeper said breezing into the kitchen on hearing Marianne's voice. 'Something she ate.'

'Goodness, that sounds worrying – is it serious?'

'The doctor has been and will return later today, so we will know better then, but It means Lucy is needed here today, in the kitchen with Mrs Blair, when she finishes her other chores – she will have to have her day off another time. You may as well go home - everyone is terribly busy.'

'I fully understand. Is there anything I can do? I'm at a bit of a loose end now,' Marianne offered.

'You can peel these potatoes if you want,' Mrs Blair muttered.

'I'm sure we'll manage, Mrs Blair,' Molly said firmly.

Marianne saw Cook's shoulders sink. 'No, really, I'll help,' she said putting her bag down. 'Just give me an apron.'

Molly bit down on her lip. 'Well, if, you're sure,' she said, but before she had finished speaking, Marianne was peeling the first of many potatoes.

*

With Marianne's help, the pressure on the household staff eased considerably, so that they were all able to have their usual couple of hours off in the afternoon. Ruby was still sitting with Mary when the doctor had returned to see how she was fairing and everyone downstairs was on tenterhooks as to whether Mary would survive.

Molly, having first discussed it with Joe, had decided to tell Marianne that Mary had been out picking mushrooms that morning and had mistakenly picked and cooked a poisonous one, only finding out her mistake when she tasted the mushrooms.

'Gosh!' Marianne was aghast at Mary's stupidity. 'It was lucky she didn't poison the whole household then!'

Molly had nodded but had to turn away quickly before Marianne had seen the guilt on her face from telling a barefaced lie.

When footsteps approached from the hall, everyone looked up thinking it was the doctor, but it was Gabriel Trelease who walked into the kitchen.

Joe stood to welcome him. 'Hello, Mr Trelease. Can I get you anything?'

'Sorry to intrude, Mr Treen, but I'm almost finished in the drawing room. I am in dire need of a cup of tea and was told I could find one here.'

'Of course, do come in,' Joe beckoned him. 'Everyone, this is Mr Gabriel Trelease whom I told you about. Mr Trelease has very kindly undertaken the task of restoring the plasterwork in the French drawing room and, I might add, he is a famous sculptor – I am sure he won't mind me saying that.'

Gabriel smiled, nodded, and sat down in the seat Joe showed him to as Mrs Blair put down a cup and saucer and a pot of brewing tea in front of him. The mood of the room lifted at the arrival of this handsome stranger and Lucy, Dorothy, and Marianne could hardly keep the interest from their eyes.

'How is the young maid who was sickly?' Gabriel asked. Joe had already given him an update, so he knew not to say anything too much about her, especially as he knew they had a young woman helping in the kitchen from outside the household.

'The doctor is with her now. We'll know more soon,' Joe answered with a tight smile.

To keep the mood lifted, Molly said, 'Can I just say a big thank you to Marianne for stepping into the breach this afternoon while Mary is sick. Mrs Blair said you have been a godsend in the kitchen.'

Marianne smiled warmly. 'You're very welcome. I'm glad I could help.'

'Mary may not be fit to return to work for days. If Mr Treen agrees and you would like some extra work, I am sure Her Ladyship would not mind if I gave you a couple of hours work, Marianne,' Molly said hopefully.

'Oh, I would normally, Mrs Johnson, but I've just secured a job at The Poldhu Tea Room – I start tomorrow.'

Lucy turned, whooped with joy, and hugged her friend. 'Well done, Marianne, I knew you would get it.'

'Well, that is some good news today,' Joe said. 'So, you'll be working with our Betsy.'

Everyone smiled at this comment. Betsy had left the manor seven years ago to marry Ryan Penrose and assume her position at the tearoom, but she was always thought of still as one of the Bochym staff family.

'I will be for a couple of days, yes and then Betsy is taking time off before her baby is due. I am only there temporarily until Betsy comes back after the baby is born.'

'Gosh, you modern girls, having babies and going back to work,' Mrs Blair declared as she brought more cups and saucers to the table.

Marianne smiled in agreement. 'Betsy loves her job, and I suppose the money comes in handy too. Of course, she knows her children are safe with my Aunt Helen,' she added.

'Still, it was never like that in my day,' Mrs Blair muttered, clearly not agreeing with these modern ways.

'I visit the tearoom most Sundays with my little son,' Gabriel said with a smile, 'so, I shall probably see you there.'

Marianne turned and melted a smile at him, delighted at the prospect of seeing more of this handsome stranger – even though he was obviously married if he had a son. The rest of the staff had been briefed about Gabriel being left a widower with a small son, but Marianne of course knew nothing of his circumstances. 'How lovely,' she said, 'I will get to meet your wife and son then.'

Joe cleared his throat. 'I do apologise, Mr Trelease, Marianne does not work here normally, therefore knows nothing of your unfortunate circumstances.'

Marianne turned questioningly to Joe, feeling a blush rise, realising she had made something of a terrible faux pas.

'No matter,' Gabriel said with a gentle smile, 'I am afraid my wife died last year, from the Spanish flu, Marianne.'

Willing the ground to open and swallow her whole, Marianne answered, 'I am so dreadfully sorry, Mr Trelease, forgive my insensitive assumption.'

'Please, do not feel bad - you were not to know.' He smiled again at her, drained his cup, and stood up. 'I thank you for the tea, Mrs Blair and for everyone's company, around this table.'

'When will you start work proper on the French drawing room?' Joe asked.

'Soon. I have just been calculating the amount of plaster I need. It's a special kind of fine gypsum plaster, so I will have to source it. I believe the nearest place to here is Barrow-upon-Soar in Leicestershire. I will have them put it on the train to Helston. Do we by any chance have a wagon that could be sent to collect it from there?'

Joe nodded. 'We do. Just let me know when it's coming.'

'Will Mr Trelease be eating with us, Mr Treen?' Cook enquired.

Joe turned to Gabriel, who nodded. 'I shall take midday dinner with you, if that is all right, but I like to have supper with my son at home.'

Mrs Blair nodded amiably, and Gabriel took his leave of them.

'Oh, my goodness, how handsome was Mr Trelease?' Dorothy swooned. 'I think I've died and gone to heaven this week – especially as Ruby mentioned that the delectable Lyndon FitzSimmons is coming back to work here too.'

Lucy and Marianne giggled at this, but Joe gave them a warning look.

'Let's keep our relationship with these gentleman professional, Dorothy,' Joe said quietly.

'That won't find me a husband,' she muttered under her breath.

'*Dorothy*,' Molly cautioned.

'If you remember, Dorothy,' Joe reminded her, 'when Lyndon was here last, he was planning on getting married the following year, so I wouldn't get your hopes up.'

'Oh, yes, I remember now. Goodness, I am going to die an old maid,' she grumbled.

They all turned as footsteps could be heard descending the back staircase.

'That will be the doctor coming downstairs now,' Joe stood, 'I will just let him out.'

Everyone in the kitchen waited anxiously for Joe's return and when he did, he was smiling.

'Mary is still very sickly, but Dr Martin believes she's out of danger. She's been purged several times and he's given her an antidote to counteract the….' he glanced at Marianne, 'mushrooms. We will just have to wait and see how she fairs now.' He sat down and smiled when he saw everyone relax.

*

When Marianne took her leave of Bochym to go and tell her mother her good news – her mind was still on Gabriel. She wondered if he was in any way related to Mr and Mrs Trelease for whom her mother cleaned. They were wealthy and lived in Cove House, an impressive building overlooking Polurrian Cove not far from where Marianne's family lived in Mullion. But of course, he must be, they were gentry and he, although he was working for a living, was clearly a gentlemen. Come to think of it, her mother kept moaning at her that her workload had doubled since the Trelease's relatives had come to stay.

Although she had made that dreadful faux pas and had barely lifted her eyes to look at Gabriel again, there was no doubt about it - she had felt a thunder bolt run through her the moment he had walked into the kitchen. He was a truly handsome man, with his broad shoulders, strong arms, blonde hair, and kind open face. Marianne felt well and truly smitten with him and what is more, she would be able to see a little more of him, when he visited the tearoom. Marianne smiled to herself. With a rich gentleman in her reach, life was definitely looking up.

4
London
Friday 12th July 1919

Lyndon FitzSimmons had exhausted all his available relaxing techniques to try and calm his tremulous breathing as he negotiated the crowds walking along the streets of London. A master hedger by trade - a man who normally worked with nature, he felt desperately out of his depth in this metropolis. A wave of nausea engulfed him, and he closed his eyes momentarily, knowing an attack in his head was imminent. He faltered slightly, swaying a little, and began to take deep, measured breaths as the doctor had instructed. It had been eight months since the Great War ended, but Lyndon was still there – deep in the battlefields, knee deep in mud and faeces, constantly fighting the demons in his head.

The Spanish flu had finally dissipated, and the streets were crowded, even though it was early evening. Motorcar horns parped, sirens rang out and people shouted and cursed at each other. The noise and heat coupled with the stench of the open sewers all brought the hell of the trenches back to him.

Jenna, the love of his life, was on his arm, and she was acutely aware of his body trembling from the worried looks she was giving him.

'Are you well, Lyndon?' she asked.

He answered with a nod, which was totally in conflict to the constant internal struggle to keep his wits about him.

'You're as white as a sheet, are you sure?'

He nodded again.

'We should have got a cab,' Jenna muttered softly.

Lyndon remained silent, but thought, *I should never have agreed to come on this trip to London – this is not my world.*

He was here with Jenna to support her at her first major art exhibition in The Black Gallery on Bond Street, having travelled up from Cornwall on the Night Riviera train. He was hot and extremely uncomfortable – dressed to the nines. Jenna wore a dress by Jeanne Paquin - a leading French fashion designer who had opened The House of Paquin in London in 1897. Lyndon, for the moment, was dressed in clothes borrowed from his good friend Matthew Bickford's wardrobe until his own set of fine clothes, for which he was to be measured on Monday in Savile Row, had been made. This, along with many other things he was conflicted by, did not sit easy on Lyndon's conscious. Lyndon had not worked since the war ended, because he had been mistakenly reported dead following a mortar attack. In fact, he had suffered severe concussion to a point that for five months after the war finished, he knew not who he was. He had floundered in a military hospital in London until someone recognised him and alerted his family on the Trevarno Estate in Cornwall. It took a further month for the familiarity of his home to jog his memory so that he remembered who he was and how to work again. Because of this, he had no jobs on his books at home, therefore no money coming in to pay for such luxuries as new clothes. Jenna had dismissed his money worries – she was now the wealthy widow of the author James Blackwell, but Lyndon was a proud man, he did not want Jenna to buy him clothes – nor did he think he needed the wardrobe she had suggested. He was quite happy in borrowed clothes should the occasion call for them - which he hoped would not be too often.

It struck Lyndon that neither he nor Jenna vaguely resembled the two star-struck lovers who had met in a Cornish meadow in late summer 1912. Oh, but for those heady days in the sun before everything went so terribly wrong and they were torn apart. Without doubt the years had been unkind to them both. Lines formed by horrors at home and the separation of war were etched into their still relatively young faces, but a glimmer of hope for a future together had materialised three weeks ago. Lyndon had received a letter from James Blackwell - who had fallen seriously ill with emphysema only six weeks after marrying Jenna and had written it from his deathbed. The letter was ingrained in Lyndon's brain - to a point that he knew it off by heart – it read:

My friend,

I feel I have done you a great injustice and I very much want to make amends. I recently learnt from your friend Matthew Bickford, that the woman I married was romantically attached to you. I swear I knew nothing of your attachment when I married her.

The circumstances of our marriage were complicated. In February, my name was to be linked to a very public scandal and Jenna - remarkable woman that she is - pushed her own happiness aside to help me in my hour of need. I am telling you, Lyndon, that Jenna has been my wife in name only.

When I learned from Matthew that Jenna was the woman you loved, it grieved me deeply to think I had taken her from you. To think you waited so long and patiently for her, only for me to whisk her away from under your nose. I hope you will forgive me in time.

I admit, I should have released her from her commitment to me the moment I found out, but I thought perhaps you would grant me the luxury of keeping her until my end came. If you are reading this letter now, it will be because I have died.

I know Jenna is lonely, and someone as lovely and caring as she is, should not be alone. I plead to your good judgment and sensibilities to visit her. It is my dearest wish that now all obstacles are removed, that you will take your place by her side and be together forever. It will be the last fitting love story this author can hope for.

I leave her fate in your hands.

Your obedient servant

James Blackwell

So, Lyndon had duly gone to her and found her swimming in the sea which was glittering in the late afternoon sunshine at Church Cove, Gunwalloe. In the cool gentle waves of the Atlantic that day, he had taken her back into his arms in a hope that the years could peel away, and nothing would, or could ever, part them again. How wrong could he have been?

*

Jenna knew the signs - that unmistakeable tremble running through Lyndon's body as she linked arms with him. She had seen it before, years ago, when they had spent their one and only night together - the night before they had sent him back off to war after being injured and they feared they would never see each other again. One minute he had been laid in her arms in bed - then the next he was under the bed, head in his hands shouting for his rifle. It crossed her mind now that she should not have brought him with her to London.

'It's not far now,' she assured him with a smile as she squeezed his arm tighter. Then the unthinkable happened! The most appalling racket started up when a one-man-band crashed and clanged cymbals between his knees. The shock of the noise almost made Jenna jump out of her skin and then she realised Lyndon was no longer by her side. Momentarily disorientated, she frantically looked up and down the street for Lyndon, but he had gone.

The boom of the man's drum resonated down the street, making people sidestep him and his contraption, although one or two were throwing money into his cap. Desperate now as to what had happened to Lyndon, Jenna's eyes settled on a girl clutching a basket of flowers who had quickly emerged from a dark alleyway - though her attention was clearly focused on where she had just come from.

Jenna ran up to the girl. 'Have you seen a man come in here?'

The girl nodded her head in the direction of the alleyway and Jenna found Lyndon by a rubbish bin, curled into a ball, his hands covering his head, crying. When she touched him, he shrank back from her, and then he grabbed her and pulled her down to the ground.

'Keep your head down, *keep it down*!' Lyndon's hand pressed her head to the floor. 'My god where is everyone?' he shouted as he looked wildly around for his comrades.

Struggling to pull herself from under the weight of his hand, Jenna spoke gently, 'Lyndon, darling, it's me, Jenna. Everything is fine I promise, you're not under attack.' She touched him again – more gently this time. 'Come on, my love, come to my arms,' she encouraged him and very slowly he moved to her embrace, clutching her body as though his life depended on it. The minstrel's drum continued to boom, making him shudder with every strike. 'It's all right, my love,' she said as he wept openly in her arms - tears, and mucus awash on his face. 'Hush now, you're safe with me.' She cradled him, and though his body was shaking uncontrollably, his weeping eventually ceased. His clothes were drenched with sweat, and they were both soiled with urine and goodness knows what else which covered the ground of the stinking alleyway. Feeling him settle, it was time to try to make him stand.

Jenna had not seen the girl approach, but as she began to encourage Lyndon to his feet, the girl put down her basket of flowers and grasped Lyndon's other arm for which Jenna shot her an appreciative look.

'We need to hail a cab.'

The girl nodded and together they staggered with Lyndon from the alleyway. Jenna had stripped him of his soiled jacket to make him more presentable but could do nothing for the spoils of her dress. At the roadside, they hailed a cab, but twice the driver took one look at the state of Lyndon and drove off. When the next one came to a halt Jenna pleaded with him.

'Is he drunk?' the driver asked.

Jenna shook her head. 'Shellshock.'

'Oh, I see,' the driver nodded, 'I have suffered myself, though to a lesser extent than this chap I suspect. Hop in.'

They bundled him onto the seat, and Lyndon buried his head in his hands.

Both Jenna and the girl were soiled and damp now. 'If you wish to come with us, we can clean ourselves up. I live in Bellevue Gardens,' Jenna said to the girl.

The girl looked down at her stained frock and nodded. 'I'll just get my basket,' she said running back down the alleyway.

As they made the short journey home, Jenna held Lyndon in her arms, speaking soothing words to calm his troubled soul, all the while realising, he would be in no state now to accompany her to the exhibition.

*

The commotion of entering the hall at Bellevue Gardens brought Mrs Hemp the housekeeper, running towards them.

'Goodness, gracious, mercy me, Mrs Blackwell, whatever has happened to Mr Fitzsimmons?' Mrs Hemp fussed.

Lyndon broke free from their hold and made for the stairs but did not ascend them - he just sat on the second step clutching his head in his hands.

'Everything is fine now, Mrs Hemp,' Jenna said without explaining further. 'I wonder, could you be so kind as to help,' she looked at the young girl, 'I'm so sorry, I don't know your name.'

'Emily, Emily Hardy.'

Jenna smiled and nodded. 'If you could take Emily to the guest room and help clean her up. I'm afraid she's spoilt her lovely dress. She very kindly helped me when Mr FitzSimmons fell ill.'

Emily curled her lip in amusement. 'It's hardly lovely, missus,' she said pulling at her old dowdy dress.

Jenna smiled. 'Nevertheless, you soiled it assisting me.' Quickly assessing Emily's height. 'I'm sure I have something suitable to fit you. I'll just help Mr FitzSimmons up to his room and then I'll come and find something for you.'

'Does Mr FitzSimmons need a doctor?' Mrs Hemp asked anxiously.

'No, thank you. We had a long and tiring journey last night, and the hot weather today is not helping.'

'Aye, It can be rare stifling in London sometimes,' Mrs Hemp agreed as she and Emily squeezed past Lyndon to ascend the stairs.

*

Once alone, Lyndon gave a deep shuddering sigh and looked up at Jenna with bloodshot eyes. The shaking had thankfully stopped, and he felt recovered enough to get up and walk unaided up the stairs. Jenna, bless her, seemed to know when to help and when to leave him be, but it heartened him that she was following him closely.

When they had arrived together earlier that day, Mrs Hemp had shown Lyndon to James's old room, but Jenna assured him they would sleep together and tonight would be the night they would rekindle their love affair at last - the separate rooms were just for decency's sake due to Jenna's recent widowhood. So, it was James's old bedroom which Lyndon headed for. He knew now he would not be fit to go anywhere this evening - these episodes when they happened, drained him completely, leaving his head feeling as though it had been locked in a vice. He knew from experience that the residue headache would see him prostrate in a dark room for hours. First though, he needed to rid himself of his soiled suit, and took himself off behind the dressing screen to strip and swill the dirt from his hands, face, and hair. Wrapped in one of James's housecoats, he emerged from behind the dressing screen and sat dejectedly on the bed.

'I'm sorry but I need to lie down.'

'Of course,' Jenna answered pulling the sheets back for him to crawl in. When his head rested on the pillow, she placed her cool hand on his forehead.

'That feels nice, thank you,' he said closing his eyes. 'I'm sorry, Jenna.'

'There is nothing to be sorry about. This is not your fault.' She kissed him tenderly on his lips – they felt paper dry. 'How many times does this still happen?'

'Too many,' he murmured.

'I'll make you a cup of tea. Will a headache draft help?'

Lyndon shook his head, and groaned, immediately regretting the action. 'Tea will suffice. I just need to rest. I'm sorry though, I'll not be fit to accompany you to the exhibition.'

'No matter. Matthew and Hillary will be there to support me. You just rest my love.' She kissed him again, but he was too weary to respond.

5

Jenna quickly discarded her beautiful dress and hung it up for Mrs Hemp to work her magic on, and then stepped into the shower to wash away the alley filth. Selecting another dress to wear, she quickly tided her hair. Although terribly late now for her exhibition, she wanted to thank Emily for her help tonight - two more minutes would not harm.

Knocking softly on the door of the guest room, a timid voice beckoned Jenna in. Jenna found Emily wringing her hands nervously in the middle of the room in a spare dressing gown. Jenna smiled at her, opened the wardrobe door, and selected a pretty cotton dress, which she laid on the bed.

'There, I think this will fit?'

'Yes, missus, I think it will, but I can't wear it, it's too posh. I'll mucky it back on the street selling flowers.'

'It's fine, it is yours now if you want it. Take it as a thank you for helping me.'

'Ah, but everyone will think me all la-di-da and not buy from me if I wear it!'

Jenna stifled a laugh. 'Well, I should think Mrs Hemp will have washed your dress, so you can't put that back on yet. You're very welcome to stay until it is dry.'

'What, 'ere?'

'Yes, of course.' Jenna smiled.

'But it might take all night to dry, missus!'

'And you're welcome to stay all night.'

'Really?' Her eyes widened and glanced around her. 'But where will I sleep?'

Jenna glanced at the bed and frowned. 'Well, if I were you, I'd use the bed!'

This time Emily's mouth dropped at the prospect.

Jenna glanced at the clock – knowing she must leave soon, or her agent Francis Knight would be cross with her. 'I need to go out now, Emily. Go down to the kitchen and

Mrs Hemp will make you something to eat if you're hungry.'

Gasping in astonishment, she said, 'You're going to leave me 'ere? I could be a thief!' She clamped her mouth shut - clearly regretting her rash statement.

Jenna raised an eyebrow. 'Well, don't be. It would be a very rude thing to steal from someone who offers you help.'

'Oh, I'm not, missus, and I wouldn't,' she tried to appease. 'I was just,' she tipped her head, 'you're very trusting, aint you?'

'I am.' Jenna smiled. 'I'll see you in the morning, Emily, for I shall be late home.'

'Yes, missus,' she answered sheepishly.

Jenna stopped and investigated the contents of Emily's basket. Thinking at first that they were real flowers, but on closer inspection she found them to be beautifully crafted from silk and wire. 'These are lovely, where did you get them?'

'I make 'em.'

Jenna felt the silk between her fingers. Emily did not look like someone who could afford to buy silk.

Pre-empting Jenna's thoughts, Emily quickly added, 'I found a silk petticoat in a dustbin and made my first ones with wire the ironmongers were throwing out. Once I sold 'em, I bought offcuts from the dressmakers and made some more. Fashionable ladies buy 'em off me.'

Jenna smiled with amusement. This street urchin was a regular little businesswoman.

'How much are they?'

'Tuppence.'

Dropping a shilling in her basket, Jenna selected a cream rose, and fitted it into the drop waistband of her dress.

Emily looked agog in the basket and retrieved the shilling, 'Oh, thank you, I can get loads of silk bits with this!'

After bidding Emily goodnight, Jenna checked on Lyndon, who was now fast asleep, glanced at the clock and walked back out onto the busy street to hail a cab and into Francis Knight's wrath.

*

The crowd at the exhibition was larger than Jenna could ever have imagined – and felt quite overwhelming – especially as this was her first solo exhibition.

'There you are, darling.' Hillary Stanton kissed Jenna and thrust a glass of champagne into her hand. 'You had us all worried as to what had become of you on your special night.'

Before she could answer, Matthew Bickford, Hillary's fiancé, appeared at their side – still using his stick following an injury to his pelvis in the war. He frowned deeply. 'No Lyndon?' he asked, looking over Jenna's shoulder for his good friend.

'I'm afraid not. He's not feeling well. He had an episode on the way here,' she whispered, 'we had to return home. The noise of London attacked his nerves.'

Matthew nodded knowingly.

'Jenna, Jenna, there you are.' Jenna turned to Francis Knight and braced herself as he rushed towards her in a cloud of cologne. 'My god, but you are very late, punctuality and all that, you know!' he chided.

'I'm so sorry, Francis, it was totally unavoidable.'

'But you're public awaits you, darling, you simply cannot keep them waiting like that.'

'Oh, leave her be, Francis,' Hillary interjected, 'she has had to deal with an illness in the family. Anyway, the trouble with being punctual is that nobody is there to appreciate it. See,' she gestured to the crowd, 'everyone is pleased to see her now!'

Francis Knight pursed his lips, decided to drop his chastisement – knowing to his cost that Hillary always came out tops in any argument.

'Come, come, Jenna, talk to your guests.' He placed a hand on the small of her back to lead her away.

'But what do I say?' Jenna shot Hillary a 'help me' look as she was practically dragged to greet her public.

Francis put a firm arm around her shoulders and said with a flourish of hand, 'Just be your gorgeous self, dear girl and tell them what you feel when you paint.'

Oh god give me strength! Jenna could feel her heart thumping in her chest as she took a deep breath and stepped into the breach. It was times like this she wished that James was by her side – he would know what to do and say. As if conjuring up an old friend, she felt a hand touching hers and turned to find James's friend - and long-time secret lover - Christian Jacques, by her side.

'Christian!' She wrapped her arms around him and kissed him on the cheek. 'I can't tell you how wonderful it is to have you here.'

His embrace was warm and restated how grateful he was for what she had done earlier this year for both himself and James.

'Well done, Jenna for this marvellous exhibition. James would be proud of you. Now I am sure Mr Knight will hold no objection to me accompanying you tonight.'

'Not at all,' Francis said, eyeing Christian with interest.

Christian was a natural at speaking, and Jenna felt completely at ease with him by her side as she listened to him speaking on her behalf, with statements such as, "As you see, Jenna has a strong emotional connection to the landscape wherever she is. Her paintings make you want to walk into them and beyond, do you not agree?"

As the night progressed, he helped and cajoled Jenna into talking about herself and soon she was engaging with everyone around her. Overall, the whole exhibition was an enormous success. All the paintings were sold, commissions had been taken and both Francis and Jenna were utterly thrilled at the outcome.

At the end of the night, Jenna kissed Christian on the cheek. 'I could not have done it without you.'

'I am sure you would have managed quite well without me, but I knew that James would want me to be here tonight, Jenna. But remember there is nothing you cannot do. James is with you in spirit always, just as he is with me. With him in our hearts, nothing is insurmountable.' He smiled, but the sadness of his loss was palpable. 'Now, let us arrange lunch. I understand your friend,' he raised his eyebrow, 'is with you in London. Do bring him along - I would love to meet the man who *really* holds your heart.'

Jenna smiled. 'Then you should look in the mirror if you want to see that man – you and James will always hold a special place in my heart.'

Christian smiled warmly. 'Shall we say Tuesday at one - our usual place? I will book a table.'

*

Declining Hillary and Matthew's invitation to go on somewhere, Matthew found Jenna a cab to take her home to Lyndon.

'I hope Lyndon feels better by tomorrow,' Matthew said as he kissed her goodnight. 'From what I remember of his previous episodes he will be better after a good night's sleep. Tell him, we will go out somewhere for dinner tomorrow evening if he feels up to it.'

'I will, Matthew, thank you.'

'Oh, and Jenna, I must ask your forgiveness for doubting your commitment to Lyndon. I was too quick to denounce you when you married James. I did not know the truth of why you married him then.'

Jenna raised a questioning eyebrow. 'And you do now?'

'No, not entirely. James could see there was conflict between us and asked me outright what the problem was. I told him, that Lyndon had returned from the war when we all thought him dead, only to find that you, the love of his life, had married James. James was shocked to hear that, and though he did not tell me the circumstances of your marriage to him, he told me that you had unselfishly married him to help him out of a dreadful situation. He also told me that although he loved you dearly, he was not in love with you. He said that he would be forever deeply indebted to you and that you were a remarkable woman.' He took Jenna by the hands and squeezed them. 'I can see that now, and I wish you only the best of luck in the future now with the man I know you truly love.'

'Gosh, Matthew, I cannot tell you how relieved I am that we are friends again. I hated to think you thought ill of me. Bless James for being our guardian angel.'

With that, he kissed her lightly on the cheek, bid her goodnight and helped her up into the cab.

*

It was late when she got back to Bellevue Gardens, and the house was quiet. Shrugging off her jacket and hat, she kicked off her shoes and climbed the stairs. Mrs Hemp would be safely ensconced in the annex flat, so Jenna slowly turned the door handle to Lyndon's room.

'Lyndon,' she whispered, 'are you awake?' She tiptoed to the bed but found him sound asleep. "He'll be better after a good night's sleep," Matthew's words rang in her head.

'Good night, my love.' She blew a kiss and left him to his slumber.

*

Lying alone in her bed, with her hands behind her head, the events of the day played in her mind. She had hoped this trip to London would be a great adventure for them both - but she had been wrong. It simply had not crossed her mind how noisy and busy London was and how it would affect Lyndon's nervous disposition. Of course, he could not help the terrible shellshock he was afflicted with, but this was not how Jenna had envisaged she and Lyndon would spend their first night together for over three years. Again, it seemed, the barriers were up against them.

It had been an impulsive decision for him to come to London. Jenna needed to attend her first solo art exhibition, and Lyndon had agreed to accompany her. They both thought it would be an ideal opportunity to reconnect with each other - a time to really be alone together, away from Loe House, in Cornwall where James's other house was situated. Although they had been joyously reunited three weeks ago, they had not had the opportunity to spend any time together. As James's widow and still in mourning - it would not do to flaunt another man in front of the good people of Gunwalloe only weeks after James's death. No one knew of course the circumstance of her marriage to James – that she had offered to marry him to stop a rather damming and criminal article from being reported in the newspaper about his relationship with Christian Jacques. Both men would have gone to prison and Christian's wife and two daughters - who were oblivious to his love affair with James - would have had to live with the shame, had Jenna not stepped into the breach. It was the least she could have done for them. James had taken her under his wing when she had nowhere else to go. He had seen her potential as an artist and had opened doors for her that she would never have thought possible.

'I miss you, James.' she sighed. She missed his company, his wit, and his kindness. He died too soon, the emphysema a result of being gassed in the war. A dreadful death for one who lived his life to the full. It was true when Christian said that his spirit would stay with her, for she felt his presence keenly both in this house and at Loe House. He was a gregarious man, so full of life and laughter - it was hard to imagine ever enjoying a party without him, of which there had been many, here and down in Cornwall. The friends who had attended, called themselves the Sundowners when they were in Cornwall as Loe House was the perfect place to watch the sunset. James had left her everything he owned, and with it came both houses, more money than she knew what to do with, plus a host of bohemian acquaintances. Her life was vastly different from the girl Lyndon met and fell in love with in that meadow in 1912. Could he settle into this new life she was leading? Could a master hedger, a man at one with nature, and she a wealthy artist now flitting between Cornwall and London, find a way to be together? She hoped with all her heart that it would be so.

6

As the Cornish dawn broke over Bochym Manor, Mary opened her eyes to greet another day. It had been forty-eight hours since she had tried to take her own life and she had been under constant watch even though the doctor had told Ruby the risk to her life had abated. Mary had never felt so wretched. She still felt terribly ill - her raw throat felt as though it had turned inside out. The very worst thing though was that she could not hold her bodily functions and had to endure the deep embarrassment of having to be cleaned up by either Ruby or Molly every time she soiled herself. The doctor told her this would pass, but the damage she had done to her body would mean her health would suffer for some time to come.

She lifted her eyes to meet with Ruby's and as she lowered them again, she whispered, 'I'm sorry.'

Ruby put her hand gently on her brow. 'I'm sorry that things became so bad that you were driven to this.'

'Does everyone think I'm wicked?' she rasped.

'No, everyone is terribly worried about you.'

'Will I lose my job?'

'I can't speak for the Earl and Countess, but I'll fight your case. You must put all thoughts of ever doing anything like this again out of your mind!'

Mary closed her eyes.

'Mary, promise me.'

She nodded. 'I never want to go through this again.' She belched, pardoned herself and shuddered at the foul smell.

'The doctor says you must start to eat something. Though he warned you may be sick again, the sooner we get nourishment into your stomach, the sooner you will feel much better.'

Mary smacked her dry cracked lips and nodded.

'I'll get Mrs Blair to grind some oats and make a smooth porridge for you, and you must drink plenty of water.'

Mary's face crumpled at this request. 'But I keep wetting myself.'

'It *will* pass. Now you're fully awake and lucid, we can use the bed pan, until you feel strong enough to get up and use the pot.'

'Am I going to prison?'

'No, everyone has been warned that they must not say anything, otherwise they will lose their position here. Everyone understands your predicament, Mary - none of us are insensitive to it. But you know, Thomas would not want you to have done this. Thomas loved life - he would be angry with you for what you have done. I know it is a harsh thing to say, but he would. You're a lovely young woman, Mary. Thomas has gone I'm afraid, and you know what Mr Treen said – his death is not how it was reported.'

'But to have my brave husband's name omitted from that plaque in Cury is not fair! The committee clearly said in that letter, that he had been left off because….' She began to sob and could not say the word.

'Can I see the letter?'

Mary nodded and pointed to her drawer.

Ruby could not hide the disgust she felt at what she read. 'Mary, the people who knew and loved Thomas, know what a brave man he was. You do not need his name on a plaque to commemorate him. You must do that here,' she pressed her hand against her heart. 'That is where it matters – your heart is where your brave husband and our dear friend's name will be forever ingrained.' She handed her a dry handkerchief to wipe her tears.

Mary's body shuddered with a sob, then her eyes widened in alarm. 'Oh no, I think I'm going to wee.'

Ruby pushed the bedpan under Mary's bottom, just in time. 'There see, you're obviously getting some control over your bladder. Things will only get better from now on,' she said retrieving the bedpan.

'Will they, though, will they ever get better without Thomas?' Mary dabbed her eyes.

'You may not think this, but you will love again and perhaps have a family. Please do not let what happened to Thomas define you.' She kissed her on the forehead. 'I shall fetch you something to eat.'

'Ruby.'

'Yes, Mary.'

'Thank you for always being you. I shall miss you when you leave us again.'

'I'll miss you too, Mary, and I would never have got over your loss had you succeeded the other day.'

'Who found me?'

'A young man who is working here. Gabriel Trelease is his name. He's a famous sculptor, but he's restoring the French drawing room.'

'Will he keep my secret?'

'He will – he too has known sadness like yours. His wife died of the Spanish flu last year and left him with a little son to rear alone.'

'The poor man – he must be in purgatory.'

'Well from the look of him – he's coping well. You will meet him soon and you can see for yourself.'

Mary's face paled more than it was already. 'I don't think I can face him.'

'Yes, you can. He was genuinely concerned about you. I think it might be nice to thank him for helping you. We are all so grateful that he was walking the gardens that day, otherwise – well, it does not bear thinking about.'

*

In London, at Bellevue Gardens, Jenna too had been up and about since the sun rose, though she could see little of its morning glory over the buildings surrounding the London residence.

Hoping Lyndon had had a more settled night, she decided to let him sleep a little longer and once dressed, she knocked quietly at Emily's bedroom door. When no answer came, she entered. The room was tidy, and the bed made, in fact the bed did not look as though it had been slept in!

The only other person to rise before Jenna was Mrs Hemp, and Jenna found her preparing breakfast in the kitchen.

'Where is Emily, Mrs Hemp?'

'The girl left first thing this morning, Mrs Blackwell. She came down for her dress and said to say thank you very much and then left. She said she had work to do.'

'Her bed hasn't been slept in!'

'No, I thought at first, she had just made it, but the sheets have not been disturbed. I reckon she slept on the floor.'

'Why ever would she do that?'

'I really don't know, Mrs Blackwell.'

'Is that the dress I gave her there?' Jenna frowned at the laundry basket. 'I told her she could keep it.'

'Well, she handed it back and said, "Ta very much, but no one will buy from me if I'm dressed posh."' Mrs Hemp smiled. 'Bless her.'

'Did you get a chance to speak with her last night, Mrs Hemp?'

'Yes, she came and sat in the kitchen. I gave her a bowl of soup and bread. Poor little mite looked as though she had not eaten properly in a long time. Wolfed it down, she did.'

'Did she say where she lived?'

Mrs Hemp shook her head. 'I reckon she does not actually live anywhere. Her dress was very dirty - as though she sleeps in it – outside,' she added. 'I tried but could not get it clean, but it was fresher than when she handed it over.'

'I see. Oh, well,' Jenna sighed, 'some people you can't help. As for those we can, could you make a breakfast tray up for Lyndon please? I'm hoping a good night's sleep has recovered his health.'

*

Lyndon had in fact been awake for some time. He had been deep in a dream, working on the Trevarno Estate where he'd grown up. The fields surrounding the estate were lush green and ready to harvest. A blackbird was singing high up in the canopy of trees. The warmth of the summer sun beat down on the back of his neck and his hands, pitted with cuts and sores, were doing the honest work of a hedger. He felt genuinely happy, crafting and pleaching the branches like his grandfather had done before him, and then he had been woken in the early hours by the noise of the traffic and people out on the streets of London. Try as he might he could not hear a single bird singing the dawn chorus as they did at home.

Nursing a terrible headache, always an after effect of an *episode,* he hated these attacks and losing control in front of people, it shamed him, though it was a small price to pay. At least he had been one of the lucky ones who had come home from the war. These thoughts took him back to the trenches - to the death and destruction of good men, it depressed him to think of the men who did not come home. It also depressed him that he had let Jenna down, first when she needed his support last night at the exhibition, and again here in this bed, where they had hoped to spend the night together to rekindle their love. How dreadfully feeble he felt in front of her when he was trembling, weak as a kitten. How could he lumber her with this mess of a man he had become? He glanced around this room – James Blackwell's room with its fine drapes and bedspreads. All this opulence and decadence did not sit easy with him.

The knock on the door made him start so he was trembling slightly when Jenna put the breakfast tray down on his lap.

'Are you not feeling any better?' she said cupping her soft hand sympathetically over his. 'You're still shaking!'

'I'll be fine, Jenna, don't fuss.' He knew his words wounded her because she retracted her hand and nodded apologetically.

'If you feel up to it, I thought we could take a cab to Bond Street to see my exhibition - it appeared to have been an enormous success. The gallery is closed today being Sunday, but Francis Knight the owner told me he will be there this morning. Afterwards, we can take another cab to the park – so we can walk somewhere less noisy,' she said gaily.

'If you wish.' He smiled weakly. 'I'm glad everything went well for you last night – I'm ever so sorry....'

'Do not apologise. It is not your fault. Matthew and Hillary have asked us to dinner at a restaurant this evening – do you think you'll be able to go?'

His eyes glazed over but nodded. 'Just keep me away from street minstrels en route,' he joked. 'If I come across that noisy beggar again, I'm likely to thump him.'

*

Francis Knight at The Black Gallery was his usual demonstrative self, air kissing and congratulating Jenna as soon as she walked in. Her exhibition had been an enormous success, a complete sell-out, and he was clearly happy. After the praising subsided, Francis cut his eyes to Lyndon and his eyebrow rose questioningly.

'And who have we here then?'

'This is Lyndon FitzSimmons – a long-time friend of mine.'

'Is he now? He looked down his nose at him. 'Well, I am pleased to meet you, Mr FitzSimmons,' he said without sincerity, but held his hand out for Lyndon to shake.

Lyndon noting Francis's insincerity disliked the man instantly but offered his hand to him. He allowed himself a wry smile when Francis quickly retracted his hand from his, on feeling how rough and work worn Lyndon's felt against his own soft hand.

'Darling, a moment in the office, if you please,' Francis said cradling his hand as though to sooth the chaffing inflicted on it. 'I'm sure your *friend* would like to take a look around, while we conduct a tiny bit of business.'

While they disappeared into the office, Lyndon wiped his hand down his jacket. His own hand may be as rough as bark, but Francis's insipid, damp handshake made his lip curl disdainfully. Turning his attention to the paintings, he began to walk slowly around the gallery, astounded at the work Jenna produced. He had only ever seen the sketches she had done when he had first met her, and of course the paintings his good friend Matthew had commissioned from Jenna which now hung pride of place in the Trevarno orangery. These, well, these were something else! Vibrant and life-size, Jenna seemed to be able to capture a moment in time to depict a scene that one could almost step into.

When Jenna returned from the office, Lyndon looked upon her with renewed admiration – she had come a long way from the girl in the meadow who used to grid her sketch pad into four so that she could get more drawings on one piece in order to save paper!

'Well,' she tipped her head for his reaction, 'do you like them then?'

'They're wonderful, Jenna. I'm enormously proud of you.' He reached for her hand, kissed it tenderly and looked deep into her eyes. For a moment they almost forgot themselves, and Lyndon felt quite bruised when Jenna, realising Francis was watching them, quickly pulled away from him.

'I'll see you before I leave for Cornwall, Francis.' Jenna kissed him on the cheek.

'I'll need more paintings soon you know,' Francis glanced at Lyndon, and then back to Jenna. 'Your late husband, James, assured me you were committed to your art. I do not expect *anything* to distract you for quite some time yet.' He gave her an unashamedly direct warning stare.

Lyndon could see Francis had wounded Jenna with his inference, for she flinched visually. Feeling duty bound to speak in her defence, he opened his mouth, but halted when Jenna lifted her chin, pulled a smile from the depths of her resentment, and retorted, 'My paintings have my undivided attention as always. Goodbye, Francis.' She then ushered Lyndon out of the gallery without a backward glance.

They walked briskly until they were a few yards from the gallery before Jenna stopped and stamped her foot. 'Oh, that man!' she seethed with indignation.

'I wanted to say something to him back there, but I didn't want to jeopardise your working relationship,' Lyndon offered, clearly seeing her anger.

'Thank you, but I'm glad you did not. Francis has the power to stop my rise to fame just as quickly as he instigated it. It's the price I must pay I suppose for his patronage.'

'You may work for him, but he does not own you! He had no right to berate you like that.'

'I agree, but Francis has never been like that with me before. Perhaps he sees me as moving on too quickly after James's death – he was, after all, a good friend of his. He's just looking out for him.'

Lyndon felt his bile rise. 'My God! But it just seems to be one thing after another. I'm sure James did not bring us together to have to climb over all these obstacles. We came here to be together but still find we must pussyfoot around everyone and pretend we are not together. And while we are on the subject - I thought I was more than a long-time friend to you, Jenna.'

'You are!' Jenna said her voice cracking slightly, 'but it's early days.'

'Then I should not have come to London with you!'

'Oh, Lyndon, please don't say that.'

He saw her eyes fill with tears and felt instantly regretful of his words. 'I'm sorry.' He pulled her into an embrace right there on the street. 'It is just that I can't bear it Jenna,' he spoke into her hair, 'I'm here with you, but we could not be further apart.'

'I'm sorry too,' she murmured into his neck.

He held her for a moment and then lifted her chin to kiss her tenderly on the lips. He could feel her mouth tremble under his touch and berated himself for getting cross with her - It really was not her fault. He kissed her again and smiled.

'Come on, I thought you were going to take me to Hyde Park to show me the mighty Crystal Palace.'

7

They returned to Bellevue Gardens - after their visit to Hyde park - though not totally unscathed in Lyndon's case. They had to negotiate crowds of people milling around someone who had collapsed in the heat on the pavement. Alarm bells could be heard as an ambulance approached and there was an altercation between a motor car and a horse drawn vehicle. A fire somewhere heralded the fire brigade to be out in force, racing past and clanging the bells for people to make way.

By the time they reached Bellevue Gardens, Lyndon's mouth was as dry as an autumn leaf and his lips were white.

Jenna put her hand gently on his arm. 'I'll see if Mrs Hemp can make us some tea and sandwiches, shall I?'

Lyndon nodded, unwilling to speak in case his voice wavered. In his bedroom, he splashed cold water on his face and looked at himself in the mirror. His eyes were bloodshot, and his weather tanned face looked pale and tired.

'Lyndon,' Jenna knocked on his door, 'luncheon is in the parlour.'

Luncheon? Lyndon glanced at his pocket watch – it was one-o-clock - dinnertime in his world.

*

In Cornwall, The Poldhu Tea Room was buzzing with activity. The cove was full of visitors -many of them sea bathing. Ellie's husband Guy was sitting outside on the shady part of the veranda with his twelve-year-old daughter Sophie. They were sharing a table with Betsy's husband Ryan. He was entertaining his six-year-old daughter, Josie, who was constantly fidgeting and squirming in her seat.

Betsy grimaced when she came in from serving them tea. 'My little Josie is proving to be more of a challenging handful every day – Ryan says she acts as though she has ants in her pants. I'm going to be more worn out trying to keep up with her once I leave here than I am serving all day!'

'She's no different to what my Agnes was like. That girl never stopped from dawn to dusk. Guy says she's just the same thatching. She can lay a thatch faster than any of them and still do a sterling job.'

'Any chance of Guy taking on Josie at the tender age of six then?' she mused.

Ellie laughed. 'You will miss their antics when they grow up.'

Betsy raised a doubting eyebrow.

They watched as Marianne moved around the tearoom and the outside veranda - this was only her second day, but she worked with the efficiency of someone who had worked here years. She was clearly loving her new job, and both Ellie and Betsy were happy with her progress.

Her help in the tearoom allowed Betsy to sit down for a few minutes every now and then to take the strain off her back.

'You'll not want me back after this one arrives, Ellie!' Betsy patted her tummy. 'I think Marianne has already made the position her own.

'I will, Betsy, have no fears about that. I never thought I could find anyone to replace Jessie, but you have more than filled her shoes,' she said placing a teapot and two pieces of cake on the tray.

Betsy beamed a smile. 'Talking of Jessie, I got a letter from her yesterday, did you?'

'I did, how wonderful that she and Daniel are expecting another baby – this will be there third! Jessie joked in her letter that she just has to look at Daniel and she's pregnant again. I'm so happy she found someone to love after her disastrous marriage to Guy's brother.'

Marianne came in to pick up the tray, and smiled, 'Are you speaking about Jessie, who used to work here?'

'We are,' Ellie smiled, 'she's written to tell us she's expecting her third child. Did you know her?'

Marianne shook her head. 'I know of her. She met her gentleman husband at the tearoom, didn't she?'

Ellie's lip curled into a smile. 'She did yes.'

'I wonder if I'll find my husband while I'm serving tea and cake,' she grinned as she took the tray out to the customer.

Betsy and Ellie exchanged amused glances.

'Methinks she's definitely on the hunt for a husband here – I had to make her wash off the perfume she was wearing this morning. Don't get me wrong, Betsy, she smelt lovely, but I want the customers to enjoy the aroma of tea and fresh baked cakes, not the waitress. Perhaps it's time to tell Jake Treen to come and enjoy the delights of the tearoom.'

*

Lyndon often found it was the small noises that irritated him after an episode - the clock ticking loudly on the mantelpiece in the front parlour at Bellevue Gardens was doing just that as he sat opposite Jenna. Although the room was richly decorated and comfortable, he was feeling terribly uneasy. He got up abruptly, picked up the clock and took it out into the hall.

'Sorry,' he said as he came back. 'It was just…'

'It's fine, I understand - I'll put it out of the way later.'

He sat back down and took a deep breath to settle his unrest.

'Lyndon,' Jenna said tentatively, handing him a cup of tea she had just poured, 'James's friend Christian has invited us to luncheon on Tuesday – he'd like to meet you.'

'Me, why?'

She laughed. 'Because he's my friend too - a special one and he's my lawyer, I think you should meet, you'll like him.'

'On Tuesday, you say?'

'Yes.'

Lyndon smiled weakly and nodded – unsure if he could stay in this dirty, noisy metropolis until Tuesday.

*

At Poldhu, Marianne had been delighted when Gabriel Trelease arrived at the tearoom, just after one o clock. She'd been more than a little annoyed that Ellie had made her wash off the perfume she'd put on that morning for that very eventuality. She could not remember the name of the perfume she had filtered off from Lady Martha's dressing table, she just knew it was expensive.

Gabriel had arrived with his little son, but by the time Marianne had got to him to take his order and perhaps have a little chat, she was dismayed to find that he had been joined at the table by Justin and Ruby Devereux from Bochym. Hopefully there would be time later to speak to him alone.

'How is Mary?' Marianne directed the question to Ruby, holding her pen and pad aloft.

Ruby glanced nervously around the table and answered quietly, 'She's better thank you, Marianne.'

'How foolish can you get? She's a cook's assistant – I cannot understand how she managed to pick a poisonous mushroom *and* eat it – everyone knows what to look for.'

'What's that?' Ellie had overheard the conversation. 'Is Mary ill?'

'Oh, it's nothing she won't recover from,' Ruby interjected before Marianne could say more on the subject.

Marianne though was determined to continue berating Mary and turned to Ellie, 'The silly girl, picked a poisonous mushroom and ate it! She could have poisoned the whole family!'

'Thank you, Marianne,' Ruby said sternly to quieten her, and then lowered her voice. 'It was a genuine mistake, and I don't think Mary would appreciate you bantering this unfortunate incident around. Remember, it made her incredibly poorly.'

Marianne coloured up as Ellie gave her a stern look. 'Marianne, go and take the order to Betsy please, and then wait for me in the back kitchen.'

Marianne's eyes darted around the table to see if anyone would speak in her defence.

'Now, please, Marianne,' Ellie reiterated.

As Marianne scurried off indignantly, she heard Ellie give her best wishes to Mary for a speedy recovery. She slapped the order down on the counter for Betsy, folded her arms and went to stand in the kitchen until Ellie joined her.

'First rule of this tearoom. You must always, always, keep your opinions to yourself!' Ellie said sternly.

'But...'

'*Always!*' Ellie practically shouted at her. 'Do you understand?'

Marianne nodded.

'Go back to work then.'

Marianne seethed as she went about her work but managed to redeem herself with Gabriel's table when she presented them with the bill at the end of their stay. Her handwriting was beautiful and never failed to make a good impression– even if she said so herself. Lady Martha had instructed her in the art of calligraphy, and Marianne decided to apply this technique whenever she wrote down an order and again afterwards when she jotted the amount up – she found it always brought a good tip.

The table had agreed to split the bill and when Marianne had presented it. Gabriel called Ellie over and said, 'It takes the sting out of paying when one is presented with a bill so beautifully written. It's so lovely, I might frame it,' he mused. 'It's rather worth coming back over and over to get another of these masterpieces.'

Marianne stood quietly to the side, drinking in the admiration – hopefully, this would put her back in Ellie's good books now.

Ellie laughed. 'I would rather it was my delicious tea and cakes which brought you back to us, but yes, I admit, Marianne is an asset when it comes to handing out these beautifully written bills.'

As the occupants of the table rose to leave, Marianne made sure she spoke up within earshot of Ellie.

'Please tell Mary, I hope she has a quick recovery, and I'm dreadfully sorry I spoke out of turn earlier. It was only on account of Mary being a friend, and we would normally, if she could, exchange silly banter like that.'

'It is fine, Marianne. I will pass on your good wishes,' Ruby said, gently touching her on the arm.

As the group left the veranda, Marianne turned to Ellie who smiled and nodded approval of her apology. Although awarding herself a little smile for redeeming herself – Marianne still thought it was odd, and not a little bit stupid, for Mary to have picked and eaten poisonous mushrooms!

8

Lyndon and Matthew had been friends since childhood, having grown up together. Matthew Bickford was the heir to the Trevarno Estate, Helston, and Lyndon, was the son of their gardener, but the class divide had never disrupted their friendship. Matthew was, and always would be, Lyndon's touchstone and vice versa. They always knew they could rely on each other – they had a shared history, not only growing up together, but in the war too where they had joined up and fought together. Despite this, it was with great reluctance that Lyndon got ready to go out for dinner with Matthew and his fiancée Hillary that night. Thankfully, Jenna had organised a cab to pick them up outside the door – that would lessen the chance of another occurrence like the one last night.

'My goodness,' Jenna smiled as he emerged from his room, 'I never thought I would see the day that Lyndon FitzSimmons wore a dinner suit!' She moved forward to fix his lobsided bow tie for him. 'There, you look just the ticket.'

'I look like a penguin and it's flipping uncomfortable.' Lyndon's eyes travelled the length of Jenna's body appreciably, she was dressed in a shift of dark blue satin. 'You look lovely – that dress is beautiful, but what the devil is in your hair?'

'It's petroleum jelly.' She screwed her nose up. 'I know, it's a bit strange, but it keeps the waves in my hair. I don't really want to cut it into the fashionable bob all the girls are wearing, so if I pin my hair up and do this to the front it looks similar. She secured a clasp of feathers in her head and turned to show him. 'There!' She posed like a model in a magazine.

'Well, you do look spectacular, and I must admit, I'm enormously grateful you haven't chopped your beautiful blond curls off. All the other young women hereabouts look like boys!'

'No, they don't' she laughed, 'It's just the fashion! Anyway, are you ready?'

He nodded resignedly and reached out for her hand.

*

The restaurant was thankfully quiet and cool with subdued lighting, so Lyndon began to finally relax. His friend Matthew had recently become engaged to Jenna's new and very likable friend Hillary, and though he had met her before briefly at Trevarno, this was the first social occasion he had been with her - and found her to be highly entertaining.

After dinner there was dancing - the band was good, though loud, and although Lyndon had recovered from last night's episode, he still had a residual headache, and each beat of the drum began to reverberate through him.

Jenna beckoned him to dance with her, which he did tentatively, as his knowledge of dancing consisted of a ceilidh and the odd reel at a folk dance. It was nice to feel her in his arms again, though twice her Vaseline hair brushed against his face which was not at all pleasant.

'This is the first time I've danced with you since the Harvest supper at Farmer Ferris's, in 1912,' he said.

Jenna looked up and smiled with a twinkle in her eyes. 'You proposed to me that night.'

'I did, but we had no idea what lay in store for us, did we?'

'Gosh, no!' Jenna answered gloomily.

'If I remember, you said yes to my proposal.'

'I remember,' she murmured.

'So, when is our wedding to be?'

Jenna laughed softly but did not answer, and Lyndon felt a great sinking sensation in the pit of his stomach at her reticence.

After dancing a couple of dances, Lyndon sat back down, leaving Jenna to dance with several young and eager men. The room began to feel stuffy with tobacco smoke and Lyndon watched as Jenna was waltzed around the room.

'A far cry from the girl we once knew, Lyndon,' Matthew said leaning back in his chair.

Lyndon nodded sadly. 'I don't begrudge her a single thing, after what she went through with that dreadful first husband of hers, Blewett. But oh, Matthew, how I miss that girl I first saw and fell in love with - the girl who drew pictures in meadows full of flowers – who had the sun in her hair, instead of grease and feathers.'

Matthew nodded in agreement.

'Don't get me wrong, I'm so proud of what she has become, it's just....'

'What?'

'I'm not sure we fit together anymore. This life - this decadence! London!' The band started up again with a screech of trumpet and Lyndon felt his body shudder.

'Are you all right, my friend? Matthew rested a hand on his shoulder.

'In truth, no. I can't stand the noise and the crowds here in London. I look around at all these people and think only of the men who fell at my feet on those muddy, bloody fields of war. What did they all die for? And what of those who survived, coming home with devastating injuries to both body and mind. Was it just so this lot could live it up as though it never happened? Was this going on while we were fighting for our lives?'

Matthew tightened his hand on Lyndon's shoulder. 'No, it wasn't. These nightclubs, jazz clubs and cocktail bars began to flourish just after the war. Yes, you're right, it's a hedonistic lifestyle, but it's perhaps an escape from reality. If you look around, these people are still young - I suspect they missed the war, being too young to fight. Perhaps they are living it up for older members of their families who weren't perhaps lucky enough to survive. They need to enjoy life to the full, because so many other young lives had been lost on the battlefields.'

Lyndon shook his head. 'Well, I can't bear it. I need the sun on my back. I need to work, Matthew. I need the Cornish air searing through my lungs, and I need to feel branches in my hands, not glasses of champagne. I want to go home, where I belong.'

'Without Jenna?'

He nodded. 'She needs to be here for a few more days - I understand that, but I need to be elsewhere.'

Hillary and Jenna returned with florid faces from all the dancing.

'What are you two so secretive about?' Hillary asked as she beckoned the waiter over for more champagne.'

'We were just talking about Cornwall.'

Jenna flashed Lyndon a worried look.

'Ah, you can take the man out of Cornwall, but you cannot take Cornwall out of the man,' Hillary replied.

Lyndon lifted his glass. 'No truer word said.'

'We are just going to powder our noses and then we'll decide where to go next,' Hillary said as she pulled Jenna with her.

'Do you want to go on to a nightclub, Lyndon?' Matthew asked.

'No. I would rather like to go home. Do you mind? I would like to go now before Jenna comes back – I do not want to ruin her night. If you could make sure she gets home safely.'

'Of course, she'll be disappointed though, if not a little angry with me for letting you go.'

The trumpet blared again, and Lyndon shuddered. 'I'm sorry, I need to go now!' He got up and picked up his jacket.

Matthew stood up too. 'I'll walk with you, to get you into a cab.' Outside, he put his hand on Lyndon's shoulder. 'Listen, my friend, I am driving back to Cornwall in the morning. You're very welcome to accompany me.'

'Yes please,' Lyndon answered without a moment's hesitation. 'Don't say anything to Jenna yet, I'll tell her when she comes home.'

*

Jenna's heart felt as though it had dropped to her shoes when Matthew came back from seeing Lyndon off. Their little adventure up to London was not boding well for either of them. She knew she should have given him a definitive answer that they would marry, just as soon as she felt a decent amount of time had passed since losing James, but she knew how frustrated he was about having to keep their distance from each other. She would speak to him when she got home, and they would make plans she decided.

Hillary filled her glass up again from the new champagne bottle.

'Chin, chin, darling' she said chinking her glass with Jenna's.

Jenna put her glass down. 'Sorry, Hillary, I feel as though a light has just gone out of my life.'

'He has only gone home – London is always overwhelming the first time anyone visits – you must remember. It's not that long since James and I took a young Cornish girl out of her environment and look at you now. Stop worrying. Matthew said he had a headache that is all. All will be well.'

They decided not to go onto a nightclub in the end and Jenna only stayed for another half an hour, because in her heart she knew she should have gone with Lyndon.

*

When she returned home, she quietly knocked on his bedroom door, and found him awake but pensive.

'I thought you would be later than this,' he said sheepishly.

'I couldn't settle without you. You should have waited, so I could have come home with you.'

He sighed heavily. 'I didn't want you to come. I told Matthew to tell you to stay and enjoy yourself.'

She climbed onto the bed.' I want to be with you, Lyndon - that is why we are here.' She snuggled into his strong arms, but there was a marked reserve in his hold. He wore no clothes, and she stroked the auburn silky hairs on his chest, but he grasped her hand in his to stop her caress.

'I'm going home tomorrow,' he whispered.

Jenna could not trust herself to speak. Sitting back from him, she noticed the suitcase on the chair already packed – there seemed to be no negotiating this. Feeling the tears well, she asked, 'Are you saying you don't want to be with me.'

'Not at all. I'm going home with Matthew. My nerves are on edge constantly. The noise is too much.' He paused for a moment. 'I love you, Jenna, please don't think I don't, but I can't be here with you. I can't bear all this sneaking around Mrs Hemp. I want us to be together, somewhere that is ours, and not…. James Blackwell's.'

'But we had things planned - what about the clothes you were going to be measured for in Savile Row tomorrow?'

'I have no need for new fancy clothes, nor do I have the means to pay for them,' he halted her when she was going to interrupt him, 'I know you have money to pay for them, but I do not want them. I'm sorry, but this world of yours is not for me.'

'But Lyndon, even in Cornwall there will be social occasions when you need to dress up – if you want to be with me down there, that is part and parcel of my life now.'

'Then if the occasion rises, I'll borrow off Matthew again. But a social diary of luncheons and dinner parties are not for me – I'm a hedger earning a crust when I'm working, and happy to do it. I do not want to be indebted to you – you of all people know my character and know that it does not sit well on me not to pay my way.'

Jenna nodded. 'I'm sorry.' She moved towards him again and let her head rest on his chest.

He gently put his hands to her hair, but his fingers stopped when they ran into the petroleum jelly Jenna had put in her hair to make it wave. 'Ugh!' Unable to hide his disgust, he pulled his hands away and looked for something to wipe them on.

Jenna pulled back. 'Oh, Lyndon, I'm sorry,' she handed him her handkerchief, 'I had forgotten that I had put that in my hair. I'll go and shower it off. I'll be back in a tick.'

'No, Jenna, just go back to your own room. I'm tired. I'll see you in the morning.'

A crushing feeling constricted her heart as she climbed slowly off the bed. She leant forward and with trembling lips kissed him and then left the room. Only when she was out on the landing, did she allow her tears to fall.

9

It was early, six a.m. and Jenna watched tearfully as Lyndon gathered up his last few possessions.

'Please don't go, Lyndon,' she said softly.

He stopped fastening his suitcase, stood up straight but did not turn to look at her; she could see by the way his shoulders were heaving that he too was finding this difficult.

'Please, Lyndon.'

He picked up his suitcase and turned slowly. 'I can't be here, Jenna. I can't live the way you live here or stay in *this* house. I'm sorry, please forgive me for leaving you like this.' He moved towards her, put his suitcase down and gathered her into his arms. 'I'm sorry,' he whispered into her hair.

Trying to stop the tears from falling, Jenna held onto him as though she was going to lose him again forever.

'I'll come home at the weekend.'

'No. don't rush, Jenna. Do what you need to do up here and I'll see you in Cornwall when you do get back.'

'Promise?' she said searching his eyes hopefully.

He grasped her hands in earnest, his own eyes pooling, and nodded.

They both turned when they heard Matthew pull up outside Bellevue Gardens. Lyndon picked up his suitcase again and set off down the stairs.

Both Matthew and Lyndon kissed her goodbye on the cheek before they climbed into the car and drove off. With a powerful sense of foreboding, she watched the car drive away, wondering how and if their relationship could progress now.

*

Christian Jacques QC sat in his London office – the heady smell of lavender polish, as always, eased his troubled mind. He was grieving for the death of his dear friend, James Blackwell, and because of the nature of his friendship, it was a grief he could not share with anyone other than James's wife, Jenna – the only other person who knew. Alas, he could not even talk to Jenna now – they were due to have luncheon together the next day, but she had her friend with her who would also be attending. A knock on the door pulled him from his reverie and his secretary came in and smiled.

'I have a gentleman outside who wishes to speak to you about James Blackwell.'

Christian felt a nervous frisson run through his body. 'Did he give a name?'

'No, sir, he would not disclose it.'

Christian nodded. 'Send him in.'

A tall familiar looking man walked into his office and Christian felt his breath catch – he was the image of James Blackwell, albeit older.

'Can I get anyone any refreshments?' Christian's secretary asked, but before Christian could answer, the visitor said a firm 'no,' dismissed her and closed the door on her.

Christian drew a deep measured breath. 'Please take a seat, Mr Blackwell.'

Blackwell sat down on the deeply buttoned leather seat and gave a cursory glance around the room. 'You know me then?'

'You are undeniably, James's father.'

'I'll not beat about the bush then - I am here to contest my son's will,' he said sternly.

Christian said nothing for a moment and then leant forward and steepled his fingers.

'The will is incontestable. His wife Jenna inherited everything by legal right.'

'Oh,' he laughed shortly, 'come, come, I think we all know it was a sham marriage to cover up his dirty little secret.' He narrowed his eyes as he spoke.

Christian felt his heart constrict but managed to keep a cool head.

'I can assure you - Jenna and James were incredibly happy in the brief time they had together. James was emphatic that you would not benefit from his will. It is my understanding that he hated you and that you cut him out of your own will because he would not marry the heiress you had chosen for him.'

'Yes,' he sneered, 'we all know why that was now, don't we?'

Unperturbed, Christian continued, 'Lyndon's wealth and property were accumulated by him alone since he left your family. It accrued solely from his successful career as a writer and Jenna Blackwell, as his legal wife, is the beneficiary.'

'She was a gold digger – and by all accounts she was a scullery maid.'

'Jenna Blackwell is a fine artist!'

'Helped by my son's money.' He folded his arms. 'You appear to know a lot about my son to say you are just his lawyer.'

James and I have been friends a long time.'

Blackwell laughed without humour

Christian tipped his head. 'I see friendship is perhaps a context with which you are not familiar.

'You were more than friends - I'll wager.'

'Be careful, sir, or I shall sue for libel.'

'I think not. I have had you watched you know – a private detective has documented your comings and goings from Bellevue Gardens before James died.'

'Then you have wasted your money.'

'I am not arguing about this, Mr Jacques, I am telling you. I want that grubby little trollop out of his properties, or I shall bring this matter to the magistrates.'

'There is no case to answer here.'

'Oh, but I think there is! That floozy he was married to is already courting advances from another man – I have had her watched you see. Rest assured; Mr Jacques I shall do everything in my power to have this overturned to gain what rightly belongs to my family. You need to remember your position in this - by all accounts you have a wife and family.'

'And you need to remember to whom you are speaking. I am a man of the law.'

'You're a fag..!' Blackwell stopped himself from using the word, pursed his lips, got up and brushed himself down as though soiled in Christian's presence. 'I'll bid you good day – you'll be hearing from me.'

*

In Cornwall, at Bochym Manor, Mary had recovered enough to eat a little now without vomiting, albeit very gingerly as her mouth was full of ulcers and her lips covered in sore blisters. Thankfully, she had more control over her bladder - though not enough that she could risk leaving her room for chance she disgraced herself. She had assured both Ruby and Molly that they no longer needed to watch her, promising that she would never do anything like that again – and indeed, she wouldn't! Never had she witnessed anything as dreadful and traumatic as having salt water forced down her gullet. She knew now what torture the suffragettes campaigning for women's rights must have endured in prison when they had gone on hunger strike. Sitting at her bedroom window, her senses seemed to be heightened for some reason. She could hear the twittering house martins as they flitted about catching insects on the wing. She shaded her eyes from the sun climbing in the sky, dappling through the trees, their leaves seemed to be more a vibrant green than she had ever seen. Without doubt she was glad she had been found and saved, though she was still terribly upset about Thomas, but killing herself was not the way forward. Glancing down into the kitchen courtyard, she dearly wished she could sit out there in the shade, but embarrassment would not allow her to go downstairs and face everyone. Soon though she may have to leave the manor in disgrace. The Earl and Countess were due back the next day and for sure, they would not look too kindly on one of their maids committing a criminal act. A pang of self-pity engulfed her, and she wept brokenheartedly for everything she had lost and was about to lose.

*

After spending the rest of Monday alone, painting in the studio in Bellevue Gardens, Jenna woke on Tuesday morning in dire need of some company and looked forward to her lunch with Christian at The Ritz.

The restaurant was full as Jenna allowed the maître d to lead her to Christian's table.

He stood and kissed her warmly on the cheek. 'You're alone, I see,' he asked with a raised eyebrow.

Jenna nodded sadly. 'Lyndon went home yesterday morning.

'Earlier than expected?'

'Yes.'

The waiter took their order, both having a salmon mousse to start with, veal for Christian and chicken for Jenna for the main course.

'So, what went wrong?'

Jenna took a sip of the fine wine Christian had ordered before she spoke - it was smooth and fruity, easing her throat which was dry from anxiety.

'Lyndon is a man of nature. He is also suffering from shell shock. We thought London would be a good place to rekindle our love, but it proved to be too busy and too noisy for his shattered nerves. I should have realised he would be like a fish out of water here. I couldn't take him to James's house in Cornwall – having only lost James a month ago. I can't flaunt another man there so soon.'

Her words must have caught at Christian's heart because she saw him close his eyes momentarily to stem the feeling of loss.

Presently he said, 'I'm actually glad he has gone home - I think perhaps it is not the right time to be seen with Lyndon.'

Jenna blanched. 'Do you not approve of us?'

'It's not that at all – all I want is for you to be happy, just as James did, it's just…'

'What?' Jenna tipped her head.

'Oh, Jenna, I have been in two minds whether to tell you this or not, but I think now I must. James's father came to see me on Friday – he is trying to contest James's will.'

'Oh!' Jenna took another sip of wine. 'And can he?'

'Not normally, no, but…,' he lowered his voice, 'he is making allegations about James's sexuality, the legality of your marriage to him, and…. *my* relationship with him.'

Jenna felt the colour drain from her face. 'On what evidence?'

'It was he who had Bellevue Gardens watched and the consequential threat of the story breaking in the newspaper that time.'

'But we sorted all that out when I married James.'

Christian pursed his lips in disdain. 'Graham Blackwell believes that your marriage was a sham - a cover up to hide James's sexuality.'

Jenna tapped her lips with her manicured fingernails. 'Has he any real evidence of James's sexual orientation?'

'Only what he thinks he believes. James may have told you he refused to marry that heiress to secure their estate in Hertfordshire. James told me his father questioned his sexuality then, but James, point blank refused to admit it. Nevertheless, his father threw him out of the family home, cutting him out of the will on that assumption. I have made enquiries and Graham Blackwell is soon to be declared bankrupt. He obviously sees that James's acquired wealth would shore up the Hertfordshire estate and he is determined to fight you for the money.'

'What am I to do? No one could ever know what really went on in our marriage so he simply can't prove ours was a marriage of convenience.'

'He called you a gold digger. I think he has been having you watched and believes you to be moving on to someone else too soon after James's death. That and only that, is the reason I implore you to distance yourself from Lyndon for the time being. The only way he can build a case is if he can find out James *was* a homosexual and that will of course expose me.'

'None of James's friends would expose him - you know that, and in truth I don't believe anyone knew. When I married him, almost everyone mentioned that they just thought James was a confirmed bachelor. Only Hillary joked that she had wondered if 'he batted for the other side.'

'Yes, well it's jokes like that that fuel the fire,' Christian said seriously.

Hillary is an astute woman, if she thought anyone was trying to smear James's name, well, god help them – she will annihilate them!'

Christian smiled for the first time since they sat down.

'Honestly, Christian, James was fortunate in his love for you. He wasn't promiscuous, he told me he was totally committed to only you for all those years. He told me you were his first and only love, and neither of you have ever given the slightest hint of your relationship. If James's father has his spies out, they are going to be extremely disappointed. I know of not one of James's friends who will sully his name.'

'What about your friend Lyndon – does he know?'

'I think he suspects after what James wrote in the letter - I assume you saw that before it was posted.'

'I did, yes. It could be incriminating! Will he say anything?'

'No. Lyndon would not do anything that might incriminate me.'

'He must love you very much.'

Jenna smiled and nodded.

'That still leaves you in no man's land – unable to love the man you want to.' He reached out and cupped his hand over hers.

'Lyndon and I have endured many separations – this will be just another one we will have to surmount,' she said sadly.

'It will not be forever, Jenna. It is quite acceptable for widows to marry again within six months of losing a husband. Life is short and fragile – a court would throw his claim out if he tried to contest the will on your re-marriage. I trust you *do* want to marry Lyndon eventually?'

'More than anything.'

'Then if you can wait, all will be well.'

They both placed their napkin on their respective laps as the first course was served, though both were preoccupied with the very real threat that all might not be well.

10

At Bochym Manor, Mary sat anxious and trembling. It was almost five o clock – the Earl and Countess would be home from London very soon. Glancing around the bedroom she'd shared with one maid or another for the last twelve years – well apart from those few precious nights the mistress had allowed her and Thomas to spend in one of Bochym's vacant cottages after their hasty marriage – she was in no doubt this would be her last week here. The mistress was a good lady, Mary felt sure that she would be given time to recover well enough to find some alternative work and accommodation. It was hoped that she would also get a reference, after all, her work had been unblemished until…. Lowering her eyes, she thought of how kind they had been with her since Thomas died – they had given her time to grieve and accommodated her melancholic moods when they had overwhelmed her, but with this, she had done something truly wicked, and she could not be forgiven for it - no matter what Ruby said she would try to do for her.

Glancing out of the window she saw that the master's car had returned and was being driven to the back of the manor to where it was kept undercover. Sitting on her hands to keep them from trembling, all she could do was wait to hear her fate.

*

Mary had to wait over an hour to hear her fate and when finally, Her Ladyship entered her room, Mary burst into noisy tears, in fear of what she was about to be told.

'I'm so sorry, Mary,' Sarah said sitting on the bed next her.

'Oh, please, my lady, don't dismiss me,' she cried.

'Mary, calm yourself.'

'Please, please, don't dismiss me.' Mary began to sob brokenheartedly.

'Mary.' Sarah's words were drowned in her howling wails. 'Mary!' Sarah grasped Mary's hands to try and calm her. *'Mary, please listen.'*

Mary took several deep hiccupping breaths and lifted her stricken face to Sarah's. 'Please don't make me leave.' She caught her breath with a sob.

'Nothing could be further from my thoughts.'

Mary hiccupped again. 'But you said sorry, I thought....' her voice trailed.

'I am only sorry that this has happened to you.' Sarah pulled Mary into an embrace.

Mary's sobs abated as she melted into her mistress's arms. She smelt wonderful - of fresh soap, silk and expensive perfume, and her arms held her safely as a mother would a daughter.

'I'm sorry that we did not see the signs that things were getting too much for you, Mary. I have spoken with the Earl, and we will do everything to support you through this terrible time. I admit, we thought because three years had passed since you lost Thomas that you were managing – but we were clearly wrong – grief I expect takes as long as it takes, and we will be here for you every step of the way.'

Mary could not speak for the lump that had formed in her throat, only a final sob emerged.

'Now, Ruby tells me the doctor thinks you need rest and fresh air and, by the feel of your bones through this dress, good nourishment. So, you will take this next week off - and if you feel well enough and while the weather is good, you must take yourself out into the garden if you wish, find a shady spot, and read and heal. Mrs Blair appears to be managing with the help of Ruby and Mrs Johnson in the kitchen, but hopefully you will be strong enough to come back to work next week.'

When Sarah gently released her from her arms, Mary sat up straight and finding her voice now said tremulously,

'Thank you, my lady. Thank you for your kindness. I am so sorry I brought shame on the household.'

Sarah shook her head. 'The shame is on us for not seeing the signs. All will be well, Mary. Your secret will not leave this house. As for the letter which prompted this dreadful event, Ruby has shown it to us, and rest assured it will be dealt with.'

*

Back downstairs, Peter, Sarah, Ruby, and Justin had gathered in the Jacobean drawing room for a pre-dinner drink.

Ruby had shown them the dreadful letter which had been sent to Mary from the *C O C* - the Cury Organisation Committee. Peter read the content again, shaking his head – it read as follows:

Dear Mrs Ellis,

We as the committee, were astonished at your letter, and in fact quite offended that you believed that we should even consider your shocking request. If your husband has been left off the list to commemorate the fallen, that can only mean that he died dishonourably and in disgrace. Good god, Mrs Ellis, you cannot seriously expect his name to sit with all the brave and wonderful men and boys who fought so gloriously for our freedom. Shame on you for asking and shame on your husband. Therefore, the answer to your request is a quite definite no.

Miss Clementine Boldwood - Chair of the C O C

Peter threw the letter down on the table. That damn committee is made up of bitter and twisted old maids, who had about as much idea of what went on in the trenches as that piano over there. I have no doubt these were the same women who were quick to hand out white feathers to those men who could not, for whatever reason, go to war.'

'Is there anything you can do, darling,' Sarah asked gently.

'Oh yes! I shall make them wish they had never sent that letter. Sarah, could you write and summon *Miss*

Clementine Boldwood *and* her cronies here on Friday morning at eleven, please?'

'Of course, with pleasure, my darling,' Sarah said with a smile.

*

It was Wednesday morning and Jenna had thrown herself into painting to take her mind off the conversation she'd had with Christian the day before – it also filled the void of Lyndon leaving. She longed to get back to Cornwall away from prying eyes now she knew that someone was watching Bellevue Gardens. She had had a sleepless night worrying about how on earth she was going to tell Lyndon that they could not be together yet? He would not take kindly to it, she knew that.

A quick glance at the clock told her it was half past four. She suspected that Lyndon and Matthew would have broken the long journey - booking themselves into hostels enroute for the last couple of nights. By her estimation they would probably be in Cornwall this evening. They had promised to phone from Trevarno as soon as they arrived, so she'd put off having dinner with Hillary that evening in order that she could take the call. More than anything she wanted to hear Lyndon's voice to ease her troubled mind, though she'd decided not to say anything yet to him about a longer separation – she would wait until she could see him in person. Would he wait for her just a little longer? She'd assured Christian that their love could withstand the wait – but could it? Remembering his outburst after the visit to the exhibition - she questioned it now.

*

Matthew and Lyndon were on the last leg of their journey home, though they still had over fifty miles to go. They were both sore of seat but eager to get to Trevarno.

'It's going to be about eight by the time we get home, Lyndon. Jenna will no doubt be out with Hillary, so, I'll phone her first thing in the morning.'

Lyndon nodded in agreement.

'Do you remember Peter Dunstan - the Earl de Bochym?' Matthew asked.

'Yes of course.'

'Well, he visited Trevarno last week, enquiring after your health.'

'That was kind of him.'

'When I telephoned Trevarno this morning, to tell them that we would be home later, Father told me Peter Dunston had sent a message over for you, offering you some work at Bochym Manor if you want it.'

Speaking of the Earl, this took Lyndon back to the last time he had worked on the Bochym Estate. He'd been so happy with life then, so full of hope for the future with Jenna. Unfortunately, shortly afterwards, his world had come crashing down when he found that Jenna's father had married her off to someone else to settle a debt. If the truth were known, Lyndon had not felt real happiness since that time at Bochym Manor.'

'You're quiet, are you not ready to take on a job?'

'I am – I need to, I can't live on fresh air and don't...' he stopped Matthew from speaking, 'say anything about Jenna being wealthy and that once we are married, I'll not have to work as hard.'

'I had no intention of saying anything of the sort. What I was going to say was that Peter said there is no rush – just when you are ready.'

'I'm sorry, Matthew – Jenna's wealth is just one of many sticking points between us.'

'It doesn't have to be. There is nothing to say that you both can't be your own person and earn your own money.'

'You don't understand, Matthew. I rent my house from you. I've hardly any money saved to buy a decent house for Jenna, and besides, she has two houses already, why would she want less then she already has?'

'Because she loves you, Lyndon! Trust me – she would live anywhere with you.'

'Would she though? Look at her – look how she dresses – the people in her circle – the life she lives. How can I expect her to live my sort of life – the life of an impoverished hedger?'

'You underestimate Jenna. I think she would be prepared to give up a great deal to be with you at last. Remember, she fell in love with you when you were an 'impoverished hedger' – as you call yourself. She may look different now, but she is the most unmaterialistic woman I know.'

Lyndon turned his head and looked out at the Cornish china clay mounds and fell quiet.

'Are you interested in the job at Bochym?'

'Yes, tell him, yes.'

*

When the car pulled up at Trevarno at half past eight that evening, Lyndon declined a night cap from Matthew and walked stiffly towards the cottage he once shared with his wife, Edna. Wife - what a joke that was! She had claimed to be pregnant after a drunken fumble at the harvest dance almost five years ago, even though Lyndon was positive they hadn't gone that far. The wedding had taken place in January 1914, and she'd claimed to have miscarried on their wedding day. Lyndon was not versed in such matters and believed it to be true, but then Edna would not let him back into her bed, feigning pain from the so-called miscarriage. Lyndon had not minded one jot - he loved only Jenna, so, as he couldn't be with his true love, he left Edna and joined up to a different kind of conflict. The marriage had been annulled quite recently, in fact as soon as he found out that Edna had had Jenna banished. He'd had his suspicions about Edna's virginity since another soldier had told him he'd been through a similar situation. Lyndon had called a doctor in, and a virginity test was done on Edna. Much to her dismay, she had been ordered to leave the cottage forthwith. There was still a lot of bad feeling between Edna's family and his own on the estate, but Lyndon was well rid of her.

He threw his bag on the chair, poured himself a stiff brandy and sat down beside the unlit fire. The trip to London was to reconnect with Jenna. They had only ever spent one night truly together and that had been almost three years ago. He knew it had been churlish of him to send her back to her own room that last night he'd spent in Bellevue Gardens, but she'd been drinking champagne, and her hair, bloody hell, her hair had Vaseline in it, god damn it! This was not the Jenna he wanted - he wanted the girl in the summer dress with the sun in her hair, sitting in a field of flowers. He sighed deeply – despite what Matthew had said, he was very much afraid the old Jenna had gone for good.

*

Lyndon's ex-wife, Edna, felt a cold anger as she'd watched from her bedroom window when Matthew Bickford's car drew up and Lyndon had got out. She knew where he'd been and who with. It was no secret that he'd gone running up to London with Jenna now she had been so conveniently widowed. She clenched her teeth together, if he thought he was bringing her back here, he had another think coming. Her father had made it very plain that the estate would lose his expertise as a handyman if that woman set foot back on Trevarno soil. It heartened her though, to see Lyndon was alone, and by the look on his face not very happy with life. Perhaps the bitch had spurned him, now she'd had a taste of the good life. Serves him right – she hoped they would both rot in hell. She angrily dragged the curtains closed and almost pulled them off their railings!

*

After spending a worrying night fretting that Lyndon and Matthew had encountered an accident en route home, Jenna finally got a phone call from Matthew early on Thursday morning.

'At last!' she said her voice a higher octave than usual. 'I've been worried sick that something had happened to you.'

Matthew laughed, which irritated her.

'Sorry, Jenna,' he said, 'it was eight thirty when we got back to Trevarno, so we decided to wait until the morning to call you. We thought you would probably be out socialising with Hillary.'

'Well, I wasn't! Because I thought you were going to phone me,' Jenna said irritably.

'I know that now, sorry. When I phoned Hillary later last night, I found out that you hadn't gone out, but then I thought it was far too late to call you!'

Jenna exhaled a slow, measured breath and Matthew, picking up on her mood, apologised again.

'Can I speak to Lyndon now then, please.'

'Sorry, but he is not here, I'm afraid. He's gone to do a job at Bochym Manor.'

This rendered her quite speechless for a moment. *He had gone without speaking to her!*

'Jenna, are you still there?'

'Yes, I'm here. Can you get him to phone me when he gets back then?'

'Well, I'm not sure when he'll be back. Peter Dunstan – the Earl de Bochym, has a big job for him over there. It will do Lyndon good,' he added quickly, 'he needs to work, Jenna. You've seen how he is - he needs some direction in his life.'

'Yes, I know, but I would have rather liked to have spoken with him,' she said sharply and then added more softly. 'We did not part well.'

'I'm sorry, of course you would – I didn't think. You'll be back next week though, won't you? So, it's not too long to wait. I hope you have an enjoyable day with Hillary,' he said changing the subject, 'she said that you're going to help her choose a wedding dress today.'

'Yes,' she answered flatly.

'Well, I…, I shall ring off now, and let you get on with your busy day. I'll see you very soon. Goodbye, Jenna.'

As he rang off, Jenna felt an overwhelming sense of bewilderment as to why Lyndon had not wanted to speak to her before he left.

11

Lyndon steered his wagon down the long dusty track towards Bochym Manor. It had been seven years since he'd last been here and so much had happened. He'd been so young, full of life and hope for a future with Jenna. He wished he was that young man again – unscathed by heartbreak and war. He felt troubled this morning – his reluctance to speak to Jenna last evening or this morning before he left was playing on his mind, but he simply didn't know what to say to her about their future together. Seeing her enjoying her new found wealth and fame, he wondered if it was perhaps kinder to just melt away into the distance, busy himself in work, and forget about a life with her. Perhaps too much water had gone under the bridge for them ever to find any common ground again.

He pulled the horse up outside the steward's cottage and climbed down. Mr Pearson came out to greet him with a welcoming smile.

Lyndon offered his hand, and it was shaken firmly.

'Mr FitzSimmons. It's so good to see you again after all this time.

'And you, Mr Pearson. It's good to see you fared well in that damn war!'

'Yes, I fared better than most, I was only there for a few months, managed to dodge the bullets and shrapnel. I'm physically sound, but mentally, well, you'll know – we have seen things that no human being should have ever seen! I will never forget the horrors.'

Lyndon nodded knowingly.

'His Lordship is in Truro today and is sorry to have missed you, so I'll walk you round. Hopefully if you take this commission, he'll see you another time.'

'I understand from Matthew Bickford, the job is vast.'

'Indeed, it is. The hedge you laid last time was so successful, His Lordship wants the perimeter hedged the same.'

Lyndon stopped dead in his tracks. 'But, if I'm not mistaken, you are 18 acres, are you not?'

'We are, and we don't expect you to do it all at once of course. It will be an ongoing job in-between your other jobs, but it will be a job for life if you undertake it.'

'Oh! Well, I, I'm speechless.'

'Come, we will walk the perimeter and you can see if it is feasible.'

Two hours later, Lyndon had agreed to the job, and as he had nothing on his books at the moment, decided that there was no better time to start than the present. So, his first port of call was to the Bochym Kitchen, though he felt a sense of unease at what news would be awaiting him of the friends he had made around the kitchen table all those years ago. For sure, everyone's life had been changed by the war.

As he walked across the cobbled courtyard towards the Bochym kitchen he found one of the maids sitting in the sunshine at the outside table, huddled in a blanket. Lyndon smiled at her, wracking his brain to remember her name. She wore a strange, haunted, distant look in her eyes, and her face, though hollowed out, looked familiar, and then it came to him who she was.

'Hello. It's Mary, isn't it? I remember, you're Mrs Blair's assistant.'

Mary looked up at Lyndon and pulled the blanket closer to her body despite the warmth of the day.

'Don't you remember me? Lyndon FitzSimmons – the hedger!'

Mary nodded, ran her tongue across her blistered lips as though she was about to speak but instead, hung her head slightly.

Lyndon took the seat next to her, puzzled by her demeanour. 'Forgive me, Mary, but you look quite unwell, shall I fetch someone?'

Mary said nothing, she just closed her eyes and shook her head, making Lyndon realise his presence by her side was unwanted.

'I'll leave you to enjoy the sunshine then.' He pressed his hands on top of his thighs and stood up.

The door to the kitchen was open, so Lyndon knocked and stepped through the threshold.

'Oh, lordy me,' Mrs Blair declared as she looked up from checking the suet pudding she was cooking for dinner. 'If it isn't Mr FitzSimmons the hedger at our door. Mr Treen said you would be coming back to see us. Lucy, go and fetch Mr Treen.' The cook grasped Lyndon by the arms and looked him up and down. 'I must say you look well – and all in one piece, thank goodness. This damn war took so many of the young men,' she said with a tear in her eye.

'I am well, thank you, Mrs Blair and may I say, you look well too, and by the aroma in this kitchen you are still cooking delicious dinners.'

'Beef suet pudding today! You'll stay and eat with us.' It was a statement not a question.

'Thank you, I will.'

'Forgive me for mentioning, Mrs Blair, but Mary out there, looked dreadful. Is she ill?'

Cook blanched. 'Oh no, she's all right, she's had a terrible upset tummy – it's knocked the stuffing out of her,' she said, 'She'll come brave. We're all looking after her.'

Lyndon turned at the sound of footsteps as Joe Treen followed Lucy back into the kitchen.

He beamed a smile. 'Lyndon, our friend! Welcome back.' Joe shook his hand firmly.

Lyndon instantly recognised that same world-weary look in Joe's eyes – a look all men probably wore who fought during the conflict.

'It's been such a long time and it's so good to see you,' Joe said, 'and thankfully, you survived the war!'

'Just about. How did you fare, Joe?'

'Not totally unscathed.' He sighed heavily lifting his hand to reveal missing fingers. 'I'm alive though, thank god. You're staying for dinner?' Joe glanced at Mrs Blair who nodded as she was setting another place at the table. 'You'll remember some of the old faces, and we have a couple of new ones too. Ah, and here is Juliet, my wife, you remember her, I think,' Joe said proudly as she walked into the kitchen.

'Hello, Juliet, I do remember you,' he smiled gently at this fine, confident, young woman who stepped forward and offered her hand to him. *What he did remember was that the last time he had seen Juliet, she had been a shy, timid girl who had hardly said a word to him.*

'Hello, Lyndon, It's nice to meet you again – I trust you are well.'

'Thank you, yes, Juliet – you look very well too if I might be so bold.'

There was a lot of hammering and banging going on somewhere in the house and Lyndon gave Joe a curious look.

'We have a gentleman restoring the plasterwork in the French drawing room to its former glory, you'll meet him at dinnertime. The south wing of the house was given over to officers for rehabilitation during the war – it's in a bit of a state as you can imagine. Some of the staff were lucky enough to rehabilitate here, thanks to His Lord and Her ladyship, including myself and Theo Trevail. We were conscripted in January 1916. We'd only been out there six months when I got shrapnel wounds to my left arm and hand. I had a great big hole in my lower arm as well, which meant a double-edged sword for me, I was injured, but thankfully, the war was over for me. I came back here and my lovely Juliet nursed me back to health.'

Lyndon smiled when he saw Juliet curl her arm around Joe's.

'And Theo?'

'He lost an eye three months later but is fortunate to be able to continue as His Lordship's valet.

Lyndon nodded and smiled. 'And Thomas – what of him?'

Joe's face clouded as he glanced to where Mary was sitting in the courtyard.

'Come into my office for a moment, Lyndon.'

Lyndon settled down on the worn leather seat opposite Joe, and he knew this could only mean sad news.

'Well, I'm afraid to tell you that Thomas died,' he sighed. 'He joined up as soon as war broke out, full of bravado, wanting an adventure – after all they said it would be all over by that Christmas.'

Lyndon laughed without humour. 'Many from Trevarno did the same – I included – I joined up with Matthew Bickford – although he was an officer. How wrong we all were, eh?'

'Exactly. Well, it broke Mary's heart when Thomas went. Although there had never been an understanding between them, she had always been in love with Thomas and was naturally distraught when he signed up. He came home on leave in January 1916 and astonished us all, including Mary, when he proposed to and married her. I think we all needed to have someone to live for, someone to get us through the war. I know I would not have survived without Juliet's letters.'

Lyndon nodded, thinking of the many letters he and Jenna had secretly written during the war. He felt a sudden pang of guilt now about his thoughts earlier.

'Bless them, they had only a few days together, and as Theo and I had been served our conscription papers, we all headed out to the front together. I must say Thomas's jolly persona saw Theo and I through a lot. You remember what sort of man he was – cheeky, cheerful, and full of life and wit.'

Lyndon nodded.

'We were billeted together for about six months, and a braver man I have never seen. He was a remarkable man, never hesitated for a moment to go over the top when ordered.' Joe lowered his eyes and his shoulders drooped. 'You'll know as well as I, that it is estimated that 306 soldiers from Britain and the Commonwealth were executed for cowardice during the war.'

Lyndon nodded, feeling his heart constrict.

'Well, Thomas was one of them.' Joe shook his head. 'But that man was no coward! One day the Germans sent a minenwerfer over to our trench and we were all blown far and wide by the thing. I kid you not, it blew a hole about the size of the Bochym kitchen in our dugout – the trench vanished completely, and with it most of the other men I'd been fighting alongside. We who survived, were so shattered – our nerves were shot to bits.'

Lyndon nodded. 'I understand – I had a similar experience. I relive the nightmare regularly,' he admitted.

'We survivors were taken off for hospital treatment, I was walking wounded, and as I approached the field hospital, I found Thomas sat outside on a box, he was caked from head to foot in brown mud – he looked like a statue you would see in a garden. He was totally silent and as still as the dead. I went to speak to him, to see if I could help, but he was completely dumb with shock. He couldn't speak to me, and I don't think he recognised me. I don't think I have ever seen a man more shattered and shell shocked. I went in and called one of the doctors to come out and they took him in. I honestly thought they would send the poor devil home, but two weeks later I glanced to my side and saw him there in the dugout – trembling with fear as we made to go over the top. I said to the commanding officer, Captain Jones – a small, brute of a man – army through and through, I said to him, "He's not well, he's a friend of mine and he's not well – he should be in hospital!" My pleas were ignored, and the officer just butted Thomas with the end of his rifle and kicked him up the backside to move him to the trench ladders. We were all on standby, but Thomas was shaking so much he lost his grip and fell back down into the trench. The officer yelled obscenities at him to get back in line up the ladder, but when Thomas couldn't move, the officer shouted effing coward and aimed the gun at him. I retreated down the ladder and pleaded with him not to shoot him and the officer turned the gun on me to silence me. Oh God, Lyndon, he kicked Thomas and then shot him at point blank range for cowardice. He was shot like a rat – he didn't even get a trial. I was stunned. My eyes could not comprehend that the man I had worked alongside, here in the manor, and fought so bravely with on the front line was laying there dead – killed by one of our own. Then only moments after he shot Thomas, one of my comrades, Corporal Higgins who was good mates with Thomas, turned his rifle on Captain Jones and shot him, just before we went over the top and charged into battle. He was my bloody hero, that day! As we were running, Higgins turned to me, his eyes wild with anger, and said, "I hope I have killed the effing bastard," then a moment later I saw Higgins killed by mortar fire. I was splattered in his blood as I charged a further ten yards and then shrapnel hit my left hand and arm and my war was over too.' Joe took a gasp of breath, the effort of recalling and telling the tale had shattered him.

Lyndon reached out and briefly put his hand over Joe's.

Joe hung his head. 'That was the single worst day of my life,' he muttered.

Lyndon watched as Joe sat there, deep in his own thoughts for a few seconds until he lifted his head quickly wiping a tear from his cheek.

'Poor Mary, all she was left with was a baby in her belly and a letter telling her that her husband had been shot for cowardice. She received no war widow pension and lost the baby a couple of months later – it was still born – put down to her distress, even though I'd told her and the rest of the staff what had really happened – but as they say, mud sticks. She's never got over it – she barely goes beyond the manor grounds and has recently been very ill – due to her state of mind.'

'That explains a lot – I saw Mary outside, she looked ever so poorly. Mrs Blair said she been ill – with a stomach bug.'

Joe just nodded.

'So, what happened to this Captain Jones?'

'I have no idea if Captain Jones survived the gunshot wound or not, but you know Lyndon, if I find that he is still alive, I am going to try and have that bastard prosecuted for war crimes if it's the last thing I do. I've spoken to the Earl to see if he can find him, but there is so much going on at the moment, trying to get the country back up and running again and Jones is a common name.

'Poor Mary and Thomas.' Lyndon pulled his mouth into a tight line. 'War, what the hell was it all about? Such a waste of young lives – that is all war is.'

'I agree.'

Joe checked his pocket watch. 'Come, let's eat, if you've still got the stomach for it.'

12

In London, Jenna rallied herself, though she was troubled at heart, and she set off to meet Hillary at the wedding couture house. Hillary was having her last fitting for her wedding gown and Jenna was there to be fitted for her attendant's dress.

'Darling, there you are!' Hillary kissed Jenna and then grasped her by the arms and held her at arm's length. 'Oh dear, who ate your bowl of sunshine this morning?'

Jenna laughed - she couldn't hide much from Hillary.

'Oh, it's nothing, I just have a lot on my mind at the moment.'

'Missing the delectable Lyndon Fitzsimmons, I'll wager.' She winked.

Jenna nodded.

'Never mind, I shall endeavour to take your mind off your loss and fill your day with frivolous wedding things. We will of course round the day off with a champagne lunch.'

Jenna's heart constricted at the thought of Hillary's wedding to Matthew. It was to be held on the 10th of August - less than a month away. It was a day she was both looking forward to and dreading in equal measure. The wedding was to be held in Cornwall at the Trevarno Estate near Helston and that place evoked so many memories for Jenna – though not all bad.

Sitting in the plush surroundings of the couture house, Jenna's mind flitted back to being here herself - only four months ago - to be fitted for her own spectacular wedding gown for her wedding to James. How fragile life is to change so swiftly, she mused sadly.

'Ta-da! What do you think?'

Hillary was stood in front of her in the most fabulous gown Jenna had ever seen.

'Gosh, Hillary, you've taken my breath away.'

'Well take a deep breath and tell me what you think - it is divine, isn't it?'

'It's stunning, you look fabulous.'

'I always do, darling,' she winked, 'now wait.' She disappeared behind the screens and five minutes later she had on another, equally fantastic gown. 'Right, what do you think of this one?'

'You've had two made?' Jenna asked in astonishment.

'Well, I couldn't decide. That's why you're here with me.'

Jenna's mouth dropped. 'Well, neither can I now.'

'Oh, darling, you're no use to me then, are you? Never mind – I'll sort it. Now it's your turn – I've had a little peek of your dress – it's on the hanger in here – it's divine,' she said, her eyes sparkling.

Jenna smiled. 'I have no doubt it will be.'

'Come on then, try it on.'

Moments later, Jenna was dressed in a beautiful peach-coloured organza gown, delicately sprigged with embroidered lily of the valley.

'Darling!' Hillary clasped her hands together. 'It's so good to see you in colour again and by the wedding date you'll be out of mourning.'

Jenna had to admit, she would be glad when she was out of mourning – dark clothes and hot weather did not mix!

*

Once out of the couture house, Lunch was on the agenda. As they sat down and ordered, Hillary took a sip of her champagne.

'Well,' Hillary said with a flourish of the glass, 'can you believe it, this is the first time we have had a chance to speak candidly since you came up to London.'

'Yes, it's all been a little fraught with one thing and another,' Jenna mused.

Hillary nodded. 'London can be like that sometimes! You don't mind waiting until next week to go back, do you? I am having a few alterations to my wedding gown.'

'Which gown?' she asked with a twist in her smile.

'Wait and see.' Hillary tapped her nose.

'As for waiting, I don't mind at all. In fact, I can get quite a lot of painting done with the house empty.'

'I suspect you are keen to get back to Cornwall though!' Hillary arched her pencilled eyebrow.

'Yes,' Jenna answered, glancing over her glass waiting for whatever Hillary was about to say next.

'And…, will you be seeing the delectable Mr FitzSimmons again?'

'Yes,' she answered more confidently than she felt. 'Though it will be difficult for some time - I am, after all, still in mourning for James,' she added tentatively.

Hillary took another sip of champagne but remained unusually quiet.

'Please don't think badly of me, Hillary, I know you and James were close.'

'I don't, darling, I assure you. James wrote to me before he died, you know – he said I was not to judge you if another man came into your life quite soon.'

Jenna nodded. 'It seems James did a little matchmaking before he died – he wrote to Lyndon as well telling him to come to me.'

'Did he now?' Hillary smiled. 'You know, when you brought Lyndon to London, I could see he wasn't just a guest you'd brought along, so I asked Matthew about him. He said Lyndon was about to marry you in 1912, but a dreadful incident occurred that put paid to that.'

Jenna leaned back in her chair. 'Dreadful it was indeed,' she said sombrely, 'my father married me off to a hateful man – a monster, to repay a huge debt he owed him.'

'Goodness, gracious me!' Hillary took a gulp of her wine almost choking on it.

'When I finally broke free of my marriage - by feigning my own death, Lyndon brought me to Trevarno, but by then he was promised to someone else, someone he didn't love, but a promise was a promise and I had to watch as he married her. I began working in the kitchen and dairy at Trevarno, so at least I could be near him, but then the war happened.' She paused, sighing deeply. 'We never stopped loving each other, and we wrote to each other regularly, but then,' her eyes looked downcast, 'Lyndon was reported dead, his wife found out about us, and I was banished from Trevarno'

'What?' Hillary put down her glass.

'Lyndon's wife, Edna, found out that I had been corresponding with him, and that we had once shared a secret assignation when he was home on leave. He'd written one of those 'last letters home' that was addressed to me but in the uniform pocket that was sent home to his wife. Edna's father Eric Madron was the estate's handy man, a job that had been held by the Madron family down the generations. He was a good employee and could mend anything so warned Matthew's father that he would leave if I stayed. Matthew had no option but to find me another place - which was with James, and the rest, they say, is history.'

'Well, it's no wonder you baulk every time I mention you coming to Trevarno. It all makes sense now. Is Lyndon still married?'

'No, the marriage was annulled – Edna had tricked him into marriage and then refused him his marital rights.'

'And where is this *Edna* person now?'

'She's still at Trevarno, as is her father. So, you see, me coming to Trevarno might cause problems.'

'No, it jolly well won't! Of that I can assure you,' Hillary said adamantly as she gestured for the waiter to top up the glasses.

*

While Jenna and Hillary were enjoying a champagne lunch, Lyndon had settled at the Bochym kitchen table gratefully inhaling the deep aroma of a hearty beef suet dinner. It was good to sit amongst friends again. From where he was seated, he could see the courtyard table where Mary was sitting. He watched as a footman he had not met before, took Mary a bowl of soup.

'So,' Lyndon turned his attention to the people sitting around the table, 'we have new faces I see.'

'Yes, this is our maid Lucy Hocking, she took over Betsy's role, seven years ago.'

Lucy smiled shyly back at Lyndon.

'And this here is David Harker. David is our new footman,' he nodded to the man who had come back in from delivering food to Mary.

Lyndon nodded a hello. 'Speaking of Betsy, did she marry her heart's desire, Ryan Penrose?'

'She did. Ryan went to be a thatcher with the Blackthorns at Poldhu. Betsy works at the tearoom there and they live in a beach side cottage with their little girl, Josie - they have another baby on the way.' Joe smiled.

'I'm glad to hear Ryan came back from the war all right.'

'He did, and in one piece – but the war has changed him. He is noticeably quiet now, isn't he, Juliet?'

'Yes, but his little daughter is stopping him from brooding – she is quite a handful,' Juliet answered.

Lyndon nodded. 'The war changed everyone. Didn't your young brother Jake work for Guy Blackthorn?'

Joe nodded. 'He was called up last Easter on his eighteenth birthday. I was devastated when I found out he had to go, but thankfully he survived and is back on the roof thatching.'

'That is good to hear. Does *he* have a sweetheart?'

'No, but he is mighty keen on a young lady called Marianne Enys, who has just started work at The Poldhu Tea Room, but she seems not to see him.' Joe gave Lucy,

Marianne's friend a knowing look, who in turn cast her eyes downwards. 'Apparently, Marianne is holding out for a gentleman.'

'There is no harm in aiming high, Mr Treen,' Lucy said boldly.

'*Lucy.*' Juliet gave her a warning look. 'Don't speak back to Mr Treen.'

Joe patted Juliet's hand. 'She's only fighting her friend's corner. But I suspect Marianne will be extremely disappointed. I just feel for Jake, the foolish lad is willing to wait for her.'

'So,' Dorothy, the maid, archly turned to Lyndon, 'what about you, did you marry your sweetheart before you went off to fight? I seem to remember you had a certain young lady waiting for you in Gweek – I trust that turned out well?'

'*Dorothy,*' Joe warned.

'It's fine, Joe.' Lyndon sighed and shook his head slowly. 'No, Dorothy, It didn't turn out too well actually. Several obstacles including the war put a stop to our budding romance, and we went our separate ways.'

'Oh, really!' Dorothy looked at him with interest. 'So, are you still single?'

Lyndon's mouth curled into a smile. 'For now, yes.'

'And the young woman in question - now the obstacle of war has gone,' Joe enquired, 'is there hope of a reconciliation?'

Dorothy pursed her lips at Joe's question.

'It's very complicated. She's just been recently widowed and is still in mourning.'

'Yes, the country is full of poor widows,' Joe agreed sadly. 'So, there may be still a chance with her eventually?'

Dorothy screwed her mouth up clearly not liking the direction this conversation was going.

Lyndon shrugged. 'We'll see.'

Dorothy's pursed lips relaxed into a smile.

'Are you taking the job here, Lyndon?' Juliet asked.

'I've nothing on my books yet, so yes - this is a blessing as it is an ongoing job – I shall become part of the family working here indefinitely.'

Joe smiled. 'You're already part of the family. It will be good to have you around again.'

'Yes, it will be lovely, Lyndon.' Dorothy fluttered her eyelashes.

Just at that minute a gentleman came rushing into the kitchen. 'I do beg your pardon for being late, everyone,' he said.

'Ah, this is Gabriel Trelease, Lyndon - the man making all the noise' Joe joked as he walked into the room to take his seat at the table. 'Gabriel, meet Lyndon FitzSimmons – he's a master hedger and will be working here on and off from now on.'

'Please to meet you, Lyndon.' Gabriel shook his hand.

'Likewise.'

Gabriel turned apologetically towards Joe. 'Am I making too much noise? It's a necessary evil I'm afraid.'

'Not at all, I only jest.'

Mrs Blair dished out the beef and kidney suet pudding and they began to tuck in appreciatively.

Once their meal was finished, Joe said, 'I see your friend Matthew Bickford is getting married soon, Lyndon.'

'Yes, I'm to be Matthew's best man,' Lyndon said proudly.

'His Lord and Ladyship and Mr and Mrs Devereux are going.'

'Oh, so Justin is still here then?'

'He is - in fact, I think this is him coming now. The sound of joyous chatter preceded Justin and Ruby as they walked into the kitchen.

'Good day to you all,' Justin said breezily, 'sorry to disturb your meal, we are just here gathering goodies for a picnic basket – we thought to go to Church Cove. Now, did I hear my name mentioned, as I came in.' Justin smiled as he looked around the table and then his eyes lit in delight when they fell on Lyndon.

'Lyndon, my old friend, how are you. Long-time no meet.'

Lyndon stood up and shook Justin's hand vigorously. 'I'm well, thank you. It's good to see you too. And you too, Mrs Sanders,' Lyndon said to Ruby.

'Mrs Devereux, now,' Ruby answered with a sparkle in her eye as she reached out to shake Lyndon's hand, 'but please, call me Ruby. It's lovely to see you again.'

Lyndon glanced between them. 'Oh, well, may I offer my congratulations.'

Justin laughed. 'Well, thank you, but we've been married a while now - since New Year's Eve 1912 actually.'

'How marvellous. Did you never make it back to Italy then? I seem to remember you lived there.'

'We did, for three years, but when Europe became unstable, we thought it better to come home to England to help here at Bochym with the war effort.'

'I should think Italy was very different from Bochym, Ruby,' Lyndon asked.

'Yes, it was very different - a real culture shock for this old housekeeper,' she joked. 'It was extremely hot as well, but glorious all the same. We're heading back there very soon to see if anything is left of our villa, aren't we darling?'

'We are indeed.'

'Oh gosh, I hope you find all is well. Were you conscripted, Justin? – I can't remember how old you are.'

'I was, unfortunately. I'm forty-seven now and I thought I'd got away with it, but then they moved the conscription age up to fifty and I was called up in June last year. Managed to dodge the bullets, thank god. Tell me, my friend, how long were you there for?'

'The duration.'

'Goodness me!' Justin frowned. 'And you got through the war unscathed?'

'Not unscathed - no. A hole in the hand which fortunately healed.' Lyndon lifted it to show the white scars where the bullet had gone through. 'Then just days before the war ended, I was hit by shrapnel and left for dead. My family were informed as such and I was almost buried alive until some kind soul heard me groaning, I had no idea who I was when I came around - I completely lost my memory for months. It was only because someone recognised me in a rehabilitation hospital in London and got in touch with Matthew, that I got home. He brought me back to Trevarno in April to recuperate but it took another three weeks before I regained my memory.'

'Are you quite recovered now though?' Justin asked.

'I admit, I'm struggling with the effects of war – loud noises, bangs, and such – it just takes me right back to the trenches – back to that nightmare. I'm like a gibbering wreck sometimes and I don't mind admitting it.'

Joe let out a low groan. 'I used to suffer as you, from loud bangs,' he admitted. 'Poor Mrs Blair had to keep the noise in the kitchen to the minimum otherwise I've been known to end up under the kitchen table.'

Juliet squeezed Joe's arm, the look on her face understanding that it wasn't an easy thing for any man to admit to.

'I've been lucky though,' Joe added, 'I had help. His Lordship paid for me to have treatment in Devon.'

Lyndon tipped his head. 'I wasn't aware there was treatment – we all seemed to have been left to flounder.'

'Yes, I was treated at Newton Abbott's Seale Hayne in Devon. It was set up by an army major, Arthur Hurst, who swept aside opposition to set up the centre there. He treated soldiers with shell shock with a variety of cures, including hypnosis, massage, rest, and dietary treatments - all with excellent results. He allowed men to work within the peace and quiet of the rolling Devon countryside. It was thought to be a place where the men could get over their hysteria through labouring on the land. We toiled on the farm and were encouraged to use our creative energies. Arthur Hurst even encouraged his patients to shoot. He also directed a reconstruction of the battlefields of Flanders on Dartmoor to help the men relive their experiences. It helped me enormously.'

Lyndon felt his heart quicken with hope – could he be cured of this terrible affliction?

'I'll get the information from Peter if you wish, Lyndon,' Justin offered.

'Thank you, yes,' Lyndon breathed.

13

Just before eleven on Friday morning Joe opened the door to the five remaining spinster members of The Cury Organisation Committee. The only male member, Albert Eustice had apparently died two days ago! The chair of the committee - Clementine Boldwood, a rather large, ugly, robust woman with an ample bosom was first to step over the threshold. Another rather formidable and disagreeable woman called Joan Freeman followed quickly behind. Then came a tiny bird of a woman called Clara Benny who squeaked a greeting to Joe. Next was Jocelyn Freethy who had the unfortunate countenance of a wet weekend and finally came Catherine Maddiver who looked as though she was chewing a pickled onion!

Joe showed them into the library. 'His Lordship will be with you shortly.'

'His Lordship, eh?' Clementine Boldwood raised a bushy eyebrow. 'Usually we see the Countess - still, this way I suppose we can set aside the niceties of explaining the needs of the community to the monkey and go straight to the organ grinder!'

'Clemi that is a shocking way to speak about the Countess,' Joselyn berated.

'What she can't hear can't hurt her. I shall put it to the Earl that the community hut needs a new roof,' she said walking around the library, running her fingers over the surfaces of the wood fold panelling.

'What are you doing, Clemi?' Clara asked aghast.

'I'm checking to see if this place has been cleaned properly. Especially when they employ maids who were married to cowards. I wouldn't trust a woman like that to clean my W.C.'

'Actually, I think she's the assistant cook here,' Clara corrected.

'Well in that case, I forbid any of you to eat any of the biscuits that may be served with our refreshments later.'

Joan Freeman and Catherine Maddiver both scowled at this veto.'

'I am rather disappointed in the Earl and Countess. I would have had that Ellis woman thrown out on her ear for the shame she is bringing on this community. I certainly wouldn't have her under the roof of a house as fine as this.'

'Perhaps they don't know, Clemi! Perhaps she has kept it a secret – I'd keep it a secret if it were me.'

'Well, if they don't know now, they will very shortly. I've told everybody I know. She'll get short shrift in the shops in Mullion from now on – I've seen to that.'

'Clemi, you're terrible,' Joan grinned.

*

Joe had returned to the kitchen after informing the Earl of the committee's arrival.

'The wicked witches of the west are gathered in the library,' Joe whispered to Molly, though Mrs Blair heard.

'Why have they been invited, Mr Treen,' Mrs Blair grumbled. 'I'm not happy about serving them tea after what they did to our Mary - the poor girl is distraught and hiding in the pantry.'

'I don't think it is going to be a social call, Mrs Blair – so no tea needed today.'

'Oh?' Mrs Blair cocked her head.

'Let's just say they are going to be given some home truths,' he said with a wry smile. 'So, you can tell Mary to dry her eyes – I suspect justice will be the only thing served today.'

The bell from the Earl's study, rang.

'I may be gone a while - the Earl requests my presence during the meeting,' Joe said pulling his shoulders back and lifting his chin.

*

When Joe and the Earl entered the library, he heard one of the women muttering under her breath that it was about time tea was sent for.

The Earl rested against the library desk - he had in his hand the letter sent to Mary.

'This obscenity was sent to one of my employees, from your committee,' he said.

The group of women glanced at each other, but Clementine Boldwood pulled herself up to her full size and said proudly, 'Indeed it was!'

Clara Benny frowned. 'What letter?'

'Be quiet, Clara,' Clementine warned.

'What do you have to say for yourself,' the Earl asked.

'Say?' Clementine shrugged as though not understanding his meaning.

'Have you no shame, in sending a letter like this to a grieving woman?'

'The shame is on her, and I might add on you, for continuing to employ her!'

The other women in the group gasped at Clementine's boldness.

The Earl folded his arms and shook his head. 'Treen.'

'Yes, my lord?'

'Remind us of what you witnessed in June 1916. I implore you to leave nothing out for there are no *delicate* ears in *this* room.'

Joe cleared his voice and told the tale once again in absolute graphic and bloody detail of what happened to Thomas. When he finished his account, he had to pull on all his reserves not to shed a tear. As he looked at the women in the room, they were holding their heads low and could not look Joe or the Earl in the eye.

'Thank you, Treen.' The Earl turned to the women. 'Now, what do you have to say for yourselves?'

'Well.' Clementine Boldwood pursed her thick ugly lips angrily. 'We did not know the facts when we sent the letter.'

'No, madam, you *did not*. But now you all have the facts, let me make one thing clear to you. I shall remove our patronage for anything your committee have planned in the future, *unless* Mrs Ellis receives a written *full* apology from each and every one of your members, for the disgraceful, and frankly disgusting letter you sent to her.' He stabbed his finger at them all.

'I didn't even know Clemi had sent that letter!' Clara Benny piped up.

'I said be quiet, Clara,' Clementine snapped.

'I do not want any excuses - I want a letter from every one of you and I shall make sure Mrs Ellis shows me them all. If any are less than heartfelt, you know what will happen.'

'She still can't have his name on that plaque, my lord,' Clementine said forcefully. 'We have to go with what the war office tells us.'

'Well now you know the war office was wrong, but having said that, I am intelligent enough to know that their wrong will not be amended, but I tell you this, Miss Boldwood, Mrs Ellis no longer wants her fine husband's name on your plaque. He will be honoured by this family in some other fitting way. He was a hero and make sure none of you ever forget that. Now the letter you write to her must first apologise for the insensitive way you wrote to her. It must convey your sympathies for her plight and of course you must tell her in the kindest way possible that, even though you understand the truth of Thomas's death now, you are deeply sorry that you cannot go against or overturn the war office decision. You must finish the letter by wishing her well at this difficult time. Do you all understand?'

There was a mumbled agreement.

'Good, now I have no doubt you have spread your denouncement of Thomas far and wide. So, I suggest that after you have written and sent your apology to Mrs Ellis – which I expect you to do within the next twenty-four hours - you retract your lies from whomsoever you have told. Because if I hear of one incident where Mrs Ellis is verbally abused in any way, *all* funding to your projects will *stop!* Now good day to you. Treen, please show the committee *out.*'

As the women filed out of the front door of Bochym Manor in silence, Joe's heart swelled with admiration for what the Earl had done today. He was truly blessed to work under such a fine upstanding man.

*

On Saturday morning, the postman duly delivered six letters addressed to Mary. Joe on seeing them, asked Molly if one of the other maids could take over helping Mrs Blair before sending Mary outside to read her letters.

'Who are they from, Mr Treen?' Mary said, her face stricken - letters had only brought her unwelcome news in the past.

'Just go and read them,' he ordered firmly.

Although the kitchen was a hive of action, Joe, Molly, Dorothy, and Mrs Blair watched for Mary's reaction. When it came, she lay her head in her arms and wept noisily.

Joe went out to her. 'Mary?'

She lifted her eyes to his.

'Is everything all right?'

She nodded her head and smiled through the tears as she handed the letters over to show him.

'May I show these to His Lordship? He very kindly explained to the committee what really happened to Thomas yesterday. I think he would like to see how deeply sorry they are for any harm caused to you.'

'Yes, of course,' she said dabbing her eyes. 'Please tell His Lordship how grateful I am for his intervention.'

'I will, Mary.' He patted her on the shoulder.

*

By Tuesday, Lyndon had been gone just over a week, and soon Jenna too would be heading home to Cornwall with Hillary.

There had been no telephone call from Lyndon, but then if he was working at Bochym Manor he probably wouldn't have access to a phone. Nevertheless, the silence from him unsettled her and she had no idea how their relationship stood now. Putting her paintbrush down, she sat down on her stool perusing the painting she had just put the finishing touches to. It was a painting of a summer meadow, knee deep in wild flowers with Gweek and the Helford River spanning out in front of her. Lyndon was correct when he said you could step into one of her paintings. It was not intentional, she just portrayed what her eyes saw, or in this case what she remembered - not having set foot in Gweek for over five years. Gweek was another place which evoked both pleasant and deeply unpleasant memories. This painting, done purely from memory was of one of the better memories she had there – a time emblazoned on her heart when she had been eighteen and had fallen deeply in love with Lyndon that long hot summer of 1912.

'Darling, Lyndon,' she sighed, 'will we ever be together again in that field?' *Not in the near future if James's father had anything to do with it!*

Jenna was desperate to leave London now, to get away from prying eyes. Though if anyone was watching her, they had precious little to accuse her of – she had only been out for dinner twice this last week with Hillary and the usual crowd they socialised with. Each time she had been cautious not to dance with any of the gentlemen in their group – feigning a sore knee, just in case she was being watched.

The telephone began to ring, and Jenna upset her paint pallet in her rush to get downstairs – just in case it was Lyndon. Fortunately, Mrs Hemp was there to take the call and was holding the receiver out to her.

'Miss Stanton on the phone for you, Mrs Blackwell.'

'Thank you, Mrs Hemp.' She felt her heart drop slightly as she took the call.

'Darling, do you have any more business to conduct here, after Thursday?' Hillary asked. 'The bridal couture house tells me the alterations will be complete tomorrow afternoon.'

'Oh, I see!' This meant that Jenna would have to arrange for this painting to be delivered to The Black Gallery, and to gather together the ones she'd started, but not finished, ready to take down to Cornwall.

'So, do you?' Hillary asked impatiently.

'No, but...'

'Well then, if there is no reason to stay, it's a good reason to go.'

Jenna laughed at Hillary's spontaneity. 'I'll be ready.'

'Fabulous. I am simply dying to see my delectable fiancé again. Good God! listen to me, I cannot believe I am uttering these words. London is my life! If you cut me open, you would see London through and through, like that dreadful confectionary they sell in that northern seaside town!'

'Blackpool you mean?'

'Yes, yes, Blackpool and that rock candy they sell there. Ugh!'

Jenna laughed at her remark. 'It's very popular so I am told.'

'Is it? Probably for those who care not a fig about their teeth, darling. Anyway, I digress, we will set off at first light on Thursday – I have decided to take the car. If I'm to be holed up in the sticks at Cornwall, I shall need a form of escape, to at least go to Truro shopping.'

'Do you never get sick of shopping, Hillary.'

'I shall ignore that ridiculous question. Now, I've phoned Matthew, so he knows we are about to be on our way.'

14

Lyndon had been at Bochym Manor for several days now. He had not returned home for the weekend - having no real reason to go there. He had quite settled down to life living in his wagon again – though his horse, Bramble, was getting a little too old now to be pulling the wagon around the county. He was in two minds whether to get another horse or one of those new-fangled motor wagons to get about with, though he was sure it wouldn't be half as comfortable to sleep in as his old faithful wagon. There was something rather wonderful about being on the road, just him and his horse. Goodness but he would miss Bramble when she was finally put out to grass. A smile formed remembering how Jenna had once saved Bramble from the authorities when the war office requisitioned all healthy horses to go for use at the front. She had pretended that Bramble was old and ready for the knacker's yard. Lyndon had ridden Bramble before he should have, so she had a real droop in the saddle area, making her look old to start with. Jenna had painstakingly and carefully coated several of the hairs around Bramble's nose and eyebrows with whitewash, added some to her mane and tail just for effect. Then she'd collected piles of her manure and mixed it with water to make it sloppy and poured it all over the field, especially near the gate where the authorities would come for her. Bramble always tended to hang her head as though she was exhausted - even when she had just been for a short walk. So, the morning the authorities were coming for the horses at Trevarno, Jenna had taken her on a long walk first thing that morning to really tire her out. It worked! They took one look at the horse and the loose manure everywhere and told Jenna it would be kinder to take the old nag to the knacker's yard rather than keeping a horse in that state. So, Bramble lived when so many others didn't. It was just one of the many lovely things Jenna did for Lyndon while he was at war, and he again felt a pang of guilt at the way he'd left things with her in London – he should have rung her. Turning his thoughts back to Bramble, he wasn't exactly traveling about the countryside at the moment, so for now, his horse was happy in the lower meadow enjoying the companionship of some sheep on this fine country estate.

It was late in the afternoon and Lyndon was busy pleaching his branches into the impenetrable hedges - and could probably do at least another yard before the end of his working day. An hour later, Gabriel drove his car up the dusty drive, stopped and got out to speak to him. They had hit it off almost immediately, and they had shared a glass or two in the nearby Wheel Inn most evenings.

'Gosh, is it that time already?' Lyndon checked his fob watch.

'No, I need to get something from Helston, but I'll be back for a drink if you care to join me.'

'I will thank you.'

'I've actually brought you this.' Gabriel handed over the note Joe had given him. 'I'll see you shortly.'

Lyndon opened the note which read. *A phone call from Matthew Bickford. The London constituency are coming home. They should be here on Saturday.*

He folded the note up, put it in his pocket and returned to his work.

'Mr FitzSimmons, sir?'

Lyndon turned, wiped the perspiration from his brow as an old peddler was touching his forelock to Lyndon as he approached him.

'I've a note for you, from Farmer Ferris in Gweek,' he said with a toothless grin.

Lyndon smiled – it never ceased to amaze him that no matter where he was working, he could be found if needed, simply by word of mouth. News travelled fast in this part of the world.

Lyndon nodded his thanks, took the note, and gave the man a coin for his trouble. Farmer Ferris had written to tell him that a good section of hedge in the upper meadow had fallen into disrepair whilst he'd been away at war. He'd be obliged if Lyndon could come soonest. Lyndon smiled. The upper meadow was where he had first set eyes on Jenna – she was seventeen then and the most beautiful girl he had ever laid eyes on. He remembered the sun haloing her golden blonde hair as she sat and sketched. How he longed for those heady days in the sun before everything had gone wrong.

This job at Bochym was ongoing - a long-term fill-in job between other jobs in the county. He suspected that it was the Earl's way of helping him to get back to work after the war - for sure the hedges in place around the perimeter were sound, albeit made up of tall bushes. There were no gaping holes in the present hedges, therefore no rush to complete the task. He knew the work he was undertaking was mostly aesthetic, but in the long term, a much sounder pleached hedge would compliment this grand estate and last for years to come. He would complete this section he was working on, which would take him another day and then set off to Gweek. Hopefully being in the village where he first fell in love with Jenna would help him to work through the obstacles which troubled his mind.

*

Joe Treen was sitting at the kitchen table dusting the wine bottles ready for the family's dinner that evening, whilst Molly Johnson was sitting with Mrs Blair discussing the grocery order for the week. Mary had returned to her role as assistant cook; she was a long way from recovering from her poisoning, and took medication for her stomach, but as each day passed, her face was taking on a healthier hue. All four of them looked up sharply when the Earl walked into the kitchen and they stood to bow or drop a curtsy.

'Ah, Treen, Mrs Johnson, Mrs Blair, I'm glad I've found you all together,' Peter said.

'How can we help, my lord?' Joe asked.

'I have just had a call from an old army comrade of mine - he has a friend coming down to the area - a fine chap by all accounts - a much-decorated officer I might add. He had a bit of a tough time in the war – which of course many people did,' he said acknowledging Joe with a thankful nod. 'My friend believes that a spot of time here in the quiet countryside, will be just the ticket for his friend. I know it's all very last minute, but I would like for us to accommodate him if we can. Treen, I am sure you can appreciate that, having spent time recuperating in Devon recently.'

'I can indeed, my lord.'

'He will be arriving on Friday around two-thirty. I think I can be assured that you will all make his stay here very comfortable.'

'Of course, my lord, if we may have his name, please?'

'Lord Beamish.'

'Thank you, my lord.' Joe bowed as Peter took his leave, and the household swept into action to accommodate the expected visitor.

*

After spending the previous day arranging for her new painting to be delivered to The Black Gallery, and collating everything else she needed to take with her to Cornwall, Jenna stood in the hall with her suitcase, saying her goodbyes to Mrs Hemp.

Hillary had promised to be at Bellevue Gardens at the ungodly hour of half-past-five that Thursday morning, so they could get out of London before it got too busy. When Hillary pulled up, Jenna noted the back of the car had four suitcases and two large boxes already in it.

'Why have you got all this luggage?' Jenna asked as she stood beside the car with her suitcase, a basket of food Mrs Hemp had made up for them, and a half-finished canvass. 'I've nowhere to put anything!'

'Darling, I'm going to be holed up in Cornwall for some time so I've brought as much as I could, and of course I have my wedding gowns.'

'Gowns?'

'Mmm,' she said sheepishly, 'if you remember I couldn't decide between them.'

'Yes,' Jenna smiled.

'Well, I bought them both. Don't tell Matthew, he thinks I fritter money away, what a notion,' she laughed, 'anyway, it's my money.' Hillary looked down at Jenna's suitcase. 'Is that all you're bringing?'

'Yes, I've only packed a couple of gowns.'

Hillary looked horrified. 'We haven't spent months shopping for your wardrobe for you to walk around looking like a pauper again, go back and pack all your clothes.'

'Why? It'll be highly unlikely that I'll be attending any other social soirées, other than your wedding, now James has gone.'

'Nonsense, of course you will. Wherever Matthew and I go – so too will you, being James's widow. You're part of society now and of course your reputation as an artist goes before you.'

But what about Lyndon, she thought, *where will he fit in at society soirees?*

'Come on, Jenna, stop daydreaming. I did not get up in the middle of the night for nothing,' Hillary ushered her in the house, helped her to pack her other gowns into another two suitcases and was back out of the house ten minutes later strapping them onto the back rack of the car.

'What about my canvas, where am I going to put it?' Jenna scratched her head.

'Leave it, darling, Greg is driving down in a couple of weeks for the wedding, he will bring them with him then if I call and ask him to. Leave it in the hall – if Mrs Hemp is out, he knows where the key is.'

Jenna smiled to herself as she put the canvas back - this was always an open house to all James's friends and even now he had gone, nothing had changed. She waved goodbye to Mrs Hemp and climbed into the car.

*

It was Friday morning. Lyndon packed up his wagon, bid everyone at Bochym farewell for a few days and set off to Gweek, much to the consternation of Dorothy, who had well and truly set her cap at Lyndon, albeit to no avail.

Lyndon arrived in Gweek, welcomed by a gentle summer breeze, brilliant sunshine, and an almost full tide. He pulled up outside Barleyfield Farm, hobbled Bramble and leant against the front lichen covered gate. He ran his gaze over the front lawn of the farm house where, seven years ago, he had attended the hog roast at the harvest dance and he had proposed to Jenna! Pulling his mouth into a tight line, he made his way around the back of the farmhouse where lines of washing flapped in the breeze.

After a quick cup of tea with Farmer Jack Ferris, Lyndon followed him up the meadow, the sweet smell of warm grass tinctured the air, as he assessed the damage to the hedge he'd pleached seven years ago. The badgers had undermined the Cornish wall beneath the hedge which in turn had made the hedge collapse. This was one of three damaged parts of the hedge Farmer Ferris showed him, all of which would take him a couple of weeks to mend. He rubbed his hands and set about the job with relish.

15

At two-thirty prompt, a car pulled up outside Bochym Manor and its occupant got out. The figure stood with his back to the house, looking out to the gardens, but although the man held a stick to steady himself, Joe would know that five-foot-six frame anywhere. A sudden visceral feeling of hate swept through his body, and he was back in the filth of the trenches reliving a horror above all the other horrors.

'Are you well, Treen?' The Earl said as he stepped out with the Countess to greet their visitor,' you look a little peaky.

'Yes, I'm fine, my lord. David, if you could get Lord Beamish's luggage and take it to the Tweed Room,' he instructed the footman.

'Yes, Mr Treen.'

When Beamish strode up to shake the Earl's hand, he shot a brief look of recognition at Joe, which Joe, in turn, ignored.

'I shall leave you two to talk war,' Sarah smiled, made her excuses that she had business elsewhere and instructed Joe to serve refreshments in the library.

As soon as Sarah had left, Beamish asked, 'Where's your pot, Dunstan, I need a pee.'

'Treen, if you could be so kind as to point Lord Beamish in the right direction,' the Earl instructed.

'When Beamish returned to the hall, Joe tried to guide him into the library, but Beamish had noticed the door was open to the French drawing room and voices within. Without invitation, Beamish stepped over the threshold, so Joe quickly went to inform the Earl.

Justin and Gabriel were sat on a plank between two ladders chatting and eating an orange each when they looked up at their unexpected visitor. The room was filled with the zesty smell of citrus oil, and Beamish wrinkled his nose.

'And what do you think you two are doing?' he demanded authoritatively.

Both Justin and Gabriel looked up, segments of orange hovering at their lips.

'I said, what are you two doing?' Beamish reiterated.

'Minding our own business, as you should be,' Justin snapped back.

With Joe in quick pursuit, Peter entered the drawing room straight into the ongoing conflict.

'Ah, Dunstan, glad you're here to witness this. I found these two, wasting time. You need to keep an eye on workmen you know – they are all wastrels.'

Peter looked momentarily flustered and then regained his composure. 'This is actually my brother-in-law, Justin Devereux – he's a famous artist.'

Beamish looked Justin up and down. 'Never heard of you, but then I have no interest in art. It is all a waste of time daubing paint if you ask me. A man should have a decent job if he is going to work, but as you're related….' He offered his hand to shake which Justin refused to take.

Beamish snorted and dropped his hand.

'And this is Gabriel Trelease,' Peter said. 'He is a renowned sculptor and is restoring this room to its former glory.'

'Is he?' Beamish gave a look of disdain, and this time did not offer his hand – instead, he sniffed and turned to Peter. 'Refreshments, I think are in order, Dunstan.' It was a demand rather than a request.

As Peter gestured Beamish out of the drawing room towards the library, he turned to offer Justin and Gabriel an apologetic look.

'Obnoxious bastard,' Justin declared under his breath and Joe nodded his head in agreement. 'Is he the one staying for a few days, Joe?'

'Yes.'

'Well, I think Ruby and I might take ourselves off down to the Dower Lodge for a few days then,' he said dryly.

Joe followed the men into the library and two glasses of whisky were poured, but it took every ounce of Joe's resolve to stand in the same room as this man.

Beamish drained his glass in one and held it up, 'Drink,' he demanded, but Joe felt rooted to the spot.

'Fill it up, man,' Beamish growled, but still Joe stood stock still.

'Treen?' Peter frowned at him.

'I'm sorry, my lord.' Joe bowed and made to leave the room.

'*Treen,* come back here at once,' Peter demanded, but Joe shook his head and quietly left the room. 'What the devil...?' Peter stood and rang the bell for assistance, but none came.

'Can't get the staff nowadays, I find – they are all feigning shell shock – bloody cowards the lot of them,' Beamish said. 'I was shot in the war,' he tapped his leg with his stick, 'but I don't go crying about it.'

Peter topped up Lord Beamish's glass and excused himself briefly. He found Joe in the corridor refusing to let the footman or anyone else from entering the library.

'*Treen,* what the devil are you playing at?' Peter fumed.

'I can't serve that man, my lord.'

'You *can,* and you *will* – it's not for you to decide who you are to serve.'

'It is in this case, my lord.'

'Good on you, Joe,' Justin said as he and Gabriel joined them in the corridor.

Peter scowled. 'Justin, I know Lord Beamish was out of order in the French room, but this is not helping matters.'

Sarah came out of her drawing room to see what was amiss. 'Is something wrong, Peter?'

'I'll say - Treen here point-blank refuses to serve Lord Beamish.'

Puzzled, Sarah turned to look at Joe enquiringly.

'It's true, my lady and I shall tender my resignation forthwith.'

A small group had gathered at the kitchen door and Joe heard Juliet give a gasp of shock at this statement.

'I'm sure it won't come to that,' Sarah said calmly, 'but if you could please explain yourself.'

Joe took a deep breath – he could feel the anxiety building again which he thought had been brought under control in Devon.

'Come on man – I haven't got all day, spit it out!' Peter demanded, but Sarah put her hand on her husband's sleeve to quieten him.

'Lord Beamish in there was the Captain in our regiment – he is the Captain Jones who shot Thomas at point blank range for cowardice.'

There was a collective gasp from the rest of the staff gathered, and Mary, who had joined them gave a shocked cry.

'Are you sure?'

'Absolutely, my lord.'

Peter's lips whitened with rage as he turned to the footman. 'David, have Lord Beamish's luggage brought back down and put in his car.'

'Yes, my lord.'

'Treen, please come with me.'

The library was billowing with cigar smoke and foul air when they entered - Beamish had clearly broken wind.

'Are there you are - I was beginning to think I had been abandoned. I know I have come here for some quiet respite after that dreadful war, but I did not expect to be left alone to entertain myself quite so soon.' He glanced at Joe and smirked. 'I trust you have been *suitably* reprimanded for your appalling manners?' He drained his glass and shook it at Joe to refill, but Peter took it from his hand and put it down on the table.'

Beamish frowned at the gesture. 'What? What is this? What sort of hospitality do you call this?'

'My home does not entertain murderers,' Peter answered coldly.

'What?' He gave a great belly laugh and broke wind again. 'We're all bloody murderers – god damn it – you too, Dunstan. We have all killed people over these last four years - that is what war is about.'

'*I* did not shoot my comrades in cold blood at point blank range – unlike you.'

Beamish cut between Joe and Peter. 'What the devil are you talking about?'

'Have you forgotten that you shot Corporal Thomas Ellis at point blank range in the trenches.'

'Who?'

Peter folded his arms. 'I rather think you must remember shooting one of your own in the trenches – or was it a regular occurrence?'

'If they were shot it was because of cowardice and I abhor cowards.'

'They! You mean, you did actually shoot more than one chap in the trenches – without a trial?'

'I'm an officer for Christ's sake! How the hell are we expected to win bloody wars with cowardly cry-babies shirking their duties? God damn it man, what the hell is this – the Spanish inquisition?'

'No, it's me ridding my household of monstrous scum like you.'

'Now just you wait a minute,' Beamish blustered as he stood up and faced Peter, 'I will not tolerate been spoken to like this. I was a respected officer in the British army, as, I understood, were you!'

'Respected! How can anyone who kills their own men *ever* be respected? You are an insult to the rank and uniform of an officer.'

'I have no idea what all this is about,' Beamish roared, 'but I'll not hear another insult from you.'

'You killed Corporal Thomas Ellis, at point blank range!'

'Yes, so you said, what is it to you?'

'Thomas was our footman – a man who had proudly joined up as soon as war broke out. A man who bravely fought in every battle he was sent to until, by all accounts, the Germans sent a minenwerfer over. Treen here was in the same unit of men who were blown far and wide by the thing. Thomas was so badly affected with shell shock he should have been sent home – his war *should* have been over, but it wasn't, he was recalled to the front – a man so traumatised, he could not speak or move, and you,' Peter prodded him hard in the chest,' shot him because he did not have the physical strength to go over the top. Treen here saw it all happen.'

Beamish narrowed his eyes at Joe. 'Ah, yes, I remember you now. You were all for turning tail as well that day, until I threatened you with the gun.'

'I was trying to stop you from killing a decent man,' Joe spat the words at him.

'Decent man?' he sneered, *'he was a coward through and through!'*

'He was not!' Peter growled, 'but now his good name is sullied for eternity by your actions. Now, get out of my house.'

'He was a bloody coward I tell you - shirking his responsibility to King and Country – he deserved to die. We all went through the trauma of shelling – it's just that some men were weak and feeble – cry-babies – that's all they were!'

'Get out.'

'Don't worry, I'm not staying.' He brushed himself down as though he'd been sullied by the request. 'Bring my bags.'

'They are already in the car,' Peter said coldly.

'I shall make this known in the Officers' Club, you know,' Beamish threatened, 'I shall tell them how you insulted me.'

'Do just that because I shall enjoy putting the record straight on why I did it. Now get out!'

Joe stood with the Earl and watched as his car drove away at great speed.

'Can I get you anything, my lord,' Joe asked following him into the library.

'You can open that window and pour us both a whisky,' Peter answered.

They chinked the crystal glasses. 'My actions today will not clear Thomas's name, but we did a little something to fight for justice for him.'

'Is there anything else we can do, my lord? Mary is in a terrible state because they won't commemorate Thomas on the Cury war plaque'

'I don't know, Treen – I simply don't know.'

*

Mary was beside herself; she had heard every dreadful word of denouncement of her beloved Thomas coming from the row in the library and had turned and fled out from the corridor and across the kitchen courtyard.

'Oh, no, Mary, come back.' Ruby made after her, but Gabriel stopped her.

'I'll go, Ruby,' Gabriel said, we have a mutual understanding of grief, I might be able to help.'

Gabriel set off after Mary and found her not, thankfully, heading for the front meadow where the foxgloves grew, but leant against the mossy wall at the back of the stables, her eyes cast downwards.

'Mary,' Gabriel said gently.

She looked up startled - her eyes wide and fearful like a deer caught in the headlights of a motorcar. Her face was stricken but she was too shocked for tears.

'He is gone. His Lordship has sent him packing.'

'That man, that awful man killed my Thomas.' She began to sway as though she was going to faint and began to slip slowly down the wall she was standing against. Gabriel moved forward and knelt to break her fall, pulling her into his arms to ease the terrible trembling of her body.

'Mary,' he said sympathetically, 'I too have known this despair. Nothing will bring Thomas back - what has been done has been done. Take my advice and hold on to only the good memories – they alone will get you through this, I promise.' He felt her thin body relax in his arms and thought for a moment that she had in fact fainted, until she curled her arms around his waist and held onto him as though her life depended on it. Gabriel remembered that feeling well - the want for a female's arms around him in his case, so that momentarily everything felt normal again. He did not move or pull away - Mary would take the comfort she needed from him for a few moments to help her through this next terrible stage of her ongoing grief.

The back of the stables was dank and shady, and they were both sat on grass untouched by the warmth of the sun. Gabriel could feel the damp seeping through the seat of his pants, but he did not want to move until Mary was ready. Eventually she too must have felt the discomfort because very gently she released him from her hold, and lifted her sad, thin face to his.

'Thank you for understanding, Gabriel.'

'Everyone understands, Mary.'

'I think you do more than most.' She smiled weakly.

'Are you ready to come back inside?'

She nodded and he helped her up. He held her bony hands briefly. 'It's time to start healing, Mary.'

'I'll try.'

'Heal for yourself and start living for Thomas now. I know that is what my darling wife would say to me if she could. I had my little boy to live for.'

'I lost my baby, the doctor said he was a little boy – I named him James.'

'Then they are together in heaven.'
She nodded and gave a sad smile.

*

When Gabriel had made sure Mary was happy to return to work, he too made his way to the French drawing room but was called back by Peter who beckoned him into his study.

'Is Mary all right? Treen said you followed her.'

'Yes, I think so. It was just a shock for her to know the man who had killed Thomas was in the house.'

Peter offered him a drink, but Gabriel declined.

'Thank you, but no. Alcohol and scaffolding do not mix.'

Peter nodded and poured himself one, this time putting a little more water in it than the one he'd had earlier. He cleared his throat. 'This business has upset me, and I will of course try to put Thomas's case to my superiors, but I do not hold out much hope. None of these men left their desks to go and fight – they have no idea what our men went through – they just got fat and gave orders. It sickens me – absolutely sickens me.'

Gabriel nodded.

'Gabriel, I know this is not what we employed you for, but I do not want to engage the services of the same stonemason who is doing the memorial plaque in Cury, but I wondered, could you find the time to carve a memorial stone for Thomas? I've a mind to erect it somewhere in the garden – at least then poor Mary will have his name commemorated in the place where he worked and was thought highly of.'

Gabriel smiled widely. 'It would be an honour, my lord.'

'As a captain in the army myself, it grieves me deeply how some of my contemporaries felt fit to act that way towards their subordinates. To shoot these men in cold blood and without trial, it just appals me. Those men were clearly at the end of their tether. No man who fought in that bloody war should ever be called a coward. I suspect in years to come, when the world wakes up to the horrors of what went on, these poor men will be pardoned, but I suspect it will not be in our lifetime, therefore all too late for the immediate families of these poor men who are now denounced.' Peter fell quiet – lost in his own thoughts so Gabriel got up to take his leave.

'I'll order some black granite and work on it as soon as it comes.'

'Thank you, Gabriel – you'll be paid accordingly.'

'You pay for the stone – I'll do my bit for Mary free of charge.'

16

Lyndon worked under the warmth of the sun, birds filled the air with twitter and chatter, and high above, gulls, brought in by the high tide, cried on the wing. It had been a long, sweltering day and the dust from pleaching had left Lyndon parched.

He settled his pony and wagon on land owned by local cabinet maker Kit Trevellick and walked the familiar road to The Black Swan. It was then he saw his friend and fellow army comrade Charlie Williams and his father Eric walking towards the inn.

'Charlie, my friend,' Lyndon called out as he quickened his pace towards him to slap him friendly on the back.

'Lyndon, my god, but you're a welcome sight, I'll tell you. When they took you away from the front line, we all thought you were dead. I wept for you - I don't mind admitting it.'

'I was very nearly buried alive - if I hadn't groaned when I was dragged from the wagon of bodies to be buried, I...' he shook his head, 'well, it doesn't bear thinking about.'

'When we heard you had been found, I wept again – you made me into a regular cry-baby. God, but it's good to see you though. Come. Let's have a drink.'

As they raised a glass to toast lost comrades, Lyndon smiled at Charlie.

'So, did you marry your Lizzy? I remember it was going to be the first thing you were going to do after the war.'

Charlie's smiled widened. 'Not yet, but very soon. Lizzy's Ma took a turn for the worse just after I came home at Christmas, and Lizzy has been nursing her these last months. Poor woman had been ill for years on and off and died in May, so we have planned our wedding for Wednesday August 6th. I sent an invitation to Trevarno for you – did you not get it?'

'No, I've been working at Bochym Manor, but yes, I will happily attend this long-awaited wedding.'

'And what about you, my friend?' Charlie winked. 'I seem to remember you had someone very secretive. I know you got letters from her. Have you set a date?'

Lyndon put his glass down. 'Ah, well, that all turned out to be complicated. I can tell you now, the woman I was corresponding with was Jenna Trevone, and of course everyone in Gweek thought her to be dead. It's a long story, but Amelia and I got her away that night you all thought she had drowned.'

'Good god, you really did keep that quiet. And of course, she was still married to Blewett, so you wouldn't have been able to marry, would you,' Charlie interjected.

'Precisely, but not only that, I was promised to another woman – terrible mistake! Jenna changed her name to Jennifer Penvean and came to live incognito in my father's house at Trevarno and when I went to war, it was her letters that kept me going. My wife never wrote to me unless to complain about something! When they thought I was dead, the 'just in case the worst happens' letter that we all wrote to send to our loved ones, was sent to my wife, but of course it was written for Jenna. My wife had Jenna sent away from Trevarno and Jenna, thinking I was dead, married James Blackwell the author shortly after George Blewett's demise.'

Charlie rolled his eyes. 'The day that bully died we all cheered in this village, I can tell you. And then later that day, Amelia told us that Jenna was still alive! So, it was good news all round. So, you lost her again then? I'm that sorry for you, Lyndon – you two were meant to be together.'

'Well now, there is a twist. I had my marriage annulled, for reasons I would rather not say, and James Blackwell died six weeks ago – a complication to his lungs after being gassed. Before he died though, and when he knew it was terminal, he had learnt from Matthew Bickford that I had been found safe and well and that Jenna and I had been once romantically linked. He penned a letter to me giving his blessing to our union after he had gone.'

'What a thoroughly decent thing for him to do.' Charlie raised his glass. 'So?'

'Well, Jenna is still in mourning, so we cannot do anything yet.'

'But you *will* bring her to the wedding?'

'Well….'

'We would all very much like to see her again, Lyndon, you must.'

'Well, I'll ask. She was always very fond of you and Lizzy.'

Charlie smiled in remembrance. 'We all went to school together. There is a lot of history between us.'

They all turned as the door opened from the snug where the ladies sat, and Amelia Pascoe the village stalwart appeared. 'My, my, if it isn't Lyndon Fitzsimons if I live and breathe. I'd heard you were back in the village.'

Lyndon went to greet her. 'It's good to see you, Amelia.' He kissed her warmly on the cheek.

'Goodness, but it does my old heart good to see you alive and well,' she grasped him by the arms and squeezed him affectionately, 'so many poor young men didn't survive, did they?'

'I'm afraid they didn't.'

Amelia shook her head. 'I'm sorry you and Jenna never found your way to each other, especially after what you'd both endured. You do know she has been widowed, don't you?'

'I do.'

Amelia's face brightened. 'So, have you seen her?'

'I have. James Blackwell wrote to me before he died and asked me to come to her afterwards.'

'He was a good man – and did you?'

Lyndon looked downcast.

Amelia narrowed her eyes in concern. 'Would you like to come to my cottage for a spot of supper later to tell me all about it?'

'Amelia, I would want for nothing more. You helped us before – perhaps you can work your magic again.'

'It has nothing to do with magic, I generally think people just need a push in the right direction.'

*

While Lyndon was catching up with old friends in Gweek, Hillary and Jenna stopped to rest for the night on the outskirts of Plymouth, having found an inn to their liking. Though bone tired from driving, unfortunately Hillary had spent a broken night's sleep, hence on Saturday - the final day of their journey, Hillary was beginning to look very tired before they even reached St Austell.

'Are you all right, Hillary?'

'I'm just wondering if we should overnight again somewhere – I'm finished,' she said giving a mighty yawn.

'Shall I drive?' Regretting it as soon as it was said.

Hillary's head snapped round. 'I didn't know you could.'

'I can't, but it's not that hard, is it?'

'Well, darling, if I can do it anyone can do it.' She stuck her hand out and flapped it up and down to indicate that she was slowing down. 'Come on, swap places.'

Jenna nervously settled in the driver's seat and looked down at her feet.

'Lift your skirt a little so I can show you which foot does what.' Hillary began to instruct her on the basics of driving.

After only a few minutes of instruction, Jenna tentatively moved the motorcar forward. For the first few hundred yards, Hillary constantly grabbed the steering wheel to move her out of the ditches at the edges of the road.

'Stay on the smooth bit of road, and yes, I know, the whole road is awfully bumpy, but keep out of the ditches or else you will tip us out. And remember, darling, in this instance, if everything seems to be coming your way, you are in the wrong lane! Look, there is a car coming towards us, give him room, Jenna - *GIVE HIM ROOM!*' Hillary pulled on the steering wheel to get the motorcar out of the way, just as the other car tooted his horn.

'That was a bit rude of him, wasn't it?' Jenna complained shaking her shoulders as if ruffled.

'Well, you were using his side of the road,' Hillary said smoothing down her hair.

Jenna glanced at Hillary. 'Isn't it meant to be ladies first?'

'Not when you are driving, darling. The road is for everyone to use,' she grimaced.

Jenna sighed and when the next car came towards her, she made sure she gave him space.'

'Good, you're getting the hang of it now.'

'Are you going to take a nap, Hillary, now that I am driving?' Jenna asked with her eyes glued to the road and her knuckles white as she held onto the steering wheel.

'Perhaps not. I'm really rather awake now!' she said, her own eyes glued to the road.

'Do you not trust me?' Jenna gave a little smile.

'With my life, darling – literally at the moment.'

'How much further is it?'

'About forty miles.'

'How long will that take?'

'We will be home by sundown. Gosh,' Hillary clutched at her chest, 'what I wouldn't give for a sundowner, right now.'

'You and your sundowners,' Jenna smiled.

'Well, there is something rather splendid about enjoying a cool alcoholic drink as the sun slowly sets over the sea, don't you agree?'

'I do. I just hope Mrs Inman has ordered a block of ice for the gin.'

*

They arrived at Loe House at half-past-seven that evening, tired and hungry and in Hillary's case a trifle traumatised by the latter part of the journey. Still, everyone had to start driving one way or another and barring a couple of near misses, she thought Jenna did quite well.

Jenna, for her part, thought she had done jolly well, and as James had a car parked here at Loe House, she was determined to drive it from now on. Having sent a telegram to Mrs Inman the housekeeper that they were due home that day, they did indeed find a block of ice in the cold cellar. They also found the larder stocked with essentials, and to their infinite pleasure - freshly made beds. Once they had freshened up - they embarked on the much-anticipated sundowner on the terrace, while they watched the sun fade into the western sky.

'I always feel as though James is with us on this terrace, don't you, Jenna?' Hillary dabbed at a stray tear.

Jenna stood elbow to elbow with her. 'I do, I feel his presence in the house, too. He was such a larger-than-life character, it's no wonder.'

'Are you saying the house is haunted?'

'No, it's nothing spooky like that. It's just, you know, a nice, comforting feeling.'

'Right, well, I'm famished,' Hillary said draining her glass, 'shall we head up to The Halzhephron Inn to take supper?'

'Good idea!'

*

They had returned home to Loe House within the hour the previous night. Normally the life and soul of any gathering, Hillary was too tired to do anything other than eat her supper, even too exhausted for a nightcap! They had bid each other goodnight and Jenna sank into her feather bed, thankful that she was home at last, safe from prying eyes, and she'd smiled to herself - closer to Lyndon.

After breakfasting on coffee and eggs late the next morning, Hillary bid Jenna farewell as she set off to the Trevarno Estate, in Helston.

'I shall seek out this nemesis of yours, what did you call her, Edna? One step out of line and she will be gone, you mark my words.'

Jenna raised an eyebrow. 'There is her father to consider you know.'

'I shall call that one's bluff. No reasonable man would leave a perfectly good job!'

Jenna bit her lip. 'The Bickford's might not look kindly to you dismissing staff before you become part of the family. Don't upset the applecart at Trevarno for me – you must live there.'

'And I intend to make it a harmonious place for my special friend to visit. No one shall keep you away anymore. Toodaloo, darling - I shall see you very soon. Gosh, but I'm so looking forward to seeing my gorgeous husband-to-be again – he is simply divine.'

*

At Poldhu, the tearoom was busy that Sunday. Marianne was fizzing with delight - Gabriel Trelease had reserved a table on the veranda today - after the disappointment of him not turning up the previous Sunday. After a fortnight working here, she had proved herself to be a real asset as she moved around with ease and efficiency, clearing tables, taking orders, and had even shown her skills as a baker, producing lovely cakes to sell.

Marianne's hair shone having been washed the previous night, so she knew she looked her best, she also made sure she smelt lovely too, although Ellie had once again berated her for wearing perfume at work. She claimed that it wasn't perfume - it was the highly fragrant soap she had bathed in the night before.

'Well please bathe in less perfumed soap in future,' Ellie had said crossly. 'It's off putting to customers.'

Marianne nodded meekly, at least she had not been made to wash it off this time.

'Marianne,' Ellie said as she breezed back into the tea room, 'Jake Treen has sat down on the veranda, would you like to take his order? He did me a great favour earlier this week so there will be no charge,' she added.

Marianne, unaware that Ellie had invited Jake to a free tea for no other reason than to try and get these two young people together, twisted her mouth resentfully. Knowing that he held a candle for her, she didn't really want to serve him and give him any encouragement. After all, she was not remotely interested in him. Still, she must do as asked, so she grabbed her pad and pen and painted on a smile she kept for customers she didn't particularly want to interact with.

'Hello, Marianne.' Jake's eyes sparkled.

'Jake,' she answered nonchalantly.

'How do you like your new job?' he asked with a smile.

'Very well, thank you, what can I get you?' No sooner as she had asked, Gabriel came walking over the dunes towards the tearoom with his little son. A flush warmed her face as her stomach flipped like a pancake and then she realised that Jake was speaking to her.'

'Sorry, what?'

'I said I would like a cream tea please.' As Jake spoke, he followed Marianne's gaze as she watched Gabriel Trelease settle at the table nearest the beach.

It was Ellie who took Gabriel's order. She had her own reasons for not allowing Marianne to take his tray to the table. Instead, Ellie told Marianne to make up Jake's order and serve him.

Try as he might to engage Marianne in conversation, she simply refused to interact with Jake and thankfully after an hour, he gave up, finished his cream tea, and left. Unfortunately, it was at the same time as Gabriel bid farewell to them.

Marianne knew Gabriel had plans for the day - she had overheard him telling Ellie they were going over to Church Cove. She could not wait to finish work at the tearoom to go over to Church Cove herself, and as he hadn't told Marianne his plans, at least if she met him on the beach, he would not think she had followed him. So, once the tearoom was spick and span, Marianne took off her apron.

'Well, it's a lovely day,' Ellie said. 'What are you planning on doing this afternoon, Marianne?'

'Oh, a walk and a paddle perhaps,' she answered trying not to blush.

'Have a lovely time then, and I'll see you on Tuesday.'

Marianne made to walk down the beach to the sea at Poldhu until she was confident Ellie was out of sight and then picked up her skirts and ran back up the beach to join the coast road over to Church Cove.

*

As Ellie had made her way home from the tearoom, Jake walked towards her, having been waiting for her amongst the dunes.

'Hello, Jake.' Ellie smiled at him but could see the disappointment in his eyes.

'I've been waiting for you, to thank you for trying, and for the free cream tea today, it was delicious but,' he sighed, 'I think it's all in vain.'

'So, are you just going to give up on her?' Ellie said thumping her fists into her hips.

Jake just shrugged his shoulders.

'Faint heart never won fair lady you know.'

'I think Marianne has her sights set on someone with a little more class than I possess.'

'Oh? Anyone in particular?'

Jake eyes scanned the dunes undecided as to whether to tell her.

'Jake, who has she got her eye on?'

'Gabriel Trelease.'

Ellie laughed. 'Then you have nothing to worry about, Jake. Gabriel is lovely but is far out of Marianne's league and she will surely get her fingers burnt if she thinks Gabriel is the man for her. And let me tell you something - don't ever put yourself down, Jake Treen. You are more than a match for any man.'

'But what am I to do? Watch her get hurt by him? He might even use her and leave her!'

Ellie shook her head. 'I've known Gabriel and his family for a while now - since his parents moved down here from Hertfordshire six years ago. Marianne is undoubtably beautiful, but he is a decent man and will not take advantage of her, nor will she become his next wife, of that, I am sure. My advice is to wait until she gets the knock back that is so obviously going to happen, because she will need someone's loving arms around her.'

'That would make me second best,' he said sadly.

'No, it will show her that you are the best of men.'

17

Once Hillary had left, Jenna stood on the terrace of Loe House and sighed, although Bellevue Gardens was in a highly desirable area of London, the peace and tranquillity of Cornwall always filled her heart with joy. She looked up as the vast pale-blue sky looked down on her, birds cried and floated on the breeze before dipping into the turquoise sea glittering in the sunshine. It was a day to spend outside. Gathering her sketch pad and pencils, she decided to go to Church Cove, a mile down the coast. Normally she would have walked the coast road, but now she knew how to drive, she decided to get in some more practice and take the motorcar. Poor Jack, the landlord's son from The Halzhephron Inn, he'd been so disappointed to learn that Jenna could now drive the car herself. He used to enjoy driving her about – it got him out of other duties at the inn. Jenna had been quick to assure him that she had no intention of dispensing with his services completely, though now she had a taste of independence she rather thought she would not use him as much.

James Blackwell had been laid to rest at Winwaloe Church, which was situated at the bottom of a rocky headland on Church Cove, Gunwalloe, and this is where Jenna made for first. She'd picked a posy of wild flowers from the cliff path near Loe House and now placed it on the mound of earth which still only bore a wooden cross with James's name. It would be a while before the stonemason had the headstone ready.

There were shrieks of childish laughter coming from the water's edge and Jenna smiled. 'Life goes on, James,' she said, putting her fingers to her lips and then to his name on the cross. 'You should not be buried in the ground – your readers need your stories.'

Standing up, she brushed her skirt down – the weather was warm, and she felt hot in her dark clothes, although she wore blue now rather than mourning black. She took off her jacket and walked to the dunes to see where the laughter was coming from.

There was a man and child walking in the surf. The man was in his shirt sleeves, with his trousers rolled up his legs. The child with him wore only shorts – his little body, white against the blue of the water.

Jenna sat down and watched them for a while, pondering on her own future now she was back in Cornwall. A little time spent outdoors painting en plein air would sooth her troubled mind until she decided what to do…. about…. well, about everything. Closing her eyes, she turned her face to the sun and let the rays warm her skin.

*

At the top of Poldhu Head, Marianne stopped to catch her breath from the run up the coast path. She peered over the cliff to see if she could see Gabriel, but he was nowhere to be seen. Carefully picking her way down the coast path towards Church Cove, she was already half way down before she spotted him, and her heart did a happy little leap. *All right, Marianne,* she told herself, *walk casually onto the sands and pretend you haven't seen him.* He was bound to recognise her and would surely shout out to her. Then she would offer to build sandcastles with his little son as a way of spending a bit of time with him. The self-satisfied smile on her face fell when she saw Gabriel's son running towards a woman who was sitting on the beach.

*

Jenna, who was basking in the sunshine, opened her eyes when she heard a man shouting, to see the small boy racing towards her.

'Robbie, Robbie, stop!' the man shouted.

'Mama, Mama,' the boy cried – his arms open wide.

Jenna glanced behind her, but there was no one there, suddenly her heart constricted. Was she dreaming? Was this boy calling *her* Mama? A strange visceral feeling passed over her, wondering if this child was the spirit of the baby, she had borne her violent husband, now grown, and coming back to berate her for her neglect in letting him die. Jenna braced herself as the child neared at breakneck speed and suddenly, he was upon her. The boy was breathless, cold, damp and covered in sand, as he flung his arms around her neck. 'Mama,' he cried into her neck.

Speechless, Jenna was shocked to the core to have this strange child suddenly in her arms. As she saw the gentleman running up the beach towards them, she cradled the trembling child. Suddenly, she heard the boy inhale – but not to check back his tears – he was smelling her! Suddenly the child pulled back. Great fat tears filled his eyes, and his chin began to wobble.

'You're not Mama, are you?'

'I'm afraid I'm not, darling,' she answered gently.

The child began to back away, treading more sand into her skirt, just as the gentleman reached them.

'I'm so sorry, he just took off when he saw you,' the gentleman said breathlessly as the boy flew towards him, clinging to his leg - sobbing heartbrokenly. He crouched down and wrapped his arms around the distressed child and turned back to Jenna. 'Your clothes – he's made a terrible mess of them, I'm so sorry.'

Jenna got up and brushed the sand from her dress. 'No need to apologise – its fine. It brushes off.' She smiled gently. 'See.'

The man looked down at his son and then back at Jenna.

'He thought – you look similar to his mother, you see – your hair,' he said nervously, 'it's the same colour.' He cleared his throat. 'My wife died a year ago from the influenza - it's been understandably hard for us both.'

Jenna's heart constricted. 'I can only imagine - I'm so terribly sorry for you both.' She glanced sadly down at the little boy who was staring up at her woefully.

The man stepped forward. 'Forgive me, let me introduce myself. Gabriel Trelease.' He held out his hand.

'Jenna Blackwell.' She took his hand to shake.

'And this is my son, Robert - Robbie.'

Jenna crouched down to the little boy, who shyly moved a little more behind his father's leg. 'And how old are you, Robbie?'

Robbie looked up at his father for guidance.

'Tell the nice lady.'

The little boy tipped his head shyly and said, 'I'm nearly six.'

'Gosh, you're a big boy for six, aren't you?'

The child nodded and moved a little further behind Gabriel, but he couldn't take his eyes off her.

'Do you live locally, Mr Trelease? I haven't seen you on the beach before,' Jenna asked to divert the situation.

'My parents live on Polurrian cliff, but I am working at Bochym Manor, restoring plasterwork in one of their rooms. It had been used as an officer's rehabilitation retreat and took quite a few knocks. My normal line of work is sculpture, but I trained in restoration.'

'I understand Bochym Manor is a grand house.'

'It is. Forgive me – but you said you were Jenna Blackwell? Are you any relation to the author James Blackwell's family, by any chance?'

'Yes, but...'

Gabriel was so enthused he spoke over her. 'Oh, my goodness, James Blackwell, well, how is he? I have not seen him for an age. Our estates in Hertfordshire bordered each other when we lived there and we went to university together, though I lost touch after that. Is he faring well? I understood he got married quite recently,' he asked meaningfully.

Jenna's smile faltered.

'I'm afraid to tell you, James died.'

'Gracious me!' He paused and scrutinised the wedding band on Jenna's finger and her dark clothes, and then took a step back. 'Oh, I do beg your pardon, I have the awful feeling that I have made a terrible faux pas. James was your husband, wasn't he?'

She smiled softly. 'He was, yes.'

Gabriel's face dropped. 'Oh, my goodness, forgive my insensitivity for enthusing about him.' He raked his fingers through his hair. 'I'm so sorry.'

'Please, do not feel awkward. James was a larger-than-life character and seems to evoke the same response in anyone who hears his name. He was a fine man, a good man, who enjoyed life to the full. I am glad he is remembered with joy and affection.'

'Was it sudden - recent?'

'Six weeks ago, but he suffered for a while – a problem with his lungs after being gassed in the war, though at first we didn't know his condition was terminal.'

'Goodness, so you were only…'

'Married less than a month,' she said with sadness.

'I am so dreadfully, dreadfully sorry. You are obviously still in mourning, and we have imposed upon your quiet reflection.'

'I can assure you that you haven't – it has been a welcome diversion. James is buried in the churchyard here – I've just brought flowers. He didn't want for any of us to grieve or be unhappy.'

'Nevertheless, we shall leave you.'

'There is no need, really. I'm glad of the company.'

'Oh, well, we were just about to make a sandcastle, weren't we Robbie?'

The small boy had appeared from behind Gabriel's legs and was staring intently at Jenna.

'The lady looks like Mama, doesn't she, Papa?'

'A little, yes,' Gabriel shot a crooked smile to Jenna.

Jenna shook her head to say it didn't matter and crouched down to come level with the boy's face. 'Would you like me to help you and Papa to build a sandcastle?'

The boy bit his lip and looked up to Gabriel for guidance. 'Would Mama mind?'

Gabriel smiled and shook his head. 'No, she wouldn't. So, Mrs Blackwell we would love you to join us.'

'Jenna, please. We're all friends now.'

*

Marianne dropped back and hid behind a wall covered in dead thrift heads. Damn it! Why did there have to be someone else on the beach. Still, she could wait, the woman was dressed in dark clothes and would be uncomfortable in this heat if she stayed too long. But as she sat and waited, she realised after an hour she couldn't have been more wrong.

*

After moving further down the beach to where the tide had been and gone, and the sand was firmer, Jenna, Gabriel and Robbie had sat under the shade of the cliff and spent a glorious hour moulding and building a great castle with a moat.

As they worked, Gabriel said, 'I've heard of your rise to fame in the art world – well done, but I understand you use a different name.'

'Yes, Trevone – my maiden name. My success was all down to James to tell you the truth – he introduced me to the right people.'

'Do not do yourself an injustice – I have seen what you do. I too exhibit my sculptures in The Black Gallery, and you, have a rare talent.'

'You're too kind. I know your work. James bought one of your sculptures – it's in the house in London.'

'Then I thank you for that.' He gave a chivalrous bow. Did your first exhibition go well? I was going to attend, but did not manage the trip up to London, though the Earl and Countess de Bochym went up briefly to see it.'

'It did go well – it was sold out.'

'There you go then.'

She laughed lightly. 'What brought you down here?'

'Once my wife died, I felt the need to bring Robbie somewhere safe – away from the Influenza which was so rife in London. It felt important that Robbie spent time with his grandparents once he had lost his mama and my mother does spoil him to death.'

'Well, that's what grandparents are for. Are you still managing to sculpt down here?'

'I admit, I haven't done much since I came home from the war. I have rather had my hands full.'

'How long were you at war, Gabriel?'

'I was conscripted in 1916, as an officer, but when my wife died last June, I was released from my commission to come home and look after Robbie.'

'This war has been a terrible thing for mankind.' Jenna leant back and brushed the sand from her skirt.

'Your clothes are in a terrible mess now I'm afraid,' Gabriel said.

'No matter – I've had a splendid time.'

'You're very good with children – I'm sorry you weren't married long enough to have your own family.'

Again, the pang of the death of her first born stabbed her. *Good with children – hardly! Didn't she let her own baby son die in the arms of another woman, unloved and unwanted? She cast her eyes downwards – the child had been a product of rape – despite the act being inflicted on her by her brutal first husband. Her son had looked like a miniature George Blewett, its face red and angry with the world, and Jenna could not bear the baby to suckle her. It had died three days after birth because of a weak heart – though George had blamed his death on Jenna's neglect. Indeed, she would no doubt be punished for her sins on that dreadful Day of Judgment.*

Gabriel, noting her sorrow, reached out to her. 'Jenna, are you well? I'm sorry, I feel that I have been yet again insensitive speaking of such things.'

'No, not at all, I've enjoyed my time with Robbie.' She looked down at the child – he was six, the same age her child would have been. 'He's a lovely little boy.'

'He is – he's my joy in this strange uncertain world. Well, then Robbie, It is getting late – it is time we went home now.'

'Oh, Papa, do we have to?'

'Yes, grandmama will have tea ready.'

'Can we come to the beach again next week?'

'Yes of course.'

'Will you come play with us again, Jenna?' he asked boldly.

'I'm sure Jenna is a very busy lady, Robbie.' Gabriel smiled apologetically at Jenna.

Jenna smiled and ruffled the boy's hair. 'I'm not sure about next week, but yes, I'm sure I will see you again soon.'

18

On Monday morning, the postman arrived at Loe House with two letters for Jenna. One was from James's publishing house telling her that his latest novel would be published posthumously on the 2nd of September. The other letter was from Lyndon and his words settled her heart a little.

Friday 25th July
My darling Jenna,
Matthew tells me that you should have arrived back in Gunwalloe on Saturday, so I trust this letter finds you well. Forgive me for not getting in touch before now, but I have secured a job at Bochym Manor. Having said that, I am over in Gweek working at the moment, and as I would like to get the job done as soon as possible, I won't arrange to meet you just yet. I'm writing to tell you that I have met with Charlie Williams, and he and Lizzy are getting married at 3.00 p.m. on Wednesday 6th of August and would very much like us both to attend. Amelia Pascoe has offered you a room for the night on the 6th if you wish to stay with her. Let me know by return post, via the Gweek Post Office and I'll make the necessary arrangements. As I will most likely be still working here on the 6th, we could meet on the village green at a time convenient to you and we can go to the wedding together. Do say yes. I so look forward to seeing you again, my love
Lyndon x

Jenna put down the letter. So, it seems her fears that she was going to lose Lyndon again were unfounded, though she felt a curl of unease as to how he would react to her news that they would have to stay apart a while longer. So, Charlie and Lizzy were getting married at last! Jenna smiled fondly - those two had been in love since their school days. She remembered them being chosen as the Gweek wassailing king and queen to bless the apple crop that first year Jenna had been married off to Blewett. She had so envied their choice to love each other. Everyone knew they would marry one day – she just wondered why it had taken them so long. They were the same age as her – twenty-five. Perhaps the war would have got in the way, remembering that Lyndon wrote to say he was fighting alongside Charlie at the front line, but still, she was amazed they had not married before he was conscripted. She felt a deep sense of relief that Charlie had survived when so many hadn't. Charlie had been her saviour twice in her life. Once when she got stuck in the mud flats at Gweek, he rescued her moments before the tide came in to drown her. The second time, he'd wreaked vengeance on George Blewett, Jenna's hateful husband, after George had beaten her almost senseless when their baby had died. It was rumoured that when George stepped into The Black Swan after he had attacked her, Charlie administered a blow so hard with his fist, he'd sent Blewett flying over several tables and back down the front steps of the inn, and in doing so, had managed to inflict a compound fracture on Blewett's right leg, a broken left arm, collar bone, and several ribs. This in turn gave Jenna, Amelia and Lyndon, weeks of breathing space so she could mend her own broken body and plan her escape from her torturous marriage. For that she would be eternally grateful.

Yes, she would go to the wedding, she would love to see them both again – though the thought of going back to Gweek after all these years made her tremble – even though her hateful husband was dead now. So, Jenna sat down to write to Lyndon, accepting the invitation to the wedding and Amelia's kind offer of a room, and that she would meet him at 2:00 that day.

*

After Marianne's disappointment the previous day, she was determined to present herself in front of Gabriel somehow, so took herself off to Bochym Manor on Monday afternoon. Her friend, Lucy's half day off coincided with her own, and because the Bochym Arts and Craft members were not utilising the lake that day, they had been given permission to take a flask of tea and a piece of cake down to sit beside it. If she were lucky, Marianne would see Gabriel, coming to or from the garden. Lucy had told her last week that Gabriel liked to take his tea out to the front garden, but Marianne and Lucy could not go in there, because the staff were not allowed in the front garden unless the family were away from home. Marianne suspected that although Gabriel was working at the manor, he must have been given permission to wander around the flower borders because he was a gentleman. Lucy also told her that he'd been invited to dinner with the Earl and Countess on more than one occasion. Oh, Marianne clasped her hands together, but how she would like to be dressed as a lady and sit around the Bochym dining table at Gabriel's side. It wasn't a fantastical dream, she told herself – Ruby the manor's previous housekeeper had married the Countess's brother, so there was absolutely no harm Marianne pursuing her quest for a gentleman – namely Gabriel Trelease.

The afternoon was sublime as they lazed by the boating lake. A thrush was busy in its task to crack a snail from its shell on one of the rocks surrounding the water. A blackbird filled the air with its sweet song and over the thick Cornish wall, the wheat and barley crops were basking in the August heat - towering towards the sun. Harvest was always a little later in Bochym than the surrounding fields, sometimes as late as September and October. Fortunately, they were normally the sunniest and driest months of the late summer. This year though, because of the long, hot summer, there was talk of harvesting a lot sooner. Marianne, tired of watching for Gabriel to come out of the house, flopped down on the rug and shaded her eyes from the sun, only to be nudged by Lucy a moment later.

'Afternoon, ladies.' Gabriel smiled down at them.

Marianne quickly tidied her hair and skirts.

'Good afternoon, Gabriel. It was nice seeing you yesterday at the tearoom.'

'I should think you'll be seeing me quite a lot then – Robbie and I never normally miss.'

'Tell me,' Marianne asked nonchalantly, 'does Robbie like to make sandcastles?'

'He does. We spent a rather splendid day on Church Cove doing just that yesterday.'

'Well, if Robbie ever wants help making them, I'm always happy to oblige. There is nothing I like more than spending time on a beach, and of course I love children.'

Marianne didn't see the puzzled look on Lucy's face, but did hear the snigger she made, which annoyed her, and she gave her friend a sharp look.

Gabriel laughed. 'I might keep you to that. Good day to you, ladies.'

When he was out of earshot, Lucy turned to Marianne. 'What on earth did you say that for? You don't even like children, or like sand in your toes, you've told me.'

'Hush!' Marianne hissed as she watched Gabriel walk towards the front garden. It was then she saw Mary walking towards the garden with a tray of tea.

'Lucky Mary,' she mumbled to herself and watched in vain for Mary to return. 'How come Mary can go into the garden and we can't?' she asked petulantly.

'Her ladyship gave her permission. She says the flowers will benefit Mary's healing process after the poisoning, she's been terribly ill.'

'What? For eating a tiny bit of a toxic mushroom! It would hardly kill her. Anyway, you said yourself that day she was sick straight away – it can't have done her much harm!'

'Nevertheless, Her Ladyship has been very sympathetic towards Mary. In truth we all thought she might be dismissed!' As soon as Lucy said it, she bit her tongue.

Marianne rolled her eyes. 'It's hardly a reason for dismissal. It's not as if she tried to poison the whole family, is it? The foolish mare poisoned herself before she served it!'

Lucy seemed reluctant to say more on the matter.

Marianne frowned. 'So, does she go in the garden often?'

'Yes, she sits and has her tea there.'

'With Gabriel?'

'Sometimes,' Lucy answered cautiously.

Marianne chewed the inside of her mouth. 'I hardly think Mary's conversation would be scintillating to Gabriel – he must be bored to tears with her.'

'He's not actually,' Lucy said picking a daisy, 'they share a mutual experience of grief you see.'

'How very dull.'

'I think they're helping each other, and you know, Mary is an intelligent woman – Ruby helped her with her education when she first came here. I think she can hold her own in any intelligent conversation she might have with Gabriel!'

Marianne prickled, feeling a pang of jealousy build inside her. *Mary couldn't speak French and play the piano forte like she could, and that was what a gentleman would look for in a wife. Well, if Mary thinks she is going to get her mitts on my Gabriel, she'll have a fight on her hands.*

Having watched and waited for a good hour, neither Mary nor Gabriel had come back from the garden. Marianne had had enough, she got up in a huff, brushed her skirt down angrily and announced she was going home, much to Lucy's consternation – who had no idea what was annoying her.

Stomping home across the fields towards Mullion, Marianne worked herself into a frenzy with jealous thoughts going around in her head. Whatever Mary was up to, she would have to nip it in the bud, and soon. Just because she was Her Ladyship's favourite, didn't mean she could put on airs and graces and flirt with Gabriel – he was hers! And why has she been given carte blanche to wander about the gardens just because she was stupid enough to eat a poisonous mushroom. *To benefit from the healing process of the flowers!* Lucy had told her. She flung her arms in the air. 'What a load of phooey,' she yelled, frightening a pair of wood pigeons. Unless, she thought, the Bochym staff were hiding something from her! Perhaps the poisoning wasn't accidental. No, Mary wouldn't do such a wicked thing – would she? But now the seed had been planted, she would wheedle it out of Lucy if it were the last thing she did.

*

On Tuesday morning, Jenna was stood in front of her open wardrobe door looking at the array of beautiful gowns Hillary had made her bring with her. Knowing she could not attend Charlie and Lizzy's wedding in one of these, she decided to get Jack to drive her into Helston to see if she could have a simple dress made for the occasion.

*

The man at the bar of the Halzhephron Inn nodded a greeting to Jenna when she came in looking for Jack the landlord's son.

'Can you spare Jack to take me to Helston?' she asked, Richard the landlord.

'Now?' He raised an eyebrow.

'If possible. I'll drive myself if he can't but….'

'No, no, it's fine. Jack,' he shouted down the cellar, 'Mrs Blackwell is in need of your services.'

Jack came out of the cellar beaming.

'Ah, you might well be smiling now,' Richard said, 'but I'll leave the scrubbing of the cellar floor for you to do later.'

Jack's face dropped and Richard winked at Jenna.

After they had left. The man at the bar asked, 'That was Jenna Trevone, the artist if I wasn't mistaken.'

'Aye, though we know her as Mrs Blackwell.'

'Ah, yes, the poor lady was widowed – I read it in the newspaper. She was married to James Blackwell the author was she not?'

'Aye, and a fine author too – died far too young.'

'Did you know him well then?'

'As well as anyone, I suppose,' Richard said polishing a glass.

'I always think of authors as people who keep themselves to themselves, sitting alone in silence all day.'

Richard laughed. 'Well, James Blackwell certainly did not fit into that mould - a more gregarious man you could not meet.'

'Wild, was he?'

'His parties down at Loe House were legendary.'

'What you mean lots of ladies?' the stranger winked knowingly.

'God no, nothing like that, they were an arty mixed bunch, but all highly entertaining. I shouldn't think Jenna will host them now, she is widowed.'

'Oh, I don't know, a beautiful woman like that, will attract the interest of men far and wide. Don't you agree?'

'She might, but I doubt she will be interested – its only six weeks since James died. She's still grieving!'

'Oh, it was a proper love affair then?'

Richard narrowed his eyes. 'Yes, it was!'

Noticing the landlord's displeasure at his question, he said, 'Forgive me, it's none of my business. I always thought James Blackwell was a committed bachelor that's the only reason I said it.'

'Well, you thought wrong, didn't you?' Richard turned away from him to polish the bottles on the back shelf.

The man cleared his throat. 'I'm down from Gloucestershire, I'm sightseeing.'

Richard did not respond, instead continued to be busy with his bottles.

'I'm doing a bit of walking, a bit of driving, a bit of this.' He lifted his glass of ale and grinned when Richard half turned around. 'I've only just arrived. Can you recommend anywhere to stay?'

'Afraid not, it's the summer, everywhere is booked. You'll be better off in Helston,' Richard answered shortly.

Seeing he'd outstayed his welcome he drained his glass and took his leave.

When he'd gone, Ida, Richard's wife tipped her head with a questioning look.

'I know, I know, Ida, it was a great fat lie. Celia Inman only told me this morning that she had a room vacant at Toy Cottage. It's just that there was something about him, I didn't like. If he comes in here asking questions again, you're to let me know.' Ida nodded. 'Right, hold the fort here, Ida, while I go and scrub the cellar floor. I reckon our Jack will be gone most of the day.'

19

Helston was a quaint town, quiet and clean after the noise and stench of the London streets. Jenna had made enquiries with Celia Inman, her housekeeper, as to where she could get a dress made, and had been given directions to Mrs Tonkin's haberdashery.

Mrs Tonkin's eyes widened at the sight of a stylishly dressed woman entering her shop.

'Good day to you, Mrs Tonkin. I understand your shop has a reputation for making good clothes.'

'The best,' Mrs Tonkin said, with a proud nod of her head.

'Would it be possible to make me a dress in time for next Monday or Tuesday at the latest?'

'We can certainly do it for Monday. Now, we have some fine silks, satins, and lace here,' she said pulling bolts of rich fabric from her shelves.

'I'm actually looking for something plain, perhaps navy cotton.'

'Oh!' she turned and gave Jenna a disheartened look.

'I'm in half mourning you see, for my husband and I've been invited to a country wedding. I need something fitting for the occasion.'

'Oh! I see. My deep condolences for your loss,' Mrs Tonkin answered, trying not to show her deflation.

After half an hour in the shop, having chosen the material and a pattern for the dress, Mrs Tonkin took Jenna's vital statistics and promised a fitting on Thursday for a completion the following Monday. Jenna stepped out of the shop into the bright sunlight just in time to see Matthew and Hillary walking arm in arm down the street.

Matthew greeted her with a kiss on the cheek, and Hillary hugged her.

'Darling this is well met, isn't it, Matthew? We are about to take tea at Mrs Bumbles Tea shop in Coinagehall

Street. I understand her cream teas are good enough to rival the ones down at The Poldhu Tea Room.'

'Oh, well, I can't say I've sampled a cream tea in either of those establishments.'

'Then you must join us today, and we'll take you to Poldhu to have one there another day – we can decide then which is the best,' she smiled.

'Well, thank you, I'd love to.'

'As they settled at the gingham covered table by the window, Mrs Bumble, a jolly, rotund woman took their order.

'We were going to telephone you this evening,' Hillary smiled, 'we'd like you to come to Trevarno for dinner with Matthew's parents on Friday evening.'

Jenna felt the colour drain from her face. It was enough to attend the wedding there, but to actually go to dinner with Matthew's parents!

'Oh no! I can't, Hillary. Tell her, Matthew. I can't turn up for a dinner party. I was the Trevarno kitchen maid there less than a year ago!'

'But, darling, you are now the widow of a famous author, and an artist in your own right! We have sent word to Lyndon to come. I'm sure he will. My friend Glen is coming too. He will arrive by train on Friday morning. As he is going to give me away, he wants to come down to make sure I am marrying into a family who will look after me, bless him.' She grinned.

'He wants to check out my wine cellar more like,' Matthew joked.

'Yes, and that.' She slapped Matthew playfully. 'Anyway, we thought it would be lovely to all get together – you know, best man, maid of honour and stand in father-of-the-bride.'

Jenna audibly groaned at the thought.

Matthew reached out and placed his hand on hers to assure her. 'Everything will be fine, Jenna. In truth, Lyndon has never set foot in the house proper either and we have been friends for years, so you will not be alone in facing my family. I shall make sure my parents are on their best behaviour.' He winked.

Clenching her teeth, Jenna silently prayed for guidance. 'Very well then, I will, *if* Lyndon comes.'

'He will. I'll send a car for you on Friday afternoon about half-past-five. It will drop you off at Home Farm on the estate. Hillary is staying there until the wedding, so you can partake in some Dutch courage before you come up to the house. You can stay the night there if you want too.'

'Well then, that's all sorted, tuck in,' Hillary said as the warm aroma of scones preceded the cream tea at their table.

*

The next morning, Celia Inman, Jenna's housekeeper, and the owner of Toy Cottage

B & B, stormed into The Halzephron Inn.

'Richard Tredinnick we are supposed to be helping each other, are we not?' she barked.

Richard stopped polishing the glasses behind the bar and looked up. 'I thought we did.'

'Then why is it a gentleman came to my door last evening asking if I knew where he could rent a room, having been told,' she stabbed an angry finger at him, 'by *you,* that there was nowhere in the village to stay.'

Pulling his mouth into a tight line, Richard asked cautiously. 'So, did you give him a room?'

'Yes, I did, and no thanks to you,' she answered angrily. 'It sounds like he is staying for a while as well - you could have lost me so much income.'

'I'm sorry, Celia, but he was asking too many questions about James and Jenna for my liking.' Richard paused when he saw Celia's face blanch. 'And by the look of it he's been asking you much the same.'

'He's interested in them that's all. They are – were - a notable couple!'

'It's an unhealthy interest if you ask me.'

'Oh!' Celia began to climb down from her high horse.

'I suspect he asked if their marriage was a happy one, and if you always thought James was a confirmed bachelor.'

Celia pursed her lips.

'I thought as much. I don't know what is going on, Celia, but that man is not on holiday and in my opinion, he's out to harm Jenna in some way.'

'Oh god! Why didn't you let me know before he came knocking?'

'I told him to go to Helston - I didn't think he'd hang around.'

'What am I to do, Richard? Tell me what to do?'

'Tell him absolutely nothing from now on and I will put it about that there is a nosey parker about. No one likes one of those.'

'Shall we tell Jenna?'

'I don't think so, Celia. We don't want Jenna to feel uncomfortable here.'

'Well, I'm going to give him his marching orders and damn the income. We need him to know that his sort is not wanted around here.'

*

On Wednesday afternoon when the Friday dinner guest list came down to Mrs Drake - the Trevarno cook - it was delivered by Mrs Kent the housekeeper who practically threw it at her indignantly.

'Look, look who's on this list,' Mrs Kent said, spittle forming at the corners of her mouth.

Mrs Drake scoured the list and smiled inwardly as Mrs Kent snorted, 'Only Mrs Jenna Blackwell - Jennifer Penvean as was the name she used here when she was - *our kitchen maid*!'

Gina FitzSimmons, Lyndon's father's new wife looked up from where she was working at the mention of Jenna's name.

'Well, she is Miss Hillary's special friend, isn't that right Gina?' Cook said matter-of-factly.

Gina nodded.

'Well,' Mrs Kent's nostrils flared, 'if she thinks she can come swanning in here, expecting me to bow and scrape to her – she has another think coming.'

'I am sure she will not expect you to do any such thing, but I'd be careful if I were you, making statements like that,' Cook warned. 'Miss Hillary will be mistress of this house when she marries Master Matthew. Besides, what have you got against Jennifer? She was a flipping good worker – the best kitchen hand I ever had, and no one, but no one, could make clotted cream like her.'

'Have you forgotten how she stole poor Edna's husband from her?' Mrs Kent answered.

Edna was standing with her arms folded nodding in agreement behind the housekeeper.

Mrs Drake put down the list. 'Let me tell you something, Mrs Kent. Edna tricked Lyndon into marrying him?'

'I did not!' Edna answered adamantly.

'Oh yes you did! You tricked him, and said he had got you in the family way.'

'He did get me in the family way – I lost the baby on my wedding day.'

'No, you did not, and you know you didn't!' Mrs Drake had abandoned making dinner and was in full throttle now. 'And not only did you trick him about the baby, but you also didn't have the decency to let him into the marital bed for the duration of your marriage! Nor did you write a single letter to him while he fought for us all at the front line. Is it any wonder you forced that poor man into Jen's arms?' she paused when she saw Edna's face turn bright red. 'Yes, well you might blush, girl, I know it all.' Pushing Mrs Kent aside, Cook glowered over Edna. 'I know that when Lyndon came back from the war and regained his memory - he brought a doctor in to examine you and found out that you were still a virgin. Marriages do not get annulled for much else you know!'

The housekeeper spun around and looked questioningly at Edna.

'Lyndon FitzSimmons is a decent man and Jen is a decent woman,' Mrs Drake shouted, 'but you, Edna Morton, do not know the meaning of the word.'

Mr Brown the butler had come out of his office to see what the commotion was.

'Mrs Drake,' he ordered, 'that's enough!'

Edna's eyes widened as she turned, picked up her skirts, and flew out of the kitchen, past everyone standing open-mouthed having heard the quarrel.

Mrs Drake seemed to swell to twice her size. 'And I have had enough of everyone badmouthing Jen! So, if I hear another lie coming out of Edna Morton's mouth about her husband's mistreatment of her - I'll not have her in my kitchen a moment longer, and I shall tell Miss Hillary why. Nor do I want to hear you, Mrs Kent, endorsing Edna's lies, now you know the truth! Do I make myself clear?' she said stamping her foot. She did not wait for an answer but began to beat the hell out of the Yorkshire pudding batter.

When everyone else had left the kitchen, Gina came to stand beside Cook.

'I'm sorry, Gina, I know you told me all that about Edna in confidence, but I just could not keep it in any longer.'

'I'm proud of you, Mrs Drake,' Gina patted her on the shoulder. 'It's time to pave the way for Lyndon to be able to bring Jen back home.'

20

The chauffeur arrived at Loe House at half-past-five on Friday evening to take Jenna to Trevarno. She had been fraught and anxious all day at the prospect of dining with the more senior members of the Bickford family, but James had always told her that it was good to do something that frightened you – every hurdle completed would make her stronger. So, she stood at her mirror, took deep breaths, and tried her best to channel James's way of coping with things. *Goodness me*, she thought, *pull yourself together, Jenna. Men have risked their lives in the trenches of war – you are just going out to have dinner.*

With everything put into perspective now she tipped her head and scrutinised her outfit. Being still in half mourning, Jenna had dressed in a drop waist midnight blue satin dress trimmed with black lace. It was vastly different to the new dress Mrs Tonkin had fitted on her the previous day, but she had been pleased with how well made it was and thought it could rival any of the couture dresses Jenna now owned.

After dressing her hair by piling it simply on her head, she secured a clasp of small, purple, blue, and black feathers. There, perhaps they would not recognise her as the dairy maid who made the clotted cream to their liking.

As the chauffeur helped her into the back of the car, he said, 'We need to drop into Gweek to pick up Mr FitzSimmons. Master Matthew said you would not mind.'

'That's absolutely fine, thank you.'

Jenna felt her heart begin to hammer as the car came slowly down the hill into the village – she could not decide which was worst – coming back to Gweek or going back to Trevarno! Fortunately, the car didn't go into the centre of the village because Lyndon was stood waiting for them outside Barleyfield Farm.

Before the chauffeur could get out and open the door for him, Lyndon had climbed in beside Jenna. Once he'd settled himself and saw how beautifully dressed Jenna was, he shifted away from her slightly.

'Oh, gosh, sorry Jenna, you are all dressed and ready. I thought you would change at Trevarno, if I'd have known, I would have got in the front with the driver. I was late finishing – I've not washed the day's dust off yet.'

'Lyndon it's fine, honestly,' she said, surreptitiously curling her hand around his rough, work-worn fingers to see if he would pull away – thankfully, he didn't.

Inhaling deeply, she savoured the scent of musk and sweet meadows which clung to his clothes. His lovely wild auburn hair was damp to his face and neck and his scarlet neckerchief was stained dark with a day's perspiration. She rubbed her thumb on the calluses of his hands. 'I think I need to find you some lanolin again.'

Lyndon laughed gently glancing down at his grimy hands, ingrained with dust and dirt from his work. 'I've had nobody to keep them soft for.'

She squeezed his hands affectionately. 'Until now.'

He turned and looked deep into her eyes. 'It's good to see you, Jenna. I'm sorry I left London so suddenly.'

'It's all right, I understand. London was a terrible mistake - I can see that now. I'm so sorry I put you through it.'

Lyndon shook his head. 'Let's not speak about it tonight. I must say, this evening's dinner is going to be very strange. Although I've known Matthew all my life, I've never set foot in the big house before.'

'I'm quaking in my shoes too – I'm not afraid to admit it. The staff below stairs won't be happy about me being back, especially as I was their kitchen and dairy maid.'

'Not all staff will be unhappy to see you back. If you have time to visit, I am sure Gina, and my pa will be glad to see you.'

Jenna looked askance at him. 'Gina perhaps, I'm not sure your pa has forgiven me for marrying James. He never wrote back to me when I sent word of my marriage, though I did get a kind letter from Gina. She wished me luck but told me how disappointed your pa was with me. I can understand his hurt, but it made me so sad that we were no longer friends – we spent a great deal of time together, your pa and I, and always got on well.'

'Well, I showed him the letter James sent me – and although none of us know the real circumstances of your marriage, now he knows it was one of convenience to James – I can assure you - he *has* forgiven you.'

Jenna smiled with relief. 'Well then, yes, I would love to see them both - though I feel terribly overdressed.'

'Well, if you wait for me once we get to my house while I wash and change - we can both visit together dressed to the nines. James has let me keep the dinner suit he lent me to go to London with. He thinks that now Hillary is about to become part of the Bickford family, you, and I – *if* there *is* going to be a you and I,' he looked seriously at her, 'may be invited to a few of these events.'

Jenna looked shocked. 'Please don't doubt our future?'

Lyndon sighed heavily. 'I do admit to wondering if our lives can ever find common ground again.'

'I'm still me,' she whispered curling her soft hand over his.

'Are you?' His eyes searched hers.

'Yes, I just need time - *we* just need time. This is just a period of adjustment, that's all.'

*

Edna was struggling with the heavy pail of pig swill when the Bickford's chauffeur pulled up outside Lyndon's house. Her mouth tightened as she watched Lyndon jump out of the car and then reach back in to help a woman out of the car. Edna felt a frisson of anger rise when she recognised Jenna. She'd known she was coming of course - they were all working late because of this dinner the Bickford family were hosting, but to be so blatantly with Lyndon was just too much – and her recently widowed. That woman had no shame! Hopefully, people would look down on her – surely people in mourning should not be socialising. Normally she would have shared her condemnation with Mrs Kent, but since Cook had so spectacularly disclosed Edna's wicked secret, everyone including Mrs Kent had been very cool with her. She narrowed her eyes as Jenna followed Lyndon to the cottage that once was her marital home. One way or another, Edna was going to make her pay for stealing her husband.

*

Lyndon unlocked the cottage door and ushered Jenna into the kitchen. It felt stifling inside on such a warm evening, so they left the door ajar. A note was waiting for him on the kitchen table.

'Ah, good old Gina, she'd heard I was coming home today and lit the range for me, she says there are a couple of pails of washing water in the warming oven.'

Jenna smiled. 'She always was practical. I'm glad she and your pa got together in the end.'

'It's like he has a new lease of life.' Lyndon grinned as he put a couple of cloths in both hands to pick the pails up from the warming oven and took himself upstairs to wash and change.

Jenna walked slowly around the sparse kitchen of Lyndon's home, listening to him filling a bath tub. She could hear him scrubbing away and suspected he was trying to get some of the ingrained grime out of the palms of his hands.

The kitchen was clean and tidy to say he lived alone here – though when she thought back – the wagon he slept in when he was on the road was always fastidiously tidy. She'd spent a couple of nights in the wagon when he had helped her to escape from George Blewett, and found that because the space was tiny, there was a place for everything and everything in its place. Sweeping her eyes around the room, Jenna found herself mentally placing a nice bright rug in front of the fire and comfortable cushions on the hard wooden seats beside the hearth. Her paintings on the wall would brighten the place. *Could I live here with Lyndon?* She thought. *Not with Edna on the doorstep, no!*

He came down twenty minutes later, clean, shaved and dressed in a full dinner suit. Jenna smiled at the transformation. His hair was still damp, and he looked dreadfully uncomfortable in his tight collar.

'You certainly scrub up well.'

'Not as good as you do,' his eyes twinkled at her.

'Thank goodness I wasn't wearing this when I had my episode in London. It would have been ruined. My other suit must have been thrown away, was it?'

'No, Mrs Hemp worked her magic on it and it's as good as new. I brought it back for you but left it at Loe House I am afraid.'

'Gosh, she must have worked a miracle on it,' he answered remembering the state he'd been in that night. He turned from the mirror. 'Jenna, can you help again with this thing?' he asked, struggling with the bow tie.

Fortunately, Jenna had tied many such bows for James in the past and produced a very neat bow that any self-respecting valet could have achieved.

Lyndon turned to the mirror to inspect it and then turned back to face Jenna. Very tenderly he cupped her face in his hands and kissed her on the lips. The kiss was warm and tender – a hint of things to come. She wrapped her arms around his familiar body and rested her head on his chest.

'All these houses we have between us and none we can spend the night in,' she murmured.

'I know. I just long for the day you are by my side in bed again, Jenna.'

'It's my wish too, Lyndon, eventually.' *Though god knows when.* She wondered if she should bring up what Christian had suggested, but something stopped her.

Lyndon glanced at the clock on the mantelpiece – it was seven.

'We're not expected at the house for half-an-hour, shall we go and say hello to Pa and Gina before we meet Hillary?'

Jenna laughed nervously. 'I thought for a moment you were going to suggest taking me to your bed now and to hell with the lot of them.'

'Believe me I would in a heartbeat, if I didn't think hundreds of eyes were on this house at this very moment.' He smiled and kissed he again trying not to smudge her lipstick.

*

Lyndon knocked and walked into his pa's cottage, tentatively followed by Jenna.

'Evening all,' he said brightly.

'Ah, Lyndon, we knew you were home, five people have mentioned it in passing! The jungle drums are out in force,' Gina said looking up from the kitchen sink.

Lyndon raised his eyebrows at Jenna as though to say, 'I told you so.'

Lyndon's pa put down his newspaper and turned to greet his son with a smile, but his smile faded slightly when he heard Gina say, 'Oh, and Jenna too - what a lovely surprise.' Gina moved to hug Jenna warmly. 'My goodness, look at you both, we'd heard you were both on the list for dinner at the big house tonight. Don't you both scrub up well?'

'Hello, Gina,' Jenna said gently, walking further into the room she never thought she would step into again. 'It's good to see you again. And Michael, it's good to see you too.'

Michael stood, put his pipe down and brushed the tobacco from his trousers. She could see his eyes watering at the sight of her again, but all he could say to her was her name with a nod of the head. *He hasn't forgiven me*, she thought, and her heart constricted.

'Come and sit down – I expect you're killing time before the dinner,' Gina gestured to the chairs around the table.

Jenna saw Michael watch as Lyndon took Jenna's hand and led her to one of the chairs for her to sit down.

'Thank you, Lyndon.' Her eyes cut from Michael to Lyndon and she smiled lovingly at him.

'So,' Michael said cautiously, 'are you two back together?'

'Not officially, Pa. Jenna is still in half mourning for James.'

'Oh, I see.' A cloud passed over his face. 'And then?'

Gina laughed. 'Michael, stop interrogating them. It's enough to see them together and happy at last.' Gina grasped and squeezed Jenna's hand. 'Goodness, but I've missed you so much, Jenna. This place isn't the same without you.'

'I've missed you too, Gina. Michael, as to your question, Lyndon and I have a lot to sort out, but we are taking one step at a time and we both believe it's in the right direction.'

Michael nodded, and Gina patted his hand.

'He's just worried something else will happen to come between you two again,' Gina explained. 'Goodness knows - the gods have kept you apart for the last seven years. So, we hear a lot about your success in London, don't we, Michael?'

Michael gave a short sharp nod.

'Yes, I've been lucky in my acquaintances – they have helped to further my career as an artist.'

'What is it like to live in London – I've never been – is it wonderful?' Gina said excitedly.

'Yes and no. It's noisy and dirty, but full of vibrancy.'

'So, will you have to go up and down there for your work?' she asked.

'I expect I will on occasions, yes.'

'And where do you fit in with Jenna's new life as an artist *in* London, Lyndon,' Michael asked stiffly.

Lyndon smiled tightly, but his silence spoke volumes.

Jenna reached out to Lyndon, curled her fingers around his hand and smiled. 'We *will* find a way,' she spoke the words to Lyndon, not Michael, and Lyndon smiled gently and kissed her tenderly on the cheek.

Michael watched the exchange and sighed.

'I suspect there were rumblings in the kitchen when the guest list came down to the kitchen and they found that I was on it?' Jenna turned to Gina.

'I'll say! In truth though, there was only really Edna and Mrs Kent who were opposed to you in the kitchen, but Mrs Drake gave them a piece of her mind when they tried to criticize you.'

'Oh, bless Mrs Drake – I always got on well with her,' Jenna said.

'I'm afraid that while they were denouncing Jenna, Mrs Drake revealed Edna's misdemeanours that I shared with her in confidence, Lyndon. I'm sorry.'

'Good! Don't apologise. It needs to be known – I don't know why I haven't exposed her myself.'

'Because you're a decent man, Lyndon, that's why, and everyone knows that to be true.' Gina smiled at him. 'I think you'll find most people are on your side now, Jenna, with the exception of Mr Brown the butler who is po-faced with everyone at the best of times. I must say though, I would love to be a fly on the wall in that dining room when he serves you tonight.'

'Oh, don't, Gina,' Jenna put her hand to her heart, 'I'm quaking in my shoes at the very thought of it.'

'And on that note,' Lyndon said getting up, 'I think we should make our way to Hillary's house – we can all walk in together then.'

21

True to form, the face of Mr Brown the butler, was a picture when Jenna walked in with Lyndon, Hillary, and Glen. The footman who took their coats was new - so did not recognise Jenna and therefore was perfectly courteous. As they walked through the hall towards the drawing room, Jenna glanced at the door to the servant's stairs and was sure she saw Edna's scowling face peeping around the door.

Being based in the kitchen and dairy while she worked here, Jenna had never been in the main house before, she looked around with admiration. The hall was large with huge Turkish rugs adorning the highly polished floor. A great oak staircase swept up to the gallery where generations of Bickford portraits stared down at her.

The group were shown into the richly ornate drawing room where Matthew and his father Andrew were already enjoying an aperitif.

Andrew Bickford welcomed them as he would any other guest in his house – without a hint of superiority - immediately settling Lyndon and Jenna's nerves. No sooner had they been offered a drink, Eleanor Bickford, Matthew's mother, could be heard outside the room complaining bitterly about attending this dinner.

Andrew Bickford blanched and excused himself to join his wife in the hall, but the conversation continued well in earshot of the group in the drawing room.

'Good god, Andrew,' Eleanor complained, 'do I really have to dine with a hedger and an artist? And who is this Glen Courtney chap Hillary has brought? I spoke to our daughter on the phone this morning about him, and she says he is nothing but a socialite – I mean, what is the world coming to?'

The group heard Andrew Bickford say, '*Eleanor*, our guests are already here!' and the conversation ceased.

Lyndon and Jenna exchanged furtive glances, and Glen looked deeply affronted.

Matthew sighed and shook his head. 'I apologise to you all now for Mama – she is a terrible snob,' he said.

Jenna felt the anxiety rise in her throat. *I should not have come.*

Eleanor Bickford sailed into the room in a swoosh of dark green taffeta and a painted-on smile. Andrew followed her with an equally apologetic smile.

Eleanor was fifty-two-years-old – her beauty fast fading with the years, though she gave a hint of her former beauty when she smiled – which was not often. Her eyes settled on Jenna's beauty and youth and could not hide her envy of her.

'Mrs Blackwell, Mr FitzSimmons and Mr Courtenay, so pleased you could join us in this celebration,' Eleanor gushed. Jenna, Lyndon, and Glen nodded back to her courteously. 'Charmed, I'm sure,' she said disingenuously and took a seat by the fireside.

Andrew poured another whisky for himself and a sherry for his wife. With the drink in hand, Eleanor pursed her lips and turned her nose up as though an unpleasant smell had entered the room.

'It must be hard putting makeup on two faces,' Hillary whispered to Jenna who had to stifle a chuckle.

Old Mrs Bickford was the next to enter and she looked down her spectacles at the ensemble in the room.

'Eleanor, who are these people?' she demanded.

'They are Matthew and Hillary's friends, Mama – they're here for the wedding.'

'What wedding?'

'Matthew and Hillary's, Mama – you know, the one you have just had a dress fitting for.'

'I thought that was next week!'

'It is - we are just having a dinner to meet them.'

The old woman sat down, banged the end of her walking stick on the floor in annoyance and sighed impatiently. Once a drink was put into her hand, the old woman turned to Eleanor and whispered, albeit not quietly enough, 'It's a big mistake this wedding you know.'

'Mama, not now,' Eleanor warned and looked up at everyone with an embarrassed smile.

'Matthew deserves better. Hillary is far too flighty – did I not see her driving a motor car – what is she thinking?'

'Hush, Mama!' Eleanor scolded.

Andrew Bickford, world weary of his mother-in-law's loose tongue, glanced apologetically at Hillary, who seemed quite unperturbed by the old woman's rantings.

Matthew moved to Hillary's side for moral support. 'I'm sorry, darling,' he whispered, 'she's old and doesn't know what she is saying.'

Not convinced for a moment, Hillary grinned. 'Don't worry, Matthew, I shall endeavour to ignore her so hard she will start doubting her existence,' she said chinking her glass with his.

Thankfully at that moment the dinner gong went.

Lyndon placed a discrete hand on the small of Jenna's back as they walked into the dining room and whispered to her, 'Good grief, we haven't even sat down yet, but I'll be glad when this dinner is over.'

You and I both she thought, *though she suspected things were going to get a deal more uncomfortable soon - the Bickford's had not recognised her yet.'*

*

Jenna was, to her ultimate relief, seated between Lyndon and Glen at the dining table, so she was not short of conversation. If looks could kill though, Mr Brown the butler would have assassinated Jenna by the time the soup course was over. He practically snorted over Jenna's shoulders as he served her, and Jenna could see he was convinced she would not know how to use the cutlery correctly - and she was right - because almost as soon as the soup was ladled into her bowl, Brown leaned into her.

'If madam would like to start from the outside of the cutlery,' he whispered, almost sotto voce.

Glen, who had been speaking to Jenna, dropped his mouth open when he heard this exchange and Jenna prickled with indignation - she was well versed in eating in polite society and had already picked up the correct soup spoon when Brown spoke.

Fortunately, Andrew Bickford, who was sat opposite her seemed to have the hearing to rival a bat. He lifted his head in astonishment. '*Brown!* What the devil are you thinking – telling a guest which item of cutlery to use?'

Mr Brown looked flustered. 'I do beg your pardon, sir - Mrs Blackwell looked as though she was struggling to know which of the spoons to use.'

'What absolute rubbish,' Glen piped up. 'Jenna was holding the spoon when you uttered your nonsense.'

Jenna shot Glen an appreciative look.

'I do beg your pardon, sir, madam.' Brown bowed and retreated from the table, 'I must have been mistaken.'

'In future, speak, only when you're spoken to,' Andrew scolded. 'Mrs Blackwell, I am dreadfully sorry if he caused you any embarrassment.'

'Not at all,' Jenna said graciously trying hard not to look at Mr Brown, for she knew he would be shooting virtual daggers at her.

As Lyndon reached his hand over and curled it around hers in solidarity, Eleanor Bickford sniffed the air haughtily – she did not care for her staff being berated in public.

The main course arrived, and Jenna was served with roast duck with cherry sauce, dauphinoise potatoes and French beans. She smiled, remembering that this was Mrs Drake's signature dish - a meal she cooked to perfection.

'My compliments to the cook – this meal is delicious,' Jenna said to the Bickford's.

'Hear! Hear!' Andrew Bickford agreed waving his fork in the air.

There was a general nod of consensus, and Matthew turned to the butler. 'Please send our compliments down to Mrs Drake.'

'Yes, sir,' he sneered.

Jenna smiled inwardly, there was no love lost between the butler and the cook – the compliment would no doubt stick in his throat as he delivered it.

'So, Mr Courtenay,' Eleanor turned her haughty nose to Glen, 'I'm told you are a socialite.'

'When I'm not assisting my brother, the 17th Earl of Devon to look after our vast estate, yes, I do find time to socialise a little!'

Eleanor cleared her throat. 'You... you are related to the 17th Earl of Devon?' she asked swallowing hard. 'I see, I hadn't realised we had someone so distinguished at our table.'

Glen brushed the comment away casually. 'I don't make a big thing of it.'

Hillary's face lit with mirth – *Glen, related to the 17th Earl of Devon!* – he was no such thing - it was a great big fat lie, but she loved him for it.

Eleanor Bickford smiled uncomfortably and turned her attention to Jenna.

'So, tell me, Mrs Blackwell, who are your parents?'

Jenna paused eating and glanced at Matthew, who nodded for her to tell.

'My mother was a talented artist, and my father was a fisherman.'

'A fisherman?' Mrs Bickford frowned, 'you mean he owned a fishing fleet?'

'No, he fished from Gweek with the other men of the village.'

Puzzled now, Eleanor asked, 'And your mother was an artist you say?'

'She was, yes.'

'Do I know of her work?'

'I very much doubt it – she painted for pleasure but taught me well.'

'And you went to school where?'

'Gweek.'

'Yes, yes but where did you finish?'

'Finish?'

'Your *education*, my dear.'

'I *finished* school in Gweek when I was fourteen and then kept house for my father – my mother died when I was eight,' she answered honestly.

'Oh, I'm sorry for your loss. So, your rise to fame has been quite recent so Matthew tells me.'

'It has.'

'Did you go to London to study art?'

'No, I worked in your kitchen and dairy here.'

Both Hillary and Lyndon grinned broadly at each other for her honesty.

Andrew Bickford looked up and scrutinised Jenna, as Hillary dabbed her mouth with her napkin to hide her amusement.

Flustered now, Eleanor Bickford glanced at Mr Brown, who nodded that it was true. 'I don't understand - how on earth have you risen from service to the so-called heights of the art world then?'

'Because your son, Matthew, saw my potential as an artist and commissioned the paintings hanging in your orangery.'

Eleanor paled significantly and put down her napkin. 'Is this true, Matthew?'

'It is, and you admire them daily you will recall.'

'So, are you responsible for Mrs Blackwell's career, Matthew? I should have thought you were too busy with this estate, for such things.'

'No, I just showed the paintings to James Blackwell when he visited. He too saw Jenna's potential.'

Feeling a little braver now, Jenna picked up the thread. 'James took me under his wing – so to speak, and introduced me to some people who helped my career in art.'

Eleanor took a deep measured breath. 'And then married you,' she said haughtily.

'He did.'

'By all accounts, James Blackwell was a very successful author – you, as his widow must have been left very comfortable,' Eleanor said taking a sip of her wine.

'I am, but I'm poorer for his loss.'

'Nevertheless, it must have been a rather advantageous marriage for you – a dairy maid.'

'Jenna was already a successful artist before she married James!' Matthew interjected.

'Well, how very fortunate for you – I'm sure many in your position are not that lucky.'

'There was no luck involved, Mama,' Matthew interjected. 'Jenna has a rare talent and has just had a sell-out show in London.'

Eleanor pursed her lips - she could not argue with that.

'And we haven't had a decent pot of clotted cream since you left, my dear.' Andrew Bickford winked which made Jenna relax.

'What are you all talking about, eh?' Old Mrs Bickford demanded. 'Who is making clotted cream?'

'Nobody,' Mama,' Eleanor replied tersely.

'More is the pity,' Andrew interjected.

'Well, enjoy your wealth while you can, Mrs Blackthorn, you are young and beautiful - you will not be able to hold onto your new-found position in life for long.'

Jenna put her cutlery down, her appetite fast diminishing with this altercation. 'I don't think I understand your meaning.'

'I see you are still in demi-mourning for your husband, but once you are in the market for another husband, your new-found wealth will bring opportunists out of the woodwork.'

Jenna felt Lyndon's body stiffen next to her, so she reached under the table to hold his hand.

'It is true, someone will come along, charm you and sweep a woman like you off her feet, marry you and your wealth will automatically go to your new husband. It is the law my dear – you probably do not know that, coming from your *humble* beginnings,' Eleanor said authoritatively.

'I am well aware of the law - I am represented by one of London's top lawyers. It is you, who is not well versed in the law. What you refer to, changed fifty years ago, when the Married Women's Property Act 1870 was brought in, to allow married women to be the legal owners of the money they earned and to inherit property.'

'Touché,' Hillary said under her breath.

Eleanor flushed and glanced at Andrew for confirmation, who nodded that it was correct, and Jenna felt Lyndon's hand slacken in her hold.

'However,' Jenna continued, and grabbed Lyndon's hand again tighter, 'when the time comes and I do marry again, it will be for love, and my wealth will be ours to share.'

'Well said, Jenna,' Hillary smiled, but Jenna felt Lyndon pull his hand from hers.

Eleanor was thankfully quiet for the duration of the meal and the talk turned more congenial. Andrew spoke about their daughter Mellissa who was, at the moment, holidaying on the Italian Riviera with friends. He told them of the new mare he had bought her as a surprise to replace her beloved Star when the authorities took her away for the war effort. He even jokingly asked Jenna if she could set a pot of clotted cream before she left the next morning.

At last, Jenna began to relax but she'd noted that Lyndon had fallen noticeably quiet since the exchange about her financial position – and that worried her.

22

When they finally took their leave of the dinner party, Lyndon said his goodnights to Jenna on the doorstep of Home Farm.

'I feel utterly drained,' Jenna said holding her hand to her forehead.

'I thought you managed yourself very well, Jenna,' Lyndon answered.

'I meant what I said about sharing everything with you.'

'We'll speak about it another time,' he answered flatly.

'Shall we speak in the morning before we go home?' she asked hopefully - there was clearly an issue here they needed to sort out.

'No, I'll be gone at first light, I've arranged for a car early, I need to get back to work.'

'I see, well, I'll see you at Charlie and Lizzy's wedding then?'

He nodded, and instead of the loving kiss they had shared earlier, he kissed her chastely on the cheek as a brother would a sister.

'Goodnight, Jenna.'

'Goodnight, Lyndon.'

He turned and walked away, and Jenna felt the chasm between them had grown ever larger.

As Lyndon left, Jenna saw Matthew walking Hillary up to the gate of Home Farm, and she stepped into the hall so that they could say their goodnights in private.

'Is that you, Hill,' Glen shouted through from one of the rooms.

'No, It's Jenna, but Hillary is just coming.

'Come in, come in and make yourself at home. I have.'

Glen beckoned Jenna into the small, but very compact drawing room, where he was already enjoying a nightcap before he returned to his own lodgings.

Hillary breezed in shortly afterwards. 'You were magnificent tonight, Jenna, I'm so proud of you,' she said pouring two glasses of brandy and pushing one of them into Jenna's hand.

'I wasn't magnificent, I felt down right rude, speaking back to Eleanor Bickford like that. What on earth must Matthew think of me?'

'He applauds you, darling, for standing up for yourself. He has said himself that his mother is a snob. Glen was the best though, what a hoot, brother to the 17th Earl of Devon, eh? Naughty boy. I almost choked on my syllabub when you said it.'

'Well, it takes enormous effort to be a socialite – I will not have my position demeaned in any way. Anyway, I might not be the brother of an Earl, but I do claim to be a distant relative of his, so I have aristocratic blood in my veins. I was certainly not going to tell her I am an antique dealer – she would have looked down her nose at me,' he said wryly. 'I will be long gone before she finds me out. I hope it doesn't make things awkward for you, Hills - with my little white lie.'

'Nonsense, everyone has the right to be stupid, but she was just abusing the privilege. She deserved it. I just hope she doesn't find out before the wedding, otherwise she will hound you off the estate and I will not have anyone to walk me up the aisle. Oh, but it was a joy to see her bow and scrape to you afterwards though, once she thought you were higher up the pecking order than herself.' She lifted her glass to toast him.

'*Hillary,* you're marrying into this family, remember. You must try to get on with them,' Jenna warned.

'The only person who matters is Matthew, but having said that I adore his father Andrew, as for Eleanor and her mother - they really don't like me, but that's all right, not everyone has good taste!'

'Eleanor's mother was quite insulting towards you though,' Greg frowned.

Hillary wafted her hand dismissively. 'In order for her to insult me, I must first value her opinion – and I don't.' She drained her glass.

Glen too finished his drink and stood up. 'Right then, I'm going back to my lodgings, otherwise being here with two gorgeous ladies will invite gossip. So, good night to you both and thank you for an entertaining evening – I genuinely thought it was going to be a bore. What fun to be had, putting the snobs in their place, eh?'

*

Jenna slept until eight the next morning. Although the previous evening had drained her until she felt bone-tired, Lyndon's reticence had bothered her greatly and she had lain awake until four that morning worrying about it.'

Jenna dressed more casually for breakfast, in a dress she would normally wear to walk the coast in. Hillary had yet to rise, but breakfast had been sent over from the big house and was being kept warm on warming plates, so she selected scrambled eggs on toast and had just finished her coffee when Matthew called.

'Have you time to come walk with me, Jenna,' he requested.

They walked through the kitchen courtyard towards the path to the high meadow and waved at a couple of people she had known and worked with. Tommy Teague, Gina's son who had been blinded in one eye in the war, gave her a hug, and Fred Saunders, Ethel the kitchen help's husband, tipped his hat to her.

They settled down at the edge of the barley crop. The sun was hot, the day peaceful and bees buzzed nearby.

'Do you remember the last time we sat here, Jenna,' Matthew said circling his knee with his arms.

'I do,' Jenna said picking at a cornflower. 'You were on leave from the war, and you told me about the dreadful conditions Lyndon and his comrades were suffering in the trenches. I take it we've come back here because you need to speak candidly to me again.'

He laughed softly at her perception. 'I took Lyndon back to Gweek this morning. I had business in Helston first thing, so it was just a quick detour.'

Jenna looked up at him. 'Forgive me if I have got this wrong, but I got the distinct impression from him last night that he finds my inherited wealth problematic.'

Matthew pulled his mouth into a tight line. 'He doesn't begrudge you anything you have achieved, but yes your inherited wealth and property does cause a problem.'

Jenna looked out over the field swaying in the soft breeze and sighed heavily.

'Lyndon is a proud man, Jenna. All he ever wanted was for you to be his wife and for him to provide for you.'

'What do you suggest I do? Give up my art - give away my wealth?'

'No, but he is struggling with the fact that you have more wealth than he could ever dream of accumulating - of that there is no doubt.'

'Well, he'll have to get used to it, Matthew – I am what I am now, and we live in a very different world from 1912!'

'It is not for me to lecture you both. I am just saying you need to find a compromise. I've told Lyndon the same. I've watched you two over the last seven years, desperately wanting each other, but not being able to be together. I do not want to see your chance of being together slip away again.'

Jenna picked a dandelion head and threw it as far as she could. 'What do you suggest then?'

'I don't know, Jenna, it is up to you two to find a way through this, but you need time together – time to talk. You have a chance now – do not let anything, especially money, get in your way.'

As they walked back towards the stables and courtyard, Gina came out of the dairy with a ripe cheese and beamed at them both.

'Jen, you're still here!'

'Yes, but I'm leaving within the hour.'

'Oh, Mrs Drake will be sad to have missed you. She was as pleased as punch when word was sent down from the dining room complimenting her dishes. She reckoned you might have had something to do with it.'

'She did,' Matthew said, 'and I feel berated that I don't send my compliments down to the kitchen enough.'

'If you'll excuse me, I must go and put this down. Come back soon, Jen, we all miss you.'

'I will,' Jenna kissed her on the cheek and let her go back to the kitchen. 'Gosh, I'd love to see Mrs Drake, but I can hardly go in the kitchen to her, can I?'

'I'll fetch her,' Matthew suggested. 'You wait here.'

With Matthew gone, Jenna turned to gaze with affection at the dairy she had worked in for so long. The yard was busy with brown hens clucking around her feet, so she didn't hear the click of boot heels on the cobbles at first. It was the sound of someone huffing with disgust which caught her attention. As she turned, there, stood before her, was the skinny frame of Edna with the vegetable basket in hand and venom visible in her eyes.

'You've got a nerve coming here,' she snarled,' look at you dressed like lady muck, sniffing around my husband like a bitch on heat. Don't think you are coming back here to live because you're not. My father will make sure you are banished again! We might have to put up with your unwelcome presence at this bloody wedding next week, because you are friends with Miss Stanton, but once that is over, I am warning you not to show your shameless face here again.'

Matthew had appeared from the kitchen as Edna was in full throttle.

'One more word out of your evil mouth, Edna Morton and you will be looking for new employment,' Matthew growled.

Edna's face drained as she swung around to face Matthew.

'Oh! Master Matthew. I was just kidding - it was a joke that's all.'

'Get out of my sight. NOW!'

Edna's chin trembled as she put her head down and ran to the kitchen.

'Are you all right, Jenna?' Matthew put his hand comfortingly on her arm.

'Sticks and stones you know.' Jenna brushed the incident away, though the confrontation had unnerved her.

'I'll dismiss her if you want you know.'

Jenna shook her head. 'She's just a very bitter and twisted young woman – I doubt she'll reiterate any of it to me again.' Just at that moment Mrs Drake came bustling out of the kitchen with genuine tears of happiness in her eyes at seeing Jenna.

'Oh, my lovely girl, how wonderful to see you.' She gathered Jenna into her enormous bosoms as a mother would a child. 'Gosh, but I've missed you.'

'I've missed you too, Mrs Drake.'

'I wish I could stay and chat, but I've luncheon cooking on the stove.'

'I'll be back next week for the wedding – we'll catch up then,' Jenna smiled.

Mrs Drake wiped a stray tear from her cheek, grasped Jenna's hands, smiled, and nodded before lumbering back into the kitchen.

*

Sunday dawned a glorious day – it looked like the summer was set fair for a few days yet. Jenna was keeping her fingers crossed that both the weddings she would be attending this coming week would be blessed with sunshine.

After deciding to walk to Church Cove, she had gathered a posy of white flowered elder, and pink campion and set off. At the top of Halzhephron Cliffs, she sat a while to gaze out across the silvery sea, letting her hair stream around her face in the soft breeze. The tropical smell of the yellow gorse scented the air and puffs of dandelion seed floated past her. Up here on the cliffs she could leave all worries behind.

*

Unbeknown to Jenna a man was following a short distance behind her. After thinking that he had secured a room for the duration of his stay down here, Mrs Inman, the silly woman, told him she had double booked his room and he would have to leave. He knew she was lying, perhaps he had been too forward in his questions about the Blackwell's. As he could find no one else to offer him a room - even though they were showing vacancy signs outside their premises, he was forced to find somewhere in Helston. That morning though, he had driven back and parked up on the road to Berepper in order to watch Loe House for sign of movement. If people wouldn't speak to him, that was no problem, he was quite versed in gathering his own evidence.

*

At The Poldhu Tea Room, Marianne could not contain her excitement when Gabriel called her over to his table to speak with her.

'Forgive me, for being so bold, Marianne, but you know you said the other day that you like to build sandcastles.'

'Yes,' she said excitedly.

'I wonder if you could help Robbie build one today on Poldhu Beach when you've finished your shift?'

'Gosh, yes, I'd love that,' she enthused.

'There you go, Robbie, isn't that nice of Marianne.'

The boy nodded and pushed another piece of cake into his mouth.

Marianne could not wait to finish work – and had been going over and over in her mind what she would speak to Gabriel about. She hoped he could see that she was well read – this was her chance to make a good impression on him – *this* was the start of their relationship.

'You look like the cat that got the cream,' Ellie said, as Marianne skipped out of the back room having changed from her uniform into a pretty dress.

'Gabriel Trelease has asked me to join him and Robbie on the beach today,' she said proudly.

'Ah, yes, he mentioned to me that he was going to ask you. It's kind of you, Marianne. If you find you need me for anything, pop back to the house.'

Why would she need Ellie for anything? 'I'll be fine,' she said.

'Well, have a nice time then,' Ellie called after her.

'I will.' As she stepped out of the door, her heart gave a little somersault when she saw Gabriel and Robbie waiting for her at the bottom of the veranda steps.

As they walked down the beach, Marianne found to her dismay that she could not think of a single thing to say that had a modicum of intelligence – her mind had gone blank in his presence.

'Can we build it here, Papa?' Robbie asked.

'Is here all right with you, Marianne?'

'Of course,' she said kneeling down with the child.

'Well, be a good boy for Marianne, Robbie. I will not be long.'

Marianne turned sharply. 'Are you going somewhere?'

'I will only be an hour at the most. Thank you, Marianne, I really appreciate you giving your time up to help me with Robbie. My parents are out today, and I remembered that you like children. I will of course pay you for minding him.'

'But…' She twisted her mouth with a sour expression.

'Sorry, I must go.'

Marianne flared her nostrils, seething at being used as a childminder. She watched him walk up the beach to climb into his car and drive up Poldhu Hill.

'Where is your papa going, Robbie?'

'He needed to go over to Gunwalloe for something. I wanted to go with him in case Jenna was over there again today, but he would not let me,' he said sulkily.

'Who is Jenna?'

'Jenna Blackwell. She is lovely, she looks just like Mama, and Papa likes her too. She made a lovely sandcastle with me last week.'

Marianne felt the tears prickle behind her eyes. To think he had left her here to mind *his* child while he goes courting another woman! What a fool she had been.

'Are you going to help me build this sandcastle then, Papa said you would?'

'Of course, I am,' Marianne said through gritted teeth. 'I'm sure I can build a better one than Jenna Blackwell.'

23

When Jenna reached St Winwaloe Church, she found a fine, white horse tethered to the gatepost. She stroked its nose, it tossed its head and snuffled at her coat pocket as though she had a treat for him.

'No, no, no.' Jenna laughed and pulled her posy away from its mouth before it decided to chomp on the flowers. After a last pat on its withers, Jenna lifted the church gate latch, stepped through into the peaceful graveyard listening as the gate clicked quietly behind her. Keeping her eyes to the ground so as not to stamp on the flowers growing wild between the graves, she was surprised to find someone else standing over James's grave. The woman who turned and smiled at Jenna, was incredibly beautiful, her skin was like porcelain and her clear blue eyes shone with friendship.

'Mrs Blackwell, is it?'

'Yes,' Jenna answered stepping forward.

'Good afternoon to you, forgive my intrusion, I just wanted to lay a posy of flowers for James. I'm Sarah Dunstan, from Bochym Manor.'

'Oh, the Countess de Bochym!' Jenna bobbed a curtsy.

'Yes,' Sarah smiled warmly, 'but no need to stand on ceremony. I am so sorry for your loss. We knew James, your husband, very well. We had to decline the kind invitation to your wedding because we were setting off to France to visit my husband's sister and only returned at the end of June, so we were understandably shocked to hear the news of James's death on our return.' She reached out and placed a comforting hand on Jenna's sleeve. 'My heartfelt sympathy goes out to you, my dear. James was a wonderful man.'

Jenna's heart caught at Sarah's genuine sympathy. 'Thank you,' she breathed.

Sarah observed Jenna's attire. 'I see you are in half mourning still. Are you attending social engagements?'

'I am, yes. I believe James would have wanted me to. I've just returned from London - I had an exhibition there.'

'Yes, we saw it a fortnight ago – we travelled up to London briefly. I must say your work is remarkable.'

'You're too kind. Thank you, very much.'

'Unfortunately, for us - but not for you, the exhibition had sold out, so we did not get a chance to purchase any of your work – I do hope you are working on some new canvases.'

'I'm trying.'

'We have a fine array of craftsmen and women within our Bochym Arts and Craft Association, although like many, we lost two of our dear friends from the association in the war. You are very welcome to look around sometime. In fact, come to tea the week after next and I will show you around. Would Tuesday the 12th of August be convenient?'

'That would be lovely thank you.'

'Three-o-clock then, shall I send the car for you?'

'No, I'll drive myself, thank you.'

Sarah put her hand to her heart. 'Goodness, I admire your bravery – the motorcar still frightens the life out of me – give me horseback any day. I will leave you to your thoughts now. It was lovely meeting you.

Jenna placed her posy next to the beautiful bouquet of flowers Sarah Dunstan had left and knelt to tell James all about the dinner at Trevarno. Presently she stood up and brushed her skirt down. It was then she wondered if she might meet Gabriel and Robbie again on the beach – she could certainly use the company.

As she rounded the church, she stood atop of the steps which led down to the beach from the churchyard, but they were nowhere to be seen. She turned to walk back up the steps and smiled when she saw Gabriel walking up the church path towards her. As he neared, there was surprised delight in his voice, and his dark eyes softened when he looked at her.

'Good afternoon to you, Jenna, this is well met. I was about to drive over to Loe House to see you, and it was only by chance I spotted you in the churchyard.

Jenna smiled at the fact that the hope to meet had been mutual.

'No little Robbie today?' It amazed her how sorry she was to not see the child again. The little boy had well and truly found a place in her heart.

'No, I left him with a child minder briefly because I wanted to speak with you alone.'

Jenna tipped her head intrigued.

'I know it is an imposition, but I came to ask a huge favour of you.'

Jenna smiled. 'You can ask and if it is in my power I'll help if I can.'

Gabriel took a deep breath. 'It's Robbie's birthday on Thursday – the first without his mama.' He paused and Jenna could see him struggling to keep his emotions in check. 'His mama died two days after his last one.'

Jenna's eyes flickered with sadness. 'Poor little lad.'

'Robbie has spoken about you many times since he mistook you for his mama last week. So, I wondered if … would it be possible if…'

'What?' Jenna laughed at his wavering.

'Well, I wondered if you could join us for a birthday tea at The Poldhu Tea Room on Thursday.'

'Oh!' Jenna was overwhelmed to be asked. 'Well, I…'

'I know it is a lot to ask of you. Robbie hinted that he wondered if you might be able to come. I did not want to get his hopes up until I'd spoken to you, hence he is not with me today. Say no if you need to.'

'You misunderstand my hesitancy, it's just that I am attending a wedding on Wednesday in Gweek – I'm staying over but,' her face broke into a smile, 'yes, yes of course I'll come to tea with you both - I would be honoured.'

'Shall we say, half past two then? If the day is nice – and this weather looks like it will last a while longer, you drive to the church here, say at two and we could all meet and have a nice walk over Poldhu Head all together.'

'Sounds wonderful. My but I seem to be popular today – I've just been invited to Bochym for tea the following Tuesday.'

Gabriel gave a wide smile. 'Ah, I thought I saw Sarah riding over the hill when I drove down. Well, I might see you there as well.' He smiled with a twinkle in his eyes.

*

On Monday, Marianne was still disgruntled with Gabriel for tricking her into looking after Robbie and was in two minds as to whether she should take a walk up to Bochym that day to try and see him again. But then that would cut off her nose to spite her face.

She and Lucy had to take their flask and cake and sit in the barley field that day because the Bochym Arts and Crafts members were lazing by the lake. As they skirted the lake towards the stile to the field, Marianne saw Gabriel with them. Standing quite visibly at the top of the stile so that he could see her, she was disgruntled when he did not look her way. *At least he isn't entertaining Mary today*, she thought, but then gritted her teeth when she spotted Mary walking towards the gardens with a tea tray – a moment later Gabriel followed her.

'Are you ever going to jump down off that stile, Marianne?' Lucy moaned, 'I'm dying for a cup of tea and a bit of cake.'

'I've just seen Mary going into the garden again!'

'Yes, she serves Gabriel there most days with the weather being fine – I told you that last week.'

'Is there something going on with those two?'

Lucy laughed. 'Don't be daft, she's not got over Thomas.'

'Well, they are much in each other's company! People will talk.'

'What people?'

'People, when this gets out. It's not proper for two people to be alone together when they are not married.'

'Oh, pipe down Marianne, they are just helping each other through their grief.'

Marianne turned to look at Lucy and gave her a hard stare. 'I still don't understand why Mary is allowed to go into the garden when you lot can't.'

'I told you; the doctor says she needs fresh air and rest - she's still not got over her illness.'

'Illness! Fiddlesticks, she only ate a funny mushroom!'

'It upset her insides – she was really poorly with it.'

'I don't believe it - unless she is feigning illness to get favours. David Bray – a boy I went to school with, ate a poisonous mushroom once and he was only off school sick for a day. I think something else happened that day - something that you're keeping secret from me.'

Lucy laid the rug at the edge of the field but did not respond.

'Aren't you?'

'Don't be so ridiculous, Marianne. I'm going back to the house if you don't stop this nonsense.'

Marianne ceased her questioning, but she could plainly see Lucy was hiding something from her. She'd get it out of her one way or another.

*

Mary was not in fact sitting chatting to Gabriel as Marianne thought – not that they hadn't shared a conversation or two in the past. She had enjoyed spending time with him on the occasions he *had* taken his tea with her. It was good to speak to someone who understood her predicament. Gabriel was working on something down in the old barn at the bottom of the orchard, so he would meet her to say hello, and then take his tea to the barn where he would spend an hour every afternoon. Mary would sit and read amongst the fragrant flowers, listening to him tap, tap, tap. She surmised that he must be chiselling something out of plaster down there to replace the damaged pieces in the French drawing room.

*

Gabriel stood back to admire his handy work. He had been chiselling the memorial stone for Thomas for the last five days and was rather pleased with how it was taking shape. Another week and it would be completed and Mary, bless her, would have something to lay flowers against. He and Peter had decided to erect the finished stone at the bottom of the cut flower garden. It was a nice quiet spot where Mary could go without being disturbed.

He smiled at the thought of Mary, he had taken as much out of their conversations as Mary had from him. They found that they could both talk about their dear departed spouses without tearing up now – so that had to be a good sign. He would miss her when he'd finished this job – still, he had Jenna to talk to now and she did seem keen on Robbie, and he with her. He felt a little pang of longing in his own heart for someone to feel keen on him again. He so missed the company of his wife – he missed her for Robbie's sake, and if the truth be known, in every part of his life too, but especially in bed. He yearned for the closeness of a woman again and Jenna, lovely Jenna, had opened his heart to think he might love again.

24

On Wednesday the 6th of August, Jenna drove into Gweek at midday. Knowing there would be nowhere to park her car at Amelia's, she pulled to a halt on a piece of waste land near Barleyfield Farm. From here she could just see the roof top to the cottage where she had lived throughout her childhood. A shiver ran through her veins – it was also where her father had hung himself, shortly after Jenna had feigned her own death. Having been married off to Blewett to settle her father's debt, Amelia had written to her to tell her that Blewett had demanded that her father settled the debt with money this time, and her father being destitute, had taken his own life. It had been hard for Jenna to come to terms with her father's death – for she believed she was solely responsible. If she had stayed with Blewett, her father would still be alive. It was just another thing she would no doubt be punished for on that dreadful day of judgment.

It had been over five years since she left this village and her nightmare marriage, and her friend, Amelia Pascoe had helped her escape with Lyndon that night. She had never thought that she would ever step foot on Gweek soil again, and indeed would never have done so had George Blewett not been killed by a horse he was treating roughly whilst shoeing it. It served him right, the man died as violently as he had lived. Jenna shuddered at the thought of him, but as she walked down the lane towards Amelia's door, she had the strangest feeling she was being watched. Something made her turn, and her body gave an involuntary shiver – there, stood at the door of the Blacksmiths Forge was Blewett! Feeling her mouth dry, it took a moment to realise it wasn't a ghost, but Sam Blewett – George's younger brother. He was the absolute spitting image of her evil dead husband. Suddenly she was back there in her hell with that man - battered, emaciated, broken – a woman without hope. Her life was so different now, but the sight of this man brought back all the horrors of that time.

'Jenna,' Amelia called out and dragged her from her hellish reverie.

Jenna ran into Amelia's embrace. 'Oh, goodness, I thought Sam was George for a moment.'

'Yes, they do look alike,' Amelia said grimly, guiding her into the house. 'Sam took over the Blacksmiths when George was killed.'

'I remember him to be quite unsavoury. Has he turned out as awful as his brother?'

'Not quite – he has a temper though, and his poor wife Alice, always looks hard done by – she hasn't looked a bit well since her one-year-old son, Harry was born. Anyway, enough about the horrible Blewett's. Come, you know where the spare room is, I'll pop the kettle on.'

Upstairs, Jenna stood in the small but neat bedroom she had taken refuge in on occasions during her marriage, when Amelia and Dr Eddy had rescued her from Blewett after his violence towards her had rendered her in need of sanctuary and medical attention. Shaking the thoughts from her head, Jenna unpacked her things and hung up her outfit for the wedding. The dress Mrs Tonkin had made her was beautiful in its simplicity - perfect for a rural wedding. Although it was navy, it was made of cotton, so hopefully she would not be too warm in the heat, and she had brought a navy straw hat with her to shade her from the sun as the Cornish heatwave showed no signs of abating.

Having washed her hair that morning, it now lay in a tumble of blonde curls down her back - at least Lyndon would be pleased with that. Having not seen him since the Friday night dinner at Trevarno, she wondered how he would be with her – would he push his concerns about her wealth to one side so that they could enjoy the day? Over the last few days, she had mulled over what Matthew had said to her about her money and property and had almost come to at least one decision - namely about the London residence. She would need help from Christian as to how to implement her plan and of course it all depended on whether James's father was successful in contesting the will!

*

Downstairs Amelia set down the tea and a homemade cake and it was just like old times.

'So, how are you, Jenna? Are you bearing up after the loss of your husband?'

'I do miss James terribly.'

Amelia nodded. 'My sister Celia misses him too - he was a good employer. You know, I hope you don't mind me saying this, but I must say I was so surprised when you married him. I met him a few times when I was over at Celia's in Gunwalloe and there was no doubt about it, he was a lovely fellow, but I never thought you were the right woman for him. Celia worked for him for many years and thought he was a confirmed bachelor. Were you happy with him, albeit for a brief time?'

'I was, yes. He gave me everything I ever wanted and was inordinately kind to me. Everything I am now, is because of his doing. He introduced me to people of influence, and I have never looked back. Those few months I shared in his company - turned the world I once knew upside-down.'

'I can see that, with your fancy clothes. I can't help wondering though, where is that young woman who Lyndon Fitzsimons fell in love with as she sat in a meadow sketching.'

'I think she is still there somewhere.'

Amelia smiled. 'Lyndon will be pleased to know that.'

Jenna lowered her eyes but made no comment.

'Will you be keeping the house on at Gunwalloe?' she asked topping up her cup.

'Houses - for there is one in London too. I don't know what I'm going to do yet. *If James's father has his way, she would lose them both, but she wasn't going to tell Amelia that – that was her problem.* I have this new career in art which takes me away from Cornwall, but in truth, part of me wants to go back to the simple life.'

'With Lyndon? He's told me that James wrote to him about wanting you two to get back together.'

Jenna chased a piece of sugar around the tablecloth with her finger. 'We have a lot of hurdles to climb first.'

'Take my advice – push all hurdles to one side and find somewhere where you two can be together, just as soon as you're out of mourning. Lyndon FitzSimmons is the only man for you.'

Jenna looked up – her eyes glittering with tears. 'I know.' *It just wasn't going to be as easy as that.*

*

Five miles down the road, Meg Williams, who used to work at the tearoom, had come to help Marianne because Ellie and Guy were attending a wedding in Gweek. Betsy, who was heavy now with child was helping behind the counter too. They watched as Marianne flitted about from table to table, but all the while her face looked set in stone.

'Marianne looks like she lost a shilling and found a halfpenny today,' Meg said as she brought an order into Betsy.

Betsy nodded. 'Ellie said she'll be glad when I come back to work because Marianne can be very moody sometimes,' she whispered to Meg.

'What *is* the matter with her today?'

'Ellie says Marianne has set her hat at Gabriel Trelease, but he's not interested in her. He popped in yesterday, when I was having a cuppa with Ellie, to ask if she could add an extra seat at his table tomorrow as someone else was coming to join them for his son's birthday tea. Marianne was fluttering her eyelashes at him the whole time he was here, but he took not a jot of notice of her.'

Marianne came in with a tray of dirty plates and realised they were both looking at her.

'What? Have I got something on my face or something?' she asked.

'Unfortunately, your face is missing its usual pretty smile today - is everything all right,' Betsy asked.

'Yes, I'm just busy that's all,' she answered shortly.

'My Ryan said Jake Treen is keen to walk out with you one day. He might restore that lovely smile of yours. He's a nice man.'

Marianne sighed heavily. 'Yes, he is a nice man, Betsy, but I am setting my hopes on a gentleman. It happened for Jessie who used to work here, and for Ruby at Bochym Manor, so there is no reason why it should not happen to me.'

'But a local lad would love you just as much, you know, perhaps more so if you come from the same background.'

'Ah, but I don't. Although I was a foundling baby, I believe my mother was gentry who perhaps had an unfortunate rendezvous with someone she loved but could not marry. When she realised that I was on the way, she must have had me secretly and decided to leave me at The Poldhu Hotel where someone nice would pick me up.'

Meg folded her arms. 'What makes you think your mother was gentry though.'

'Because of the shawl I was found in – it's beautiful and clearly worth a lot of money!'

'Do you still have the shawl?' Meg asked.

'Of course - it's all I have of my real mother.'

'Maybe you could bring it one day to show us.'

'I will, and then you will know I am right about my real mother.' She flounced off with a tray of teacups as the two women exchanged glances.

'She can certainly spin a good yarn. Does anyone hereabouts know her real parentage?' Meg asked.

'No, Ellie said there was an extensive search at the time, but no mother was found. Susan Enys, who found her, and eventually adopted her, told Ellie once that Marianne's umbilical cord was tied with a grubby piece of cloth and the doctor said it had been cut with a rusty knife – he had to trim it again to stop infection.'

'That doesn't sound much like the act of a gentle lady,' Meg grimaced.

'No, I think our Marianne has delusions of grandeur.'

*

Lyndon was waiting for Jenna on the village green at two. He was dressed in his Sunday best clothes, a dark suit, waistcoat, white shirt open at the collar and a clean, red, and white spotted neckerchief around his neck. Jenna saw him smile appreciatively as she approached in her new navy cotton dress and navy straw hat.

'You look lovely – more like my Jenna now.'

'Thank you,' she said, forcing herself not to touch him.

'I want to kiss you so much, but I know I must wait.' He smiled sadly.

Returning an equally gloomy smile, she turned as Amelia, also dressed in her finery, joined then.

'I've arranged for a lift to the church in the wagon for you, me and Amelia,' Lyndon said straining his neck to see if the wagon had returned from taking another group of guests up.

'Oh, I have the car with me, it's parked at Barleyfield – I thought we could all go in that,' Jenna offered.

Amelia shot a panicked look at Lyndon, which did not go unnoticed by Jenna.

'So, you can drive now as well?' Lyndon asked in astonishment.

'Well, I'm beginning to doubt my ability, no one believes I'm able to because I'm a woman, but yes, I drove over from Gunwalloe, and I am still in one piece.' *Unlike the gatepost at Loe House which will probably need some attention after she hit it. Still, it was the only thing she hit driving over here! She remembered James took the same gatepost out twice when he was learning to drive.*

'I don't doubt you can do anything, Jenna. Another string to your bow, eh? You astonish me on a regular basis.'

Jenna wondered if Lyndon's voice held a slight note of regret.

'I wonder though, would you mind if we go on the wagon today,' he asked tentatively. 'It's just that I'd like us to join in with the celebration with everyone else right from the start – I'm not sure I could do that if we arrive in the car – it sort of sets us apart from everyone else,' he added with a whisper.

'Of course,' she answered, 'I didn't think, but I fully understand.'

As she climbed on the wagon, she decided that she must make a conscious effort to be her old self here, if only to show Lyndon that she was still that woman.

*

There were gasps of disbelief when Lyndon walked into the church beside Jenna – most people had only recently heard that she had not, as they all thought, drowned in 1914! As they settled on a pew, Jenna could hear the incessant whispers about her, which only died down when Lizzy walked down the aisle on the arm of Eric Williams. Having lost her own father many years ago, Lizzy had lived and worked with the Williams and had always been thought of as the daughter they never had.

The church service was beautiful and as the happy couple took their vows, Jenna and Lyndon surreptitiously glanced at each other and smiled. Very tentatively Jenna moved her hand to rest on Lyndon's and their fingers entwined with each other's. They thought they had done it out of sight, but Amelia, who was sitting next to them, had seen the movement from the corner of her eye and a smile formed on her face.

*

As the wedding guests gathered in Constantine Churchyard to throw rice on the happy couple, Jenna felt a sharp tug on her sleeve - when she turned, she found Meg Bolitho at her side.

'Well, mercy me,' Meg declared, 'I thought I was seeing a ghost when you walked into the church earlier.'

'Hello, Meg,' Jenna said tentatively. The last time she'd seen this woman she had acted as a wet nurse for the baby Jenna had rejected. Bracing herself, she waited for the inevitable condemnation of the neglect of her baby - but it never came.

Meg smiled gently at her. 'When we heard you had drowned - many did say it was a blessing for you to be away from that brute of a husband Blewett - especially after he battered you so cruelly after your poor babe's death. The whole village was shocked you know after the beating, and most turned against him. His death couldn't have come sooner for everyone – hateful man that he was.' She smiled as her eyes swept up and down Jenna. 'And now look. Here you are,' she squeezed her arm, 'flesh and blood real. I'm that happy to see you looking so fine and well. I know this is a happy occasion and I don't want to bring awful thoughts back to you, but I just wanted to say how sorry I was that I couldn't save your babe. Poor little mite – I tried my best you know, but he wouldn't suckle. I'm that sorry I couldn't bring him brave for you.'

Jenna felt a lump build in her throat. 'Meg, you have nothing to be sorry for. You did a wonderful thing by taking the baby when I was unwell and unable to deal with him. I thank you for all you did, truly I do. You're a wonderful human being.'

Meg seemed to swell in pride at her words. 'I'm glad I could help you. You know you're not the first mother to find it hard to bond with a babe and you certainly won't be the last. It comes eventually, I'm just so sorry he didn't live long enough for that to happen to you.'

Now Jenna's tears were dangerously close to the surface hearing this woman who had nursed so many babies, offer her kindness and understanding to a plight she fully believed she would be condemned for.

Meg's parting words to her were, 'Ah, bless you - I can see you are welling up. Now Blewett is dead – perhaps you can marry again and bring a fine and healthy baby into the world, and if you need any help, you know where I am.' She winked.

'Oh, Meg!' Jenna felt her heart constrict as she tried to keep the despondency from her voice. 'Thank you.'

Amelia approached to tell her they were ready to go back to Gweek and as Jenna climbed onto the wagon to sit beside Amelia, she glanced over at Lyndon sitting opposite her. Meg's words had pierced her heart. Although Meg had not condemned her, she rather thought God would not give her the joy of bringing another baby into the world - especially after she had so neglected and rejected the last one. If that was so, it was a fitting punishment she was ready to accept, but what about Lyndon? If they did marry – they may never be blessed with a family - was that fair to him?

Glancing again at Lyndon, he must have seen the consternation in her face because a frown had formed.

'Are you all right,' he mouthed.

She nodded and smiled weakly. Little Robbie had woken her maternal instinct, and now her heart began to ache for the children she and Lyndon might never have.

25

The wedding breakfast was held at the Williams Dairy Farm. A fine buffet of good wholesome food was set out at the back of the barn, which had been swept clean and whitewashed ready for the occasion. Straw bales had been pushed to the edges of the building for people to sit on, but as the day was so glorious, everyone milled about in the hot afternoon sunshine. A hog was roasting around the side of the farmhouse – a pig large enough to feed the whole of the village, which was necessary as the whole village seemed to have been invited. Several kegs of ale and cider had been set up in the dairy where it was cooler, along with jugs of elderflower cordial, apple juice and fruit punch – which, Jenna thought, had a fair amount of alcohol in it and so she decided to limit herself to a couple of glasses!

While Jenna waited for Lyndon to bring her a drink, Sam Blewett walked past her with his downtrodden wife Alice in tow. Sam narrowed his eyes, but said nothing to her, and Jenna felt relieved when Lyndon joined her again with a glass of elderflower cordial.

'Are you all right, Jenna? You looked a little distressed back there on the wagon.'

She nodded. 'I'm fine don't worry.

Standing on the side-lines of the wedding, Lyndon whispered, 'This brings back memories, doesn't it? Being back in Gweek I mean.'

'A lot of bad ones, perhaps.'

Lyndon turned to her in dismay. 'I try to only remember the good times.'

Jenna nodded. 'Yes, I'm sorry. The time I spent with you here was the happiest I have ever been. It's just,' she paused to give herself a moment to settle the unrest still inside her, 'It's the horror that followed, it mars those memories. It has brought it all back to me being here - the terror of being Blewett's wife. I thought of nothing but you, you know, and our days in the sun, whilst he subjected me to the most horrendous acts of violence. You were my safe place. If I were with you in my head, I could try to blot out my wretched situation.'

'Oh, Jenna.' He reached out to touch her arm but retracted it when she pulled back. 'I cannot envisage what you went through.'

'You've been through it too, Lyndon. The horrors you described in the war, still plays on your mind – I know it does – I saw it in London. We have both been damaged by the horrors in life.'

Lyndon nodded. 'You're my safe place too, you know. When the tremors hit me and a noise takes me back to the hell in the trenches, you're the one I try to think about. The softness of your soothing voice, the touch of your hand, the image I have fixed in my brain of your beautiful face – all these things bring me back from hell, because you are heaven on earth.'

'Darling, Lyndon.' Jenna wanted nothing more than to reach out to hold Lyndon's hand, and it grieved her that she couldn't. 'I fear we are going to struggle to find our safe place together. Matthew spoke candidly to me of your reservations about my money,' she said tentatively.

'I'm a proud man, Jenna, I do not know how we are going to overcome this enormous wealth you have acquired. It does not sit easy with me to be a kept man.'

Jenna was just about to say that nothing was insurmountable when Eric Williams called out to Lyndon to help him with another barrel of ale.

Jenna sighed– there was always something or someone getting in the way of them talking through their problems. Her gaze fell upon her old friends Lizzy and Charlie, meeting and greeting everyone, so she did not see Sam Blewett approach, until a sudden chill ran down her spine at the sound of his voice behind her.

'You're a sly and conniving bitch, aren't you?' Blewett growled.

Jenna turned to face Sam – whose timid wife was pulling at his sleeve to leave her alone. Several people had heard his comment and turned to see what the altercation was.

'You left my poor brother George, grieving for your loss, and all the while you were shacked up with someone else.'

Jenna felt the adrenaline rush of fight or flight kick in. From out of the corner of her eye, she saw Lyndon fighting his way through the crowd to be by her side, but Jenna was not going to let this brother of a bully get the better of her. Narrowing her eyes at Blewett, she channelled her friend Hillary's way of dealing with unsavoury characters. Holding the flat palm of her hand in front of his face, she hissed, 'Whatever permission you thought you had to speak to me, I hereby remove. Now I suggest you crawl back from under the stone you came from, you slimy toad.'

Blewett's wife smirked at the insult, and Blewett's mouth dropped open when Jenna flicked her hand at him as though to swat away a nasty smell. The crowd which had formed roared with laughter at her counter insult, and Jenna lifted her chin and moved swiftly and confidently away from him.

'Well said, Jenna?' Lyndon smiled proudly at her as he took his place back at her side. 'Eric Williams is about to send him packing from the wedding.'

'Hateful man – hateful family,' she said with a shudder.

'Do *you* want to leave?' Lyndon whispered.

'Goodness, no! The Blewett's ability to make my life a misery is well and truly over,' she said, though now the adrenaline was wearing off, she felt thoroughly drained. 'I do think I might have something a little stronger to drink though.'

*

The village gossip, Minnie Drago was watching Jenna with interest. Having once been instrumental in scuppering

Jenna's original plans to run away with Lyndon before Blewett married her, Minnie resented seeing her so well and happy, especially as she thought her to be dead! It took all her resolve to keep a civil tongue in her head, but she had seen Eric Williams oust Sam Blewett from the party for what he had said, and she wasn't going to pass up the chance of free drink and food.

'What was all that about then?' A man Minnie did not recognise, asked as he came to stand by her side.

With a swift look she gave him the once over, and never one to keep gossip to herself was happy to share Jenna's story with him.

'That woman there, Jenna Trevone or Blackwell as she is calling herself now, feigned her death in 1914 to run away with Lyndon FitzSimmons – that's him who is standing beside her now. That man who was berating her and has just left, was her brother-in-law Sam Blewitt. She has a nerve speaking back to him like that. Her husband, George Blewett was beside himself when he thought his wife had died.'

'So, Jenna and Lyndon have been lovers for years, have they?'

'Yes, by all accounts she ran away to be with him, even though Lyndon was married at that time! And now, apparently, she's not two months widowed, and here she is, bold as brass, fraternising with Lyndon again.

'Shocking state of affairs isn't it?' the man said with a tut.

'Aye.' Minnie looked him up and down again. 'And who might you be – you're a stranger to these parts.'

'Oh, me? Just someone passing through. I saw this mass gathering so I thought I would take a look. The argument intrigued me, that's all. I'll bid you good day,' he said doffing his hat.

*

While Jenna steadied her nerves with a glass of punch, Amelia came to her side.

'I'm proud of you Jenna. Sam Blewett needed taking down a peg or two.'

'I'll not stand for being bullied anymore. The old Jenna has well and truly gone!'

'I hope some of her has stayed,' Lyndon said wistfully.

Jenna's eyes twinkled. 'The Jenna who fell in love with you is still there.'

'Amen to that!' Lyndon and Amelia said, chinking glasses with her.

'Look, Jenna,' Amelia exclaimed, 'here is someone you know well.'

Jenna's heart filled with gratitude for Dr Eddy as he walked up to her and took her by the hands.

'Jenna, I cannot tell you how wonderful it is to see you again – especially as we all thought you were dead. Amelia kept your secret close to her chest - even though she knew we were all grieving for your demise.'

'I'm so sorry our secret caused you any grief and distress, doctor, but you'll understand - it was a necessary evil.'

'I do, my dear, and look at you now – you look wonderful. The last time I saw you, you had bald patches in your hair and your poor frail body was recovering from the beating Blewett had given you. I'm just so sorry we could not prevent a lot of what happened to you.'

'You did everything you could for me, Dr Eddy, I will never forget the kindness you and Amelia bestowed on me during that very difficult time.'

The doctor squeezed her hands affectionately. 'Well, may the rest of your life be the best of your life.' He glanced between Jenna and Lyndon.

'Thank you, doctor.' Jenna smiled.

Suddenly a bell was sounded, and everyone was beckoned into the barn for the cutting of the cake ceremony.

Eric Williams raised his glass, and everyone did the same.

'May you all join me in toasting Charlie and Lizzy. If two people were ever meant to be together then I reckon it's these two. They won't mind me saying it, but they have been in love since they were thirteen. So, I give a toast to two people who have waited for each other for a long time. May your future together be worth the wait.'

Amelia whispered behind Lyndon and Jenna. 'They're not the only ones to have waited *too* long to be together. Sort yourselves out you two – I'm not used to my matchmaking going awry.'

26

After the cake was handed around, everyone went back outside into the sunshine. As Lyndon went for more drinks, Jenna commented to Amelia on how beautiful Lizzy looked, as they watched the bride and groom continue to greet their guests. Lizzy was dressed in a froth of white lace, the gown had a dropped waist, ornate beading, and embroidery on the bodice and was finished off with a Juliet headdress and long flowing veil - a more radiant bride Jenna had never seen.

'Lizzy's wedding dress was especially made for her by Sophie Trevellick who used to work with her many years ago as a dairymaid,' Amelia explained. 'Sophie has always been a fine seamstress but has now made a name for herself as an embroiderer specialising in Italian quilting. She works under the prestigious umbrella of The Bochym Arts and Craft Association.'

'Well, to be sure, I've seen no better gown in a couture house in London. I vaguely remember Sophie Trevellick – she and Kit live in Quay House, don't they? Our paths never really crossed though. Is she here?'

'She is somewhere,' Amelia said scanning the crowds, 'Ah, yes, look, Sophie and Kit are coming now with Guy and Ellie Blackthorn.'

Jenna was introduced to them all, including their children.

'Ellie here owns The Poldhu Tea Room,' Amelia explained.

'Really! I've heard wonderful reports about your tearoom,' Jenna enthused.

Ellie smiled. 'You must come and see us then.'

'I will, and very soon, I promise,' Jenna said smiling secretly.

'Guy is a thatcher, and so too is their daughter Agnes now,' Amelia continued, 'and this is Sophie Trevellick, her husband Kit, and their two children, Selene and Christopher.'

Jenna shook hands with them all, just as Lyndon arrived back with drinks.

'Actually, I know Kit,' Lyndon said as Jenna introduced them, 'having shared at glass or two of ale in The Black Swan.' He winked. 'But Guy, I've not had the pleasure.' He shook his hand. 'I know of you, you're a thatcher, I believe. I'm a hedger, so in that we are kindred spirits in keeping ancient workmanship going.'

'There's not a lot of us left,' Guy said woefully, 'so it's up to us to keep the next generation in the trade. My daughter, Agnes here has turned out to be a fine thatcher,' he pulled his daughter into a hug.

'Yes, I had heard. It's nice to meet you, Agnes.'

'And this is my son Zack, he is an apprentice cabinet maker working with Kit.'

'Excellent.'

'And you, Lyndon – you have children to teach the trade to?'

'Not as yet, no, hopefully one day though.'

Jenna felt her heart constrict, and quickly cleared her throat and asked. 'I trust you both came through the war without injury?'

'In truth, neither I nor Kit went to the front, thank goodness,' Guy admitted.

Jenna gave them both a questioning look.

'I was deemed medically unfit due to a puncture to my lung nine years ago,' Kit explained. 'I very nearly died at the time – I still suffer from a little breathlessness. It was terrible at the time, but alas it saved me from a worse time.'

'And I fractured my spine in 1901 after a fall, and in truth still suffer terrible back pain, so I too was deemed medically unfit,' Guy explained.

'It didn't stop the white feathers from arriving at our doorstep though, did it?' Ellie added bitterly.

'I suppose not everyone knew our circumstances, Ellie, and if their men had to go to war, it must have embittered them to see me still here.'

Kit agreed with Guy.

'Well, I went, and I'm not embittered at all that you two were spared,' Lyndon patted them both on the arm, 'I wouldn't wish it on my worst enemy.'

Lyndon fell into conversation with Guy and Kit, so Jenna turned to Sophie.

'I was admiring the beautiful dress you've made for Lizzy.'

Sophie steepled her fingers and glanced over at Lizzy with a smile. 'I am rather pleased with it myself.' Turning back to Jenna. 'I remember you, Jenna, you went to school with Charlie and Lizzy, but the age difference stopped us from knowing each other socially.'

'Yes, I vaguely know you too. Amelia tells me you are part of The Bochym Arts and Craft Association.'

'I am, so too is Ellie here who makes lace, and my husband Kit. We all work remotely from Bochym - but for them.

Jenna smiled. 'I've been invited to tea at Bochym Manor next Tuesday - the Countess wants to show me around the workshops.'

'So, are you a crafts person yourself then?'

'I'm an artist. I show at The Black Gallery in London. I've just had an exhibition.'

'Goodness, but we've just come back from London and saw that very exhibition – it was astounding and a sell-out, if I remember. So, I take it you are Jenna Trevone - James Blackwell's wife!

'I am yes.'

'May I offer my heartfelt sympathy, Jenna. James was a mutual friend – a fine gentleman, I'm sorry we didn't get to meet you socially as a couple.'

'Yes, I'm afraid he died too soon, but he was the best of men.' Jenna saw Lyndon look up from his discussion with Kit at the mention of James.

'I cannot believe he isn't with us anymore. He was always dining at Bochym whenever he was in Cornwall - we had many a jolly evening with him. Are you with anyone here today?'

'Yes, I'm accompanying Lyndon here. We've been friends since before the war.' Jenna smiled at Lyndon, but his smile back did not quite reach his eyes.

'We received an invite to your wedding,' Sophie said, 'but Christopher my youngest was quite ill and we were worried he had the influenza – thankfully, it just turned out to be a dreadful cold. We were sorry to have missed it - I understand it was a grand occasion.' She placed a comforting hand on Jenna's arm. 'You must miss him very much.'

Jenna nodded. 'I do, yes.'

'I read all his books. His readers will be lost now,' Sophie added wistfully.

'As it happens, the novel he had just finished before he died will be published posthumously on the 2nd of September. I thought perhaps it would be fitting to have a little get together at Loe House to celebrate it. I'll send an invitation to you.'

'Thank you, that would be very kind of you.'

When Kit, Sophie, Ellie, and Guy moved away to speak to someone else, Lyndon moved back to her side.

'You're more popular than the bride today,' he joked, 'everyone wants to speak to you.' He took a sip of beer and looked as though he was mulling over something he wanted to say.

She tipped her head. 'Is something bothering you?'

'You didn't say you were throwing a party for James's new book.'

'It's not a party, it's a book launch, and to be fair, Lyndon, I only found out last week it was going to be published and we haven't had a great deal of time to speak about anything – you left in rather a hurry on Saturday morning.'

Lyndon looked sheepish and nodded. 'Sorry about that. I wanted to get back here to finish the job, but only so I can spend a little more time with you,' he added. 'We have an awful lot to discuss.'

'Quite obviously! And have you finished your work here?'

'I will have done by Friday.'

'By which time we'll be heading back to Trevarno for Matthew and Hillary's wedding.'

'We could speak tomorrow morning. I thought we could walk up to our meadow.'

'No, I'm afraid I have somewhere to be tomorrow.'

'Oh, I see,' he said dejectedly, 'maybe after Matthew's wedding then?'

Jenna nodded just as Charlie and Lizzy approached them.

'Jenna!' Charlie grinned.

'Hello to you both and congratulations. You look beautiful, Lizzy.'

'Thank you, I feel like a princess,' she said swaying gently. 'I don't ever want to take the dress off.'

Charlie reached for her hand and kissed it. 'I shall treat you like a princess every day of your life.'

Neither Lyndon nor Jenna doubted that fact.

'Come here, Jenna, let me give you a hug,' Charlie said, 'I'm sure my bride won't mind.'

Jenna was pulled into a great big bear hug which made her laugh.

'I must say, Jenna, you look a lot better than the last time I saw you. What a god-awful time that was for you! And then we thought you had drowned!'

'I have you to thank you for my freedom, Charlie. If it had not been for you putting Blewitt out of action with all those injuries, I might never have got away.'

He bowed gallantly. 'It's always a pleasure to help a maiden in distress.' He winked. 'We were so happy when we learned that you were still alive. Now, we must apologise and leave you for a while – we have so many people to meet and greet. Enjoy the rest of our wedding day,' he glanced between Lyndon and Jenna, and lowered his voice, 'and we shall expect an invitation to your wedding one day soon.'

Whereas Lyndon smiled happily, Jenna just gave a non-committal smile.

*

Ellie Blackthorn, who had been in earshot of the whispered comment, but had not seen Jenna's response to it, smiled happily at stumbling upon their little secret. She turned to go in search of Guy or Kit – they would know if a little romance was on the horizon for those two.

*

As the afternoon progressed, the music started and the dancing began. Owing to her state of mourning, Jenna did not think it appropriate to dance these country reels – though her toes were tapping to the music. Instead, she settled herself on the side-lines and enjoyed watching everyone else. As the sun set, she cast her eyes around this beautiful village. Before her troubles here, Gweek was the only place she wanted to be and she would often sit high above the village in the lush green hills surrounding the valley to drink in its beauty. Yes, there were many industrial workings on the river bank – it was a living, breathing working village, but beyond that, stood forests of oaks flanking the winding Helford River down to the sea. She had enjoyed this day of celebration, enjoyed meeting everyone she had grown up with again and enjoyed the freedom of spending time with Lyndon, even though they were trying to keep a respectable distance.

When everyone waved Charlie and Lizzy off to the Williams farmhouse to start their married life together, Lyndon walked Jenna and Amelia back to the cottage.

Amelia left them alone to say their goodnights, but when Lyndon leant forward to kiss Jenna, she pulled away. *It may be dark, but she knew from experience, nobody missed anything in this village.*

He sighed heavily. 'Will we ever be able to be together again? Will I ever wrap my arms around you in bed and make love to you?' he whispered.

'Yes, Lyndon, that time will come – I promise.'

'And will I find the girl I fell in love with in the meadow behind this building?'

'Yes, though it will be a rather world-weary version of her.'

'As long as she knows I too am world weary,' he smiled.

'I want to kiss you, Jenna, and I need to speak to you. Are you sure we can't meet in our meadow tomorrow morning?'

'Lyndon, I'm sorry - I told you I really need to leave in the morning.'

'Where can you be going that is more important than staying here to sort things out?'

'I'm sorry, Lyndon, but I just need to be somewhere else tomorrow. We'll speak soon. I too have something important I need to discuss with you, but we'll make the time to do it at Trevarno at the weekend.'

When reluctantly they parted ways, the shadowy figure who had been listening to their conversation, dropped back into the hedges.

27

Ellie Blackthorn unlocked the door to the Poldhu Tea Room and turned to find Marianne behind her with a parcel under her arm.

'Did you have a nice wedding yesterday, Ellie?'

'We did, thank you. How were things here with you and Meg.'

'Busy, but we managed. Betsy popped in as well and helped behind the counter.' Just as she spoke, Meg and Betsy walked up the veranda steps.

'We thought we would come and help you set up for the day while you tell us about the wedding,' Meg said cheerily.

Marianne's face fell, she had brought her shawl for them to look at, which was much more important than some country wedding, so she presented the parcel to them.

'Before all your wedding talk, I've brought my shawl for you to look at – the one I told you about yesterday – the one I was found in,' she said proudly pulling it out of the bag and presenting it to them.

Ellie picked up the lace shawl. 'Oh, my goodness!' she gasped audibly.

'See, I was telling Meg and Betsy how lovely it was, and it is, isn't it?' Marianne said proudly.

'It's my shawl!' Ellie declared.

'No, it's not! It's mine!' Marianne snatched it back from Ellie. 'I was found in it!' she said petulantly.

'No, what I mean is, I made it, many years ago, see.' Ellie reached towards it, but Marianne pulled it away sharply. Ellie dropped her hands to her side. 'If you look, I have a signature pattern I weave into the lace, so it can always be traced back to me. I always put a ring of ivy on every piece I make. On this particular shawl I put it in the middle.'

As Marianne inspected the shawl for the ivy lace, Ellie reached over and pointed it out to her. 'It was my second-best piece of work.'

Marianne moistened her lips and asked tremulously, 'So, who did you sell it too?'

'Nobody, I lost it in 1902. We had a great storm which ripped through the tearoom destroying half of the building. My chest of drawers which held all my handmade lace was swept away in a huge wave. I got some of it back when it was washed up – including, thank goodness, my wedding dress which I had spent years making, but a lot of my pieces were never found. This is one of them. Whoever found it was your mother.'

Marianne pursed her lips and stuffed the shawl back into the bag and tucked it safely under her arm. 'I'll go and bake the scones,' she said flouncing away to the kitchen.

This twist in the story angered Marianne – that would mean her mother could be anyone – not a genteel woman, for a genteel woman would never scour the water's edge for flotsam and jetsam – unless…. someone found it, and seeing it was a work of art, sold it to a fine house – yes, that's what must have happened! She stepped closer to the kitchen door to see if they were laughing at her and her shawl, but they were chatting about the wedding now. Not being particularly interested in this wedding, Marianne set too and began to make the scone mixture until she heard something that made her ears prick up.

'I met Jenna Blackwell, James Blackwell's wife, well, widow now, yesterday. I never got to meet her when they were married,' Ellie said.

Jenna Blackwell, wasn't that who Gabriel's son mentioned? Marianne thought as she moved her bowl of scone mixture nearer the door to listen.

'What is she like?' Betsy asked.

'Very beautiful. She came with Lyndon FitzSimmons - did you not say you had met Lyndon at Bochym Manor, Betsy?'

'I did, yes and very handsome he is too! Dorothy and Lucy used to swoon when he came into the Bochym kitchen when I was there. Juliet tells me he is working there again so with Dorothy and Lucy not married yet, I suspect they will have resumed their quest to make him fall in love with one of them, though there is rumour that he is still hankering after some woman he knew before the war.'

'Well,' Ellie lowered her voice to a whisper,' that woman was Jenna Blackwell, or Trevone as she was then. Both she and Lyndon were at the wedding together yesterday, but not together - if you know what I mean. Jenna is still in mourning for James, so I think for decency's sake they have not yet resumed their relationship, but from what I understand Lyndon and Jenna were in love many years ago. I heard a whisper that there will be a wedding on the cards soon.'

'Gosh, Dorothy and Lucy will be devastated at that news,' Betsy declared.

From where she stood in the kitchen - this news made Marianne's heart sing. If Jenna married Lyndon, then there could not possibly be anything between her and Gabriel.

'Anyway, keep it to yourself for now about Jenna and Lyndon,' Ellie said to the others. 'Now ladies, thank you for helping to get the tearoom ready. I'm going to make a birthday cake for Gabriel Trelease's little boy, Robbie. It's his first birthday without his mama and they are coming to tea this afternoon.'

*

Jenna decided to wear the same dress to the tea party as she had worn to the wedding yesterday. Being navy and cotton, it was perfect for the occasion without being overdressed.

She had enjoyed meeting everyone again from her schooldays in Gweek and the welcome they had given her made her less wary about visiting her childhood home again. It was nice to have spent time with Lyndon too, who seemed more relaxed with country people. She was sorry she couldn't meet him in the meadow this morning, it would have been good to discuss Christian's suggestion of a longer separation and get it out in the open, and she knew he was disappointed, but she had something important to do today for a little boy. Be it guilt or what, but because she had neglected her own baby, she felt inclined to make Robbie's day special and she had gone to Helston that morning to buy a wooden train for him. A smile broke on her face at the thought of him and she hoped he would like the present she had bought.

*

Gabriel had taken the day off from working at Bochym, so that he could spend the day with Robbie to make his birthday special. He had been heartened when Jenna had agreed to come to tea – he hadn't told Robbie yet, though the little boy had mentioned twice that day that he wished Jenna could have come to his birthday tea. If the truth were known, Gabriel was looking forward to spending time with her again too. Somehow Jenna had finally managed to pull him from his grief and despair. It took all his resolve though to not think about the future, but without doubt her beautiful face had been the last thing he had thought about at night and the first thing in the morning. He looked up at his reflection and berated himself for thinking too far ahead – he had only known her a week or so and met her only twice, but how long did a man need to know his heart's desire?

His mother Catherine smiled softly at him when he came downstairs – he could tell she knew there was a change in him – nothing normally got past her.

'You look nice, son,' she said holding him by the arms. 'You smell nice too. Your father and I will meet you and Robbie at The Poldhu Tea Room after you have collected Mrs Blackwell. I must say, it was kind of her to agree to come, she must like little Robbie very much.'

'Yes, I believe she does.'

Gabriel could see a glint in his mother's eye, which said that she hoped that Mrs Blackwell liked her son very much too.

*

Gabriel and Robbie set off over Mullion golf course, slowly driving down the rutted lane to Church Cove.

'Why are we going the wrong way to Poldhu, Papa?'

'I thought we could park down here and walk over to Poldhu, as it's such a nice day, and I know it's your favourite walk.'

Robbie clapped his hands together with glee. 'We might see Jenna at Church Cove!'

'You never know, we might.' Gabriel smiled.

As they parked the car near Dollar Cove, another car approached and Robbie's face lit up when he saw Jenna get out.

'Jenna,' he squealed in delight.

'Happy Birthday, Robbie,' Jenna said as he rushed towards her to wrap his arms around her legs.

'We're going to The Poldhu Tea Room for my birthday, Jenna,' he said, his cheeks rosy with glee.

'Well, that's a coincidence because I've been invited to a special little boy's birthday tea there too.'

Robbie's mouth formed an astonished O as he looked to his papa who nodded in confirmation. Without a moment's hesitation Robbie reached for Jenna's hand and then for Gabriel's and they set off over to Church Cove and the magnificent cliff path to Poldhu Cove.

At Poldhu Head they stood to take in the vista. The turquoise sea glittered in the afternoon light, lapping at the dark cliffs beneath the impressive Poldhu Hotel.

'Gosh,' Jenna breathed.' What a magnificent sight!'

'Have you not been up here before?' Gabriel asked in astonishment.

'No, I've never gone further than Church Cove – I haven't lived on this coast long.'

'We shall have to show you more of our beautiful coastline then,' Gabriel's eyes twinkled. 'Incidentally, my parents are meeting us at the tearoom, I hope that is all right with you.'

'But of course, I shall be delighted to meet them.'

*

Ellie Blackthorn had just seated Gabriel's parents at the reserved table on the veranda when she saw Gabriel walking with Robbie and, if she wasn't mistaken, with Jenna Blackwell! Pushing aside her surprise at seeing Jenna, she greeted her like an old friend, though they had only met yesterday.

'Jenna! How lovely for you to come and see us so soon,' then lowered her voice, 'I must say, I'm suffering from a slight headache after that fruit punch yesterday – I'm sure there was a lot of alcohol in it.'

'I know,' Jenna laughed, 'I refrained after one glass and stuck to elderflower cordial for the rest of the day.'

'Gosh, I wish I had!' Ellie groaned. 'You didn't tell me you were coming today with Gabriel and Robbie,' she asked searchingly.

'No,' she smiled, 'it was a surprise for Robbie.'

Ellie bent down to Robbie's level. 'I understand it's your sixth birthday today.'

Robbie beamed with delight and nodded.

'Well, your grandparents are waiting over here for you.'

Robbie's smiled broadened as he ran towards them, pulling Jenna with him.

Ellie watched with interest as Gabriel put his hand to Jenna's back to steer her to her chair – he was courteous in every way, and if she was not mistaken – totally enamoured with her too. It was a strange scenario and after seeing her with Lyndon yesterday, Ellie could not make out what was happening here - nothing seemed to tally. She turned to Marianne who for some reason looked stony-faced.

'Marianne, can you take the Treleases's order when they are ready?' to which Marianne gave a reluctant nod.

*

Gabriel proudly introduced his parents to Jenna once they were seated and Jenna produced the present she had in her bag for Robbie. His eyes widened as he unwrapped the unexpected gift and cradled the toy train to his chest.

'Thank you,' Robbie said climbing down from his chair to wrap his arms around her. As she bent to embrace him, he kissed her on the cheek.

'That is very kind of you, Jenna,' Gabriel said meaningfully.

'Well, special little boys need special toys, and you, my little friend, are very special to me.'

Gabriel saw his parents exchange a delighted smile. Jenna was obviously a hit with them too.

When Marianne came to their table to take their order, Gabriel said, 'Mama, Papa, this is Marianne - the kind young lady who looked after Robbie last week, while I was arranging for Jenna to come to Robbie's birthday. Marianne likes making sandcastles, don't you?' Gabriel looked up at Marianne who smiled through gritted teeth.

Once they had given their order to Marianne, Catherine turned to Jenna. It is lovely to meet you Mrs Blackwell.'

'Likewise, but please, call me Jenna.'

'Thank you, Jenna. We have heard a great deal about you from both Robbie and Gabriel.'

'All good I hope,' Jenna joked as her eyes twinkled at Gabriel.

'Oh yes!' Catherine said emphatically. 'Robbie especially seems quite enamoured with you.'

'As I am with him.' Jenna looked down with kindness at the boy, unaware of how her words would be misinterpreted.

*

Ellie sent Marianne over to them with a tiered plate of sandwiches and scones, and mused that if jealous looks could kill, Marianne would have killed Jenna!

After eating their fill, Ellie presented a surprise birthday cake she had made for Robbie.

'I don't know if you want to share it now or take it home for later,' Ellie said, but they all decided to have a sliver now, despite already eating their fill.

'I think I am in dire need of a walk after all that cake,' Gabriel said patting his tummy. 'Jenna, would you accompany us down to the water's edge?'

'I'd like nothing better,' she said excusing herself from Gabriel's parents.

Ellie watched with interest as Jenna and Gabriel each held one of the little boy's hands to walk down the beach - they already looked like a tight little family unit - and she clearly wasn't the only one to think that. As Ellie cleared a table near to Gabriel's parents, she noted they too were watching them.

'Oh Grant,' Catherine Trelease clasped her hands together, 'don't they just make a wonderful couple, Jenna and Gabriel?'

'Now, Catherine, don't be jumping to any conclusions yet,' he parried.

'Well, both Robbie and Gabriel are totally enamoured with Jenna, and you and I like her do we not? I think she would make a lovely mother and wife. Yes, I know she is still in mourning for her poor husband, but just look at them together. God knows those two boys need some happiness in their life, and do you know, I think Jenna is the one to bring the joy back to them. I shall be surprised if there is not a wedding before the year is out.'

Marianne suddenly dropped the tray she had been loading up on the next table, making a loud clatter as one of the cups rolled onto the floor and smashed.

Flustered, Marianne looked up at Ellie and mouthed. 'I'm so sorry, Ellie.' As Ellie bent down to help her pick up the pieces. Marianne's eyes were brimming with tears as she added, 'You must take the breakage out of my wages.'

'Hey, now, don't get upset,' Ellie smiled gently, 'we all do it from time to time. No wages will be deducted, I promise.'

Once the mess was cleared away, Ellie glanced again at Mr and Mrs Trelease, happily watching their son and grandson walking with Jenna along the water's edge and felt a strange foreboding. Still unable to make out what was happening here, Ellie brushed down the front of her apron and got on with her business - as this was none of hers! Picking up her tray, she glanced at Marianne who too was looking in the direction of Jenna and Gabriel. The girl looked stricken, and perhaps not by the breakage of the cup. Ellie sighed - if Marianne was still harbouring fantastical thoughts of Gabriel taking her as his wife, it seems there would be great disappointment in more than one camp soon.

28

Gabriel smiled at the way Jenna casually discarded her shoes and stockings and gathered her skirt up so that she could walk with them in the cold surf. His heart caught when she laughed openly with Robbie as a wave broke unexpectedly over them, splashing their clothes. With the damp sand shifting beneath his feet, Gabriel felt a shift as another layer of grief peeled away.

*

They returned laughing from the beach, and it took all of Marianne's resolve to compose herself when Gabriel called her over for the bill.

When she presented her usual, beautifully written bill to him, Gabriel smiled at everyone around the table.

'This is the one place I enjoy receiving my bill. Just look at Marianne's beautiful handwriting.' Gabriel showed it around for the others to admire.

Marianne felt her lip tremble – *it was a shame he couldn't see all her other beautiful traits.*

When they got up to go, Gabriel's parents kissed Jenna warmly on the cheek.

'We are going away for a couple of months, Jenna, but you must come and dine with us when we return,' Catherine said.

'Thank you, I'd like that.'

Gabriel, happy that she had said yes, smiled openly as he handed over the money to Marianne for the birthday tea, along with a big tip.

Marianne, ignoring the tip, watched them walk away as her heart felt as though it would implode.

The man, sitting alone at the other end of the veranda put down his newspaper when Marianne came to clear his table.

'That was a nice little family, wasn't it?' he nodded to Gabriel and Jenna walking back over the dunes toward the coast path.

Marianne looked up but could not trust herself to speak.

'Are you quite well, my dear?'

With a nod of her head, she began to clear the debris of his cream tea.

'I'm sure I recognised the lady – isn't she a famous artist – Jenna Trevone – or Mrs Blackwell as she is now?'

'Apparently,' Marianne said bitterly.

'Oh, dear, do you not care for her work?'

'I don't know of her work,' she said glancing around to see if Ellie was in earshot.

'I believe it is very good. I understand she has been recently widowed from James Blackwell the author. I must say though it looks as though she is coming through her grief to a brighter future.'

That was it - Marianne could hold the tears back no longer.

'Oh, my dear, whatever can be distressing you?' He placed a gentle hand on hers, but she pulled it away quickly. 'Come, now, what could be troubling a pretty young lady like you? You can tell me,' he smiled. 'After all I am just a stranger passing through on a walking holiday - you'll never see me again. I do enjoy listening to people's troubles. A problem solved is a problem halved as they say.'

Marianne's bottom lip trembled and glanced around to see where Ellie was before she spoke. 'Mrs Blackwell appears to be stealing the future I thought I would have with Mr Trelease,' she blurted.

'Mr Trelease?' He tipped his head.

'Gabriel Trelease - that is who she was with today.' She nodded to them as they headed towards Poldhu Head.

'So, you think Mrs Blackwell, *is* romantically involved with Mr Trelease?'

Marianne nodded sadly. 'And she is betrothed to someone called Lyndon FitzSimmons as well. It's not fair,

I tell you, that I must sit back while she decides which man she wants.'

'It certainly isn't fair, my dear,' he said gently. 'And this Mr FitzSimmons, what do you know about him?'

'Only what I've recently heard - that Mrs Blackwell has been in love with him for years.'

'How strange then that she married James Blackwell.'

'I don't think she can help herself. She sees a man she wants and to hell with the consequences.'

The gentleman rubbed his chin thoughtfully. 'It was probably for money - it often is!'

'Most probably, she seems to be a scheming individual,' she hissed, *though she knew this statement had no foundation.*

'Marianne,' Ellie called over to her and she turned guiltily towards her. 'Do you think you can take this order here?'

'Sorry, Ellie, yes.' She smiled at the man. 'I'll have to go.'

'Of course. It was nice speaking to you, Miss - sorry I didn't catch your name.'

'Marianne Enys.'

'Well, Marianne, don't fret your pretty little head. Someone very soon is going to sweep you off your feet and Mr Trelease will be a distant memory.'

Marianne's lip trembled, *that is not what she wanted at all.*

'You were deep in conversation with that gentleman, who was he?' Ellie asked when Marianne brought the order in.

Feeling guilty at revealing so much about a customer, Marianne lied, 'Oh he is on a walking holiday, I couldn't get away from him – he kept me talking. I was so glad when you called me away.' A blush rose from her neck to her cheeks at the lie, so she turned swiftly to go and clear another table.

*

Jenna drove to Trevarno on Saturday afternoon and parked outside Home Farm where Hillary was staying.

Greg and the others, who had arrived for the wedding by train that morning, were encamped in another property on the estate.

Hillary met her at the door. 'Darling, Jenna, come in,' she kissed her cheek and ushered her through to the drawing room. 'I'm so glad you're here, now my wedding party can really begin. Matthew and I have had a divine week. He has shown me all around the estate and even got me into gumboots, would you believe! I must say, I love it here – not that I am giving up my life in London- and neither should you!'

Jenna flopped down on one of the Queen Anne chairs and at once regretted it - for it was jolly uncomfortable. 'Ouch!'

Hillary grimaced. 'My sentiments exactly! Flipping aristocratic furniture - why didn't they do comfort?'

'It's to make us all sit up and be strait-laced,' Jenna said sitting up straight.

'Well, I am having none of that in here. Matthew and I are having everything refurbished while we are in Italy. I want it to be as homely as your house in Gunwalloe.'

'Yes, Loe House does rather wrap its arms around you when you enter, doesn't it? I'll be sad to see it go.'

Hillary gave her a hard stare. 'Does it have to go?'

Jenna traced her finger along the arm rest. 'Lyndon doesn't want to live there.'

Hillary tipped her head and shook it. 'Why wouldn't he want to?'

'Because it was James's house.'

'Then the man is a fool. No one owns a house - we just look after it until the next person takes possession.'

'Lyndon is no fool, Hillary – he's just a proud man.'

'Well, pride comes before a fall and if he does not see sense soon, he could lose you by his foolishness. I know Matthew has spoken to you about him, but I believe Matthew is wrong as well! Why should you give up your houses and wealth? You are your own woman now, Jenna.

The wealth you have gained you earned, just as Lyndon earns his money from his job.'

'Yes, but my wealth surpasses Lyndon's by hundreds of pounds.'

'Lyndon chose that profession and by all accounts loves his work as you love yours. Times are changing – and if Lyndon wants to be with you, he will have to change too!'

Jenna lowered her eyes.

Hillary gave a heavy sigh. 'Sorry, I'll be quiet now - I've said my piece.'

'No don't apologise, I know you're right.'

'I'm seldom wrong, darling, you must know that by now,' she winked. 'Oh, but I must say though, all this talk of James is making me incredibly sad. I so wanted him at my wedding.'

'I know, I miss him too.'

Hillary sighed. 'We all miss that wonderful man keenly. I must say, It's going to be nice to see you out of dark clothes tomorrow.'

'For propriety's sake I shouldn't be out of mourning until Thursday.'

'Fiddlesticks, James won't mind,' Hillary whispered. 'Now, let's forget the tea, and start the celebrations! Let's have a gin and tonic outside in the courtyard garden – its rather lovely out there.'

'Who else is coming tonight?' Jenna said, settling in a much more comfortable garden chair.

'Caroline and Jane, you remember them – they spent Christmas at Loe House last year – though they stayed at Toy Cottage. They are all staying at Namskerris on the estate with their husbands Robert and Gerald. Anyway, they will be joining Glen, Lyndon and his father, and Matthew and his father at The Crown Inn down the road.

'I should think Glen will miss you when you marry.'

'I know, he is feeling very put out now I am not on his arm, bless him. He has tried all week to talk me out of marrying Matthew and take him up on one of the many proposals of marriage he has made me over the last few years. Not that he dislikes Matthew, he thinks he is wonderful, he is just not keen on handing over his partner in crime.'

'Did you never consider Glen?'

'God no, he is my best friend. It would never work. I do not know what he is fretting for. We shall still peruse the London scene together when I get bored down here in the sticks.'

Jenna grimaced. 'Won't Matthew mind?'

Hillary shot her a look that said, 'Let him try.'

'So, does that mean, Eleanor Bickford and Melissa will be coming here tonight?'

'No, thank goodness! Eleanor says she is far too busy with the wedding and Melissa is not arriving home from Italy until later this evening. So, we do not have to watch our P's and Q's. Chin, chin darling.' Hillary raised her glass and chinked Jenna's. 'Here is to me finally netting the delectable Matthew Bickford – god knows I've waited long enough for him to ask me.'

*

A telephone call came in from the main house at five that afternoon to see what Hillary wanted to order for dinner that evening. Poached salmon, new potatoes and French beans were duly delivered on platters by Mr Brown, the butler, the footman, and Gina!

As soon as Mr Brown and the footman left, Jenna hugged Gina and introduced her.

'Hillary, this is my friend, Gina who's married to Lyndon's father.'

'Hello, darling.' Hillary embraced her gently. 'Any friend of Jenna's is a friend of mine. Oh, do stay for dinner, I am sure the lovely Mrs Drake has sent us more than enough.'

'Oh, err, no, thank you,' Gina blustered. 'I'm still working for another half an hour and then I need to get

Michael his dinner before he goes out with the others to The Crown.'

'Then you must come after, my dear.' Hillary flourished her hand.

'Oh, but….'

'I insist,' Hillary said, refusing to take no for an answer.

Gina looked to Jenna for help, but Jenna just smiled. 'There is no arguing with her, Gina. I'd love you to come too.'

*

Gina had put on her best Sunday dress and took a deep breath as she knocked on Holme Farm door, worried that she was going to be far out of her depth at this gathering. She need not have worried about a thing though, everyone welcomed her in, a drink was handed to her and within a quarter of an hour, she was laughing with everyone.

By the end of the evening, as Gina and the others were leaving, Hillary declared Gina to be her new partner in crime whenever Jenna was away.

'I don't know what Michael will say about that,' Gina giggled - slightly inebriated.

'All I can say, Gina, is don't try to fight it. Hillary's friendship is something to behold. I'll see you tomorrow.' Jenna kissed her friend goodnight.

29

The next morning after Eleanor Bickford's lady's maid dressed Hillary and Jenna's hair, Jenna stood back to admire Hillary in her wedding gown.

'You look stunning, Hillary,'

'It does work, doesn't it, though I'm still undecided about this and the other one.'

Jenna shook her head. 'For goodness' sake, forget the other dress and put your headdress on.'

'You look wonderful too, Jenna, I knew that peach colour would compliment your hair and skin.'

'Well, I've never known you to be wrong when it comes to dressing me.'

'It's a gift darling - a pure gift,' Hillary said with a flourish. 'Having said that, I now want to work my magic on your friend, Gina, and take her shopping.'

'Oh, Hillary, don't say that to her, or she will think her clothes are shabby and I know she makes them herself. She and Lyndon's father, Michael, have little money, and Gina works in the kitchens remember. The clothes you want her to dress in would be lovely, but unsuitable for her life here. It's not that I don't want her to have new clothes, but if you take her under your wing, she will face opposition from those who work here and perhaps Michael too. I know - it happened to me when Matthew introduced me to James.'

Hillary rolled her eyes. 'You're right of course – it's just that she is so pretty, and a well-made nice dress would look wonderful on her, and….'

Jenna raised an eyebrow, and Hillary's lip curled into a smile. 'All right, all right, I won't.'

Jenna turned to the mirror to admire herself and felt a pang of sadness for Gina – more than anything else she wanted Gina to feel what it was like to be dressed in silk and satin.

Hillary tipped her head and smiled at Jenna. 'Lyndon will be bowled over when he sees you, darling.'

'I think he would rather me be in a plain old country dress if the truth be known,' Jenna said, putting the finishing touches to Hillary's veil.

'Then that man needs to give himself a serious talking to.'

*

When the car came to take Jenna to the church, she left Glen partaking in a bit of Dutch courage in the drawing room.

When Hillary came down the stairs, Glen stood at the bottom, shaking his head sadly.

'What is it – what's the matter,' Hillary asked in alarm.

'Nothing, except that you're making me give you away to someone else today!'

'And I can't think of a better person to do it, darling.' She kissed him on the cheek.

Glen took a deep breath. 'It's just that I always hoped you'd marry me one day, Hills.'

'Darling, Glen, you couldn't handle me even if I came with instructions.'

He pursed his mouth. 'I know you better than anyone, and you know that too!'

'You're my best friend – my partner in crime, why spoil a good friendship with marriage.'

'Well, that doesn't say much for Matthew then.'

'Matthew is different. I am completely and utterly in love with Matthew. I love you dearly too, but come on, Glen, it would be like bedding my brother if we were to get married.'

Glen grimaced. 'Well, I don't think of you as a sister, you will always be my one and only love.'

Hillary kissed him again, only this time on the lips.

'Then it is time to let me go, Glen. Go and find someone who makes you tingle inside, but tell her, you and I have a special bond that cannot be broken. Whoever she is, she will have to understand that, because I might be getting married, but there is a whole lot of partying to do, and I cannot think of anyone to party with better than you. Now, straighten your face, and take me to church.'

*

While Jenna waited at the church door for Hillary to arrive, her attention was caught by a gentleman walking up the church path. He was dressed, as all the other gentlemen were, in a full morning suit and he nodded an acknowledgement to her. She was sure she'd seen him somewhere before, though could not place it. Straining to hear whether he said he was a guest of the bride or groom; she was sure he hesitated a moment too long before saying bride. She would ask Hillary later who he was. A moment later her attention was pulled away from him when Hillary and Glen arrived in a horse drawn carriage and waved at her.

Greeting Jenna at the door, Hillary grumbled, 'Good grief, Jenna, give me a car any day of the week to travel in, that carriage was the most uncomfortable ride I've had for a long time. I do believe I've acquired a bruise on every bone in my derriere!' she said, as she linked her arm through Greg's while Jenna straightened her friend's gown at the back.

'Right, come on you two. The party cannot start until I walk in.' Hillary grinned.

*

The wedding was beautiful and throughout the ceremony, Lyndon's loving eyes kept drifting to Jenna – he could not get over how lovely she looked. Since they had reconnected with each other, she had been dressed in dark clothes – apart from when he first came to her and found her swimming at Church Cove. Now here she was, dressed in peach silk with her lovely hair adorned with flowers – she was as beautiful as any bride. Hopefully, they would be able to make their own wedding happen one day, now she was out of mourning. But first there was the seemingly insurmountable problem they must overcome with her acquired wealth - for he would not be a kept man.

*

The reception was held in the grounds of the estate. A great white marquee had been erected for the wedding breakfast, but as the weather was fine and hot, trestle tables were set outside under the shade of gazebos holding vast ice buckets full of champagne to serve to the guests.

Hillary had engaged Jenna to speak to a group of people Lyndon did not know, although Jenna seemed to be well acquainted with them. She really did look beautiful today and he yearned for her. His heart lifted as Jenna turned to smile at him, and as she walked towards him, he knew he must take this opportunity to speak candidly to her.

He took two glasses of champagne from one of the waiting staff and handed her one, chinked her glass, and took a sip.

'God knows I cannot find this stuff palatable – the damn stuff comes back down my nose.'

'You need to sip it.' Jenna smiled.

'You look beautiful, Jenna. Can I hope that now you're out of mourning for James, we can spend time together?'

'Ah well, I need to speak to you about that.'

'That sounds ominous. I am seriously wondering if we will ever be together.' He looked deep into her eyes as he saw them cloud over. 'Will we?'

'Yes, yes of course, but not quite yet. There is another problem you see.'

Lyndon's shoulders dropped. 'What? What problem can there be?'

'Well for a start I know there is a money issue between us.'

Lyndon took a deep breath. 'I'm a proud man, Jenna, you know that, and I won't live on your money.'

'So, what do you suggest, Lyndon - what exactly do you propose I do with the money?'

'I don't know.'

'Then don't come to me with a problem you have no solution for, because I cannot help the fact that I make money now. You encouraged my art when I was eighteen. Do you resent that I made it in the art world?'

'No of course not, it's not what you earn, it's just….'

'What, what is it, Lyndon?'

'It's the money and property James left you. I don't know how to deal with it.'

'Well, you might not have to.' Her face suddenly set hard.

Lyndon looked stricken for a moment, fearful that she was going to end their relationship. 'What do you mean?' he asked cautiously.

'James's father is trying to contest the will.'

'Oh!' Lyndon felt the colour return to his face.

'He thinks I am a gold digger and only married James for his money. He is trying to take the houses and the money James left me.'

'What are you going to do?'

'I'm going to fight for it. You might have a problem with my inheritance, but James wanted me to have it, and he definitely did *not* want his father to benefit from it. So, as I say, we might have to wait a little longer to be together, until this is sorted out, I'm afraid.'

'Oh, for goodness' sake, Jenna. You either want to be with me or you don't. Is the house and money more important to you than our future happiness? God damn it, I have a house we can live in - you don't need his flipping money and from what I can see you are making money hand over fist all by yourself.'

'Hush, Lyndon.' Jenna held her hands out to try and calm his mood. 'It's more complicated than that.'

'Why, why is it?' he answered trying to keep his voice calm.

'Christian, James's lawyer, says James's father believes we had a sham marriage and is trying to gain evidence that we married to cover up an indiscretion.'

Lyndon tipped his head, as his mind took him back to the letter James had sent him - his words branded into his brain.

The circumstances of our marriage were complicated. In February, my name was linked to a very public scandal, and Jenna - remarkable woman that she is, pushed her own happiness aside to help me in my hour of need. I am telling you, Lyndon that Jenna has been my wife in name only.

Lyndon lowered his voice. 'Was he homosexual?'

Jenna glanced around to make sure no one was in earshot and gave a quick nod.

'I see. Well, I know nothing about the law. So, can his father contest it? I shouldn't think so with you being his legal widow.'

'Christian thinks that James's father might try to find a way of speaking to you, and in fact, all James's associates to find out the truth.'

'How does he know about me?'

'I believe he has had us followed in London and suspects that I am moving on to another man too quickly after James's death. If he can find any evidence that we did have a sham marriage, and that I am planning to marry again, he *will* be able to contest it. It was James's father who had James watched at Bellevue Gardens and reported his findings to the newspaper that time.'

Lyndon raised his eyebrow. 'He must have hated his son very much.'

Jenna nodded. 'The feeling was mutual. Apparently, James had refused to enter into an alliance with a rich socialite to save their family pile in Hertfordshire. His father never forgave him for it, he cut James out of his will and sent him packing. I don't think he realised what a success James would make of his life. Lyndon, you must understand, I cannot let James down in this. I must fight for James's fortune; James would not want his father to have it, and for sure he will use the money to shore up the estate in Hertfordshire. Apparently, his father bullied James when he was growing up. He put his mother into an early grave with his temper when James was only eight, and then quickly remarried. His father and new stepmother had James sent to Rugby school, and James said it was the single most dreadful thing that ever happened to him, and never forgave them for doing it. So, you see, I must do this for James, to save his reputation, and you're right, I don't need his money, but he wanted me to have it and I want to do something special with the fortune he left me – though I know not what at the moment.'

'But what about me, what about us? Are we never to be together?'

'Of course, we will. Christian says that the courts will throw his contest out, just as long as his friends,' she looked hard into Lyndon's eyes, 'do not betray him.'

Lyndon frowned. 'So, can you be sure everyone who knew him will lie for him?'

'I believe no one knew about, you know…. they all thought he was just a confirmed bachelor. You met him, did you know?'

Lyndon shook his head. 'No, I didn't. Although he spoke to me once about love and how he too knew heartbreak. He didn't offer up his story, even though I had told him my sad story of losing you.'

Jenna smiled gently. 'Did you?' She reached out and very nearly touched him.

'Yes, he spent a morning with me once, watching me pleach a hedge. It was the only time I ever met him,' Lyndon's eyes lowered. 'I thought he was a jolly decent kind of chap.'

'He was – he was the best of men.' Jenna's eyes watered at the thought of him.

'Did you know he was a homosexual?'

'No, not at first. He was very discreet for obvious reasons. It was pure chance that I found out, and when he knew I did not judge him, that cemented our friendship indelibly. That is why I offered to marry him when his secret was about to come out. His lover has a wife and family you see. Therefore, it's imperative that we wait until all this is cleared up, you must understand that.'

Lyndon raked his hands through his hair until it stood on end. 'Why does our love always have to be so complicated?'

'I'm sorry, Lyndon - it won't be forever.'

Their conversation halted when the Earl and Countess de Bochym came over to meet them.

'Jenna,' Sarah Dunstan addressed her like an old friend as she approached with Peter. 'And Lyndon too. Good afternoon to you both. What a glorious day for a wedding.'

'Good afternoon, my lord, my lady,' Jenna and Lyndon said in unison.

'No, no!' Sarah flapped her hand. 'Do not stand on ceremony. We are all friends here, please call us Sarah and Peter. Darling, this is James's wife. I told you I met her at St Winwalloe Churchyard.'

'Ah, yes, terrible loss. My sincere condolences to you. James was a great friend. We were sorry we did not make your acquaintance socially before his untimely death.'

'I'm sorry too,' Jenna said. 'He spoke very fondly of you both and your lovely house.'

'Speaking of the house, Jenna is coming to tea on Tuesday, Peter. I'm going to show her around the workshops,' she added, 'but I would like to extend the invitation to a little drinks party later that evening, Jenna if you could join us. My brother Justin and his wife Ruby are setting off back to their life in Italy and we are having a little send off for them. Lyndon, you will join us too I hope.'

'Oh! Thank you, my lady,' Lyndon said in all astonishment.

She laughed. 'Sarah *please*,' pressing the emphasis home.

'Thank you, Sarah,' he smiled genially.

When they walked away, Lyndon gasped. 'What on earth do I wear to a drinks party at Bochym Manor?'

'The clothes you wore for Charlie and Lizzy's wedding.'

'Oh god, I am not well versed in these things.'

'You'll be fine, Lyndon.'

Hillary approached them, beckoned to Jenna and Lyndon nodded for her to go. He took another sip of champagne and looked around to see if there was something more palatable to drink other than a glass of bubbles. It was then he noticed his ex-wife, Edna, serving the punch and suddenly the champagne became more palatable.

'Lyndon, my friend.' Justin approached with Ruby. 'How are things? Have you and your lady friend surmounted the hurdles yet?'

'No not quite. She's here though.' He nodded in the direction Jenna was standing. 'She is Hillary's best friend – the Maid of Honour.'

'Goodness, I can understand why you fell in love with her,' Justin said appreciably. 'What is keeping you apart now? She looks as though she is out of mourning.'

'She is, but both Jenna and I feel it is still a little too soon to be seen together. If we had somewhere to go, where we were not known, perhaps that might help. I naturally don't want to go to the house she shared with James, it would not be proper.'

'Then you should go away somewhere. Spent time alone away from both of your lives here.'

Lyndon laughed softly, remembering how London panned out.

'Look, as we told you the other week, Ruby and I are heading back to Italy next Wednesday.'

'Yes, Sarah and Peter have just invited us to your farewell drinks party.'

'Splendid. Now if all is well with the villa, Matthew and Hillary are coming over to see us in September – on a belated honeymoon. Matthew does not want to leave the estate during the harvest. Why don't you and Jenna tag along – we have plenty of room for you all – and I think it is just what you need to find yourself again.'

Lyndon laughed. 'I'm not sure that Matthew would relish us tagging along on his belated honeymoon!'

'I think he would – it's a long journey, best undertaken with good friends, as you so obviously are. Think about it. I genuinely believe you and Jenna need to spend some quality time away from both of your normal lives. A little time under the Tuscan sun will set you on the right path. I will speak to Matthew, and once we know all is well over there I will telegram and then you can start packing.'

'Well, thank you, but let's just see if Matthew and Hillary are happy first,' he stalled, wondering how on earth he could pay for such a trip. He turned to look for Jenna and saw to his dismay that she was heading to the drinks table, and that Edna had spotted her too.

30

Feeling slightly delicate from the night before, Jenna went in search of a glass of water. She saw Ethel the kitchen hand and headed for her, but before she could ask her for a drink, Edna interjected and sent Ethel off for some more ice.

Edna scowled at Jenna. 'I see you still haven't got an ounce of decency,' she hissed, 'by my reckoning you should be still in mourning for your poor dead husband, but no, here you are, dressed to the nines, flirting with my husband again!'

'I didn't order a glass of your opinion, Edna,' Jenna said coolly.

'Oh, very witty answer, but the truth hurts, doesn't it?'

Unbeknown to Jenna, Hillary, Matthew, and Lyndon had all noted there was something of an altercation going on between Jenna and Edna. Unwilling to continue the interaction, Jenna turned her back on Edna to see Hillary approaching her in full sail.

'I'll sort this one, darling,' Hillary hissed, pushing her champagne glass into Jenna's hand, and moving her aside.

Jenna had clearly obscured Hillary from Edna's view, because although Edna had checked to see if anyone was watching before purposely hitting the end of the punch tureen spoon so that it fired its contents down the back of Jenna's dress, she had not envisaged Hillary stepping into her line of fire.

Hillary shrieked as she was splattered from head to foot in bright red fruit punch, and everyone turned, shocked to see her beautiful wedding gown ruined.

Edna stood aghast. 'Oh, my goodness, please forgive me, Mrs Bickford,' she cried desperately, 'I am so dreadfully sorry, my hand slipped, and I knocked the spoon out of the tureen. It was a pure accident.'

Hillary kept her cool and narrowed her eyes at Edna as she flicked the drips of punch from her face.

'*That* was no accident,' Hillary said scowling darkly.

'Yes, it was, I promise...'

'*Be quiet!* You are about to exceed the limits of my patience.'

Edna, silenced by the ferocity of Hillary's voice, looked up at Matthew as he approached. 'It was an accident, sir, a pure accident, I'm so sorry,' she pleaded.

Matthew leant towards Edna, regarding her reproachfully. 'That was no accident, Edna, and you know it! I saw you do that purposely and I think we all know who you were aiming for. Now, *get out of my sight immediately!* I shall deal with you presently.'

'But, but...'

'*Be gone, woman,*' Matthew roared.

Mrs Kent approached to deal with the incident but seeing the anger on Matthew's face and the state of Hillary's wedding dress, she knew she could say nothing to calm the situation, so she steered Edna away from the wedding party.

Matthew turned to Hillary and raked his hand through his hair, as he took in the great red stain across her wedding dress. He shook his head. 'My goodness, darling, I'm at a loss as to what to say to you - your beautiful dress. I will get mother to send her lady's maid over to Home Farm to see what can be done.'

'I'm fine, Matthew.' Hillary reached out to him. 'Just go and deal with the cause and I will deal with the dress. Jenna, be a darling and come with me to help me change, please?'

Hillary walked slowly between the wedding party guests to audible gasps of shock when they saw the extent of Edna's actions. Everyone knew the expense of a wedding gown such as this, and everyone agreed that Edna should face grave consequences for what she had done!

Jenna was distraught by the time they stepped over the threshold of Holme Farm. 'Hillary, I am so sorry, that ladle of punch was clearly aimed at me.'

Hillary turned to her with a wicked smile. 'I know, that is why I stepped in front of her aim.'

Jenna's step faltered. 'You knew what she was going to do?'

Hillary nodded. 'I could see the glint of malice on her face.'

'But your beautiful wedding dress, its ruined!'

'Ah but,' she patted the side of her nose, 'I do have another one – this way I will get to wear them both. This will clean - I have seen worse stains erased from garments.'

'But why?'

'I have spoken to Matthew about dismissing Edna. I do not like her manner towards me – she hasn't said anything, it is just the surly way she looks at me, and darling, if I am to reside here at Trevarno, I will not tolerate such behaviour from one such as her. Nor do I want you, my friend, to be uncomfortable visiting me here. Matthew wanted to dismiss her - he does not like her either – especially after what she did to Lyndon, but that did not merit a dismissal from the household. This,' she swept her hands down her dress, 'will give Matthew the ammunition he needs. So, darling, I present you with a fait accompli!'

*

Matthew, normally the most placid of men, was livid. Try as he might he could not settle back into the wedding party until he had dealt with Edna – this was simply too much, and she had gone too far this time.

Andrew Bickford, seeing his son's consternation, patted him on the shoulder. 'I will go and deal with the silly girl, Matthew. You go back to your guests.'

'No, Father, *I* will do this. You want me to take over the running of this estate, then let me deal with the rot that has set in with some members of staff below stairs. But you must back me up on what I am about to do.'

Andrew nodded. 'Do what you must then.'

'Thank you, Father. I will be back soon.'

When Matthew went in search of Edna, he heard voices in Mrs Kent's housekeepers room, Edna and Mrs Kent were in deep conversation, and Matthew held back in the shadows for a moment to listen in.

'What in God's name did you think you were playing at, Edna?' Mrs Kent demanded.

'I couldn't help myself. It just gets my goat to see Jen swanning about - lording it up over us all – and so soon after her poor husband's death. But that is what she is like, isn't she – she's heartless. But oh god, Mrs Kent, I'm in trouble now though, aren't I?

'I know, I know, I cannot abide the woman either, but look, I do not condone what you have done – and in truth I was shocked to hear Mrs Drake tell me what you did to Lyndon, but you're a good worker, and we have always got on. So, I will say I saw what happened and that it was an accident, but you must never, ever do anything like that again.'

'Thank you, Mrs Kent.'

'Everything will be all right. You must tell the master how deeply sorry you are, but your hand slipped, and I will back you up.'

Matthew stepped into the housekeeper's doorway and both women looked up startled. His face darkened with rage. 'I think we have all heard enough of Edna's lies to last a lifetime.'

'Oh, sir, Edna is very, very sorry,' Mrs Kent pleaded.

'Be quiet, woman. I want Edna off this estate by first light tomorrow.'

Edna started to cry, her shoulders heaving.

'But!' Mrs Kent exclaimed in alarm.

'I said *be quiet*!' and Mrs Kent pulled her lips into a tight white line. Matthew turned to Edna with cold anger in his eyes. 'You have managed to ruin our wedding day and destroy my new wife's beautiful wedding gown – a dress that cost four-hundred-pounds I might add, all because of your nasty efforts to spoil Jenna's day here. Both Lyndon and Jenna have had their lives blighted by your previous actions. I will not tolerate you blighting my wife's. Now *get out* and never, ever, darken Trevarno's door again.'

Distraught, Edna picked up her skirts and fled from the kitchen.

'Mrs Kent, fetch Brown. I want to see you both in the library, *now!*'

Matthew was seated at his father's desk when they both shuffled in.

'This is a disciplinary, Mrs Kent, which is why I have brought Brown in.' Mrs Kent shifted nervously. 'As housekeeper, you are in the privileged position in this house to oversee the domestic staff, and what you have allowed to happen is unacceptable. Secondly, I heard you offering to lie for Edna, and do not try to deny it. I expect better from you. Edna may be the one dismissed today, but if I find that you continue with your denouncement of my good friends Lyndon and Jenna, you too will be looking for new employment. Do I make myself clear?'

'Yes, sir,' Mrs Kent said tremulously.

'Brown.'

'Yes, sir?'

'I am not unaware of your subtle resentment towards Jenna either.' Matthew saw Brown's Adams apple move as he swallowed hard. 'So, I give you the same final warning.'

Brown cleared his throat noisily. 'Yes, sir.'

'Jenna is my wife's best friend, and from now on she will be a regular visitor to Trevarno. If I hear of one hint of resentment from either of you, you know what will happen, and, I might add, I have my father's full backing in this matter. Remember, no one is indispensable, nor do I care how long you have served this family. I will not tolerate insolence of any kind.' He slammed his hand down on the desk. 'Now, Edna is to get her wage owed up to yesterday, but not a penny more, nor is she to have a reference. She must learn to become a decent human being and so, I might add, should you two. Now get out of my sight, both of you. I will not allow you to ruin my day further.'

*

Bypassing the wedding party on the front lawn, Matthew took himself off to Home Farm to see if all was well with Hillary. There, he poured himself a stiff whisky – dealing with and firing staff had not been in his remit before, but he felt liberated, for he knew he had done the right thing. He could hear Jenna and Hillary upstairs and was heartened to hear their voices were bright and lively.

'Is everything all right, ladies?'

'Everything is sorted now,' Hillary said as she descended the stairs in her other gown.

Matthew gaped incredulously. 'Hillary, where the devil did you get that gown from?'

'It's my other one, darling.'

'You bought two wedding dresses!'

'Of course. One for daytime and one for evening.' Hillary narrowed her eyes. 'Bought with *my* money, I might add. A woman must be ready for all eventualities. Now, enough about my dress. What have you done with the little minx?'

'Dismissed her!'

'Bravo, that is the best wedding present I could have had.' She kissed him full on the lips and his mood softened. 'Now, our guests are awaiting us, darling.'

*

More champagne was brought round and as Hillary collected two glasses, she handed one to Jenna.

'Problem, sorted.' She winked. 'Nothing to keep you from Lyndon now.'

Jenna smiled but her face clouded.

'What is the matter, Jenna? You look pensive.'

'That man, over there, stood on his own. I saw him come into the church while I was waiting for you, and I know I've seen him somewhere before. I overheard him saying he was a guest of the bride.'

Hillary narrowed her eyes. 'He is certainly no one I know, and I knew everyone on the guest list that Mama gave me.'

Ellie, Guy, Sophie, and Kit moved towards Jenna and Hillary. 'Are you discussing that gentlemen over there by any chance?' Kit asked.

'Yes, I believe he is an interloper,' Hillary said coolly.

Kit nodded. 'I did wonder because he approached us earlier and started to ask probing questions about James Blackwell.'

Jenna and Hillary's eyes cut to each other.

'Such as, Kit?' Jenna asked tentatively.

'I was just exchanging small talk with him mostly about the wedding in general at first. Then he asked about the incident with that maid and that it seemed deliberate, to which I told him I didn't know why it happened, but then he moved the conversation to you, Jenna, about you being James's widow and how he'd know James all his life and couldn't understand why he'd married you after years of being a confirmed bachelor. He said something about James never being a lady's man. I did not like his inference, so I excused myself and left him.'

'What the devil is he implying?' Hillary was aghast.

Jenna knew exactly what he was implying.

'Hillary,' Matthew said as he and Lyndon approached them, 'in five minutes we need to lead everyone through to the wedding breakfast.'

'Matthew, darling,' she kissed him on the cheek, 'before that, I need you to do something else for me. We appear to have an interloper at our wedding. See that man over there, he has been asking our guests probing questions about the feasibility of Jenna's marriage to James.'

Lyndon shot a worried look in Jenna's direction.

'What?' Matthew said incredulously.

'I know, what a notion,' Hillary said affronted. 'He claims to be on my guest list, darling, but I don't know him, do you?'

'No, I don't,' he said grimly. 'Good grief, are we going to get through any hour of this day without incident?' He turned and called Brown the butler over. 'Fetch Dunnett and Goodman would you, and have that man over there removed from my land.'

'Yes, sir, right away,' Brown said authoritatively.

Matthew smiled at Hillary. 'Do not worry, my steward and gamekeeper will see him off. Come, wife, I'm ravenous!'

'Ooh, for me or for food?' Hillary teased,

Everyone laughed as Matthew coloured slightly.

'Good god, woman, whom have I married?'

'The woman of your dreams, Matthew,' Hillary said, kissing him on his hot cheek.

When Jenna, Lyndon and the rest of the party began to follow everyone into the marquee, the interloper had been approached by the gamekeeper and steward. As the man turned to leave, without - by the look of it - any fuss, he shot Jenna a look that convinced her that she was not safe from prying eyes even in Cornwall.

*

It was only after the wedding breakfast, that Lyndon found the opportunity to tell Jenna about Justin and Ruby's invitation to Italy.

'I can't afford the ticket of course, I've only been back working a couple of weeks, and no, Jenna, you are not going to pay.'

'Damn your pride, Lyndon! This would be a wonderful opportunity for us to be together and sort things out – away from prying eyes. You saw that man. I'm being followed again. I'm desperate to be with you, Lyndon, and this is an ideal opportunity. Just think, a month in the sun – making love.'

Lyndon's eyes melted with yearning, but he shook his head. 'I can't let you pay, Jenna, I'm sorry, I just can't. Anyway, we cannot possibly encroach on Matthew and Hillary's honeymoon.'

'Of course, you can, my friend.' Matthew had arrived by their side and patted him on the back. 'I've just spoken to Justin and Ruby, and you *are* coming, and I'm paying your passage, and I will not,' he held his hand up, 'take no for an answer. You have given me much more than money could ever buy with your enduring friendship, Lyndon. You have been like a brother to me. I could not have got through the war if you had not been by my side – let me do this for you. Now, both Hillary and I want you to come with us. It is time to see life beyond Cornwall.'

Jenna looked hopefully at Lyndon.

'I am being ganged up on here, aren't I?' Lyndon smiled.

Everyone nodded.

'Well, yes, then. We would like that very much,' he said.

31

While the grand wedding was going on at Trevarno, it had been a busy day at The Poldhu Tea Room. This long hot summer brought many visitors to the cove and business was brisk.

Ellie and Guy had gone to Matthew and Hillary Bickford's society wedding that day, so Meg was in charge of the tearoom. Betsy had come in again to help, but she kept having pains, and Meg was worried that she would give birth behind the counter. Betsy just laughed and promised her that she would go home at the first sign of baby coming.

Marianne, having been disgruntled with Gabriel for a few days, felt her tummy do its usual somersault when Gabriel and little Robbie settled on the veranda outside - especially as Jenna was not with them. Marianne was desperate to serve them, but Meg got there first! Thankfully, she was able to take their order to the table. With a quick tidy of her hair and apron, she put on her best smile and picked up the tray.

'Thank you, Marianne.' Gabriel smiled warmly as she placed a tray of tea and cake on their table. 'No Ellie today?

'She's gone to a fancy wedding.'

'Ah, let me guess, at Trevarno?'

Marianne held the order pad aloft and nodded.

'It seems everyone who is anyone has gone to that wedding,' he mused.

Marianne would have taken that as a slight if not for the fact that Gabriel had not gone.'

'How come you were not invited? After all you're a gentleman!'

Being a gentleman does not get you an invite to every social occasion going you know,' he teased. 'Having said that, I did get an invitation, but with my parents being away, I could not find anyone to leave Robbie with.'

'I suspect though being a gentleman gets you into more social soirées than I go to nowadays.'

'Nowadays?' He asked with a slight turn up of his mouth.

'Yes, when I was a lady's companion to Lady Martha Jefferson, I attended many such occasions – I rather miss that life.'

Gabriel raised his eyebrow. 'Forgive me, Marianne, you appear to have a vastly different background to the one I believed you to have had. Is your mother not employed by mine to housekeep?'

Marianne felt her eye twitch at the inference that she was no better than a char lady's daughter.

'They're not my real parents. I was a foundling baby, and they very kindly took me in. But it has been said many times that my intelligence must have been inherited from my birth parents as neither of my adopted parents did well at school. I, however, did very well at school you see – I could have been a teacher, but Lady Martha personally asked me to be her companion. I can speak French and play the piano forte – *though she did not add how badly she played*.

As though assessing her claims, he spoke to her in French. 'Je vois que vous avez des qualités cachées.'

He looked impressed when she answered. 'Yes, Gabriel, I do have hidden qualities.'

'I can see I have underestimated you.'

'Many people do,' she said petulantly. 'So, have you no guests with you today?'

'Not today, no. As I said, and your mother may have told you, my parents have gone away to the continent for a couple of months, so it is just me and Robbie to fend for ourselves.'

'Well, it's another lovely day again,' she said almost biting her tongue for not thinking of anything more interesting to say rather than commenting on the weather.

'It is, indeed, Marianne, this heatwave looks set for some time to come. Perfect for a day on the beach after tea and cake - that is what we're going to do, aren't we Robbie?'

Robbie nodded brightly.

'What are your plans for later when the tearoom closes today, Marianne?'

Marianne felt a frisson of pleasure that he seemed interested in what she was doing and felt a little guilty that she had been so angry with him since Thursday.

'Oh!' she smiled brightly, 'I thought I might take a walk over to Church Cove. I will take my book and perhaps have a little paddle.'

'That sounds like a splendid idea. We often do much the same, don't we Robbie?'

'Yes, Papa,' he answered licking the jam from the side of his slice of Victoria sandwich.'

'Eat it properly, Robbie otherwise Marianne will think you have no manners.'

The boy licked his lips and took a bite.

'Well, I hope you have a wonderful day at Church Cove, Marianne.'

'Oh, I think I will.' She picked up her tray and walked a few steps away just as Robbie spoke.

'Jenna won't be there to make sandcastles though,' he sighed.

Marianne felt a curl of annoyance at the mention of Jenna's name.

'No, Jenna is at a wedding today, never mind, we can see if anyone else will help us.'

'I want Jenna, Papa.'

'I know you do. You like Jenna, don't you?'

He nodded. 'Jenna hasn't gone to marry anyone today, has she?'

'I don't think so,' Gabriel laughed and then whispered, 'I hope not, otherwise she won't be able to come and play with us again.'

'Are *you* going to marry Jenna, Papa?'

Marianne paused and gritted her teeth, waiting for the answer, but Gabriel just ruffled Robbie's hair.

'Marianne, are you daydreaming or something,' Meg spoke, 'that table over there would like you to take their order.'

'I'm going, I was just catching my breath,' she answered crossly.

*

Marianne was eager to finish her chores once the tearoom closed, which it did earlier on a Sunday. Unfortunately, they were a little later than normal, as a crowd of ladies seemed in no hurry to leave that afternoon. Thankfully, Meg politely, but firmly, told them that she needed to close as her husband was taking her out for the afternoon. They quickly apologised and got up to leave.

Once the last cup and saucer was washed and put away, Marianne changed into her prettiest dress which she had happened to bring with her, and it was with great excitement, that she set off towards Church Cove. By the time she reached the top of the cliff and looked down onto the cove, her heart was thrumming with anticipation. She practically ran down the rocky coast path to the beach. There she stood, her hand shielding her eyes from the sun, scanning the beach, but they were not there. Deeply disappointed, she first checked the church to see if they were in there before walking over to Dollar Cove. When she couldn't find them, she despondently walked back to Church Cove and flopped down on the dunes, cradling her knees with her arms. Gazing out across the sea silvered with the sun, she sighed heavily – she would wait. It was then she saw a man walking across the beach towards her. Her heart leapt - Gabriel was coming, and he was alone!

*

Jake Treen had taken a huge gamble to follow Marianne. He had been waiting on the dunes at Poldhu for her to finish work, in the hope of speaking to her, but she was late coming out. He must have momentarily taken his eyes off the tearoom because he had not seen her leave, and it was only by chance he noticed her running up the hill towards Poldhu Head. Marianne was the most beautiful woman he knew. With her long nut-brown curls tumbling down her back and her lovely figure, she did something to him that no other woman had managed. He loved everything about her – the way she took care of her appearance - always so neat, tidy, and so very well brought up. She was clever too – he had been to school with her, and she had far surpassed everyone else in her class academically. The war had made a man of Jake - though he would not recommend it to other young people and hoped that they would never have to face another war like it. Jake wanted something lovely in his life now – to wipe the memory of those dreadful days in the stinking trenches of France and the horrors he and thousands of other men had witnessed. He wanted Marianne so much it hurt his heart. His dreams were filled with images of her – wild imaginations of touching her perfect face with his fingers. Oh, to feel her next to him in bed – to see her hair spread out on the pillow next her his. If only he could just make her see him. He had almost given up the chase with Marianne a few weeks ago, but Ellie's words to him, 'Faint heart does not win fair maiden' had stuck in his mind. With this thought, he felt the adrenaline pump through his veins as he made his way quickly up to Poldhu Head and down the other side.

He found her, sitting on the dunes and his heart lifted when she stood up as though to greet him - was she really smiling at him? Suddenly the smile fell from her face – he was so obviously not who she thought he was. He faltered and almost stopped in his tracks – she looked furious at his approach and began to gather up her bag from where it lay on the sand. He had to say something, to stop her from running away from him.

'Hello, Marianne,' he said, his voice cracking with emotion. 'Great minds think alike. It's a lovely day to spend on the beach.'

'Yes, yes, it is,' she answered, her eyes glancing beyond him as though searching for something.

Plucking up the courage to ask his burning question he said, 'You look all alone here, would you like some company?'

'No,' she snapped, then lowered her voice realising the sharpness of her tone and said, 'No, thank you, I'm waiting for someone.'

'Oh, I'm sorry, please forgive my intrusion.' He turned quickly and walked down towards the sea - disappointment laying heavy on his chest. He hardly dared turn around to look at her, but when he did, she was running up the hill from whence he had just come from, and Jake patted his fragile heart as it curled back into the lonely place in his chest.

*

Not wanting to be embarrassed when Jake came up the beach to find that the person she was waiting for had not turned up, Marianne had taken flight almost as soon as he had left her to walk down to the sea. Hopefully as she made her way over the cliff top, she would meet Gabriel coming the other way – perhaps he had been delayed for some reason. Whatever the delay was, she needed to distance herself from Jake Treen. What was wrong with that man? She had never given him any encouragement, so why did he persist in pursuing her? There was no doubt he was handsome, and in the normal scheme of things she would have been flattered by his attentions on her, but she was determined to stay steadfast in her want for a gentleman – Gabriel Trelease to be exact. She had not spent her time with her nose in a book bettering herself, to end up the wife of a thatcher!

*

Gabriel was in a reflective mood as he sat on Polurrian Beach, watching as Robbie patted the sandcastle he had just made with him. He wished he were at Trevarno with Jenna - though he had no claim to be at Jenna's side. He had received an invitation to the wedding, via Justin and Peter he suspected. He did not know Matthew Bickford, but he had heard of his bride-to-be Hillary Stanton. She was widely known in the social scene in London – but he could not claim an acquaintance with her, even though he and his late wife, Jane had frequented many parties in London before the war. Anyway, there was no way he could have gone now his parents had gone away. He had managed to secure the help of Helen, the lady who looked after Ellie and Betsy's youngest children in minding Robbie during the week, but Helen liked her weekends and evenings to spend with her own family. As for wanting to be by Jenna's side - well, although he had only met with her three times, she had made an enormous impact on both he and his son's life and he felt her loss keenly on the beach today. That was why he had decided not to take their normal route to Church Cove, he would have felt her loss more. It was as though Robbie could read his mind because he got up from where he'd been playing and flopped down beside him on the sand.

'I wish Jenna were here today, Papa,' he said.

'So do I, son, so do I.'

'Will she come and see us next week? Do you think she would come and have tea with us again at Poldhu?' He knelt up excitedly.

'I don't know, Robbie, maybe. She is a busy lady. She has work to do, she cannot spend all her time entertaining little boys on the beach.'

'But we have tea on Sunday – nobody works on Sunday!'

'They work at the tearoom on Sunday to serve you tea and cake.'

'Oh, yes, they do, don't they!' he said deflated. 'I miss her though.'

Gabriel pulled Robbie into a hug and looked out to sea. *I am missing her too and I should not be. She is still grieving for her husband, just as I should be grieving for Jane. But every day she seems to be filling the void in my heart that I thought no woman could ever fill again.*

Robbie turned his face up to Gabriel's. 'Will you ask her if she will come to tea, Papa, next Sunday and then she can help me build another sandcastle? I am sure she would rather do that than work all day.'

Gabriel laughed. 'Yes, Robbie, I will definitely ask her, but I can't promise anything.' With that thought in his mind his mood lifted. He knew he would see her at Bochym on Tuesday when she came to tea with Sarah, so he would ask her then.

*

Extremely disappointed that she had not met with Gabriel over at Church Cove or on the walk back over to Poldhu, Marianne walked down to the sea to paddle her hot feet. She was cross and she knew not why – there had been no offer from Gabriel to join her on the beach - she had just assumed that he would be there. Next time she would ask Gabriel outright if he would like her to come and help build sandcastles with Robbie, and then she would turn on her charm and show him that she was interested in him too. Maybe, just maybe he would see that *she* would make a better wife than Jenna flipping Blackwell! For surely, he would prefer Marianne, who was young and beautiful and untouched by another man, then someone who had been married before!

32

At Trevarno, there was a break in the celebrations at five that afternoon for the wedding breakfast to be cleared away in the marquee, in readiness for the evening celebration of drinks, music, and a buffet supper. The invitation to this event extended to all staff and residents of Trevarno – with the exception of Edna Madron.

Because Hillary and Matthew were moving into Holme Farm together that night, Jenna had packed her things ready to take them to Lyndon's cottage, as he had arranged to spend the night back in his old room at his father's cottage. Lyndon offered to carry Jenna's suitcase to his cottage, and aware that many eyes were watching their arrival, he kept his distance from Jenna and had Gina there to greet them for propriety's sake.

Gina showed Jenna to the spare room and when they came back downstairs, she said, 'If you two want a moment together, I'll go back upstairs to give you a little privacy.'

Smiling gratefully as Gina left them, Lyndon wrapped his arms around Jenna and kissed her. 'I never thought you would ever be in my arms in this house, but it's going to send me crazy knowing you're sleeping here, and I cannot be with you.'

'Well, we'll soon be spending our days in the sun,' she whispered.

They smiled at each other having decided amongst the rest of the party going to Italy that 'our days in the sun,' which was also the title of James's new novel, was to be their secret code if they mentioned Italy. No one was to know they were going, and all members of the party had agreed to secrecy.

Lyndon sighed. 'I cannot wait, Jenna.'

'You know, good things come to those who wait!'

He nodded and pulled her tighter into his arms. 'I know we have much to sort out, but never doubt my love for you.'

'I love you too. Now we can't keep poor Gina waiting upstairs so I will let you go,' she said with one last kiss.

*

While Hillary and Matthew were getting ready for the evening's entertainment, the telephone rang.

Hillary rolled her eyes. 'I'm going to take that thing off the hook tonight,' she joked. 'This place won't crumble if you take a few hours off.'

'I have no intention of doing any work other than entertaining my new wife,' Matthew said kissing her before he ran downstairs to answer the phone. He returned to her a few moments later. 'I need to go up to the house, Father wants me.'

Hillary narrowed her eyes. 'It had better be important.'

'I promise I shall be back in half an hour.'

*

Edna's father, Eric Madron, was in the library with Andrew Bickford, and Matthew noted the scowl he gave him when he walked in.

'I'm here about my daughter.'

'I gathered that,' Matthew said stiffly.

'She tells me she's been dismissed for accidently spilling a drink.'

'Let's just get this straight, Madron - it was no accident. Your daughter deliberately threw a ladle of punch at my wife - ruining a dress worth four hundred pounds.'

'Well, she says it was an accident.'

'I saw her do it with my own eyes.'

Madron's mouth twitched angrily and turned to Andrew Bickford for help.

'Mr Bickford, sir, please can you intervene. Master Matthew here would have Edna's livelihood ruined for a mistake – for being slightly overzealous with the punch ladle.'

Andrew Bickford raised an eyebrow. 'Overzealous? I can tell you that I too saw the malicious glint in your daughter's eyes the moment before she deliberately flipped the ladle from the bowl. Matthew has dismissed her, and I fully agree with his actions. Your daughter has been a thorn in the side of a very respected member of our community for too long. She leaves tomorrow!'

Matthew felt his chest inflate – he had never been prouder of his father.

'Well, I'm here to tell you, if Edna is forced to leave in the morning, I too will resign my position as estate handyman,' he said holding his chin high.

Andrew glanced at Matthew to respond, and he in turn said, 'Well, I will be sorry to see you go, Madron, but if that is how you feel, I trust you will give us a months' notice.'

Madron blanched as he looked between the men. He had obviously not thought for one moment that his resignation would be accepted. 'You'll not find anyone as good as me to take my place you know!'

'Oh, I don't know, I understand the estate managed extremely well when you were at war.'

'And is this….' he blustered, 'is this the way you treat someone who fought in the war?'

'You seem to forget, Madron, it is you who is offering your resignation, not I, insisting on it. I seem to remember you making a similar demand a couple of years ago on behalf of your daughter Edna, resulting in the expulsion of a much loved and valued member of our staff from the estate. After today's events I know now I was wrong then to keep your family on the estate. I suggest you go home and think long and hard as to whether you want to stay here or not. As for your daughter, she *will* leave tomorrow, and she will not be welcome back here - not even to visit her parents *if* you stay. Good day to you, Madron.'

*

The rest of the wedding had passed off without further incident and there was many a sore head on the Trevarno Estate the next morning.

Lyndon had delayed his departure from Trevarno that morning to watch Edna's expulsion from the estate. There had been quite a turn out to watch her being bundled into her father's wagon to be taken off in disgrace to her aunt's house in Hayle. It was an event overseen by Mr Goodman the estate steward. The incident had brought much speculation now to see if the whole family would up and follow suit - especially as both Mr Bickford senior and Matthew had not seen fit to pander to Madron's threats to leave if his daughter were to be expelled.

At Gina's suggestion, Jenna kept well out of the way until Edna left, though she witnessed it from behind the bedroom curtain. As soon as the wagon pulled away, Jenna made her way to Lyndon's father's house to say her goodbyes. She had dressed soberly again that morning, though longed to rid herself of her dark clothes, which were terribly uncomfortable in this heat. Still, she only had to go until Thursday to complete the propriety of mourning, and as Hillary kept telling her, James would not have wished her to have done it anyway.

Jenna stood tentatively on the threshold of the FitzSimmons's cottage.

'Come in,' Gina said, hugging her. 'Don't stand on ceremony here. We hope you will come and see us more often now that Edna has gone.'

'I will. I suspect Hillary will beckon me over on a regular basis.' Jenna then glanced at Michael. 'I hope you will welcome me here too, Michael?' He nodded, but Jenna could tell he was still wary of her intentions towards his son.

Lyndon came forward to say a chaste goodbye to Jenna before he left for Bochym Manor. 'I'll see you tomorrow evening then at Bochym – for drinks!' he said with a wry smile.

'Hobnobbing with the gentry now, are we?' Michael teased. 'I don't know, what with you being invited by the Earl and Countess de Bochym to a drinks party, and my Gina here, enjoying cocktails with the new mistress of Trevarno, I'll be bowing and scraping to you all soon! Go on, you two, be off with you, before you give Gina anymore cause to become disgruntled with her life with this old gardener.'

'Now, Michael,' Gina said, kissing him on the cheek, 'you know very well that I would not swap you for all the fine trappings of the gentry.'

*

While Jenna settled back into painting at Loe House, Lyndon returned to Bochym Manor early Monday afternoon and set himself to work at once. He had been trying to process his thoughts about the trip to Italy and time must have slipped by, because he was surprised when Gabriel came striding up the long dusty drive from Bochym. He had his jacket slung over his shoulder, a spring in his step and a smile on his face.

'Hello, Lyndon, did you have a good wedding over at Trevarno?'

'Yes, it was splendid, thank you. What have you been up to? You look very pleased with yourself,' he said slapping Gabriel on the back.

'You know, I do believe I am, my friend.'

Lyndon grinned. 'I'm intrigued.'

Gabriel laughed lightly. 'Life it seems, is looking up for this poor, sad widower. I've met someone you see – she is widowed like me, very beautiful and so lovely with young Robbie - he adores her. After Jane, my late wife, I never thought I would feel like this about another woman,' he said wistfully, 'but she is just so easy to be with. I've only seen her three times, but you just know if something feels right! And she is right, she is just what we need. I'm probably jumping the gun, but I think if we continue to meet like this - and she seems very willing to do so – I think, maybe this will turn into something special for Robbie and I.'

'That is good news. Where do you meet?'

'On the beach normally, so it is in full view of people for propriety's sake. I had a lovely day last Thursday with her, when she very kindly came to Robbie's tea party at Poldhu, she bought him a gift as well, and then we had a lovely walk down to the sea. My parents were there too, and they like her very much.'

Lyndon tipped his head. 'Does she feel the same about you?'

'I don't know, maybe, I don't know. I don't like to push anything. It is early days since she lost her husband.

Lyndon nodded. 'I understand. It's probably difficult for her. Does she have a name, and does she live nearby then?'

'Yes, but I'd rather not say where or much about her. I don't want to compromise her situation in any way.'

'I fully understand. I'm in a similar situation. I'm happy that you have found someone, and I wish you well in your new friendship then.'

'Thank you, Lyndon and I wish you well too. Are you coming for a drink at the Wheal Inn? Justin and Peter are coming up too. Justin wants one last drink before he and Ruby head off to Italy – lucky devils. They're having drinks and a buffet supper tomorrow night in the manor for everyone else.'

'Yes, I too have been invited. It seems my status as Matthew's best man has elevated me to the heights of being a guest in fine houses now.' He gave a wry smile.

'You do yourself an injustice. You're as fine a man as any gentlemen I have ever come across. The world is changing, Lyndon, so too is the class divide.'

'Is your lady friend of genteel stock, Gabriel?'

'No, she is from lowly birth, but married well. If she was good enough for her late husband - who was a gentlemen - she is good enough for me.'

*

When Jenna returned to Loe House from an afternoon painting en plein air, Celia Inman the housekeeper was just putting the grocery order in the larder.

'Ah, Jenna, did you have a nice time at the wedding?'

'I did yes, thank you. It was beautiful and the weather was so gorgeous we were able to spend most of the day outside on the front lawn. Celia, you haven't by any chance encountered a man loitering here abouts have you?'

Celia's face clouded.

'You have, haven't you?'

Celia nodded and Jenna was shocked to hear what Celia told her had happened at The Halzhephron Inn, and later at her own Bed and Breakfast.

'As soon as Richard told me that the man had been in the Inn asking questions, and I realised it was the same man who had been chatting to me about you, I went back home and told him to leave – and that he wouldn't find anyone else in the village to take him in.'

'Thank you, Celia.'

'What's it all about then, do you know?' Celia tipped her head.

'I'm not sure,' she said evasively. 'It may just be that he is interested in us. James was, after all, famous.'

'And so are you now!' Celia stated.

'Yes,' she answered tremulously, feeling a curl of unease, that even down here, she could not evade prying eyes. Surely there was a law against being spied on!

Celia must have seen her consternation because she put her hand on her arm.

'Well, I don't think he'll be hanging about any more,' Celia said confidently. 'He got short shrift from both me and Richard.'

'Thank you again, Celia.'

Once Celia had gone, she walked down onto the terrace and looked over towards Porthleven. At least she knew for sure that if she was being followed and her friends were being questioned, the man was definitely not getting the information he needed to discredit her.

33

Jenna shared her concerns about the man following her when she rang Christian the next morning.

'I'm so sorry, Jenna,' he said sympathetically. 'All I can say is, if he does anything untoward, just call the police, but until he does, there is nothing we can do. How are things with you and Lyndon?'

'Understandably difficult. We have been to two social events, but have kept our distance, oh but Christian, I want to be with Lyndon so much. We have waited too long already.'

'I understand, Jenna, but if this man watching is gathering evidence that you were in love with Lyndon before and during your marriage to James, there may be a case to answer.'

'But many women lost men in the war and remarried. I thought I had lost Lyndon. I cannot be the only woman to want to marry again after being widowed. It's not as if I look for rich husbands. My first husband was a brute of a man who bought me off my father,' she paused on hearing Christian gasp, 'and Lyndon is a hedger with little or no money of his own.'

'Mmm. The latter might go against you.'

'Why?'

'The courts may think you colluded with Lyndon, to marry James knowing he was ill, to get his money so you and Lyndon could set up home.'

This stunned Jenna into silence, so much so, Christian questioned if she was still on the line.

'Yes,' she breathed, 'are you joking?'

'No, but it's something we have to be ready for.'

'But when I married James. I had no idea he was ill – none of us did, and as for Lyndon – I believed that he had died in the war when I married James.'

'Rest assured I will appoint someone to fight your case, Jenna.'

'Someone else! Not you?'

'James's father has indicated that I was involved with James – I can't defend you – I'm not even sure I can defend myself in this!'

'Oh god, Christian – what a mess. Would it be easier to just let him have everything?'

'No! James left everything to you because of what you did for us.'

'But Christian, this could ruin you.'

'Let us wait and see. If you can wait a while longer, no court will hear him.'

'Well, Lyndon and I are going to Italy in September, with Matthew and Hillary – we're staying at our friend's villa. They all know of our former relationship and as I am still newly widowed, our inclusion in the party will be kept secret, but we'll make sure we book separate cabins on our journey just in case. They are all good friends - they will not betray us. We just need to spend time together, and this will be an ideal opportunity.'

'I fully understand, Jenna. When are you going?'

'Probably early-September. We will be gone eight weeks. By the time we get back it will be five months since James's death, perhaps Lyndon and I can make plans to marry then.'

'Let's just see.'

Jenna gave a weary sigh. 'While you're on the phone,' she said changing the subject, 'I've been thinking about Bellevue Gardens - If I get to keep it, that is. I would like to set up a home for young girls who are living on the street. I would have to speak to Mrs Hemp of course to see if she is willing to be the housekeeper. But these girls are turned out on the street when they are orphaned, and they cannot get proper work because they have no address.'

'It is a lovely idea, Jenna. What prompted it?'

'A young girl helped Lyndon and I when he had one of his terrible shell shock attacks in London. She told Mrs

Hemp that she was living rough on the streets. I want to help some of them. Once they are clean, fed and housed they will be able to get proper employment and perhaps go on to meet someone and marry. Left alone on the streets, well, you know what could happen to them and the path they could be forced to take.'

'I do, yes,' he said gravely. 'Leave it with me, I will look into it for you.'

'Oh, and I'm holding a launch party here for James's new book on Tuesday 2nd September – you would be very welcome if you want to come.'

'Alas, it's best that I distance myself from anything to do with James for the time being.'

'I hope that doesn't include me.'

'Never you, Jenna, I promise.'

*

Lyndon looked up from where he was working when Jenna's car pulled up at the front of Bochym Manor. He noted that her attention was diverted by Gabriel who was walking up from the garden. He tipped his head - they seemed to have quite a bit to say to each other to say they were strangers, but then Jenna seemed to have the confidence to speak to anyone, whether she had met them before or not. He wondered what Gabriel thought of his lovely Jenna. He could not wait for the day he could introduce her to him as his future bride.

*

Gabriel smiled with delight as he approached Jenna, feeling heartened that her return smile was just as warm.

'Jenna, I'm glad I caught you. I just wanted to thank you again for the gift you gave Robbie. He has played with nothing else since.'

'I'm glad he liked it.'

'We wondered if you might be on the beach at Church Cove next Sunday. Robbie missed you this week.'

'I admit I missed him too,' she said genuinely.

'Or better still, Robbie asked if you could join us for tea again,' he added with a sparkle in his eyes.

'Well, I really should be working - I am planning on going away soon and if I don't produce some paintings, Francis Knight at The Black Gallery will lose interest in me.'

'Yes,' Gabriel scratched his chin, 'Francis can be demanding sometimes. Are you going anywhere nice?'

'Just away from Cornwall for a while,' she said evasively, 'but as for next Sunday, why don't I bring a picnic to Church Cove, and I can help Robbie build sandcastles again?'

'We would like that very much. How did the wedding go at Trevarno?'

'Very well, thank you.'

'They extended an invite to me too, but with my parents away, I had to stay home with Robbie.'

'Who looks after him while you're at work then?'

'A lady called Helen, who minds Mrs Blackthorn and Mrs Penrose's youngest children at Poldhu.'

'So, will you miss Justin and Ruby's drinks party this evening?'

'I'm afraid so. Helen likes her evening to herself – and I do not blame her.

They both turned as Sarah came down the path to greet them.

'Jenna,' Sarah greeted her warmly.' I see you have met Gabriel.'

'Yes, but we are already acquainted.'

'Excellent. Come, Jenna, we shall take tea and then I will show you around. Gabriel, I trust we will see you later at the drinks buffet?'

'Unfortunately, not. I was just telling Jenna, I have no one to mind Robbie.'

'Well then you must bring him along. Nanny or one of the maids will look after him.'

Gabriel's face brightened. 'Thank you, Sarah. That is so kind, I will. So, I *shall* see you later, Jenna.'

'I shall look forward to it.' She smiled gently.

*

The drinks party started at six-thirty and Jenna was mingling quite happily with all the members of the Arts and Craft Association whom she had met earlier when she had looked around their workshops.

Lyndon, dressed in his Sunday best clothes, hesitated for a moment in the kitchen - he had never been beyond the kitchen door before, and felt uneasy about attending this drinks party. Fortunately, Joe came to meet him.

'I feel as though I'm out of my depth here, Joe,' he admitted.

'Nonsense, His Lord, and Her Ladyship are expecting you. Let me show you through to the Jacobean drawing room where the others have gathered. You will be amongst friends - Matthew Bickford is already here, as are Kit and Guy.'

Once in the room, Lyndon was offered a drink from a tray Dorothy was holding, but he studiously averted his glance from her fluttering eyelashes. He turned and smiled when he saw Jenna, and as always, a crowd of men had drawn around her. His heart flipped when she looked up and saw him - her face glowing with happiness as though he was the only person in the room. He watched as she excused herself from her many admirers to come to his side, albeit keeping a polite distance.

'What a wonderful place this is, isn't it?' she enthused.

'It certainly is. I never thought I would be here for a social gathering,' he said staring up at the ornate plasterwork on the ceiling.

'Ah, well, Lyndon. Things are changing for both of us.'

Justin and Ruby joined them and beckoned them over to the corner of the room near the buffet table, to speak in private.

'We have just spoken to Matthew and Hillary to tell them we should dock in Naples on the 27th of August. So just as soon as we check the villa is still standing, we will send Matthew a telegram so you can book your tickets. Which means if you can be ready, you could set off the next week. The ship to Naples sails on Wednesdays, so you could be on the high seas on the 3rd of September.' Justin smiled.

'Oh goodness! That is the day after I'm holding the book launch for James's new novel at Loe House.'

'Will that be a problem?'

'No, I'm sure it won't.'

'Excellent, you'll be in Italy by the 17th and together at last,' Justin whispered.

*

Lucy, who unbeknown to Lyndon and Jenna, had been replenishing the buffet table behind them, overheard their plans to go away. Biting her lip, she realised she had inadvertently stumbled on who Lyndon's secret lady friend was. Shooting a quick glance over at Dorothy serving drinks at the other side of the room, she knew Dorothy would be devastated when she found out – as she had set her cap at Lyndon. If the truth were known, Lucy too felt a little sore of heart, she had been quietly falling in love with the handsome hedger over the last few weeks. Glancing at the beautiful Mrs Blackwell, it was clear neither of them ever had a hope of competing with her. So, with a sad heart, Lucy decided this morsel of information was best kept to herself, for Lyndon and Mrs Blackwell were still clearly trying to keep their love a secret.

*

Gabriel was a little late arriving with Robbie because the little boy wanted to look at the ducks on the lake, and when he tried to take him through to the nursery the child was reluctant to be left under Nanny's charge in this strange house.

Mary, seeing the little boy's distress knelt to him.

'Hello, Robbie, I'm Mary. Would you like a glass of milk and a biscuit?'

Robbie rubbed his fists into his eyes and shook his head. 'I want to go back to the ducks.'

Mary saw Gabriel's shoulders droop, clearly resigning himself that he would be unable to join the others in the drawing room, so she whispered to Mrs Blair, 'Can I take Robbie down to the lake?'

'I don't see why not. All the buffet food has gone in now and Lucy is keeping a check on the buffet table.'

Mary glanced at Gabriel and mouthed, 'Would you mind if he comes with me?'

Gabriel's face brightened. 'If Robbie wants to go, that is fine by me. Robbie, do you want Mary to take you back to the ducks?'

The little boy's face lit with happiness. 'But where will you be, Papa?' he said anxiously.

'I'm just going to see some friends in the other room. Mary will come for me if you need me.' He looked at Mary as she nodded.

Robbie slipped his little hand into Mary's without a second hesitation, and Gabriel shot her a grateful smile.

'I'll look after him, Gabriel,' Mary said softly.

'I know you will, thank you, Mary.'

*

Throughout the evening, and because the drinks party was a very informal affair, Jenna and Lyndon made no effort to keep apart as they joined their friends in happy company, but neither did they make it apparent that there was anything between them other than friendship. All the while Ellie Blackthorn watched with interest as Jenna chatted amiably with both Lyndon and Gabriel. Both men seemed enamoured with her, though both kept a polite distance - she really could not make out what was happening between these three people. Ellie thought it strange that neither Jenna nor Gabriel mentioned the birthday party they had attended the previous week, therefore she was mindful not to mention it herself. As she had told herself before – this was their business not hers.

*

Gabriel was overjoyed to be able to spend time with Jenna, albeit sharing her with a crowd of other people. He watched her happily engage with everyone and was heartened to see his good friend Lyndon enjoy her company too. He could not wait to introduce Jenna to Lyndon as the woman he hoped to spend his future with. Gabriel smiled to himself – he must stop jumping the gun about her. But oh, he felt like a love sick school boy - the more he looked at her, the more he wanted her to be by his side forever. Justin broke into Gabriel's reverie when he came over to him to introduce Matthew and Hillary.

'Gabriel, we have heard so much about you. We are so sorry to hear of your loss,' Matthew shook his hand.

'Thank you,' he answered graciously. 'It is lovely to make your acquaintance too. May I congratulate you on your marriage.'

Hillary and Matthew exchanged a happy glance. 'We were sorry you couldn't come to the wedding,' Hillary said.

'I thank you for the invite. I was sorry I could not attend, but I had no one I could leave my boisterous six-year-old son with. My parents have very inconveniently gone to the continent for two months,' he joked, 'so it left me in a little bit of a predicament.'

'You need to employ a nanny for your son,' Hillary suggested.

'It might be an idea, *but I might not need one soon*, he mused.

'Where is your son this evening?' Hillary asked.

'Mary, the assistant cook here, is kindly minding him. Having said that, I had better see if she is tiring of him – he can be a bit of a handful. So, are you not planning to go on a honeymoon?'

'Not just yet. Matthew is busy with the harvest at Trevarno, but we are setting off to Italy in a couple of weeks to stay with Justin and Ruby,' Hillary said brightly.

'Italy, how lovely. I hope you have a splendid time.'

When Matthew and Hillary were called away, Justin turned to Gabriel.

'You know you are very welcome to come too. You will have to wait until October though. We have a full house until the 14th but you could catch the ship on the 1st so you will arrive as they leave.'

'Thank you, that is extremely kind of you, but I have Robbie, remember.'

'That is not a problem. It will be an adventure for him – anyway you might have engaged a nanny for him by then. Think about it and send word if you are coming.'

Gabriel was genuinely grateful. 'Thank you, Justin. I will.'

With a spring in his step at the thought of a trip to Italy, Gabriel went in search of Mary and Robbie. He found Robbie curled up on Mary's lap while she read to him, and the sight made his heart catch. It was just as his wife Jane used to sit with him. Robbie had not noticed Gabriel, but Mary looked up and smiled and then went back to reading to him. Suddenly the little boy yawned noisily, and Gabriel stepped forward.

'Time to go home, Robbie, I think?'

Robbie nodded sleepily. 'Can I come and see Mary again?'

'I'm sure you can, yes,' he said lifting him gently from Mary's lap.

'I like Mary, Papa. She smells like Mama.'

Gabriel and Mary exchanged curious glances.

'What did Mama smell of?' he asked tentatively.

'She smelt of apple pie. Just like Mary does.' He rubbed his eyes with his fists and yawned again.

For a split second, Gabriel remembered the apple blossom cologne his wife Jane used, and a lump formed in his throat as he lifted Robbie into his arms and thanked Mary for all she had done tonight.

'It was a pleasure. He is a lovely little boy – thank you for trusting me with him,' Mary whispered.

34

Edna, having been banished from Trevarno to her aunt's house in Hayle, had been charged with the task of helping to look after her aunt's brood of seven children as they stood on the harbour front, helping to salt the recent shoal of pilchards brought in that morning. It was a job she hated.

'Mrs FitzSimmons,' a man's voice sounded behind her.

Edna straightened her back, shocked that someone was using her married name. Lyndon had forbidden her to use it after their marriage was annulled. She looked round to find a man dressed in plain, albeit decent quality clothing. 'Yes?'

'Might I have a word with you?'

'About what?'

'About Jenna Blackwell.'

With her interest piqued, she wiped her stinking, sore hands down her apron and followed the man to the far end of the harbour.

After listening to what he asked of her, she pursed her lips. 'What's in it for me?'

'Justice, my dear. You could help bring about her downfall and part her from her inherited wealth. Wouldn't that be justice enough?'

'I'd rather be paid for my information,' she said thumping her fists into her hips.

'Sorry, Mrs FitzSimmons, it is illegal to pay for evidence. We often find that people who tell us the truth, by proving someone has benefited money illegally – and I believe she has wronged you too, would normally be payment enough. So, I shall bid you good day and I am sorry to have bothered you.'

'Wait,' she said sharply.

The man turned and smiled.

'I have a story for you.'

*

With no social events planned before the book launch party, Jenna and Lyndon had made a conscious decision not to visit each other until then. She did, however, endeavour to send him a love letter and a sketch every few days, so that he knew she was thinking of him. Lyndon in turn received them with delight and duly sent words of love back to her at Loe House.

Jenna did however venture out to Church Cove to attend a picnic with Robbie and Gabriel. Even knowing there was someone about probably watching her at this moment, she decided she was doing nothing wrong, besides the desire to see little Robbie overtook all other worries. After all, how could she be demonised for enjoying the company of a little boy.

There had been a slight break in the weather on the Saturday before the picnic, but although it clouded over and everyone held their breath for much needed rain, only a small shower occurred, and the rain dried on the parched earth the moment it touched it. Sunday, although a little cooler until the sun burnt away the remaining clouds, promised to be another beautiful day. Jenna made up a picnic basket consisting of a selection of tasty sandwiches, and a sponge cake. She had filled a flask of tea and brought with her a bottle of her homemade lemonade for Robbie to drink. It was a spread fit for a king. No sooner had she stepped out of the car and onto the beach she heard Robbie squeal with delight.

'Look, Jenna, I have drawn a picture of you!'

The drawing was of a stick woman with yellow hair. 'Oh, my, Robbie this is beautiful. Did you do it all by yourself?'

'Yes, Papa wanted to help, but I told him it was a special drawing for you so I should do it on my own.'

Jenna's heart constricted. Perhaps she wasn't such an evil person after all, if this lovely little boy could take to her so happily. She looked up at Gabriel who was smiling back at her.

'You have made a big impression on him.'

'He is adorable.' She knelt and put her arms around the little chap.

'I love you,' Robbie whispered in her ear and Jenna felt tears sting at his declaration.

*

At The Poldhu Tea Room, there were celebrations to be had. Betsy and Ryan Penrose had been safely delivered of a son, William, born five days earlier and having his first outing at the tearoom. Everyone was doting on him – well, everyone except Marianne. Gabriel had popped in that morning for a quick cup of coffee and to cancel their usual afternoon table as they were heading off for a picnic at Church Cove.

'With Jenna,' Robbie had chipped in, but Gabriel put his fingers to his lips to silence the child.

Marianne was simmering with jealousy, but aware that Ellie could always pick up on her ever-changing moods, had to pull on all her reserves to keep her feelings under control.

It hadn't worked though. Ellie ever perceptive, was at the end of her tether with Marianne's moods, which normally darkened following Gabriel's visits.

'Now the babe is here, Betsy,' Ellie whispered, 'when are you coming back to us?' There was a desperate plea in her voice.

Betsy grinned, knowing full well why she wanted her back. 'Ah, Ellie, let me have a few weeks to enjoy my new born,' she joked.

'Well don't take too long – I have never murdered anyone before, but there is always a first time.'

*

After building a sandcastle and eating their fill, Robbie was playing happily by himself with the toy truck Jenna had bought him.

'Robbie seems more settled now. I thought with my parents going away he would be upset by the separation from them, but he seems to be adjusting to life now,' Gabriel said.

'And you, how are you adjusting to life without Jane?'

'I'm getting there too. Tell me, Jenna, how long do you think a widower, or widow for that matter, should wait before they try to find a new soul mate in life?'

Jenna smiled inwardly. 'That rather depends on the individual,' she answered looking out to sea. 'And if there is someone willing to take them on.'

Gabriel laughed and followed her gaze.

'What about you, Jenna - will you marry again?'

'Yes.'

'That was a very definite yes.'

'I know I will. What about you?'

'Absolutely,' he gave her a brilliant smile, 'and not just to give Robbie a new mother. I miss the closeness of a life partner. I want to share my life with someone again.'

'I know how you feel. It has been a while for you now, what is it – a year?'

'Yes, I'm ready now, but don't get me wrong – I will never forget Jane, she was a wonderful chapter in my life – I need someone to be the whole book now.'

'That's a nice way of looking at it.' She looked down towards Robbie playing. 'Robbie is a lovely little boy – and so loving, any woman will be lucky to bring him up as her own.'

Gabriel smiled. 'He has certainly taken to you.'

'And I to him.' She placed a friendly hand on his arm. 'And any woman would be lucky to have you as a life partner.'

Very tentatively Gabriel put his hand over hers. 'Thank you.'

Jenna pulled her hand from under his and stood up. 'I must be going now. I have a lot to do before I go away – paintings to finish and ship up to London. I also must arrange a book launch party for James's posthumously published novel. Quite a few of his friends are coming down to stay. You're very welcome to come – it's on Tuesday 2nd September from six until eight.'

'I will, thank you, can I bring Robbie?'

'Of course. After all you come as a team. I do wish it were on another day though, I'm leaving Cornwall for a few weeks on the 3rd.'

'A few weeks!' he said dismayed.

'Eight to be exact. I will be away until mid-October.'

'Goodness, but that is a long time – how shall we endure the separation?'

'It's nice to think I'll be missed, thank you.' She smiled as they packed the remnants of the picnic back into the basket.

'Robbie, come and give me a big hug,' she said holding her arms out to him and Robbie kissed her on the cheek. 'I shall see you again very soon.'

Robbie looked up at her with sad eyes. 'I'm missing you already.'

'Bless you, darling.' She ruffled his hair.

*

Gabriel too felt desolate as he watched her drive off. If it was mid-October before she came back from her holiday – that was when he was meant to be going to Italy. Perhaps he would postpone the trip until next year – for he did not want to spend the next few months without her.

*

With the previous day's picnic running through his mind, Gabriel was in a happy mood that Monday as he stood back, arms folded looking at the work he had done in the French drawing room. The work was coming along nicely and hopefully he would be finished mid-September, though he was loathe to leave this beautiful house. He enjoyed the quick and lively banter in the kitchen and looked on them all as good friends – including Sarah and Peter. He missed Justin now he had gone to Italy though, but at least he had Lyndon to share a glass of ale in The Wheel Inn with. He could also speak openly to Lyndon about Jenna and the few things he and Robbie had done with her - though he still had not disclosed her name to him. That was something he would not do until he and Jenna had come to a formal arrangement and their relationship could move on from friendship to love.

He glanced out of the window, and noting that Mary was carrying a tea tray out to the garden, he realised that it must be three o clock! Most afternoons, he would meet her down the garden, share a quick chat with her and then he would take his tea down to the barn where he would work on for another hour on the memorial stone for Thomas. He just had a few more days to put the finishing touches to the stone. Feeling a glow of pride at the thought of his work, he knew Mary was going to be so happy when she saw it. Peter and Sarah had secretly arranged a special tea for the following Monday to celebrate Thomas's life after the unveiling of the stone. He was sure it would give Mary some closure on all the dreadful things that had happened over the last three years. Gabriel had found he was very protective of Mary. They had helped each other through quite a few wobbles in their shared recovery from grief. She was so good with Robbie too. He had brought him up to Bochym on Saturday afternoon to see Mary again, and Sarah had allowed them to take a boat out onto the lake – Robbie had been in his element - he seemed to love Mary as much as he did Jenna. If only he could find someone like Mary to be Robbie's full-time governess, as Hillary had suggested. For sure they could not live with his parents down here forever and he would have to move back to his London house eventually. A governess – someone who Robbie liked - would fill the gap left by his mother and she could continue to look after Robbie even when Jenna became his wife. Perhaps he would set about searching for someone quite soon.

*

Marianne was visiting Lucy again and they were just returning from a walk from the arboretum when they saw

Mary heading for the garden with a tea tray. Marianne scowled and was even more disgruntled when she saw Gabriel practically running from the main house to meet Mary in the garden.

'I see Mary is still getting preferential treatment by being allowed to go into the garden.'

'Oh, stop your griping, Marianne,' Lucy snapped. 'What have you got against her. She's had a rotten time of late.'

'Loads of women have lost their husbands, but they don't get to take their tea in the gardens at Bochym. I'd love to have a walk around them,' she said petulantly.

'It's not just her grief, I told you, she's been quite poorly,' Lucy defended her.

'With that so-called food poisoning, you mean!' Marianne parried with a shake to her head.

Lucy turned her head away, and Marianne narrowed her eyes.

'I don't believe it, you know. I think something else happened!'

When Lucy wouldn't look at her, Marianne pulled her back to face her.

'Something else did happen, didn't it?'

'Oh, for goodness' sake, Marianne. Stop this at once. I know you're jealous of Mary because she sees more of Gabriel than you do. I'm not daft you know – you don't come up to see me, it's Gabriel you come to see, but he is busy at the moment, so you're out of luck.'

'Busy with Mary, yes!' Marianne folded her arms. 'Well, she is barking up the wrong tree there, because Gabriel has his sights set on someone else.'

'Who? You? I don't think so, Marianne.' Lucy's anger matched Marianne's now. 'You might be clever and lovely to look at, but Gabriel would never be interested in someone with a jealous personality like you have. I'm even surprised at Jake Treen's constant adoration for you. How he cannot see your faults, I do not know, because you have many of them.'

'That is an awful thing to say to me, you're supposed to be my friend. Anyway, what has Jake Treen got to do with anything.'

'If you would just open your eyes and be a bit nicer, you would see he is the perfect man for you. Forget about Gabriel – he is not for you.'

'He flipping well is! And I am not going to let Mary or Mrs Jenna Blackwell get in my way.'

'What?'

'There see, you think you know everything, but you didn't know about her, did you?'

'Now *you are* barking up the wrong tree! There is nothing going on between Jenna Blackwell and Gabriel.'

Marianne lifted her chin. 'Oh, you think not, eh?'

'I know for a fact!' Lucy snapped.

'Oh, another secret you're keeping from me, is it?'

'I'm going in, Marianne. I would rather like you to go home, and not come back until you can be a nicer person.'

*

On Tuesday morning, the weather broke with a terrific thunderstorm. Lyndon watched the sky darken, and when the low rumble of thunder began to work its way up the valley, he left his work to fetch Bramble in from the fields. The horse had always been troubled with thunderstorms, and Lyndon had spent many a storm with Bramble's head poking into the back of his wagon, while he circled her neck with his arms and spoke soothing words to calm her.

By the time Lyndon got her to the stables, a terrific crack of thunder broke overhead, which made them both shudder. Lyndon knew the signs - he was going to have an episode and turned wide eyed at the groomsmen for help.

Realising something was wrong with Lyndon, the groomsman ran for Joe who duly arrived to take control. Only after the groomsman assured Lyndon that he would take care of Bramble, did Lyndon follow Joe back through the kitchen and into his office, all the while trying to avert his eyes from everyone.

Joe locked the office door, just as another loud crack of thunder resonated through the manor.

Lyndon sat down and held his head in his hands. 'Oh god, Joe,' he said trembling from head to foot.

'It's all right, my friend, I'm with you.' Joe rested his hand on Lyndon's shoulder. 'Just remember its thunder, nothing more. We're all safe - nothing will harm you.'

The storm lasted for ten minutes and when Lyndon finally lifted his head, there were fearful tears in his eyes, and he felt drained and sick to the pit of his stomach.

Joe had prepared a headache draft for him to take and smiled gently as he pushed it towards him.

'Thank you,' Lyndon said sincerely, wiping the tears away with the back of his hand.

Joe nodded. 'That is what comrades do – they look after each other, but I seriously think you need to think about going to Devon for some treatment. It cured me!'

35

At Bochym a letter of apology came for Lucy. Marianne had gone home in a huff on Monday and spent twenty-four hours fighting with her inner self about the cruel words Lucy had said to her. In the end, she conceded – Lucy had been right, she was without doubt moody and jealous, but that was only because she loved Gabriel! However, falling out with Lucy over it was not the best card she had ever played. If she didn't go up to Bochym Manor on her days off anymore, she wouldn't be able to see Gabriel as much - even though when she did, it was from afar. Not only that, but she would also miss Mrs Blair's lovely tea and cake. So, on Tuesday evening she penned her letter and on Friday she received a reply.

Apology accepted – we are having a special tea on Monday. I will see you then.

Lucy x

*

Mrs Blair and Mary had been busier in the kitchen than normal on Monday morning because His Lord and Her Ladyship had requested a special high tea.

'Who is coming today, Mr Treen?' Mary asked.

'I think it's a surprise, Mary,' Joe said with a wink to Mrs Blair.

'Well, they are pushing the boat out – there is a deal of fancy food here! It must be for someone special.'

At three o clock that afternoon, Mary wiped her hands down her apron as the last plate of food was laid out in the library.

'Nobody has arrived yet,' Mary whispered to Mrs Blair. 'Perhaps it was so secret they forgot to tell the person to come.'

Sarah, Peter, and Gabriel came into the room and Mary and Mrs Blair bobbed a curtsy to them.

'All ready?' Peter asked Cook.

'Yes, my lord.'

'Mary, could you take off your apron?' Sarah asked.

Mary looked down to see if her apron was splashed with something, it was relatively clean, but she did as she was asked.

'Lead the way, Gabriel,' Peter said. 'Come on, Mary, Mrs Blair, we'll meet the others outside.'

Mary was puzzled, wondering where she was going. Outside, the rest of the staff had gathered at the gates to the front garden and Gabriel beckoned Mary through the gate to follow Peter and Sarah. She turned and looked at Joe and mouthed, 'What's happening?'

'We will all see in a moment.'

At the bottom of the garden, they all veered left towards the enclosed rose garden – the fragrance there was overpowering. They stopped in the corner of the garden where a sheet had been hung over something. A hush ensued but for the sound of bees buzzing in the flowers and the birds twittering high in the trees. Everyone drank in the sound of peace. Gabriel stepped forwards placing his arm gently around Mary's shoulders.

'Pull the sheet, Mary.'

'Me?' She looked around, and everyone smiled and nodded. Glancing back at Gabriel, he gestured her forward, and tentatively she grasped the cotton sheet and tugged.

Her hands flew to her mouth and she cried out, as the beautiful granite memorial stone was unveiled.

IN LOVING MEMORY OF THOMAS ELLIS
1896 - 1916
AGED 22
BELOVED HUSBAND OF MARY & FATHER OF JAMES
A TRUE FRIEND AND HERO TO ALL WHO KNEW HIM.
R.I.P

Falling to her knees, her trembling fingers reached out to trace his name on the stone.

'Oh, Thomas,' she wept, as Gabriel, Peter and Joe began to sing the words to Thomas's favourite poem by William Blake to the tune composed by Sir Hubert Parry.

And did those feet in ancient time
Walk upon England's mountains green?
And was the holy Lamb of God
On England's pleasant pastures seen?
And did the Countenance Divine
Shine forth upon our clouded hills?
And was Jerusalem builded here
Among these dark Satanic mills?
Bring me my bow of burning gold:
Bring me my arrows of desire:
Bring me my spear: O clouds unfold!
Bring me my chariot of fire.
I will not cease from mental fight,
Nor shall my sword sleep in my hand
Till we have built Jerusalem
In England's green and pleasant land

By mid-song, everyone had joined in to sing their hearts out for Thomas, while Mary wept openly for the man she loved, and who she now knew would be remembered for the hero he was by anyone seeing this plaque.

Gradually their voices fell away and the garden once again fell silent but for the sound of the birds and the bees. Sarah moved to kneel beside Mary and pointed to the white roses each side of the stone.

'The stone was specially carved by Gabriel, Mary, and these roses, have been personally selected by Mr Hubbard the gardener who also kindly sourced them for us. This one is called *Thomas* and this one here is called *At peace*. Thomas will never be forgotten by those of us who knew and loved him. Now, take your time with Thomas, but then please come and join us in the library for a celebration of his life.'

Mary turned tearfully to address everyone. 'Thank you, my lady, my lord, Gabriel, Mr Hubbard, and to everyone who is here today. Thank you. You have all been so kind and this has made me so happy – I never thought I would feel happy again or deserve such kindness after....'

Sarah, put her finger to her lips to quieten her from saying more, so Mary lowered her head and turned back to her Thomas.

*

Marianne had stood at the back throughout the proceedings as she was not one of the household. She narrowed her eyes – wondering what Mary was going to say before Her Ladyship stopped her. What did Mary mean when she said, '...or deserve such kindness after....?' She thought back to the time she had stepped into the breach when Mary fell ill - it could only mean one thing, and she knew then that Lucy and all the others in the household were keeping a shocking secret from her.

When everyone peeled off to go back to the house, Marianne stepped forward and put her hand on Gabriel's sleeve. 'I'll walk back to the house with you, Gabriel.'

'Thank you, Marianne, but I shall sit here and wait for Mary,' he whispered as he settled on the ornate bench.

'Then I shall wait too.' She settled herself next to him.

'No,' he said quite sharply. 'Go back to the house with the others.' With a gentle hand he made her move from where she was seated and sent her on her way.

As she stomped indignantly up the garden after the others, she looked back, just in time to see Gabriel put a comforting arm around Mary as she sat beside him. Once again, a curl of jealousy engulfed her.

It was about ten minutes before Mary arrived back with Gabriel and the celebration of Thomas's life began. Toasts with cups of tea were made and everyone shared a happy story about Thomas. All the while, Marianne sat quietly watching the friendly interaction between Lyndon and Gabriel. Her lip curled scornfully - Lyndon would not be so pally with Gabriel if he knew that Gabriel was planning to sweep his long-time secret sweetheart away from him. It would serve Mary right as well when it all came out, she mused, watching Mary gaze admiringly upon Gabriel. Silly girl - did she really think that Gabriel would be remotely interested in *her*? Well, she decided, the sooner everything was out in the open, and both men had seen Jenna Blackwell for the deceiver that she was, they would both drop her like a hot stone, Mary would be back in her place, and she, Marianne, would be there to pick up the pieces and offer Gabriel comfort.

*

A week later, on Tuesday the 2nd of September, Lyndon had packed the wagon to go back to Trevarno, and to get ready for the trip to Italy the next day. He had told the household staff at the weekend that he had secured work near Penzance and that he would be gone from Bochym Manor for eight weeks. Dorothy could not hide her distress at his impending departure, having looked forward to holding him in her arms at the harvest dance. Lucy though, had looked straight at him, as though she could see through the lie and knew exactly where he was really going. He dismissed this thought - she could not possibly know, only the group he was going with knew, as it had to be kept a secret.

Everyone was busy when he left, so it was only Joe, Mrs Blair, and Mary to see him off. Fortunately, Gabriel had taken a couple of days off work from the manor, so Lyndon did not have to reiterate his lie to him about where he was going. Lying did not sit easily on his conscience.

'Hurry back, my friend,' Joe slapped him on his back, 'you have become part of the household here – we will all miss you. Are you going straight to Penzance?'

'No, home to Trevarno and then onto Gunwalloe to that book launch with Matthew and Hillary – the one Mrs Blackwell is holding for James Blackwell's posthumously published novel.'

'Ah, yes, the Earl and Countess are going too. Well, farewell, Lyndon. We will see you in eight weeks.'

*

Lyndon was just approaching Helston when he fumbled in his jacket pocket for a handkerchief and found a stamped letter there. It must have come to Bochym for him, and somebody had popped it in his pocket. Checking the road ahead was clear, he unfolded the letter, noting that it had been written in a fine hand.

Dear Mr FitzSimmons,
Please forgive the nature of this letter, it is kindly meant, but I feel you must be made aware of a situation escalating that could potentially bring you a great deal of heartache. Mrs Jenna Blackwell has been meeting Gabriel Trelease on a regular basis in Church Cove and has been seen out with him in a social capacity. It is my understanding that Mr Trelease has been overheard discussing the prospect of marriage to Mrs Blackwell as soon as she is out of mourning.
Yours, a well-wisher.

'What?' Lyndon re-read the letter in disbelief. He looked up at the road ahead, trying to process everything. Gabriel and Jenna? No! But then had Gabriel not told him about his hopes of a future with his widow? Had he not told him that he met her on the beach and even invited her to tea? A burning anger engulfed him. Damn the man! He screwed the letter into a ball but did not throw it away. Was Gabriel laughing at him - making a fool of him, was Jenna doing the same? All these weeks, she had kept him at bay with her excuses, and all the time had she been meeting Gabriel? A motor car suddenly overtook the wagon and honked at him. He had taken his mind off the road and strayed over into the middle! Bramble whinnied crossly, tossed her head, and reared up.

'Whoa there, girl,' Lyndon pulled on the reins to try and calm the normally placid animal, but she reared again, snorted, and pawed the ground bringing up a cloud of dust from the road. He quickly jumped down and grabbed her bridle, stroked her head, and spoke soft words of calmness to the agitated beast. 'I know, girl, I know, you're angry, we both are, but hush now, be calm.' Lyndon was not too sure whether his words were just for his horse. When Bramble settled, Lyndon climbed aboard the wagon with the weight of the world once again on his shoulders.

36

After settling Bramble in her field at Trevarno, Lyndon made straight for his cottage, hoping that he had not been seen by his father or Gina. He needed time to think - to process his future now. God damn it he was meant to be going to Italy with Jenna tomorrow! It was meant to be their chance to be together at last – to see if they still fitted into each other's life! How could he go now, knowing what he did? The rational side of his brain told him not to jump to conclusions – a well-wisher letter normally came from a disgruntled soul who had been hurt in the past and wanted to pass that hurt on. Edna perhaps? But no, her handwriting was more of a scrawl. So, who? It was more likely to be from someone Gabriel had scorned - though knowing Gabriel's personality - as he thought he did, Lyndon was not sure Gabriel would consciously do anything to hurt anyone. He laughed sardonically at that notion – feeling his own pain from Gabriel's actions. But who knew there was a link between the three of them? Lyndon searched his memory to see if he had ever mentioned Jenna to Gabriel – he was sure he had not. So, wait a moment, if Gabriel did not know of Lyndon's attachment to Jenna, his conduct could not be condemned by him – but Jenna's damn well could if this letter was to be taken seriously. A knock came to the door and Lyndon almost leapt out of his skin. Then he felt it - the familiar onset of another episode. He walked cautiously to the door, his hand shaking as he turned the handle. There on the threshold, with a suitcase in hand, was Matthew. He saw at once the signs of panic in Lyndon's face and dropped the suitcase he was carrying and put his arm around his friend's shoulder.

'Christ! Have I brought this on by knocking? I knew I should have just called out and stepped through, you would not have minded, would you?' he said as he helped

Lyndon to the chair by the table. 'Let me get you a drink, do you want a drink?'

Lyndon shook his head. 'I'll be fine, it'll pass. It's not going to be a full-blown episode, now I know it's you and I'm in no danger.'

'Lyndon, let me pay for your treatment in Devon where Joe Treen went?'

Lyndon shook his head. 'You have already laid out money for me to go on this trip to Italy. I'm already deeply indebted to you.'

'You are not indebted to me at all! The ticket to Italy is a gift from one friend to another. I told you, over the years your friendship had given me much more than money can buy. Now, whether you like it or not, I am going to arrange for you to go to Devon on our return. You owe it to yourself to get better, for both you and Jenna before you start your life together.'

Lyndon laughed without humour, and Matthew regarded him curiously.

'Your derisive laugh concerns me. What's the matter? Very soon you and Jenna will be together.'

'Will we, Matthew? Are you absolutely sure about that?'

'Yes. Do you doubt it?' Puzzlement was evident in his face and voice.

Lyndon stayed silent - not ready to disclose what he had just learned without first seeing for himself.

'This holiday will seal your relationship again, Lyndon. It will heal the wounds that have harmed you both in the past. You just need time alone together and spending a month in the sun away from everything here will be just the tonic. Now, speaking of which, here, I've brought a suitcase for you as you said you didn't have a decent one. Inside there are a couple of pairs of light cotton trousers of mine which no longer fit but should fit you. You will need light coloured clothes to wear - for the heat is ferocious out there - even in September.'

Lyndon nodded a thank you.

'Are you worried about the holiday?'

Lyndon shrugged.

'You will have the time of your life.'

Will I? All he really wanted at this moment in time was to be left alone with his thoughts.

'We'll pick you up at five thirty to go to the book launch.'

'I'm not really sure it's my kind of thing,' he said weakly.

'Have you ever been to one?'

'No.'

'Then how do you know it's not your kind of thing. Anyway, we need to support Jenna. Hillary said she is nervous about hosting it without James. It will just be a few people who like books – I seem to remember you used to read James's books while at the front.'

'I did and I never expected to come home to find the love of my life married to him,' he said acidly.

Matthew frowned. 'Jenna would never have married him if she had known you were alive. It's really time to sweep the past under the table now. I will leave you to your packing.'

*

Jenna had been busy all day preparing for the book launch. She had sixteen guests coming, many of them James's friends who often frequented Loe House. Celia Inman, her housekeeper would accommodate six of them at Toy Cottage, the rest of them would make their way back to their own homes afterwards. Jenna would normally have bedded down a few in Loe House, but as she would be setting off for Italy the next morning, she could not really accommodate anyone and it would be unfair on Celia as she would be busy with her own guests at Toy Cottage.

*

When Lyndon arrived at Loe House, he tried at once to speak with Jenna, but she was much in demand by everyone. She had greeted him with her usual warm smile and kissed him warmly on the cheek, whispering in his ear, 'Not long now,' and then she had been whisked off in another direction.

Hillary had pushed a drink into his hand, and he realised he must patiently wait his turn. Trying his best to relax, he spent the next hour with Matthew who must have seen his unease, because he kept him engaged by speaking about the changes he wanted to implement at Trevarno on their return from Italy. When Matthew was pulled away to speak to another group, the house emptied as everyone made their way out onto the terrace. Lyndon glanced around this comfortable house of James's - now Jenna's - and found it to be richly furnished with a well-worn homely feel to it. Could he envisage himself sitting in one of those easy chairs by the fireside one day? Or was it Gabriel who would be sitting there! He struggled to tamp down his rising discontent now he had thought of the letter again and began to study the painting over the mantelpiece. It was one of Jenna's early work, but there was that same feeling of being drawn into the landscape - something she had perfected over the last few months. His attention was diverted from the painting when he heard a small child shout, 'Jenna.' He looked up to find Gabriel's son Robbie hugging Jenna and she in turn had her arms lovingly around the child. It was then he saw Gabriel and felt an unfamiliar curl of resentment against a man who had become a good friend to him these last few weeks. Swallowing hard, to tamp down the sick feeling in the pit of his stomach, he watched as Jenna greeted Gabriel as warmly as she had greeted him. Oh god! What *was* happening here?

'Lyndon,' Matthew called over to him. 'Come on, Jenna is going to make her speech on the terrace.'

*

Outside, Hillary had passed around a copy of the book to everyone; she stopped the gramophone, and chinked a glass with a spoon to gain everyone's attention. Jenna stood nervously on the top terrace of Loe House gardens, and everyone turned to watch her address

Smiling nervously, she held a copy of the book close to her heart. 'Thank you all for coming here tonight, to celebrate the launch of this book,' she lifted it up, 'Our Days In the Sun,' - James's new, and final novel.' Jenna felt the words catch in her throat. 'If James were here, he would of course make a splendid speech - he would also be well down a decent bottle of claret by now! That man knew how to party,' she added with a smile. 'I knew him only briefly, but he changed my life and I know from speaking to his friends he changed their lives too. He was one in a million. An officer, a gentleman and one of the nicest people I have ever met, and I miss him dreadfully, as do we all.' Jenna glanced at Hillary and smiled sympathetically when she saw she was weeping. 'James was desperate to finish this novel during his last few days on this earth. He worked day and well into the night, to finish it, and I know he was immensely proud of it. When I received the books from his publisher to give to you all, I was thrilled to find that he had dedicated the book to me, of which *I* am immensely honoured.'

Jenna's eyes cut to Lyndon who was standing close by. She saw him turn to the dedication page which read,

"For Jenna - the woman who rescued me from bachelorhood.
Go forth, my darling girl, live life and write the next great love story for me."

Jenna knew the meaning behind the words - James was telling the world that he wanted his wife to go out and find happiness again. Shooting a surreptitious smile at Lyndon, she noted that when he lifted his eyes to meet hers, for reasons unbeknown to her, they did not smile back at her. Jenna held the book aloft in one hand and raised a glass of champagne in the other.

'To the genius who was James Blackwell – he will live on forever in his books.'

'To James,' everyone said and raised their glasses.

*

Lyndon watched as Jenna melted into the crowd of people again – how was he ever going to get a chance to speak to her – for speak to her he must. Tomorrow they were to set off to Italy first thing in the morning. How could he contemplate spending eight whole weeks with her if this rumour were true? Even if she denied it, would he believe her? His heart lurched when he saw she had moved towards Gabriel Trelease and his young son who were standing near the balustrade overlooking the sea. Something compelled him to move closer, but he faltered when he heard their conversation.

*

Jenna leant on the balustrade and looked out to sea. The sun was setting, leaving a great orange split in the sky near the horizon. Clouds of midges danced in the twilight and the gentle wash of waves on the shingle beach made a soothing shush sound.

Gabriel turned to smile at her. 'Well done, Jenna, you make a great orator.'

She shook her head. 'I was shaking in my shoes.'

Little Robbie swapped places and stood between them, his little hand searching for Jenna's. Jenna smiled down at the boy and curled her hand around his.

'Two months away, Jenna! We're going to miss you terribly, aren't we, Robbie?'

The boy nodded sadly and put his thumb in his mouth, to which Gabriel pulled it away.

'Hurry back to us, won't you?' He turned and gazed intently into Jenna's eyes.

'I'm sure you'll find someone else to build sandcastles with on the beach.'

'You're the only sandcastle builder we want, isn't that right, Robbie?'

'Yes,' he answered and tugged on her hand. 'Are you going to be my new mama when you come back?'

Gabriel gave an embarrassed laugh, just as Jenna heard a sharp intake of breath behind her. She turned around, but all she could see was the back of someone retreating through the throng of people.

Gabriel chided Robbie for his embarrassing question and apologised profusely to Jenna.

'It's fine, Gabriel,' she smiled and crouched down to Robbie's level. 'I promise that when I come back, sweetheart, I shall meet you on the beach again to build sandcastles.'

Robbie put his arms around Jenna's neck and whispered, 'I'd like you to be my new mama.'

Jenna glanced up at Gabriel and gave him a mournful look, he in turn mouthed again that he was sorry.

*

Lyndon had barrelled through the crowd of people, this heart hammering in his chest, trying to analyse what he'd just heard. Only the other day, he had spoken to Gabriel, who had told him the widow he had been seeing would make a wonderful mother for his son and a perfect wife for him. *Oh God! What the hell is going on here? And right under my nose! They are taking me for a fool!*

'Lyndon,' Matthew caught his arm as he made his way to the door, 'where are you going in such a hurry?'

'Home, I need to go home.'

Matthew gave him a searching look. 'Are you feeling unwell? You very nearly had an episode earlier.'

Lyndon nodded.

'Come on then. We have an early start in the morning, I was just saying we should go soon to Hillary. Give me a moment to say my goodbyes.'

Lyndon then saw Jenna walking with Gabriel and his son, so he ducked in the shadows out of sight. When they got to the door, Jenna turned to Gabriel.

'Well, goodnight,' she said kissing Gabriel gently on the cheek before bending down to kiss the child. 'I'll see you very soon, sweetheart,' she said to the tearful child.

Robbie put his arms around her neck and hugged her as though his little life depended on it.

'Come on, Robbie, the sooner we let Jenna go, the sooner she'll be back with us,' Gabriel said as he walked out of the door.

As Jenna waved them off and turned to go back inside, Lyndon balled his fists in annoyance as he stepped out of the shadows to join Matthew and Hillary who too were making their way to the door.

Jenna smiled brightly at them all. 'Are you making a move too,' she asked.

'I think we must, early start and all that!' Matthew said, but Lyndon remained resolutely quiet by his side.

Jenna kissed Matthew and Hillary and then reached for Lyndon's hand.

'I'll see you in the morning, Lyndon,' she whispered, kissing him as chastely as she had the others, but Lyndon could not respond to her, and gave a curt nod before walking away.

Matthew must have noted his reaction because as he moved away, Lyndon heard Matthew say to Jenna, 'I believe Lyndon is tired. He almost had one of his episodes earlier when I inadvertently made him jump. We will look after him though, and he will be fine after a good night's sleep.'

*

Thankfully, everyone else in the party followed suit, and those staying at Toy Cottage with Celia Inman set off to finish the night at The Halzhephron Inn. All Jenna was left with was the debris of the party and a strange feeling that all was not well between her and Lyndon.

37

It was, Hillary declared, an unearthly hour to be out and about – but needs must for them to catch the train to Southampton and then to board their ship later that day. Hillary paced the road in front of Holme Farm like a caged lion as she waited for Matthew to come back with Lyndon - who should have been there when the car came. When Matthew rounded the corner of the garden, his face was full of consternation.

'What is it? What's the matter? Where is Lyndon?'

'He's coming now, but not without a great deal of persuasion. Has something happened between him and Jenna, do you know?'

'Nothing that I am aware of, no,' she said, getting into the car.

'He was adamant that Jenna would not want him to come, but refused to tell me why,' Matthew said, running his hands distractedly through his hair until it stood on end.

Hillary gave a half smile, licked her fingers, and plastered his hair back down neatly.

'In the end, I told him I would never speak to him again, if he didn't get in this car.'

'Ooh!' she pouted, 'I do love it when you are forceful.'

Lyndon arrived a few seconds later to a quick rebuff from Hillary and they finally got on their way.

*

Jake had driven Jenna to the train station that morning. He had been told that she would be in London for the next eight weeks.

There was a flurry of excited kisses, when she met with Hillary and Matthew, though Jenna detected a marked reserve in Lyndon's greeting. The foursome shared a compartment and talk was lively - mostly about the success of the party the previous night.

'Have you read the book yet, Jenna?' Hillary asked, 'I've brought mine with me to read on the boat.'

'I haven't, no. The publishers sent me a proof, but I have been too busy painting, I've not had time to read it.'

Lyndon snorted and everyone looked at him. He must have realised everyone had noted his derisory interjection, because he quickly sniffed and made to rub his nose as though something was irritating it.

'Are you all right, old chap,' Matthew said putting down his paper.

'Fine,' he answered, closing the conversation.

'I've brought my book too. I think James would have been rather pleased with his book launch party,' Jenna said, her eyes cutting to Lyndon who made no comment.

'It was almost as if he was there - it was such a James gathering,' Hillary mused. 'God but I miss him with every fibre of my body.'

Jenna nodded and saw Lyndon shift uncomfortably. She must make a concerted effort not to chat about James too much in his company. He may have brought them together, but Jenna was painfully aware that he was a thorn in Lyndon's side.

'It was nice of James to dedicate the book to you Jenna.' Hillary smiled.

'Yes, it was, I had no idea.'

'Do you think he was telling you and Lyndon to go and write the next great love story, or are you planning to take up the pen?'

'I think he very much wants me to have love in my life again.' Jenna smiled and glanced at Lyndon, but he didn't smile back. 'Are you sure you're all right, Lyndon,' she asked nervously, 'Matthew said you very nearly had another episode yesterday.'

'I'm fine,' he snapped and turned to look out of the window.

Wounded, Jenna looked at Matthew, who pulled his mouth into a tight line and shrugged.

Eventually Lyndon closed his eyes, and whether he was sleeping or not, they heard no more conversation from him until they arrived at Southampton.

*

There was a change in the weather by midday Wednesday. A cool breeze was blowing up Poldhu valley and there was a slight hint of rain in the air. The ground needed rain - the hot dry spell had lasted most of July and all of August. What the farmers did not need though was torrential rain like the thunderstorm they'd had the previous week – that would flatten the harvest! So, everyone watched the skies with trepidation.

Gabriel sat down to the midday dinner in the kitchen at Bochym with the others that day and glanced at Dorothy who had a face like a wet weekend.

'Goodness, Dorothy, whatever is the matter?' Gabriel asked, as Mrs Blair brought the teapot to the table.

'She's pining for the loss of Lyndon,' Lucy said, and Dorothy glared at her.

'Why, were has he gone?'

'To work somewhere else. Did he not tell you?' Joe asked. 'He said he got word of another job on Saturday and told us all then.'

'No, but of course I've been off four days, I did see him briefly last night at the book launch and he never mentioned it.'

Joe scratched his chin. 'How strange. Perhaps he thought he'd told you.'

'He'll be gone for eight whole weeks!' Dorothy moaned.

'Eight weeks!' Gabriel laughed. 'How strange, everyone seems to be going away for eight weeks all of a sudden.'

'Who else is?' Joe tipped his head.

'Oh, just someone I know,' Gabriel answered, picking up his knife and fork.

'Where has Lyndon gone then, for eight weeks? That is quite a big job!' Gabriel asked presently.

'Somewhere near Penzance,' Joe answered.

'Somewhere in Italy more like,' Lucy mumbled.

Everyone turned to look at her.

'What did you say, Lucy?' Juliet asked.

'Nothing,' Lucy answered, embarrassed to have spoken aloud.

'Yes, you did, you said he'd gone to Italy,' Dorothy persisted. 'Why would you say that?'

Everyone around the table waited for her to answer.

'Well?' Joe asked.

'I overheard Lyndon speaking about it to Matthew and Hillary Bickford at the drinks party.'

Joe nodded. 'Yes, I believe they are going to Italy for a belated honeymoon, they are staying with Justin and Ruby,'.

Lucy took a deep breath. 'Well, I believe that Lyndon is going too…. with Mrs Blackwell.'

'What?' Joe said in astonishment.

Gabriel felt the colour had drained from his face and he suddenly lost his appetite.

'I overheard Mr Justin say that everyone would be in Italy by the 17th of September and that Lyndon and Mrs Blackwell could be together at last.'

'Why did you not tell me this,' Dorothy said affronted. 'Instead of letting me fawn all over him like a love sick idiot!'

'Sorry,' Lucy mouthed.

'So, Jenna Blackwell is Lyndon's secret lady friend?' Juliet said.

Gabriel's eyes cut to Lucy for confirmation and felt a curl of despair form in his stomach.

'I suspect so by the way they were talking,' Lucy answered.

'Were they speaking openly about this?' Juliet asked.

'No, they were whispering about it, but I overhead them when I was replenishing the buffet table.'

Dorothy, crestfallen, dropped her head in her hands and groaned.

'Then perhaps you should not have shared this news with us until Lyndon was ready to tell us, Lucy,' Joe berated.

'Well, it just slipped out and then you all made me tell you,' Lucy said sullenly.

Mary and Cook placed plates of dinner in front of everyone, but Gabriel had heard enough. 'Excuse me,' he said, getting up quickly.

Everyone looked up, but Gabriel was out of the back door before anyone could ask if he was all right or not.

Mary watched as Gabriel set off across the kitchen courtyard and knew something was amiss.

'May I go after Gabriel,' Mrs Blair, 'I think something has upset him!'

'Yes, but don't be long, we'll need to clear the dinner table soon.'

*

Mary found Gabriel in the front garden, down by the avenue of lime trees, sat on a bench with his head in his hands. She approached him cautiously. 'Gabriel, are you quite well?'

He dropped his hands to his lap, but when he lifted his head, she saw that his face was stricken.

'Oh, deary me,' she knelt beside him, 'I fear you are not at all well.'

'Oh Mary, I'm not ill, it's just….,' he shook his head, 'I think I have been such a fool.'

Mary sighed gently and placed her hand over his, 'Oh well, you're in good company then.'

He smiled at her through his anguish.

'Was it what Lucy said about Mrs Blackwell?'

Gabriel looked at her questioningly.

'It's just that Robbie mentioned someone called Jenna when I looked after him the evening of the drinks party for Mr Justin. He said I was kind like Jenna and told me that he loved her as much as his mama, he also said he thought you loved her too.'

Gabriel lowered his eyes. 'I thought I did, and I have clearly got that little boy's hopes up as well.'

Mary frowned. 'I fear, Mrs Blackwell has been unkind to you both to do this.'

'No,' he said gently, 'there was no promise between us.' He rubbed his face with his hands and took a deep breath. 'I think perhaps I have read too much into her interest in us. Now I think of it, the relationship I had with her was all in my mind.'

'I'm sorry for you Gabriel.'

'No disrespect to my wife – whom I loved dearly, but I wanted so much to feel a woman in my arms again.'

'I understand that feeling. My arms are open for you, Gabriel, if you need holding, until you find your soulmate, as yours were for me when I needed to feel a man's arms around me.'

He looked deep into her eyes as he lifted his hand to cup her face. 'Mary, you are so full of goodness. I'm so glad I have you to speak to.'

She placed her hand over his. 'I feel the same about you, Gabriel. You helped me through the worst time of my life. I'm here for you if you need me.'

Without a moment's hesitation, he wrapped his arms around her thin body and sighed.

His warm body against hers made Mary aware of something she had not felt for a long time – a tingle of desire, and a yearning to be loved again. It would not happen of course, but she felt as though her grief was lifting ever so slightly, and it was all because of the help this wonderful man in her arms had given her.

A cloud of soft mizzle had begun to drift across the valley, coating the grass with tiny jewel-like drops.

'I think you should go in,' Gabriel said presently.

'And you?'

'I'll go home, I think. Tell the others I had a sudden headache, would you?'

'I will.' She smiled gently and as she got up he reached for her hand.

'Thank you for being here for me, Mary.'

*

Gabriel climbed into his car but did not start the engine. He looked out of the windscreen at the bleak day before him – the weather matched his mood. All his future hopes and dreams of a life with Jenna had dissolved in an instant. She was in Italy with his good friend Lyndon – he would be living the life Gabriel hoped for. He dropped his head in his hands again thinking back to the many times he had spoken to Lyndon about Jenna and how much in love he was with her, all thankfully without disclosing her name. At least that was one consolation – Lyndon would never know Gabriel had coveted his sweetheart. Goodness, but it was going to be so hard seeing them together when they got back. Perhaps it was time to return to London – he was not sure he wanted to visit Justin and Ruby's villa in Italy, now he knew that was where Lyndon and Jenna had gone to rekindle their love affair.

38

At Southampton docks, they boarded the vessel to take them to Naples and were shown their cabins. Matthew and Hillary to their executive honeymoon cabin, and Lyndon and Jenna to their equally lavish respective cabins where they were shown where their life jackets were stored. Once they had deposited their belongings, they joined the rest of the passengers to wave goodbye to England.

The captain's voice came over the public address system, informing passengers that they would commence their voyage at seventeen hundred hours and that there would be a safety drill and roll call at eighteen hundred hours, emphasising that all passengers must report to the deck in their life jacket – no exceptions.

'Goodness me,' Hillary groaned, 'I'm sure I shall look a frightful sight in a lifejacket.'

'You will look a more frightful sight drowned, my darling girl,' Matthew chided, 'now, do as you're told.'

The blast of the horn brought a great cheer, and everyone waved at friends and relatives on the dock side. But no sooner had they begun to move, Jenna felt ill.

'Right, let's find the bar,' Hillary said, 'we can toast the start of the holiday.'

'Actually, I need to go and lie down,' Jenna said, turning a strange shade of green.

'You can't be seasick so soon; we've only just set off!' Matthew joked.

Hillary bit down on her lip. 'Well by the look of it she is. Come on, darling, I'll walk you to your cabin.'

'Don't forget the roll call in an hour,' Matthew said, and Jenna groaned.

*

Hillary had stayed with Jenna, because no sooner had she opened the cabin door, Jenna had made straight for the bathroom to be violently sick.

'Oh dear.' Hillary mopped Jenna's brow. 'I'll send out for some water and I'm sure the ship's doctor can give you something.'

The public address system rang out again, calling everyone to the rollcall and Jenna groaned mournfully.

'We'll have to go, Jenna.'

'I can't, just leave me hear, tell them I'm ill.'

A knock came to the door and the steward arrived with water, and a sickness tablet?'

'I'm sorry, ladies. But we need you all on deck.'

'Can't you see, she's too ill to move?' Hillary parried.

'Sorry, Ma'am, rules are rules. It will take twenty minutes for the roll call, and she can be back here, lying down for the rest of the journey if she wants.' He handed Hillary a brown paper bag.

Hillary sighed and took the bag. 'Come on, darling, rally round. It will all be over soon.'

Jenna groaned as the steward helped Hillary to walk her up the steps to the deck. Once there she was placed on a seat with the paper bag strategically held under her chin. Her whole body was perspiring profusely by the time the rollcall had ended and Lyndon had to carry her limp sickly body back to her cabin as Hillary and Matthew followed.

'I'll see to her until she falls asleep and then I'll meet you both in the bar,' Hillary said as she fussed around her friend.

As soon as Lyndon and Matthew left, Jenna looked mournfully up at Hillary. 'Oh my god! I think I'm going to die.'

'No, you are not. Did you take that anti sickness pill?'

'Yes, I threw it up a second later.'

'I will send for ginger tea – that should settle you. You'll feel better soon.'

Jenna closed her eyes and groaned – she very much doubted it.

The ginger tea went the same way as the seasickness tablet, but eventually Jenna relaxed, and sleep prevailed.

Hillary turned her on her side, propped her up with pillows so she would not turn on her back and choke if she were sick, and then joined the men at the bar, grimacing at the state Jenna was in.

'That is the worst case of seasickness I've seen. Hopefully, she'll get her sea legs in the morning. Right, it's way past sunset and I haven't had my sundowner.' Hillary shot the bartender a dazzling lipstick smile. 'I'll have a gin and tonic, please.'

*

Jenna slept fitfully – her mouth tasted sour, but every sip of water she took, came straight back. Hillary visited her before she retired and saw her grimace at the smell of vomit in the room.

'Just go, Hillary, leave me to die in peace.'

'Don't be so dramatic. Nobody dies of sea sickness. You'll be fine in the morning.' She tenderly stroked Jenna's forehead and blew her a kiss. 'I'll come and see you first thing.'

When morning came, her first visitor was the steward with her breakfast, but no sooner had he placed the tray down, the smell of eggs turned Jenna's stomach and she spent the next few minutes retching over the lavatory.

Hillary arrived shortly afterwards, put the tray outside the cabin and called up for more ginger tea and another seasickness tablet. Unfortunately, both went the same way as before.

'Oh my god, Hillary, fourteen days of this Hell.'

'I'm sure you won't be ill for fourteen days,' Hillary said confidently. How wrong could she be.

*

After a fitful night's sleep, Gabriel deposited Robbie with the child minder and set off bleary eyed to Bochym. The sky had cleared again after the drizzle the previous day and as he came up the drive, he noted there was a flurry of activity going on with farm vehicles making their way into the upper field.

'Hello, Gabriel, I trust you're feeling better,' Peter said as he approached. 'Treen tells me you went home early with a headache.'

'Yes, Peter, thank you. I'm feeling better.' *That was a lie, his heart was sore, but...* 'Are you starting the harvest?'

'We are, yes. The good weather is breaking now, and proper rain is coming, according to the farmers here about. We normally harvest later than this, but because of the dry weather, everyone else has reaped their harvest so we can now have the use of the harvester. I am worried though. We do not have enough men to help. So many of our helpers were lost in the war.'

'I'll help, what can I do?'

The relief was palpable on Peter's face. 'That would be wonderful if you could. I will take you to Parson, my steward, he will put you to work. I am going to send down to Poldhu to see if Ryan Penrose and Jake Treen can come and help at the weekend. We need as many hands as possible.'

*

When Guy Blackthorn at Poldhu got the call for help from Bochym, he immediately halted work on the thatch they were doing which was almost complete and he, Jake, Ryan, and Agnes presented themselves on Friday morning to work on the harvest.

*

Over the next couple of days, when lunchtime came, the kitchen staff and maids brought pasties and ale for the workers, Gabriel always sought out Mary to sit with especially as she brought Robbie down to see his Papa. The domestic staff had all taken it in turns to keep an eye on little Robbie while Gabriel was working in the fields. He was a good little boy and would sit in the kitchen and draw or play with his beloved wooden tractor. Mary, in particular, was Robbie's favourite, and had become very close to her - especially as she fed him milk and biscuits and read to him in the afternoons!

As the threesome settled on a rug in the fields each day, the rest of the domestic staff, watched on with interest at the quiet companionship Gabriel and Mary shared. Mary was filling out slowly – putting a little more flesh on her bones. No more did her face hold that gaunt hollow look, instead her bonny face held a smile now and her brown eyes sparkled especially when she had Robbie with her. Everyone was so relieved that her past troubles seemed to be over. Molly the housekeeper though was particularly concerned about what would happen when Gabriel left, which he would do quite soon now the French drawing room was almost complete. How would Mary fair without him. There was no doubt about it, her recovery from that terrible incident was largely down to Gabriel. He seemed to be able to reach into her broken heart and help heal it like none of the others could.

*

At Poldhu, Marianne was busy with the Sunday clientele and had noted that Gabriel hadn't reserved his normal table.

'It's busy out there, Ellie. Shall I put the reserved sign on Mr Trelease's table?'

'No, he won't be coming, he's been working on the harvest at Bochym with my Guy, Agnes, Jake and Ryan.'

'Who is looking after his son then?'

'Mary, by all accounts.'

Marianne felt that familiar curl of bitterness towards Mary.

'Guy said Mary is a natural with the little boy. It's such as shame she lost her baby after poor Thomas died, I think she would have made a good mother, it would have helped her through her terrible loss.'

Marianne tipped her head. 'How long is the harvest on for?'

'It's the last day tomorrow and then they are having the harvest dance in the evening. Betsy and I have been invited with the kiddies.'

'Oh, well, I might go up and help tomorrow on my day off,' she said.

Ellie nodded. 'They would no doubt welcome your help. It will be a busy day in the kitchen for Mrs Blair and Mary.'

'Or I could look after Robbie for Gabriel,' Marianne said casually.

Ellie raised her eyebrow.

'What?' Marianne asked, though she knew what Ellie was thinking.

'I wasn't aware you liked children - you seem not to be interested in any of them who come to the tearoom with their parents.'

Marianne pursed her lips.

'And I seemed to remember you were quite disgruntled when Gabriel left you on the beach to look after Robbie.'

'That's because I didn't know the boy very well and I thought Gabriel was staying with us,' she said turning with a sniff, and flouncing away before Ellie could say more.

*

The next morning, Marianne arrived at the Bochym kitchen bright and early.

'I thought you might like another pair of hands, Mrs Blair.'

'Well, thank you. You can help by crimping these pasties for the lunch.'

'Actually, I thought I could take little Robbie for a walk around the gardens.' She walked towards the boy who was sitting quietly at the table.

'No, Marianne,' Mrs Blair stopped her, 'leave the boy there, he likes to be where Mary is, don't you sweetheart?'

Robbie looked up from his book and nodded. 'I love Mary.'

'If you want to help, we need it here in the kitchen. We have lunch and the harvest supper to prepare for.'

Marianne clenched her teeth and picked up an apron, but as she worked, she kept speaking to Robbie, asking him questions, such as, 'Have you been down to Church Cove lately, Robbie?' and, 'Are you going there next Sunday?'

Robbie answered, 'No,' to the first question and 'I don't know,' to the second, and then tried to go back to the book Mary had bought him.

'Leave the lad be, Marianne, he wants to read,' Mrs Blair scolded.

'He should be out playing in the garden, not stuck in here reading – it's a lovely day. Don't you want to go out to play, Robbie?' she asked.

He looked up from his book and shook his head. 'Mary will take me out later, won't you, Mary?'

'I will, sweetheart.' Mary looked up from filling the pasties. 'We'll have a nice walk after luncheon.'

'I'll come with you then,' Marianne suggested.

Robbie frowned at this idea. 'Can I just go with you, Mary, please?'

'Of course, sweetheart. Whatever you want.'

Marianne's eyes narrowed at the rebuff.

*

After a busy day in the kitchen, Marianne was feeling generally disgruntled with herself. She had spent only a few minutes in Gabriel's company, having followed Mary and Robbie down at lunch time and plonked herself down on their rug. If she wasn't mistaken, Gabriel had looked quite put out that she was there - though he was always courteous. Once they had eaten their fill though, Gabriel had taken Robbie for a little walk towards the ever-decreasing circle of crops in the centre of the field. When Marianne had offered to come with them, he declined her request, saying, that they wanted to spend a little Papa and Son time together alone.'

*

The harvest supper dance brought Marianne no better luck. Gabriel danced with her just once and was pulled away half way through to move the hog roast spit away from the seating area. The strong breeze, which had got up, had been sending sparks towards it. Marianne watched as Gabriel danced with all the other women in the group but was especially peeved when he danced with Mary and Robbie in a circle, and they all flopped down laughing on the seats at the table beside her.

Out of the corner of her eye, Marianne saw Ellie urge Jake to go and ask her to dance, so, she folded her arms and turned away from him, hoping to deflect his advance.

'Marianne.' She heard Jake but did not turn around. 'Marianne,' he persisted.

She snorted angrily and turned. 'What?'

He smiled softly. 'I would very much like to dance with you.'

She looked at him coolly, and it struck her how handsome he was, but she was adamant that she wanted nothing to do with any of the local boys. 'Well, I would very much like to sit here and not dance, thank you.'

His face dropped, but Agnes, grabbed him by the arm. 'I'll dance with you, Jake,' she said scowling at Marianne.

'Thank you, Agnes, I would like that very much. I'm sorry I didn't ask you first,' he said rather cuttingly.

Marianne turned away, pretending she hadn't heard the remark, and didn't realise Ellie had moved towards her, until she heard her voice.

'You know, Marianne, pride comes before a fall. You are very beautiful and behave as though you are very pleased with yourself, but from the view of an onlooker, your persona is very ugly. It would not have hurt you to dance with Jake. It took the lad great courage to come over to you and ask. You need to take a good look at yourself and change your ways.'

Although Ellie's words stung, Marianne just lifted her chin - people just did not realise how much better she was than them.

39

On day five of the voyage and showing no signs of getting better or keeping anything down, Jenna had been transferred to the ships infirmary and monitored there. Hillary, Matthew, and Lyndon offered to take it in turns to sit with her, but Jenna was in no fit state to entertain her visitors and shooed them away almost as soon as they came in. Only Hillary would not be swayed from staying with her.

With Jenna incapacitated, and while Hillary sat with her, Matthew took the opportunity to eventually wheedle out of Lyndon what was so obviously eating him.

Matthew read the letter Lyndon had received and shook his head.

'Jenna would not do this to you. Do you not realise that? This letter is mischief that is all. Now I do not know Gabriel as well as you do, but it strikes me he would not do this to you either.'

'Yes, but I think he has, albeit unintentionally. He didn't know that Jenna was my sweetheart, you see, and the way he spoke about his widow, he sounded like he had really fallen in love with her.'

'And Jenna never mentioned that she'd been meeting him?'

'Not once, but it's clear she has been.'

'Honestly, Lyndon. This is all going to be a huge misunderstanding. We both know Jenna.'

Lyndon's mouth twitched. 'What I do know is that she married someone only months after thinking I was dead!'

'You know there were certain circumstances around that which forced her hand there – though I know not what exactly they were, but I know for certain, that if you had come back sooner, as much as she admired James, and would have wanted to help him, she would not have married him had she known that you were alive. You are her one true love. Do not let this malicious letter come between you.'

Lyndon folded his arms. 'So, you think I should just ignore it?'

'No, I think you should speak to Jenna as soon as possible and find out why she's been meeting Gabriel.'

Hillary breezed into the bar and the conversation halted.

'Oh, yes,' she said narrowing her eyes, 'what are you two so secretive about.'

'Men's talk,' Matthew winked.

'Oh, how droll. Goodness but I miss Jenna's proper company, all she does is groan at the moment, poor love. I don't think she is going to improve until we get her on solid ground, so I'll have to make do with you two for company. So, stop the men's talk and order me a large gin and tonic. I need something to take the smell of hospital disinfectant out of my nostrils.

*

The dry spell broke in Cornwall on Friday the 12th of September and the rain came in biblical proportions. No one ventured to the tearoom for risk of getting soaked to the skin and though the rain eased off by late afternoon still no one came. Marianne thought she was going to have an easy day, but Ellie declared, 'It's a day to deep clean the inside of the tearoom.' Windows had been washed, chair and table legs wiped down with hot soapy water and the counter was scrubbed and tidied.

It was only by chance that Ellie glanced out of the window and saw the drifter woman fall that day. The old woman had been a regular visitor to the beach for as long as Ellie could remember, she would keep herself to herself combing the water's edge for wood to dry and burn. A complete loner, she lived in a broken-down hut on the outskirts of Mullion and would not accept help from anyone. Many people ignored her refusal of food and secretly left bags of bread and vegetables hooked on her door handle, the children thereabouts had theories that she lived on frogs and rodents caught and cooked on the fire. It was probably true - for a more wretched woman you could hardly find.

When the old lady didn't get up, Ellie and Marianne donned oil skin coats and gum boots to go to her aid, but by the time they got to her, the woman was moaning incoherently and as they came closer, they both recoiled from the smell she was emitting.

'We need to get her some help, the tide is coming in,' Ellie said, fearful of the surf licking dangerously close to the woman.

They turned as Meg and Tobias Williams approached, walking their dogs down the beach.

'What's amiss, has she fallen?' Tobias asked, moving them to one side.

'I think she's collapsed, more than fallen. She looks dreadful,' Ellie said anxiously.

Tobias had been a policeman in his time, so quickly took control.

'Meg, can you take the cart and fetch the doctor. Marianne, can you fetch Ryan and Guy here please. Ellie is that board still behind the tearoom – the one to fetch folks off the beach if they have got into difficulty in the sea?'

'Yes.'

'Can you help me bring it? We need to get her somewhere dry - the tide is fast approaching, and the rain is coming in again.'

As soon as Guy and Ryan arrived, they took the load of the board from Ellie, but as they reached the old woman to pick her up, they all recoiled at the stench, but they knew they must move her.

'Take her to the stables,' Guy advised. 'The straw is clean there. Ellie, get the storm lamps, the doctor will need light when he gets here.'

When the doctor arrived, he too recoiled from the stench which the others had almost become accustomed to. He held his handkerchief to his nose, and after noting her sickly pallor, said, 'We need to get her out of these wet clothes.'

Layer by layer, he and Tobias peeled her clothes from her body, each layer consisting of damp sacking, tied with rope, and infested with lice. The stench increased the nearer they got to her flesh making everyone in the stable baulk.

Ellie fetched a blanket to cover her when they had got down to her filthy underwear, but the worst was yet to come. As Dr Martin eased off one of her boots, her foot made a large squelch and came away in his hand!

There was a collected gasp of horrified shock.

'Oh, good god,' the doctor breathed as he noted that the rest of the leg was green and gangrenous. He glanced in alarm at the woman, but she seemed oblivious to what had just happened.

'Do we need to fetch an ambulance?' Tobias asked gravely.

Dr Martin shook his head – it was all too late for an ambulance. He reached out and held the woman's cold hand. 'What is your name?'

'Adrienne Cooper,' she whispered and shivered at the touch of another human.

'How long has your foot been bad, Adrienne?'

'A year or so, I think. I lost the feeling in my foot a while ago, but my leg hurts like hell to walk on.'

'Did you injure your foot?'

'A rat bit me,' she sighed wearily.

Ellie gasped. 'I admit, I've seen her limping for a long time. I should have done something for her, sooner.'

Adrienne turned her rheumy eyes on the doctor. 'Am I dying?'

Dr Martin pulled his mouth into a tight line.

'I am, aren't I?'

'You're very ill, yes.'

'I knew this morning that I couldn't go on another day. I stink, don't I? Even I can't stand it now.'

'I'm going to give you something for the pain, Adrienne.' He reached for his bag and filled a syringe of laudanum.

Suddenly her expression gave way to purpose. 'If I'm to die this day, doctor, I need to confess my sins.'

'I'm sure that is not necessary, Adrienne.'

She grabbed the doctor's arm purposely. 'I need to tell my story before it's too late. Will you hear me?'

'Very well, Adrienne. I'm not a man of the cloth, but I will hear your confession.' The doctor said softly.

She drew a deep trembling breath. 'I'd rather you hear it now, than you bring that sin eater to my dead body.'

'What on *earth* is a sin eater,' Marianne murmured at the back of the stable.

'A sin-eater was a person who consumes a ritual meal to spiritually take on the sins of a deceased person,' Guy whispered. 'A piece of bread and a dish of ale would be laid on the body of a person who had not confessed their sins before they died. The local sin eater would consume the food, to absorb the sins of that person, thus absolving the soul of the person. Sin-eaters, therefore, carried the sins of all people whose sins they had eaten - they were usually feared and shunned. The last one hereabouts died in 1903, he was called Jacob Clemins and a more unsavoury man I have never met.'

Adrienne struggled to lift her weary head. 'Yes, yes, that was his name,' she hissed, 'he was a monster!'

'Calm yourself, Adrienne,' the doctor soothed.

Momentarily she closed her eyes, took a deep breath, and then opened them again. 'Clemins was fetched, ready to eat my sins when I fell ill with the fever in January 1902. I was sixteen and beautiful then,' she looked beyond the doctor shoulders, 'just like you!' She pointed a shaky, filthy finger at Marianne.

Dr Martin did a quick mental calculation. 'So, you're thirty-four!'

Another collective audible gasp came – she looked like an old woman!

She nodded and lowered her weary eyes. 'We were passing through Mullion at the time – travelling.'

'A gypsy!' Marianne spat the word with disdain.

Adrienne's eyes narrowed at the insult. 'We were proper Romany. Didn't do any harm to anyone, just travelling through we were. But Da fell ill, and we could not travel, we were allowed to stay in Mullion, but the rest of our group had to go on ahead having been shunned by the locals. A doctor came to us, but one by one, every one of my family died of the fever in that wagon over the space of a week. Ma, Da, three brothers, two sisters and then I got it. I thought I was going to die too. It was then the doctor sent for Jakob Clemins the sin eater. I was terribly ill, but through my delirium, I saw him come to my bedside – with his long, greasy hair and ugly pox marked face. He stank because he was the night soil man too. The doctor left so he could hear my sins when I died, but instead, he lifted my skirts, climbed atop of me, put a hand to my mouth and raped me. Then he sat on the chair waiting for me to die so he could eat the bread and ale left for him. My body was in torment, but it would not give in, so every couple of hours through that night, he climbed back on top of me, until a doctor came to check on me the next morning, saw that my fever had abated, and Clemins was sent packing. I was left all alone to recover, used and abused by that hateful man. When I was strong enough to get up, I went to the sea to wash his filth from my body. My people must have come back to see if we had survived while I was out, because when I returned the wagon and horse had gone. With nowhere to go, I had to stay, but no one would give someone like me employment, and then my belly grew large, and I knew then that he had planted his filthy seed inside me.'

Ellie moved forwards and knelt next her. 'What happened to the child?' she asked.

Adrienne looked straight at Marianne before answering. 'She was born alive and well, but what could I do with a babe all alone? So, I wrapped it in a shawl I had once found in the surf and left her at The Poldhu Hotel.'

Everyone knew of Marianne's beginning as a foundling baby wrapped in a shawl, and they all turned slowly to stare at her.

Aghast, Marianne staggered back. 'No! She's lying!'

Adrienne shook her head slowly. 'No one would lie on their death bed – and this really is my deathbed this time. I left you there on 27th of September 1902.

'Liar, you're lying, she is lying, *liar!* Marianne screamed at her.

Dr Martin glanced up at Ellie. 'Could you take the young lady outside please.'

'Come, Marianne,' Ellie said gently.

'She's lying,' Marianne yelled, as Ellie put her arm around her to lead her out of the stable. 'How could she say those things – those lies in front of *all those people?*' Marianne stomped around flinging her arms in the air. 'Everyone will believe that - that, bloody wretch of a stinking woman is my mother now!'

'Marianne, calm yourself,' Ellie grabbed her arms.

'Calm!' Marianne shrugged her off, 'how can I be calm when lies are being told about me?' Hot angry tears streamed down her face which she swept away with the swipe of her hand. 'And what about who she said the father of her baby was – a stinking night soil man who ate sins for a living! Oh god! This is too much!' She clamped her hands to her head and screamed at the top of her voice. 'These lies, how could she say those lies about me. I don't even know the woman. I've never spoken to her in my life, why would she do this to me?'

'Marianne, come back to the tearoom so you can calm down a little – I'll make you a cup of tea.'

She turned on Ellie – her eyes wild with anger. 'You believe her, don't you?'

'Hush now. Let's just sit down a moment.'

'No, she screamed. 'I'm going home! She started to walk away but turned and came back. 'I don't want any of her lies bantered around, you hear me?' she threatened. 'You tell that lot in there, that they'd better not repeat a single word that liar said about me, or I shall, I shall….' Suddenly a strange guttural noise rose from her throat, and she threw up in disgust.

Ellie stepped forward to quickly grasp her hair back as Marianne retched.

'No one will say a word, Marianne, I promise,' Ellie soothed. 'Go home if you must.'

'It's not true, it can't be true, it's not true,' she turned and sobbed in Ellie's arms, but somehow as she felt the sympathetic pat on the back Ellie gave her, Marianne knew deep down in her heart that the woman's story was true.

40

Unwilling to face her adopted parents with her distress, Marianne had taken herself off to bed. The fewer people who knew the better. Damn that awful woman to have spewed her lies in front of so many people. Marianne did not believe Ellie for one moment when she told her that none of them would say anything. Of course, they would talk, and relish in her bad news, especially the local lads who she had shunned. She would be the laughing stock of Mullion when this got around, she could hear their voices in her head saying, 'Not so high and mighty now, are you?' 'Well, I *am* better than them, I'm better than everybody!' She beat her fists into her pillow and cried herself to sleep that night.

*

Ellie gave Marianne a sympathetic look the next morning when she arrived at the tearoom, a gesture which annoyed her immensely. If Ellie believed the ravings of that filthy old woman, then every single one of the people in that stable last night would no doubt feel the same.

'Adrienne died shortly after you left, Marianne,' Ellie said as she placed a comforting hand on her sleeve. 'The undertaker took her away and Guy is going to pay for the burial, which we suspect will be quite soon. Her poor body had already started to decompose so the doctor said.'

Marianne clenched her fists. 'Why are you telling me? I couldn't care less what happens to her.'

Ellie retracted her hand from Marianne's sleeve. 'I just thought you would like to know.'

'Well, I don't! It has nothing to do with me! *She* has nothing to do with me!' She grabbed her apron and took herself off to the kitchen.

Ellie had left Marianne to simmer in the kitchen as she was obviously struggling with the revelations, hence there was no more conversation to be had between them until they opened the tearoom at ten that day. The rain had eased considerably but only a smattering of regular customers were at the door first thing. Mrs Edith Eddy – a lovely lady who always had a cheery hello for everyone - was the first through the door.

Ellie welcomed her in and showed her to her seat inside. 'It's a little damp to be out on the veranda today, but hopefully the sun will come out and dry things later. I'll send Marianne over to take your order shortly,' she said.

Despite the gloomy weather, everyone who followed Mrs Eddy through that door seemed to have a cheerful disposition, and there was lively chat and laughter as people shook the rain drops from their coats ready to be seated.

Marianne could hear the bright chatter coming through to the kitchen as she was getting the scones ready to bring out. She clenched her teeth in annoyance, wondering what was everyone so flipping happy about?

'Hello, Marianne, are you all right?' Mrs Eddy said seeing Marianne's stony face as she stood with her pen and pad posed to take her order.

'Yes,' snapped Marianne,' why wouldn't I be?'

'*Marianne*,' Ellie said authoritatively. 'Go and wait for me in the kitchen. I am so sorry, Mrs Eddy. Marianne seems to have got out of the wrong side of the bed this morning. It will not happen again. Please let me take your order – it's on the house.' Ellie put the order on the counter and strode into the kitchen. 'What on earth were you thinking, snapping at Mrs Eddy like that. She is one of our best customers.'

Marianne folded her arms. 'They know, don't they? Someone has been spreading those lies that bloody woman was telling last night.

'Don't be so ridiculous, Marianne. Nobody in the stable that night would ever do that to you. They all understand how upsetting it is for you.'

'Well, I don't believe you. Someone told them. Everyone's looking and laughing at me, aren't they? I know they are!'

Ellie thumped her fists into her sides. 'Nobody is laughing at you, you silly girl.'

'Yes, they are,' she yelled, feeling her face turn hot with anger. 'I bet that old witch was spreading her stories about me long before she decided to die in your stables.'

'No, she wasn't. I would have heard if gossip were going about.'

'You believe her, don't you?'

'I do, yes. She spoke a little more about you after you left. She told me she left you at the door to the laundry and watched until someone picked you up, so she knew you were safe. She said she was sorry if she caused you distress, but she thought you should know, and she asked me to tell you that she was proud of who you had become.'

Marianne gritted her teeth. 'She should have kept her mouth shut. I hate her for what she has done to me.'

'What Adrienne did was to give you life, and then had the good sense to pass you onto someone who could look after you. You must understand - it is not where you came from, it is who you become.'

'She should not have said anything. Why did she have to tell me, *I hate her*,' she yelled.

'Marianne, stop this, now! The poor woman is dead, and I will not have hysterics in my tearoom. Now, you either calm down and go and apologise to Mrs Eddy for being rude, or you can leave and not come back.'

Marianne was stunned for a moment, unsure of what to do.

Ellie tipped her head. 'Well?'

'I'll apologise,' she said sulkily.

'See you do and put a pleasant smile on your face. If I ever hear you snap at a customer again, I am afraid you will have to look elsewhere for employment. I will not have you being discourteous to my customers.'

Marianne balled her hands into fists and painted a smile on her face as she apologised to Mrs Eddy, but for the rest of the day she felt sure everyone was talking about her. As she worked, her mind was in a whirl as she wondered how to divert the talk about her parentage - because she felt sure that Guy and Ryan would tell Jake Treen and then he would tell everyone else, because she had spurned his attentions. By the time she took off her apron at the end of the afternoon – she knew exactly what she was going to do to deflect the gossip away from her.

*

The following Tuesday morning at breakfast time, a policeman called at Bochym Manor. Mrs Blair had been the first to see him approach – her second sense telling her trouble was afoot.

'Mr Treen, look!' she said in alarm.

Joe dropped his knife and fork with a clatter and turned to Mary. 'Go upstairs to your bedroom, Mary, and stay there. Everybody else, say nothing. I will do the speaking,' he ordered as he straightened his jacket and met the officer at the door.

'Good morning. What can I do for you?' Joe asked.

'I would like to speak to Mary Ellis on a very grave matter.'

'I'm afraid Mary doesn't work here anymore,' he said thinking on his feet. 'She left at the weekend to settle up country somewhere. We were very sorry to lose her.'

'Do you know where up country?'

'The North I believe. She told us a relative was very poorly and she would have to go and look after her children.'

The officer took a deep breath. 'Could I speak to the Earl then?'

'Of course. I will go and inform him.'

Joe quickly told the Earl of what he had just told the policeman.

Peter nodded. 'Well done, Treen. Send him in and make sure Mary does not leave her room or the house.'

'Yes, my lord.'

Peter listened to the officer's report that they had reason to believe Mary Ellis had tried to kill herself with poisonous mushrooms.

'Attempted suicide is a criminal offence, you know?' P.C. Cole stated.

'I am well aware of the law,' Peter answered tersely, 'but this report is utterly preposterous.'

'Well, there has been talk that Mary has been quite unstable since her husband was shot for cowardice.'

'Who has said these things? Because if by unstable they mean grief stricken, then yes, the poor girl has suffered – as would anyone if they lost their spouse so cruelly. But we, as her employees, have endeavoured to look after her in her grief.'

'And she repays you by leaving you at the drop of a hat,' the officer said with an arched eyebrow.

'We have known for some time that Mary might have to leave us as she informed us of a sick relative who might need help in the near future.'

'So, this report is unfounded.'

'Absolutely,' Peter said adamantly.

'Then how do you account for this. It was found in the mushrooms box at Mrs Jennings grocery store.

Peter read the note, which was in capital letters.

BE CAREFUL OF THE MUSHROOMS YOU EAT.
THE DOCTOR HAD TO BE CALLED WHEN MARY
ELLIS THE COOK FROM BOCHYM TRIED TO
KILL HERSELF WITH POISONOUS ONES

'I must inform you, my lord. We spoke to Dr Martin, who confirmed that he was called to Mary in July to deal with a case of food poisoning.'

'Yes, he was,' Peter answered feeling a curl of anxiety. 'From my understanding, when Mary picked the morning mushrooms, which she does every morning, she accidently picked a Fools Funnel which grows alongside of the Scotch Bonnet. Fortunately for us, but not for her, she tasted the mushrooms before they were served as our breakfast and fell extremely ill quite quickly.' *Peter felt so relieved that he had arranged with the good doctor to stick to this story should it ever get out.*

'Very well, my lord. I am sorry to bother you. It seems this was just a case of mischief. I would of course, like to speak to Mrs Ellis, should she ever come back to work here.'

'I should think that is highly unlikely. Her relative was not expected to live. I should think her services are needed in the North.'

*

Gabriel knocked on Peter's study door later that morning to tell him the renovations were complete and found both Peter and Sarah there. From their faces, they were clearly worried about something. Picking up on their mood he said, 'I can come back later.'

'No, its fine, come in. We have had some disturbing news.'

'Anything I can help you with?'

'I am not sure anyone can help. The police have called. They have received information from someone that Mary tried to take her own life. Which, as it was you who found her, know that to be the truth. I have denied it of course.'

Gabriel slumped down in the chair without invite. 'But we have all been so careful, not to let the truth out.'

'I know. We are going to speak to everyone to see if anyone can shine a light on this allegation.'

'Have the police spoken to Mary yet?'

'No, I've had to lie and tell the officer that she doesn't work here anymore, and we have no forwarding address for her.'

'Where is she now?'

'She's in her room. But she cannot stay here, that is for sure. The police were pacified for the moment, but...'

'Poor Mary. Hasn't that poor woman been through enough!'

'We think it would be best if she went abroad. Sarah and I were just discussing whether to contact Ruby and Justin in Italy. Ruby was always very fond of Mary – she was almost like a mother to her, but we cannot send Mary alone on such a trip.'

'Well, you do know that I am taking Robbie over to Italy to see them in a fortnight, don't you? She could come with us and help look after Robbie while I can see to her safe passage.'

Peter sat back in his chair. 'I think she rather needs to go now in case the police return.'

'Then tell Mary to pack her belongings and we shall go tomorrow. I will phone through and book our tickets and we will leave first thing in the morning.'

Sarah touched Gabriel's sleeve and gave him an appreciative smile.

'Well, that is jolly decent of you, Gabriel,' Peter said.

'I have become very fond of Mary. I cannot let anything else happen to her. If you could send a telegram to Ruby and Justin, telling them we are coming. I know they have guests staying with them at the moment,' he faltered for a moment realising that he would have to face Jenna with Lyndon, 'but I am sure they can accommodate Mary somewhere at the villa, and I'll find a hotel for Robbie and myself to stay in until the other party leaves.

*

On Wednesday morning, Mary said a tearful goodbye to all her friends at Bochym Manor as she readied to leave to go to Italy. The previous day she had sat in total bewilderment after being told of the arrangements that had been made for her. Mrs Blair in particular was the most distressed at her leaving and had sat with her on her bed weeping broken heartedly – Mary had been her right-hand woman in the kitchen for over twelve years. Neither of them knew how they were going to cope without each other.

Disguised in a hooded black cloak, Mary had been allowed to go down to Thomas's memorial stone at first light to say her last goodbye to him. Though she had Gabriel and Robbie by her side, Mary was terrified of the fugitive life that stretched out before her. Never known to have a malicious bone in her body, Mary did hope that whoever had let her dreadful secret out would pay sorely for their indiscretion.

41

While Gabriel, Mary and Robbie were just starting the first leg of their journey to Italy, the ship carrying Matthew, Hillary, Lyndon, and Jenna docked in Naples in the chill of the early morning. They were the last to disembark as they were waiting for Jenna to be stretchered off and transferred to the local hospital.

After settling Jenna at the hospital, they booked into a nearby hotel and took themselves off for lunch to discuss their ongoing journey to Tuscany. They should have caught the train to Florence later that morning, but Jenna was in no fit state to travel.

'I had better send a telegram to Justin and Ruby telling them of our delay,' Matthew said. 'Hopefully, the delay will only be for another day.'

'Are you sure that's all?' Lyndon answered dubiously, 'she did not look at all well, this morning.'

'I'll speak to the doctor later when we go back to see her,' Hillary said, 'I shall insist they discharge her. I'm sure she will manage the journey and will recuperate so much better in Justin and Ruby's villa. So, here is to Jenna's recovery.' Hillary chinked glasses with the men. 'Now shall we see what delights Naples has to offer?'

*

Mary had been quiet for the first part of the train journey – lost in her own thoughts. Robbie had been sleeping in his father's arms having endured an early morning wake up, but at around eleven he rubbed his sleepy eyes and smiled at Mary.

'I'm glad you are coming on holiday with Papa and me,' he said climbing up beside her and hugging her arm. 'Papa, are you glad Mary is coming with us?'

Gabriel smiled softly. 'I am very happy. I can think of no one nicer to travel with than my little boy and a lovely companion.'

'Papa likes you!' Robbie looked up at Mary, and she and Gabriel exchanged glances.

'Are you all right?' Gabriel mouthed to Mary, and she smiled and nodded. At least she was with people who knew and cared about her.

As they ended their train journey and boarded the ship. Mary stood on the deck and said a sad goodbye to England – for she genuinely believed she would never set foot on its shores again.

*

When Hillary, Matthew and Lyndon arrived at the hospital later that evening, Jenna was sitting up in bed enjoying a boiled egg and toast.

'My goodness, who are you and what have you done with our sickly friend?' Hillary said, kissing her warmly on the cheek. She stood back and shook her head. 'What a transformation!'

'I know, once I stopped moving, I realised I was starving hungry,' Jenna gave a sheepish grin as she cracked open her second egg. 'They are going to discharge me just as soon as I have proved I can keep food down.'

'Well don't eat anymore,' Hillary pulled the spoon from her hand, 'we have a train to catch in the morning and you are going to be on it. I simply cannot wait a moment longer to lie in the Tuscan sun.'

Jenna frowned as the rest of her meal was taken from her reach. 'I'm so sorry I spoilt the journey for you all.'

'You didn't. We managed without you, though we were terribly worried, but we did miss you, didn't we?' Matthew glanced at Lyndon, who nodded.

Jenna frowned she wasn't too sure that he had – for without doubt something was niggling him.

*

On Thursday morning Ruby and Justin lay in each other's arms, within the tangle of cotton sheets as the Tuscan sun began to rise. They always enjoyed making love in the cool of the early morning, and after receiving two telegrams yesterday from Matthew, one in the morning saying they were delayed, and then another in the evening saying they would be on the train the next day, they were enjoying their last few hours alone with each other.

'Our last morning of peace.' Justin smiled and kissed Ruby on the nose.

'Much as I like having you all to myself – it will be nice to have some company, and I'm sure they will take themselves off sightseeing for a few days,' she answered.

'Well, I'm happy to take them to our favourite local spots, but I really do need to do some work soon. Is everything ready for them now?'

Ruby nodded. 'I think so yes. I'll need to go shopping this morning that's all.'

'They should be in Florence at five if they catch the train on time.'

Ruby put her arms behind her head. 'I do hope Lyndon and Jenna find this time together a catalyst for their future happiness. Lyndon has waited too long to be with the love of his life.'

'We had a long wait before we found each other,' he kissed her, 'and my goodness but it was worth the wait.'

'I hope they will be as happy as we are.'

'Amen to that.'

'You have given me a life I would never have dreamed of.'

Justin turned over onto his side. 'I just wish I could have given you the baby you so desired.'

Ruby gave a sad smile. 'If it was not to be, it was not to be. I am truly thankful to be laid in your arms every night.' She sighed, 'Oh I do hope they all enjoy their stay here.'

'Well, it will not be for lack of you doing everything possible to make them welcome. You have transformed this villa in two weeks.'

'So have you.' She slapped him playfully.

'I just did the whitewashing. You made it homely. Goodness, but when I think of what I brought you home to after we were married.'

She laughed. 'It did rather need a woman's touch.'

'And so did I. Talking of which,' he pulled her towards him and began to kiss her passionately.

'Justin Devereux you are insatiable,' she giggled.

*

Jenna had been discharged the previous evening at Hillary's insistence, so the group boarded the train to Florence early that morning. As they settled in a carriage together, everyone was feeling the stifling heat of the fierce Italian sun.

'Open that window, I'm going to melt,' Hillary said fanning herself.

'You'll acclimatise in a while,' Matthew assured her as he did her bidding.

'How long did Justin say the journey was?' Hillary asked, checking the padding on the seat.

'Two hundred and ninety-six miles.' Matthew answered.

'Good grief. How long will that take?' Hillary slumped down.

'The best part of a day. It's like going to London from Cornwall, but with comfier seats, I understand the journey is quite scenic though. How do you feel Jenna?' Matthew asked.

'A deal better now I'm not on that ship. I've lost so much weight in the last two weeks; my clothes are hanging off me.' Jenna looked at Lyndon who was studiously gazing out of the window and then glanced at Matthew and Hillary, but they seemed not to notice his reluctance to converse. 'Are you all right, Lyndon? You're noticeably quiet,' she asked.

Lyndon peeled his eyes from the window. 'Just enjoying the scenery,' he said, turning back to the window.

In all the years she had known Lyndon, she had never known him so uncommunicative. She wondered perhaps if he was trying to keep his mind settled with all that was going on around him. After all, he had not been able to deal with London. Hopefully when they got to the villa, things would settle between them – she certainly hoped so anyway.

*

As they stepped off the train into the busy station at Florence, they were greeted by a cacophony of foreign voices, people meeting people, hands gesticulating joy and sometimes frustration. They were met by Justin and another gentlemen, who Justin introduced as Barclay Graham. He was staying at a nearby villa and had offered to help drive two of the party and their luggage up to Villa Casomi.

The heat, though late afternoon, was almost unbearable and both women shifted uncomfortably in their tight corseted clothes as each car was loaded up with luggage.

'First thing I am going to do is strip to my shift, I am perspiring in a very unladylike fashion,' Hillary said to Matthew as they parted ways with Lyndon and Jenna to climb into Barclay's car.

Justin laughed. 'It is the one thing that always happens when guests arrive. Inhibitions are lost in the heat, propriety goes out of the window, shoes come off, as bare feet are the only sensible way to walk around on the cool stone floors. Having said that, the weather is changing. Rain is forecast, though don't worry, it doesn't hang around for long. It just gives some respite from the heat. Our poor neighbour Giovanni has been working flat out for days to get the grape harvest in before the rain comes.'

As they made their way out of the bustle of Florence and into the calm Tuscan hills. Jenna was filled with the desire to put paintbrush to canvas to capture the images before her.

'So, the villa stood the test of time, did it?' Lyndon asked.

'To a point. Apparently, every room housed a family of rodents due to several windows having been broken. Barclay came back to his villa almost as soon as the war finished and came to inspect ours. Once he saw the damage, he had the windows mended and arranged for someone to rid the villa of pests. Worry not though, Ruby has been cleaning the place from top to toe in readiness of your visit. So, you two, how do you like the look of Italy?'

'Gosh, but it's lovely,' Jenna enthused.

'We'll tour around another day – preferably early in the mornings when it's cooler,' Justin said. 'Is this your first time abroad, Jenna?'

'No, James and I toured the French Riviera on honeymoon.' Jenna felt Lyndon's body stiffen beside her and she shot him a sharp look which he returned with just as much severity. Beautiful country or not, Jenna was beginning to think she should not have come here with Lyndon.

When the cars wound their way up the long dusty drive and pulled up in front of the villa, all the occupants got out and gazed in astonishment, first at the beautiful red roofed, white building – its front arches adorned in a mass of crimson bougainvillea. Then almost in unison they all turned to take in the vista below them, looking down the road they had just travelled, as it snaked down through the tall cypress trees to the vast vineyards below.

'Hello and welcome to Villa Casomi.' Ruby had rushed out to hug everyone in turn. 'Come, I have put cold drinks and snacks on the terrace. Leave the luggage there for a moment. I'll show you all to your rooms after we have had some refreshments. The water closet is down the corridor and there is one just over there by the studio, should you need it,' she said in almost a whisper. 'Barclay, will you join us?'

'Thank you, my dear, but I think I'll head down to see how Giovanni is getting on.'

After a cool refreshing drink of lemonade and a few morsels of cured meats and cheeses, Justin showed Matthew and Hillary their room, as Ruby led Lyndon and Jenna further down the corridor.

'Lyndon, Jenna, this is your room – let me know if you need anything. I'll be serving proper drinks soon.' Ruby smiled as she closed the door on them.

*

Alone now, both Lyndon and Jenna were silent as they glanced around the simple but spacious bedroom. Voile curtains blew into the room with the welcome evening breeze and a large fan whirred above them. The room housed a wardrobe, a large bed with iron bedstead, dressed in crisp white linen and on the bedside tables stood two lamps and citronella candles to ward off the mosquitoes – which Ruby told them were the only nuisance in paradise.

After putting their cases down on the floor, Lyndon and Jenna looked across the bed at each other.

'I can go and find a hotel,' Lyndon said.

Jenna tipped her head, puzzled why he should say such a thing. 'There is no need, I'm quite well now.' When Lyndon's face remained stony, she added, 'Is that what you want to do?'

Lyndon looked away from her and sighed. 'No, but...'

'But what? We've come here so we can be together, Lyndon! Are you saying you don't want that anymore? If so, we should not have come.'

'I..,' he cleared his throat,' I'm not sure it's what you want anymore.'

'Why? If it's because I've not joined you during the voyage it was because I've felt extremely ill, surely Hillary told you how sick I've been.'

'Yes, yes she has.'

'What then?'

He plunged his hands deep into his pockets and tightened his jaw muscles. 'I think you care about someone else now!'

She laughed. 'I care about a lot of people!'

'Another man, I mean.'

She staired at him. 'What on earth are you talking about?'

'Oh, come on, Jenna, I know you've been meeting Gabriel Trelease.'

Jenna stepped back slightly. 'And his little son - I've become quite attached to the little lad.'

'And to his father so it seems. God damn it, Jenna, Gabriel has told me on numerous occasions that he has met and fallen quite in love with a widow - that widow apparently being *you*.'

Aghast, Jenna said, 'What nonsense is this?'

'Don't make a fool of me, Jenna, I saw and heard you with them at your book launch party.'

Jenna shook her head in astonishment.

'I heard him, telling you to hurry back – I even heard the little lad asking you if you were going to be his new mama soon. What am I supposed to think?'

'The boy is only six – he lost his own mother – I think he just craves a mother figure.'

'And I believe Gabriel looks to you as the boy's replacement mother too.'

'No, Lyndon! There has been nothing inappropriate between us and certainly no mention of any interest in me - other than a friendly meeting on the beach.'

'Well how many more widows does Gabriel meet on a regular basis?'

'It's not regular. I've occasionally met them on the beach at Church Cove. I also went to The Poldhu Tea Room with them for Robbie's birthday because the little lad especially asked me.

'I know you have, because Gabriel has told me all about you and where you go together – he just didn't mention your name. He said he didn't want to name who the woman was, because she was still in mourning for her late husband. What I cannot understand, Jenna, is that you keep me at arm's length, because you were being watched and that you are in mourning for James, but freely go about meeting Gabriel.

'And his little son!' she reiterated.

'As you keep mentioning,' he raised his voice, 'but nonetheless, you have spent time with them while I have been waiting in the background for the appropriate time until we can be seen in public together. If it's just about the little boy, why did you invite him to the book launch?'

'I invited them because Gabriel had been a friend of James's since childhood. I just thought it was a sociable thing to do. I can assure you there is no ulterior motive. I have no intentions on him whatsoever.'

'Well, I think you have vastly misjudged his interest in you. He has spoken non-stop about his *widow*. For God's sake, Jenna, he told me in confidence that he loved you, and I, stupid fool that I am, wished him luck!' Lyndon threw his hands in the air and paced the room. 'I had no idea he had fallen in love with *you*!'

Deeply concerned, Jenna flopped into the chair. 'I am sure you are wrong.'

Lyndon shook his head. 'I saw the look in his eyes when he said goodbye to you at the book launch – it was only then I realised it was *you* he loved. I must tell you – it has floored me. I almost didn't come to Italy – I'm still not sure if I should have. In fact, I am seriously thinking of returning home.'

'So, you don't believe my innocence in this?'

Lyndon lowered his eyes. 'I'm angry - I don't know what to believe.'

*

The rest of the household had gathered in the kitchen, exchanging worried glances about the altercation going on in Lyndon and Jenna's bedroom. They could hear every word spoken.

'Did you know there was a problem?' Hillary asked Matthew.

He nodded yes.

'Why didn't you tell me? I could have spoken to Jenna about this – and we could have avoided this argument they are having. If Jenna thought for one moment that Lyndon believed she was being inappropriate with anyone else, she would have addressed it before we came here.'

'I only found out on the boat journey. I knew he was pensive about coming and agitated about something, when it continued during the voyage, I forced him to tell me.'

'We were on the boat for fourteen days, Matthew!'

'Hillary darling, one argument is enough I think – we are guests here,' Matthew warned.

Hillary turned and apologised to Ruby and Justin.

'Do not worry. It will all blow over. We have had one or two guests arrive in the past only to argue as soon as they are alone – it is the journey – it would test anyone's patience,' Justin said with a smile. 'I watched those two at your wedding and from what I can see they are besotted with each other. Give them time.'

Just at that minute. Lyndon came out of the room, glanced apologetically at everyone, and walked out of the door.

Matthew made to follow him, but Hillary put her hand on his arm. 'Let him be. If, as you say, this has been simmering for a while, now he has confronted Jenna, he will need time to sort this out in his mind.'

'How come you know so much about men?' Matthew asked curiously

'I think like one, that's why. Right, I shall go and see how Jenna is.'

'So, I can't go to Lyndon's aid, but you can go to Jenna's!'

'Correct! We are a vastly different breed to you men, darling. We need to analyse things woman to woman. Men need to brood.'

Matthew's eyes cut to Ruby's.

'It's true,' she answered his questioning look, 'women need women and men need to lick their wounds on their own.'

Matthew then looked at Justin who just raised his eyebrows.

'Right,' Ruby said to change the subject, 'who could murder a gin and tonic?'

'Count me in,' Hillary shouted from inside Jenna's bedroom, and everyone laughed.

'I swear that woman can hear the top coming off a bottle of gin at twenty yards,' Matthew said wryly.

42

Hillary stood in Jenna's bedroom - her head tipped, her hands on her hips.

'Where has Lyndon gone?'

'I don't know.' Jenna flopped down on the wicker chair.

'We heard most of it, and Matthew said Lyndon had confided in him about it. I would have told you if I knew, you know I would.'

'I feel so awful, Hillary. I feel as though I must have led Gabriel on.'

'Unintentionally though,' Hillary interjected.

'Nevertheless, it seems Gabriel believes there is something between us when there really is not. Goodness, but I've been a fool, and in truth, I *have* sought these meetings, but it's not Gabriel I covet, it's little Robbie. I feel as though I have been given another chance from someone up high to see if I can care and love another child.'

'What on earth do you mean?'

'I never told you this before, Hillary, but when I was married to that hateful first husband of mine, I rejected the baby I bore him.' She shook her head. 'It was a boy, and it looked like my husband, and I just couldn't take to him. The poor little mite never knew a mother's love- because I wouldn't let him near me. He died two days after being born from a heart condition that I think I probably caused.'

'Now Jenna, how could you possibly have caused it?'

'I starved myself when I was pregnant, I didn't want it growing inside me, I don't think the child formed properly. He died never knowing a kind word or a cuddle from his mother. Robbie is the same age as my child would have been. Robbie is the sort of child I thought I would have had with Lyndon – he is a handsome little lad with an abundance of auburn hair.'

'And you *will* have children with Lyndon!'

'I won't, Hillary. I think I shall be punished forever for what I did.'

'Fiddlesticks, you're talking nonsense now. Punished by whom, God? Let me tell you, there is no god to punish you, trust me, he would have struck me down several times for my misdemeanours.'

Jenna smiled through her tears.

'Your baby dying had nothing to do with you, so stop blaming yourself. So, how does the land lie now with Lyndon?'

'Well, I have told him I had no idea that Gabriel was interested in me, but he is struggling to believe me. Gosh, Hillary, what shall I do? I love only Lyndon, and I'm sorry to say this, as I know James was your friend, but Lyndon has been the only man I have ever genuinely loved.'

*

Outside, Lyndon was sitting under the open window of their bedroom and could hear every word said inside. He buried his head in his hands berating himself for not staying to hear her explanation. *You bloody fool to doubt her!* He thumped his head with the knuckles of his wrists and then looked up when he heard Matthew call out his name with a degree of urgency. He got up and made his way to the front of the villa.

'Thank god I've found you. Barclay's here, he wants to know if we can lend a hand picking his grapes. The rain is imminent, and the harvest will spoil. Justin and I are willing, will you come?'

'Of course.' He looked towards the villa, but Matthew grabbed his arm and they set off in Barclay's car in a cloud of dust.

*

Jenna had stripped to her petticoat, her stays thrown to the chair with abandon as she cooled her hot body under the ceiling fan. There was a pitcher and bowl of fresh water in the room, she swilled her face to try and reduce the puffiness around her eyes from crying. Hillary had done her best to chivvy her along, but all she wanted was to speak to Lyndon to try and sort out this terrible misunderstanding.

Dismayed when Lyndon did not return to their room, she reluctantly slipped her dress back on, and put on a brave face as she stepped out to make her embarrassed apologies to her hosts on his behalf.

The temperature had cooled slightly, and Jenna found Hillary and Ruby on the terrace enjoying a cooling drink.

'Jenna. Come, sit down. The men have gone.'

'Gone?' Jenna's eyes widened.

'They have gone to help Giovanni get in the harvest – I suspect they will be gone all night. I've sent them off with bread, cheese, and meat, so they won't starve. Now you're here, I shall cook something for us - if you're ready to eat.'

'Thank you, Ruby, but first please let me apologise.'

'No, no need.' She held her hand up. 'It happens, tempers become frayed in the heat, but everything normally sorts itself out quickly.'

'I wish I had your confidence.'

'Before Lyndon went, and they went in a hurry, he said to tell you that he is sorry.'

'Sorry, sorry for what? For not wanting me anymore? For deciding to leave me here and return home, what?'

Hillary put a calming hand on Jenna. 'Darling, calm yourself. He is not going anywhere - trust me on this.'

Jenna's eyes began to water again, and Hillary put her arm around her. 'Pour her a drink, Ruby. I always find it helps.'

*

After a meal of pasta and mushrooms in a tasty tomato sauce, coupled with a glass of ruby red wine, so bursting with the flavour of wild berries it tingled Jenna's tongue, she felt at last her whole body relax. Tired from the journey, the ladies retired early.

Despite the fan, the room was hot and stuffy under the mosquito net and the constant whine of a mosquito somewhere in the room pulled her from sleep on several occasions. When Jenna woke the next morning, a heady aroma of coffee and sweet pastries filled the air, and she followed her nose to find Hillary and Ruby on the terrace.

Looking for the others, she asked, 'Are the men still not back yet?'

Ruby smiled. 'No, they've been out all night. I went down to them first thing this morning with figs and apples, and they were almost finished, I don't think they will be long before they return. Did you sleep well, Jenna?' she asked searchingly. 'Apart from the heat and mosquitoes, I mean.'

Jenna laughed. 'It was rather challenging.'

'You'll acclimatise soon. Come sit down and eat,' Ruby gestured. 'There is a storm brewing now and once the rain starts it's torrential and we'll not be able to sit here.'

The sky was flat and grey and decidedly chilly, and a low rumble of thunder foretold of what was to come. The lush vegetation in the gardens which everyone had commented on when they arrived, wore a muted green hue now, as though huddling to shield from the oncoming weather.

Ruby placed a hand over Jenna's. 'You look pensive. All will work out well – I am sure.'

'I just don't know what to do about Gabriel.'

'I know Gabriel, he is a decent sort of chap. Once he understands how the land really lies, he will do the honourable thing and step back.'

'But I feel now – the more I think of it – I had given Gabriel hope that there was something between us. I simply did not think he would look on me as anything other than a friend. And poor little Robbie, I should have realised when the little lad thought I was going to be his new mama that I had overstepped the line. How on earth am I going to face them now – I loved spending time with the boy – it will break my heart not to see him again.'

'Jenna,' Hillary said firmly, 'I told you last night, you will soon have your own children to love and care for - and don't shake your head, you will, I tell you. Lots of people have lost babies and I bet there isn't a mother in the world who does not blame herself at first – it is a natural thing a mother does, to ask herself "what did I do wrong?" *You* Jenna, did *nothing* wrong. From what Matthew has told me about your violent husband, you were thoroughly traumatised by him and his actions.

'You don't have to stop seeing the little lad,' Ruby interjected, 'you could be his favourite friend - a makeshift aunt or something like that.'

Jenna tipped her head. 'And how do you think Lyndon is going to like that, if they are both still in my life.'

'Lyndon is a sensible soul, and you of all people know he is,' Ruby answered, 'he will not mind, now he knows there is nothing between you and Gabriel.'

'*If* he believes me that is. I'm still not sure.'

'He will! Now to change the subject, have you brought paints and brushes with you, Jenna?'

'Yes, my watercolours – and thank goodness I did, Italy is a feast for the senses.'

'Well, while we're waiting for the men to come home, I will show you both my studio. I cannot show you Justin's – he doesn't even allow me in there normally.'

*

The studio was to the side of the villa - housed in the old outhouses. The path that led to the peeling and weathered bright blue front door, was lined with an array of different sized terracotta pots. Most were filled with scarlet geraniums, but the largest displayed a rather spindly looking cerise bougainvillea. There was a small lace covered window in the door, and as Ruby shoved her shoulder to open the door the sharp smell of turpentine fuelled Jenna's desire, she immediately wanted to push Ruby aside and claim the room as her own.

Tubes of paint lay in military precision next to a large glass-mixing pallet. Jars of sable brushes and rows of stretched canvases lay waiting against the wall - gathering dust from the last four years. Sketches covered the walls, and an old wool shawl lay discarded across the worn armchair. The easel, which was splattered with paint, held a half-finished painting of the view down the valley.

'Oh gosh, Ruby, this is a proper artist's studio!' Jenna enthused as she walked around gently eyeing up everything - her artistic juices beginning to flow.

'I thought you would like it, Jenna. You're very welcome to share my space should the urge to paint take you. Personally, I haven't had time to paint much since I returned – I needed to get the villa ready for you all, but the moment I stepped back into the studio I admit I abandoned the washing of the windows as my fingers itched to put paint to canvas again.'

'Mmm, but I know that feeling well,' Jenna breathed.

'I didn't do much painting while I was back at Bochym,' Ruby said wistfully. 'Sarah and I were so busy while the soldiers were rehabilitating – art has rather taken a back step – but now, oh….' She rubbed her fingers together in anticipation.

'Well don't let us keep you from it,' Hillary said, 'we will be happy to go exploring on our own.'

'Yes, but we want to show you everything. I do normally work in the early morning – I am so used to getting up with the dawn from when I was a housekeeper at Bochym. So, I shall have the best of both worlds and we shall all have a jolly good time.'

When they stepped out of the studio, a deep rumble of thunder rolled around the valley below and shortly afterwards the first great spots of rain splashed on the terrace. The smell in the air changed as a rich earthy aroma rose from the ground soaking up the life-giving moisture.

'What you can smell is petrichor - the smell of rain,' Ruby said, as they watched the storm drifting in from the sea. 'The word comes from the Greek words 'petra', meaning stone, and 'ichor', which in Greek mythology refers to the golden fluid that flows in the veins of the immortals.'

Within seconds of the rain starting, a bolt of lightning crisscrossed the dark clouds and the thunder clap resonated overhead. True to Ruby's prediction, when the rain started to fall in earnest, the force of it falling, coupled with the overflow from the terracotta roof, rendered it impossible for them to sit on the terrace without getting soaked through with the spray on the stone flags.

They all squealed as they picked up cushions, cups, and the cloth from the table as they ran to the door of the villa.

When they turned, all they could see was a wall of water pouring down like a waterfall from the room.

'Goodness gracious, I've never seen rain like it,' Hillary declared as they pulled up chairs to sit just inside the villa where they could experience the storm whilst keeping relatively dry.'

'It is quite spectacular, isn't it?' Ruby laughed.

'The men are going to be soaked,' Jenna said, and at that very moment, Justin came running in through the curtain of water swiftly followed by Matthew. For a split-second Jenna thought Lyndon was not with them and then he burst through into the villa panting from the exertion of the run from the car. They all stood like drowned rats, laughing, and slapping each other on the back, making a huge puddle on the tiled floor of the villa.

'We did it,' Justin said reaching for Ruby to pick her up and swing her around.

'Let me down, you're wet through,' she complained whilst laughing with him.

'We got the last basket of Giovanni De Rienzo's grapes in the barn five minutes before the rain came,' he said as he kissed Ruby before he put her back on her feet.

Brushing her damp clothes down, Ruby said, 'go on you lot, get dried and I will make you all some breakfast.'

As they made their way to their rooms, Lyndon turned to Jenna beckoning her to follow. She cast a worried look at the two other woman who urged her to follow.

Once in the bedroom he closed the door and turned to face her - his auburn hair hung heavy with droplets of rain, and his eyes were hooded with fatigue.

Before Lyndon could say a word, Jenna said tremulously, 'Don't leave me, Lyndon, please don't leave me.'

'Jenna, my Jenna.' He sighed as his fingers reached up to her face damp with tears – his touch had a lightness in contradiction to the largeness of his work worn hands as he thumbed away her tears. Taking her into his arms - the cool wet of his shirt penetrated her thin dress as he held her as though his life depended on it. 'I will never leave you, my darling. Don't ever think that again.'

'But the argument last night. I'm so sorry, I really had no idea.'

He put his finger to her lips. 'Hush, my love, it's all forgotten. It is I who is sorry, Jenna. I'm sorry I doubted you. I was a fool to think it,' he said covering her face with kisses.

'But Gabriel thinks it! What are we to do?'

'Nothing, everything will be fine. I will speak to him when we return.'

Jenna relaxed her body into his arms, and as he pulled her close, she felt his urgency for her building. Despite the dampness of her clothes from his embrace, her body responded with a passion she had not felt for many years and a primal need which matched his.

Looking up into the pools of his eyes, she shivered slightly in anticipation.

'I love only you, Lyndon.'

'I know, I know, my love.'

Her dress was loosely fitted, and he was able to very gently ease it off her shoulders so that it slipped from her body to pool at her feet. Underneath, she wore a peach-coloured silk camisole, French knickers, and no stockings. 'You're so beautiful, Jenna, I have longed for this moment,' he whispered, as he peeled his wet shirt from his body, and without taking his eyes of Jenna's, he kicked off his shoes and discarded his trousers.

Coming back to stand beside her, naked and wanting, she ran her fingers across his broad strong shoulders as he slowly undid the ribbons on the camisole. Leaning towards him with a sigh, she felt the soft auburn hair which liberally covered his chest tickle her face. With little effort he scooped her into his arms and lay her down on the bed. Thunder rumbled across the rooftops and the cool breeze from the storm fluttered the voile curtains into the room as finally after all these years, they lost themselves in each other again.

*

Entwined in each other's arms, the storm rumbled slowly over the Tuscan hills and away into the distance. The rain ceased and the breeze that cooled their hot bodies died away to be replaced by a sultry heat.

'I'm thousands of miles from Cornwall, but I feel as though I've come home now I have you back in my arms again,' Lyndon whispered, as he placed soft kisses in between Jenna's fingers. 'I'm so tired.'

'You've been working all night - I'm not surprised.'

'No, I'm tired of waiting for this. I feared that we would never be together again after I received that letter.'

'Letter?'

He moved his arm from around her and walked naked to his suitcase. She watched the muscles on his taut torso ripple as he searched for what he was looking for. She smiled at how much she wanted this man to be always near her.

'I received this just before the book launch.' He handed her the well-wisher letter.

Jenna sat up and gasped. 'Wait a moment – I know this handwriting. It belongs to Marianne.'

'Marianne!'

'Do you know her?'

'Yes, I've met her at Bochym – she's friends with Lucy, one of the maids there. She has quite a high opinion of herself if you ask me.'

'Well, she works at the tearoom – I saw her handwriting on the tea bill she wrote out.'

'When you had tea with Gabriel you mean.'

She turned and gave him a warning look. 'I went because it was little Robbie's birthday! Marianne must have read more into me being there, though how she knew I was involved with you, I simply don't know and why would she want to cause trouble?'

'Well, that's something we will have to find out. Jenna, about the boy….'

'Please don't tell me I can't see the little chap again, Lyndon.'

'I'm not going to do that - though I think you need to give Gabriel a wide berth until we can get this settled. I know how you feel about the boy, and why!'

Jenna lowered her eyes, and he gathered her into his arms so that they could lie down again. 'I overheard you speaking to Hillary after our quarrel, about a baby.'

'So,' she said tentatively, 'you heard that I might not be able to give you children?'

'I did. But my darling, all I want is you, and whether our love makes a baby is inconsequential, what matters now is that we are together. I know you want to be a mother now, but if a baby does not come naturally then we will give an orphan a chance of a family with us.'

Jenna took a deep tremulous breath. 'Thank you,' she whispered.

'Now my love,' he reached for his watch, 'it is a quarter past two in the afternoon and I have not slept for over thirty-one hours, so please let me kiss your beautiful lips again before I drift off to sleep.'

43

Jenna and Lyndon woke early the next morning entwined in each other's arms.

'Good morning, beautiful,' Lyndon said kissing her on the nose.

Jenna sighed happily. 'I think I'm dreaming – I can see you in my bed and feel your arms around me.'

'You're not dreaming, my love. We are here together at last, and we have four weeks in Italy to settle into what will be our new life together. We have much to discuss, but also nights in each other's arms. Let's enjoy being together at last.'

When Jenna and Lyndon dressed, they followed the aroma of warm bread and hot coffee out onto the terrace. They sat down to breakfast and looked sheepishly at everyone seated around the table.

'I apologise for the argument the other night, and for us not joining you for dinner last night,' Lyndon said.

'Think nothing of it,' Ruby answered, her linen dress flowing in the breeze as she put a fresh jug of coffee on the table. 'We all went to bed quite early. Did you come down for anything to eat after we retired.'

'We did, we took some meat, cheese and bread back to bed,' he said with a tinge of embarrassment.'

'Good for you. There is nothing better than a picnic in bed,' Justin laughed as he pulled Ruby towards him for a hug.

'Mmm, we have yet to experience that,' Matthew said raising an eyebrow at Hillary.

'Early days, darling,' she winked. 'I'm just enjoying the experience of sharing a bed with you, my new husband – I've no desire to have crumbs between the sheets.'

'I highly recommend it,' Lyndon said, and Jenna looked at him in mock shock.

'What say we take a trip down to Florence this morning,' Justin suggested, 'we can do a little sightseeing and maybe visit the Uffizi Gallery.

Just at that moment a cyclist arrived with a telegram. Justin paid him and opened it.

'Oh!' he said.

'What is it – not bad news I hope.' Matthew enquired.

'No, just something from my agent. Ruby, can I speak with you a moment. We need to sort something out.'

Inside the villa, Justin handed the telegram to Ruby.

GABRIEL BRINGING MARY. ARRIVE 1.10.19.
PHONE BOCHYM.

'Gabriel bringing Mary! What on earth could have happened?'

'I don't know.' Justin rubbed the stubble on his chin. 'I shall phone Peter when we go down to Florence and find out. It all sounds a little ominous. It must be something serious as Gabriel was not meant to come until the others had gone.'

Ruby looked anxious. 'After that argument the other night, which was clearly over Gabriel, how are we going to tell Lyndon, his love rival is coming?'

'In all honesty I don't think Gabriel is a love rival – you said yourself that it had been a terrible misunderstanding on Gabriel's part.'

'But there might well be ructions, when he does get here and still believes Jenna is his future.'

'Well, I don't think we should say anything yet. Gabriel will not be here for another fortnight. I think we should let Lyndon and Jenna have this time to themselves without the worry of confrontation. Their relationship will be rock solid by the time he arrives, and nothing will shake it.'

Ruby pushed her fingers through her hair. 'I hope you're right. But the other problem is, where shall we house them? We're full here!'

'Perhaps Barclay will accommodate them. Let's not worry about it now. Come, we must get back to our guests.'

*

After all squeezing into the car, they spent a lovely morning seeing some of the sights of Florence. They decided against the Uffizi Gallery due to the long queue, so they all took a leisurely lunch in a small restaurant overlooking the Arno, before taking the winding, dusty road back to Villa Casomi.

Once everyone had settled in the shade with a cool drink, Justin told Ruby about his phone conversation with Peter at Bochym.

'Good grief! Who would have done such a thing to Mary?'

'All the staff have been questioned and they all swear that they have not uttered a word of what went on. The only non-members of the household in the house that day were Marianne and Gabriel and by what Gabriel is doing to protect Mary by bringing her here – I rather think he was not responsible.'

Ruby leant against the cold wall of the villa enjoying the feel of it. 'Marianne then?'

'It seems the only possibility.'

'Goodness! Why would she do such a thing?'

'When questioned, Lucy said that Marianne has set her hat at Gabriel, but he has been spending time with Mary – helping her over that unfortunate incident. Marianne had also questioned the validity of Mary picking the wrong mushrooms. In fact, do you remember Marianne saying that day at the tearoom that she could not understand how Mary had managed to pick a poisonous mushroom *and* eat it, because everyone knew what to look for.'

'I do,' Ruby breathed, 'I had to stop her from going on about it. Damn the girl, for her unchecked opinion, and by the look of it, she was clearly jealous about Mary, when I'm sure she had no need to be.'

Justin nodded. 'They can't prove Marianne spread the rumours, but it seems highly likely.'

'Poor Mary. To be uprooted from everyone she knows by such actions.'

'Peter and Sarah apologized for sending her before telling us, but it was imperative they left quickly and thought we wouldn't mind.'

'I don't mind. Do you?'

Justin shook his head and smiled. 'As far as I'm concerned, she is very welcome.'

Ruby flung her arms around him. 'You are so kind.'

'It costs nothing to be kind – something young Marianne might like to think about in the future.'

*

Gabriel, Mary, and Robbie had been at sea for five days when the weather turned stormy. Up to that day they had enjoyed all the delights the ship had to offer. For someone who had never set foot on a sea vessel before, Mary adapted very quickly. They had all felt a little queasy shortly after they had moved out of Southampton harbour, but Mary threw herself into entertaining Robbie and by the next day, with the aid of a seasickness tablet each, they all got their sea legs. There were many forms of entertainment on the deck which kept Robbie and all the other children entertained for hours. After the devastation of being ripped from everything she knew, Mary began to enjoy this unexpected adventure. At least she was going to stay with Ruby, whom she loved as a mother – she just hoped Ruby wouldn't mind this cuckoo in their Italian nest.

Before they had set off, Molly Johnson the housekeeper had told Mary that she would be traveling with Gabriel as Robbie's governess, but she soon found out that Gabriel looked on her more of a companion than anything else. More than anything she wished she had more than two nice dresses with her, for Gabriel was a gentleman and dressed accordingly. She felt the lack of nice clothes the most when he insisted on her eating an early evening meal with them every night in the vast dining room. Afterwards they would take a stroll out on deck before she would read Robbie a bedtime story in Gabriel's cabin and then retire to her own cabin to read one of the novels she had picked up in the ship's library. Gabriel was kindness personified and Mary knew she had become very close to him over the past few weeks, and more so these last few days. If she admitted to herself, she had fallen just a tiny bit in love with him and his wonderful little son but knew she must rid all thoughts and fancies from her mind. He was just a kind man who had gone out of his way to help her in her hour of need, and she must remember that. She would miss him and Robbie though, once he had left her with Ruby. He had told her he would send a telegram once they docked in Naples for Justin and Ruby to meet them from the train in Florence, and once he had handed her over to them, he would go off and find a hotel for himself and Robbie. He had said that it was because there was no room at the villa for them all as they already had guests, but Mary knew that Gabriel was not ready to meet with Jenna Blackwell who was one of those guests. Mary felt close enough to Gabriel to know that him finding out that the woman he thought he was in love with, was in fact his friends intended, had saddened Gabriel. It was as though the spark had gone out of his life and she was deeply sorry for him.

*

The storm had hit the ship during the evening meal on Saturday. Lights flickered, glasses began to smash, and people found they were holding on to their tables when the boat had become a little unstable. The captain suggested that it was perhaps best for people to retire to their cabins and lie down, to avoid falling over once the ship hit choppy seas. Everyone took his advice and three times on the descent down the iron steps to the cabins they were thrown against the walls.

'No story tonight, Robbie,' Gabriel said. 'It will be best if Mary goes to her cabin to lie down like the captain said. At Mary's door he could see in her eyes that she was frightened. 'Will you be all right, Mary?' She nodded fearfully. 'I'll bid you goodnight then. Hopefully, the storm will pass through quickly.'

Gabriel laid on his cabin bed and gathered Robbie into his arms, but the child was fretful with every boom of wave against the ship. 'I want Mama to hold me as well,' he sobbed.

'I'm sorry, Robbie. I'm sure Mama is watching over us to keep us safe.'

'I want Mary then.'

'Mary must stay in her own cabin. We all must lie down.'

Robbie started to cry broken heartedly. 'I want her to be here with us, so we know she is safe. Please Papa, please can Mary come and be with us? I'm frightened.'

Gabriel's heart caught that Jane was not here to comfort Robbie, so there was only one thing to do, although it was highly inappropriate!

When Mary came to the door, her hair was down, and she was dressed in her nightdress and housecoat. There were fearful tears in her eyes.

'Are you all right, Mary.'

She shook her head. 'I'm terrified I am going to die here. Silly, isn't it? I wanted to die a few weeks ago and now I'm fearful of the prospect.'

Without hesitation or thought of propriety he pulled Mary into his arms to comfort her. 'Robbie will not settle without you, and it seems to me that you need company too. Would you mind coming to our cabin?' Mary had stepped out of her cabin and closed the door behind her before he had finished the sentence.

Robbie on seeing her, held his arms out, and she folded him into hers. The ship listed slightly, and they all stumbled awkwardly.

'We need to lie down like we were told.' Gabriel instructed.

Mary climbed on the bed with Robbie and pulled him close to her, whispering soothing words which Gabriel suspected were calming them both down.

Gabriel went to lie on the other bunk, but Robbie started to cry again.

'Papa, you come and hold me too, and then we will all be safe.'

Gabriel shot an anxious look at Mary who smiled weakly and nodded. Gabriel climbed onto the bed and settled down beside them. He curled his arm over his son, his hand softly brushing Mary's where hers lay, and for a fleeting second there was a moment of pure intimacy between Gabriel and Mary. The waves boomed against the side of the ship and Robbie's body stiffened in their arms, so Mary began to sing a soft lullaby.

Gabriel's eyes swept over Mary's still painfully thin body. A lock of her thick brown hair had fallen slightly over her pretty face and the tears on her eyelashes only minutes earlier had now dried. He was able to gaze at her as she sang and looked down on his son. For a moment, Gabriel could not conjure the image of his darling wife's face. Something visceral caught at his heart – the image before him was perfect. Though he had coveted Jenna to take his wife's place, seeing Mary with Robbie, this beautiful scenario of someone close to them both, giving love when it was needed, was more than any man could ever want.

Very soon the child's eyes grew heavy, he pushed his thumb in his mouth as he used to do when he was quite small, and his little body fell limp with sleep. Mary fell silent and lifted her eyes to Gabriel's.

'Thank you,' he mouthed, and she smiled her sweet smile back.

*

It was a slight movement in her arms which woke Mary the next morning. Opening her eyes, she looked around the unfamiliar room - sometime during the night she must have turned on her back. Very slowly she looked down at the child tucked in at her side and remembered then where she was. Swallowing hard to counteract the dryness in her mouth, she dared not cast her eyes to the side - knowing she had spent the night in Gabriel's bed. She had unashamedly watched Gabriel fall asleep only inches away from her. His handsome face had relaxed as his blond eyelashes fluttered closed. Very softly his breathing deepened, and his lips parted and more than anything, Mary wanted to reach over and kiss him very tenderly on the mouth.

Robbie shifted again in her arms, and she kissed his soft hair when he whimpered slightly in his sleep, and when she looked up again, she locked eyes with Gabriel. He was wide awake now and looking directly at her.

'Morning,' he mouthed.

'Good morning,' she whispered.

'It seems the storm has passed.'

She smiled and nodded and something inside her wished the storm had lasted for ever.

44

At The Poldhu Tea Rooms, Marianne had not heard a whisper of gossip about her real parentage – perhaps Ellie had been right saying that nobody in the stables that night would say anything. She momentarily felt a pang of guilt that she had tried to make trouble for Mary to deflect gossip away from herself, but then she brushed it aside - it served Mary right for thinking she could worm her way into Gabriel's affection. Thinking of Mary, Marianne was confused that no gossip had materialised about her either, especially since she planted the note in Mrs Jennings's mushroom box almost a week ago. Normally if Mrs Jennings heard a whiff of scandal it went around Mullion like wild fire. Unbeknown to Marianne it had been the local police officer's wife who had picked the note from the mushroom box, and without mentioning it to Mrs Jennings, had passed it onto her husband to deal with officially.

The tearoom was busy again that Sunday. Outside, Betsy sat with Ryan, their two children, and Meg and Tobias Williams, all of whom caused Marianne great unease - they all knew about her parentage!

Meg smiled at Marianne. 'We have just been discussing the advert in the West Briton for an assistant cook at Bochym Manor. Has Mary left?'

'I don't know,' she answered feeling a blush rise. *She certainly hoped so – Marianne could have Gabriel all to herself then.* 'I shall find out tomorrow when I go up to see Lucy.'

'I don't blame her if she has decided to move on,' Betsy said jiggling baby William on her knee, 'perhaps a fresh start somewhere will help her get over Thomas.'

Or perhaps she found that her shocking little secret had become known. Perhaps the note had worked after all. Marianne thought.

'Gabriel Trelease works at Bochym,' Marianne said casually. 'He normally comes to tea with his son on a Sunday afternoon – he'll know if she's gone.'

'He's not coming today,' Ellie said putting a pot of tea on the table, 'nor for a while to come.'

Marianne shot her a sharp look. 'Why?'

'He has gone away for a couple of months. It was all a spur of the moment thing, but he asked Sarah to send word down to cancel his regular table here.'

Two months! Marianne felt her stomach plummet.

Ellie tipped her head. 'I would have thought he'd have left word with your mother – after all, she works for the Trelease's.'

'She does,' she said tremulously,' but she's been laid up with lumbago this week.' Suddenly tears began to well, and Marianne had to quickly turn away to clear another table.

*

With Gabriel gone, Marianne was undecided whether to go up to Bochym Manor on her day off, but curiosity got the better of her. She wanted to see Lucy to find out if Mary had been banished, and if she had, Marianne would relish that her gut instinct that Mary had tried to commit suicide, had been correct. So, it would serve her right!

Practically skipping across the kitchen courtyard, she knocked and stepped through the open door, only for Mrs Blair to turn and shout, 'Stop!'

Marianne halted and looked down to her feet to see if the kitchen floor had just been mopped, but it was bone dry. When she looked up, Joe Treen was stood in front of her.

'Step outside please.' He ushered her out of the kitchen, pulled the door closed behind him and folded his arms.

Marianne gave an embarrassed laugh when he just stared at her. 'What?' She shrugged.

His eyebrows knitted with disapproval. 'I think you know what,' he answered crisply.

Marianne flushed furiously. 'I don't know what you mean, I'm here to see Lucy.'

'Lucy does not want to see you, and from this moment on, you are not welcome at Bochym Manor.'

Feeling a sickness in the pit of her tummy she asked tentatively, 'But, but why?'

'You know why.' He turned, went back inside, and closed the door on her.

For a moment she did not move. *They must know what she had done. How could they know though? They couldn't know, but....* Suddenly the consequences of her actions began to dawn on her – she would never be able to come here again. Hanging her head, she walked across the kitchen courtyard and then turned to look back at the manor. There at the bedroom window stood Lucy with her arms folded. Marianne smiled and lifted her hand to wave, but Lucy just shook her head and turned away from her.

*

For a blissful week, Lyndon and Jenna slowly found the love they had lost - spending nights of passion, and days holding hands like new lovers. As Matthew and Hillary had gone for a walk, and Ruby and Justin were working in their respective studios, Jenna took this opportunity to speak candidly to Lyndon about the one thing they had not yet addressed, money.

Sitting in the shade, on the edge of her sun lounger she cleared her throat.

'I've been thinking, if I am allowed to keep James's money and houses,' she paused momentarily when she heard Lyndon sigh heavily, 'I would like to give over Bellevue Gardens to vulnerable young girls who are living on the street. You know, girls like Emily who helped us that day in London.'

Lyndon's interest was piqued, he turned on his sun lounger to face her, so she went on to explain her plans.

'Do you think Mrs Hemp would do that?' he asked.

'I think so, yes. When Emily stayed that one night, she told Mrs Hemp about her life on the streets. It upset Mrs

Hemp to think nothing could be done for them. If it's too much for her, I can employ someone to help.'

'But you'll need somewhere to stay when you're in London, will you not?'

'I'll probably keep the studio on the top floor, but I can sleep at Hillary's place. So, what do you think of my idea?'

'It's a nice idea, and Loe House, what do you plan to do with that?'

'I'm keeping it.'

His eyes clouded. 'I don't want to live in James's house.'

'It's our house now.'

'*Yours!*'

'In truth, Lyndon nobody really owns a house,' she said remembering what Hillary had said on the subject, 'we just take possession of it and look after it until we pass it on. I thought we could keep it as a weekend retreat. James's friends can use it when we are not there. What do you say? He wanted me to have it. He wanted *us* to have it.'

'So, you want me to visit you at weekends there?'

'No, silly, she laughed. 'I want to live at Trevarno with you. In your house. We could even move to a bigger place on the estate – I believe Namskerris where Hillary's friends stayed for the wedding is empty. We could share the rent.'

Lyndon's mouth twitched at this thought.

'You earn your money from your work, Lyndon, and I earn money from mine.'

And what about the vast wealth coming in from James's estate?'

'What about it?'

'I want to provide for my wife.'

'And so, you will, from what you earn. But our life is changing, Lyndon. Hillary coming into Matthew's life, will inevitably alter our life irrevocably too. Matthew wants you at his side and Hillary wants me at hers. Though we are still that couple who fell in love in that meadow – you, a hedger, me, an artist, nothing stays the same. It will soon be 1920 - we are moving into a new era. The money James left was for us to move with the times – and he did leave it to *us!* We could do more of this,' she reached out and curled her hand around his, 'spend days in the sun - see the world, make love in countries we never thought we would ever visit.' She smiled sweetly.

Lyndon laid back and closed his eyes and Jenna watched as he digested her words.

'When do you plan to marry me?' he said with his eyes still shut.

'I thought perhaps at Christmas. You'll be in Devon for a month when we get back.'

'I'd rather marry you before I went – just in case someone else comes along and wants you for their own.' He opened one eye and looked at her.

She broke into a broad smile. 'I shall endeavour not to do anything to encourage any such interest again. Christmas would be perfect. It will be six months since James died by then, so no one could accuse me of any impropriety about remarrying too soon.'

'Jenna Trevone, I do not know how you have the barefaced cheek to speak of propriety after what you have done to me in bed this last week,' he teased.

Jenna blushed up to the roots of her hair. 'Hush, someone might hear.'

'Be under no illusions, they probably all know what goes on in that bedroom. You've a tendency to cry out when we make love.'

She slapped him playfully. 'That's a shocking thing to say, I do not cry out!'

He grinned, grabbed her arm, and pulled her towards him to kiss her. 'Speaking of which, I should very much like to make you cry out now.' He got up, took her hand, and led her into the cool of the villa.

*

Although they had fitted back into their normal routine of dining together and taking an evening stroll around the ship, there had been a shift in the way Gabriel thought of Mary since that night of the storm five days ago. It was something which caused a little uneasiness in his heart. He was not sure if he had got over the disappointment with the whole Jenna scenario and wondered if his fragile heart had compensated by looking for something that perhaps was not there in Mary. He sat on the deck now watching her playing with Robbie in the morning sun and shook his head. Those thoughts were very discourteous to Mary, after she had been so tender with his son. His heart caught as he remembered waking during that night and watching her sleep only inches away from his face, his son happy in her arms. *Come on Gabriel, you either feel something for her or you don't.* His heart answered that question as he concluded that he was very much afraid that he did feel something. He blew out a long breath. If that was the case, how was he ever going to be able to leave her in Italy?

45

On Wednesday morning another telegram came to Villa Casomi.

'I think you need to get a telephone installed,' Lyndon joked seeing the poor boy on the bicycle sweating profusely. 'You're going to kill all the young boys around here if they have to fetch as many telegrams as this normally.'

'Believe me we would, but I suspect it will be years before they install the lines out here in the sticks,' Justin said, taking the telegram from the boy and paying him generously for his troubles.

'More requests for paintings from your agent,' Jenna asked.

Justin smiled and glanced at Ruby to follow him inside.

'Gabriel and Mary will be in Florence at five. Barclay is out for the day but he's expecting them. He has left the key in the normal place. We'll fetch them from Florence, take Gabriel and the child to Barclay's and bring Mary here. Then we can explain to Lyndon and Jenna what is happening, hopefully that way we can avoid any unpleasantness.

*

Justin put his Panama hat tightly on his head and Ruby tied a scarf around her hair as they set off to collect Gabriel.

'I do hope all will be well when we tell Lyndon and Jenna that Gabriel is here,' Ruby said anxiously.

'I'm sure everything will be fine. We will break it to them gently. If they don't want to see him, I'm sure Gabriel will understand and stay at Barclays until Lyndon's group set off back to England.'

It was four-o-clock, the train from Naples was due at five - plenty of time to get to Florence – or so they thought. Half way, however, they found the main road blocked by several vehicles having stopped because of an overturned wagon full of grapes. There were plenty of helpers to right the vehicle, but it was going to take time.

They decided to turn back and take the smaller, albeit longer route to Florence but what they had not envisaged was that everyone else had had the same idea. There were cars and wagons, struggling to pass each other, farmers driving sheep, tempers flaring and no chance of getting to Florence any time soon.

*

Gabriel, Mary, and Robbie, stood outside the train station in Florence in the baking heat of the Italian sunshine.

'I'm hot, Papa,' Robbie said sleepily.

'We'll soon be somewhere cooler, Robbie. Let's have a drink in that café while we wait for Justin to come.' An hour later, Gabriel said to alleviate the worried look on Mary's face, 'I can only assume the telegram didn't get to them. Come on, we'll find some sort of transport to take us to the villa.' They walked out into the sun again and Gabriel approached a row of cars.

'Mi scusi, può portarci a Villa Casomi a Pedona per favore?'

The man nodded. 'Tin pochi minuti,' he said waving his cigarette in the air.

'Right, he is just finishing his cigarette and then he will take us.'

'Why did you use those funny words with him, Papa?'

'I was speaking Italian.'

'I didn't know you could speak Italian?'

'Ah, well, Robbie, I had an Italian friend at University, Giuseppe. He taught me to speak it. He said women would fall in love with me if I spoke Italian to them.'

'Is that why Mama fell in love with you?'

Gabriel laughed. 'Amongst other things.'

Robbie turned to Mary. 'Has it made you fall in love with Papa?'

Mary's eyes widened. 'Erm, I believe it is the language of love.'

Robbie looked from Mary to his father. 'Are you going to speak Italian all the time you are here Papa and make Mary fall in love with you?'

Gabriel and Mary's eyes locked for a moment and Gabriel laughed nervously. 'You certainly ask a lot of questions, Robbie.'

'So, how do you say I love you in Italian?'

'Ti amo,' Gabriel answered softly, trying unsuccessfully to avert his eyes from Mary.

'Ti amo,' Robbie repeated, and Gabriel nodded. 'Ti amo, Papa.'

'Anch'io ti amo,'

'What did you say then, Papa?'

'I said I love you too.'

Robbie smiled - he liked this game. 'Ti amo, Mary,' Robbie said sweetly. 'You have to say it back in Italian.'

Mary looked to Gabriel for help. 'Anch'io ti amo,' he repeated, and this time he looked directly at her.

Mary consciously swallowed. 'Anch'io ti amo, Robbie,' she said as she bent down to cuddle him to hide the blush on her face.

'Vieni adesso,' the driver said throwing his cigarette butt on the floor before grinding it in with his toe.

'Come on, it looks like we are on our way,' Gabriel bundled them and their suitcases into the car.

As they made their way up the winding roads towards the villa, Robbie fell asleep in Mary's arms, and Gabriel, too weary from the long journey, closed his eyes. Every time Mary looked at Gabriel's handsome face, all she could think of were the words anch'io ti amo.

*

After paying the driver an extortionate amount of money, they found the villa door locked. It was then Gabriel started to wonder if Justin and Ruby knew they were coming at all.

'I want a wee, Papa,' Robbie said holding himself.'

'Yes, you're not the only one,' Gabriel said. He glanced at Mary, and though she did not admit it, she too was hopping from one foot to the other.

'We'll go this way, Robbie, perhaps Mary can go the other and we can all find somewhere secluded in the garden to relieve ourselves.'

Mary had set off before he had finished speaking.

As they all came back to the front of the villa, they heard voices coming up from the bottom of the garden.

'At last,' Gabriel smiled at Mary, 'signs of civilisation I think.'

*

After an afternoon wine tasting at Giovanni and Rachel De Rienzo's vineyard, Lyndon and Jenna walked rather tipsily up through the gardens of Villa Casomi. With their arms around each other laughing about something, they were gazing lovingly into each other's eyes, when Jenna heard a child shout, 'Jenna!'

Startled, their arms dropped away from each other.

'What the devil...?' Lyndon said on seeing Gabriel.

Robbie ran to Jenna and wrapped his arms around her legs, and she crouched down to hug him.

'Did you know they were coming?' Lyndon snapped at Jenna.

'No, of course not.'

'What the hell are they doing here, then?' he hissed.

'Hush.' Jenna covered Robbie's ears to block out Lyndon's anger and pulled the boy away from the altercation that was clearly brewing. As Ellie passed Gabriel, she flashed him a questioning look and it was then she saw a woman standing by the front door.

Mary curtsied and Robbie ran towards her. 'This is Mary, Jenna, she has been looking after me and Papa on the journey here.'

Jenna smiled weakly and quickly fumbled for the key in her handbag to let Mary and Robbie into the cool of the villa just as voices began to be raised.

'This is not the welcome I thought I would get from a friend,' Gabriel frowned.

'It's the welcome you deserve after coveting my intended.'

'Oh!' Gabriel's eyes lowered. 'You know then.'

'I do.'

'Lyndon, you must believe me. When I found out about you and her, I was shocked. I had absolutely no idea Jenna was your sweetheart. She never spoke of you, she…'

Lyndon balled his fists and growled, 'Don't you blame Jenna for this, she says she had no idea you were interested in her.'

'I don't, I'm not blaming her,' Gabriel said flustered.

'So, If you know about us, why are you here then – there is nothing here for you. Jenna belongs with me!'

They both turned as Matthew and Hillary came through the garden into the fray.

'Gabriel!' Matthew said in astonishment.

Lyndon's eyes flashed angrily at Matthew. 'Did you know he was coming?'

'Don't be absurd, don't you think we would have told you?'

Gabriel put his hands out. 'Look, it is clear my presence here is not expected. Peter said he was going to send word, I thought Justin and Ruby would have told you.'

Just at that moment, Justin's car pulled up and he and Ruby raced up to them.

'Oh, dear, forgive us, Gabriel. Welcome. We are sorry we missed you in Florence. We were waylaid off the road and stuck in traffic on a tiny lane.'

'We got a lift up here,' Gabriel said - the price of it still smarting. 'Ruby, Justin, I fear I have made myself very unwelcome here.'

Lyndon turned to Justin. 'So, you knew he was coming, but you didn't think to tell me after you knew Gabriel had been a sore point between Jenna and myself?'

'Lyndon, we are so sorry. We did not want to spoil your holiday so we thought we would give you a fortnight of happiness together and then we were to pick Gabriel up and take him to Barclay's villa. We were going to break it to you gently once he was here, and If you wanted to see him to sort things out, we would have sent for him to come up.'

'But why is he here?' He turned to Gabriel. 'Why are you here?'

'Gabriel has very kindly brought Mary out to us,' Ruby answered.

'Mary?'

'From Bochym.'

Puzzled, Lyndon looked between them all.

'The police came knocking – someone had told an untruth saying that Mary had attempted to take her own life. Peter and Sarah needed to get her away somewhere safe, to someone she knew, so I offered to bring her here.'

'Oh! I see.' Lyndon's anger finally dissipating.

'Lyndon, my friend. I can only apologise for my stupidity. I clearly read more into my friendship with Jenna than was there. I just wanted the hurt of grief to go away, and I suppose spending time with Jenna – and trust me on this,' he held his hands up, 'I only spent a few hours with her honestly, it made me feel something again! God, but I wish I had told you who I had fallen for - you could have put me right straight away.'

'And how do you feel about Jenna now?'

'I still think she is lovely – but I suspect she has more feelings for my son than me,' he said with a crooked smile. 'Seeing you come up the garden together just then, reiterates that she loves you very much. I can safely say she never looked at me the way she looks at you.' He reached out his hand in friendship to Lyndon and Lyndon took it. 'You're a very lucky man.'

'I know.'

'I just can't understand why you never told me about her.'

'We have our reasons,' Lyndon answered gravely.

'So,' Justin said, feeling the tension in the air ease considerably. 'Let us show you some good old fashioned Italian hospitality, to make up for missing you at the train station. You will stay for dinner? Lyndon, will that be all right with you and Jenna?'

'It will,' Jenna said, having listened to the conclusion of the argument from inside the villa.

'It's nice to see you again so soon, Gabriel, and of course little Robbie. I'm sorry I was the cause of all this upset.'

'Please, do not apologise. I feel very foolish,' Gabriel said sheepishly.

Ruby came outside with a tray of olives and bread, as Mary brought up the rear with jugs of cold lemonade and two carafes of wine.

'Come and sit down everyone, and cool off,' Ruby said ironically. Everyone seated themselves in the shade and Mary turned to take herself off back into the kitchen.

'Mary, where are you going?' Ruby asked.

Mary gulped, and answered softly, 'I... I don't know where I should go.'

'Do you need something from inside?'

'No.'

'Then come and sit down.'

Mary hesitated. 'With you all?'

Ruby laughed. 'Yes, you're not a servant now, you're our guest – and a permanent one at that. Come on.' She moved away from Gabriel, and patted the seat for Mary to sit between them. 'Tell us all about your trip.'

'No, wait!' Hillary stood up and Mary's face looked stricken, obviously feeling that Hillary was going to object to a kitchen maid eating with them.

'What is it, Hillary,' Ruby questioned.

'Look at Mary, the poor girl is boiling in that dark dress and boots. Come, come with me,' she beckoned, 'I am sure we can find you something cooler to wear.'

Mary looked around the table as everyone looked back at her.

'You'll have to go, Mary,' Jenna laughed, 'resistance is futile. Hillary did much the same to me when we first met.'

Ten minutes later, Mary emerged with Hillary proudly showing her off. She was dressed in a loose, cream, calico dress, her hair down, and her feet bare like the rest of the guests were.'

'Ta da, my new protégée,' Hillary said. 'We will go shopping tomorrow and buy her all she needs to live a bohemian life here. Oh God, Matthew, do we have to go back in two weeks' time? I could get used to this,' she said picking up her drink.

As Mary sat back down, she glanced shyly at Gabriel, and found he was smiling warmly back at her.

46

After a cooling drink, Ruby showed Mary her room. Up until two weeks ago it had been a storeroom, but Ruby had worked her magic, put a temporary bed up and pretty curtains.

'This is lovely, thank you,' Mary said touching the bedspread gently.

'It's only temporary. You'll move into one of the bigger rooms when the others vacate. Now I think I should cook dinner.'

'May I help?' Mary followed her.

'Of course, you can, if you're not too tired. I'm just making a very simple pasta dish.'

'What is pasta?'

Ruby smiled. 'It makes a change for me to show you how to cook something. Come, I will show you the art of Italian cooking.'

While they were cooking, Ruby tipped her head and looked at Mary as she worked, she looked a little bemused at this new life she had been plunged into, but much better than when she last saw her. 'Are you all right, Mary, with all this upheaval?'

She nodded sadly. 'I miss Bochym. I miss everyone, but at least I'm with you. Thank you for taking me in, Ruby.'

'It's a pleasure to have you here. You'll be good company for me when Justin is away. How did you get on with Gabriel and Robbie during the trip?'

'Absolutely fine. Gabriel has been so kind, so very, very kind to me, and I love little Robbie more than perhaps I should. I shall miss them when they go to the other villa tonight.' She sniffed.

Ruby turned to give her a moment, but smiled secretly – did she detect a little love interest for Gabriel? She had watched Gabriel and Mary chatting earlier, there was a real easiness between them – a shared companionship. 'I'm sure they will come every day and of course they will come back here to stay with us in a fortnight when the others have gone home.'

Mary's face brightened at that.

*

Sharing a meal as the sun began to set. Gabriel turned to Lyndon.

'Can I just ask. How did you find out that Jenna was the woman I had been speaking about?'

'A mischief letter came for me, here.' He pulled the letter from his pocket and handed it to Gabriel. 'Jenna thinks she knows the hand.'

After reading the letter he handed it back. 'I know this hand too,' Gabriel said gravely. 'It's the hand of Marianne Enys.'

'I knew it,' Jenna said. 'I saw the bill at the tearoom that day.'

Justin and Ruby exchanged glances at the mention of Marianne.

'So, you were planning to marry my intended then?' Lyndon said dryly.

'Lyndon,' Jenna warned.

'Well, I cannot tell a lie, it was certainly on my mind, but I suspect Marianne had overheard my mother and father discussing it at the tearoom,' he looked at Jenna, 'they liked you very much.'

'Oh dear! I'm so sorry Gabriel, to cause this misunderstanding.'

'I'm sure my poor fragile heart will get over it,' he teased, holding his hand to his heart.

'And I'm sure someone equally as lovely will mend that heart for you soon, Gabriel,' Ruby said confidently.

'Then will I have a new Mama, Papa?' Robbie asked – tomato sauce all around his mouth.

'Perhaps,' Gabriel said reaching for a napkin to wipe his face, but Mary beat him to it.

Pushing the napkin away, Robbie said firmly, 'My new mama will have to love me too!'

'Of course, she will – it's a written rule,' Gabriel said softly.

'You love me don't you, Mary, you told me in Italian didn't you – I've forgotten how to say it though.'

'Ti amo,' the words spilled from Mary's lips as though she had been holding it in her mouth.

'Yes, Ti amo that was it. Can Mary be my new mama now that Jenna is going to marry someone else, Papa?'

Gabriel made a small, embarrassed hmph and everyone around the table laughed, but Ruby saw Mary's eyes flicker to Gabriel.

To bring the conversation back, Justin said, 'Going back to Marianne. Sarah and Peter believe that she was the cause of Mary's troubles too.'

'Pardon?' Mary's mouth dropped. 'Why would she do that to me?'

'Lucy told them that she believes that Marianne had set her sights on Gabriel and did not like the friendship he had developed with you. It seems she was jealous.'

'But we did nothing inappropriate, did we,' she looked at Gabriel.

'No, Mary, we didn't.' He smiled softly at her and then addressed the rest of the table. 'I admit, I was not unaware that she had designs on me, but I swear I never gave her any encouragement. In fact, I did everything I could to deflect her advances.'

'Goodness me, "Hell hath no fury like a woman scorned," as they say,' Justin said.

'Quite!' Gabriel answered.

*

When it was time for Justin to drive Gabriel and Robbie to Barclay's villa, Robbie naturally did not want to leave Mary.

'Mary cannot come with us, Robbie. She must stay here.'

'Why, Papa, I want Mary to read to me until I fall asleep.'

'*I* shall do that tonight.'

'But.' His chin wobbled.

Mary folded him into her arms. 'I can't come with you, sweetheart, I'm sorry.'

'Why?'

'A lady cannot be in a house with two gentlemen and a little boy – it is not appropriate,' Justin answered.

'But Mary slept with us in our cabin during the storm when there was only one gentleman and a little boy!'

Gabriel cleared his throat and glanced ruefully around the table. Raised eyebrows and interested faces glanced back.

'That was – that was different, Robbie – we were all frightened of the storm that night. Now come on,' he chivvied him along, 'say goodnight to everyone. We will see them all in the morning.'

Robbie kissed Mary on the cheek and waved at everyone.

As the ladies began to clear the table, Lyndon and Matthew shared another glass of wine.

'Well, I am glad that is all sorted between you and Gabriel,' Matthew said raising his glass.

'You and me both,' Lyndon chinked his glass with Matthew's.

'I don't think he will grieve over Jenna too long. I don't know if you noticed or not, but there was definitely a spark of something between Gabriel and Mary.'

*

The villa kitchen was a hive of activity, but Mary, weary from her long journey could not stifle a yawn.

'If you're tired, Mary, you get off to bed. It's been a long day for you. We'll clear up.'

'Oh, thank you, Ruby. I will if you don't mind.'

As she lay in her bed under this strange net, with the room smelling of lemons, she felt the loss of Gabriel and Robbie's company keenly. When tiredness prevailed, her eyelids fluttered closed, and she thought of Gabriel's handsome face. 'Ti amo, Gabriel,' she whispered into the night.

*

When Barclay drove Gabriel and Robbie back up to Villa Casomi the next morning, the others were discussing where to go that day.

'We were thinking about Viareggio on the coast,' Justin suggested. 'We could take the train from Florence – its only about an hour or so. We are just trying to sort out how to ferry people down to Florence, we cannot get everyone in the car.'

'Take mine, Barclay offered, 'Gabriel can drive it, I have no need for it today.'

'How do you feel about driving in Italy, Gabriel?'

'Fine, it can't be more hair raising than the first time I drove in Britain.'

'Don't bank on it,' Justin muttered under his breath. 'Right then, who is going with whom?'

*

After parking their cars, and a short stop over at Hillary's favourite clothes shop in Florence, where she procured three summer dresses and a pair of soft sandals for Mary, they boarded the train to Viareggio. They stood on Viareggio avenue located alongside the local beach, famed for the Carnival of Viareggio held in February before the war – a spectacular parade of floats and masks, usually made of paper-pulp, depicting caricatures of popular people, such as politicians, showmen and sportsmen.

'Let's have a cool drink and maybe Robbie would like an ice cream, then we can take a dip in the sea, shall we?' Ruby suggested,

Once suitably refreshed they made their way down to the water's edge.

Ruby, walked with Mary. 'I'm afraid there is no segregation in our little group, not like when we went swimming on our days out from Bochym at Poldhu. Are you comfortable about that?'

'I think I'm going to have to embrace many different things now I am no longer the assistant cook at the manor.'

'I think you're very brave Mary, and I will be here to help you all the way.'

'Thank you, Ruby, for everything you have ever done for me. You have always been like a mother to me.'

Ruby put her arm around Mary. 'And you are the daughter I never had.'

Robbie who was holding Mary's hand, tugged on her arm. 'Am I the son you never had, Mary?'

Mary's face broke into a smile as she glanced at Gabriel, who just shook his head in disbelief.

'Robbie,' Gabriel berated, 'you do ask some strange questions.'

'It's all right, Gabriel,' Mary said, 'yes, Robbie you are.'

The ladies went to change into their swimming attire in a changing hut, while the men changed in a large tent by the water's edge.

Embracing different things or not, Mary was slightly nervous about being in her swimming costume in front of Gabriel, especially as her arms and legs stuck out of her costume like thin sticks. Then she thought, *well, he has seen you at your very worst – covered in pink vomit and soaked in urine!* So, she held her head high, and went to join Gabriel and Robbie splashing at the water's edge.

'Can you swim, Mary?'

'Yes, can Robbie?'

'He can a little.'

'Come on then, let's go a little further in and he can swim between us.'

Lyndon and Jenna watched them play for a while and when Robbie wanted to build a sandcastle, Jenna offered to do it with him, so that Mary and Gabriel could go for a proper swim.

'Are you matchmaking, Jenna Trevone?' Lyndon whispered.

'I'm not too sure that is needed, but I'm channelling Amelia Pascoe and giving them a push in the right direction.'

Out in the deeper water, Gabriel and Mary laughed with delight, swimming side by side in the warmth of the Lirugi Sea. Though both consciously avoiding touching each other, Mary had never felt happier.

With shoulders and noses pink with the sun, the group gathered in the shade of a seafront restaurant for a late lunch. While Mary and Gabriel had their heads together to assist Robbie with his plate of sword fish, there was an unspoken agreement between the rest of the group that perhaps Mary would not be staying behind as a guest at Villa Casomi when it was time for Gabriel and Robbie to leave.

47

The next couple of weeks flew by, and with the loan of Barclay's car when not needed, they had visited Sienna, had an overnight stay in Rome – the eternal city - and listened to someone sing an impromptu aria in Lucca. Any reserves they had about a child integrating with the grown-ups were banished. Everyone was enamoured with Robbie, especially as he was so inquisitive and talkative. The boy gravitated to Jenna and Mary, but it was mostly to Mary he went to when he was tired and in need of motherly attention.

This was keenly felt by Jenna, though she didn't say anything, but Lyndon saw the want of a child in her eyes. When it was finally time for Jenna, Lyndon, Matthew, and Hillary to leave Villa Casomi, Gabriel and Robbie came over to say their goodbyes.

'When we get back, we'll collect your things from Barclay's,' Justin said to Gabriel.

'Barclay is happy for us to stay there, you know. We don't mind if you need some time to yourselves.'

'Nonsense, we want you to come, besides Mary has been looking forward to reading Robbie his bedtime story, haven't you Mary?'

She nodded happily and Gabriel's face softened at the thought. 'Very well, we would love to come.'

After a flurry of kisses with everyone, Jenna gave Robbie the biggest and longest hug.

'One day, Jenna, we will have a little one of our own to bring up, however we come by it,' Lyndon said as he gently led her to the car.

Jenna had been dreading the trip home, but Ruby had supplied her with strange wrist bands which were to be worn near her pulse spots and she promised they would alleviate any sickness. Just to be on the safe side though she had also given her a supply of sea sickness tablets and ordered her to start taking them the day before they left.

With tearful goodbyes and promises to return one day, Ruby and Justin said goodbye to them all at Florence station.

*

When the ship sailed out of Naples harbour later that evening, everyone waited with trepidation for Jenna to turn green – but to their delight it did not happen. When they all convened for dinner that night, Jenna was still upright and ready to eat a hearty meal.

'You obviously feel all right then, Jenna?' Hillary said tentatively.

Jenna snapped the wrist bands and grinned, 'I don't know whether it is these, or the pills, but I think I am going to be able to enjoy everything this voyage has to offer,' she said raising an eyebrow at Lyndon.

'Well, Amen to that.' He grinned.

*

Because Gabriel was confident to drive around Italy, Justin lent him his car when it was not needed so they could go out and about, leaving Justin and Ruby to do some much-needed work in their studios. They had settled nicely into Villa Casomi. Mary seemed to be blooming with health and happiness, and thoroughly enjoying the task of keeping Robbie entertained. Her pale skin had a rosy glow with the sun, and she insisted on cooking every other evening to give Ruby some time off. All in all, they settled into a very aimable routine.

'Do you think Gabriel and Mary will get together?' Ruby asked Justin after making love early one morning.

'They certainly seemed to like each other, and as far as we know they may be lovers already but keeping it a secret. After all they go off together most days.'

'Yes, but with Robbie in tow – they can hardly conduct a love affair in front of him.'

'Well at night then when we are tucked up in bed,' he grinned.

'No, I did hear some movement the other night when I was getting a drink of water, but it was Robbie going into Gabriel's room. Believe me, if Robbie had seen his father in bed with Mary, he would undoubtedly tell us all.'

Justin laughed, knowing that to be true. 'Maybe they need a push in the right direction,' Justin said, folding his arms behind his head.

'No, I think we should leave it to chance, they have both been through a lot, losing their respective partners.'

'What will Mary do, if Gabriel does leave her here with us?'

'I don't know. I'll speak to her when and if that happens.'

*

Never did Gabriel think he would find someone who he could be so comfortable with again, as he was with Mary. They had travelled around Italy, enjoying the sites, eating together, swimming together and he had no idea how he was going to leave Mary here when the time came. Mary for her part was serenely reserved, so that he was unsure how she felt about him. There were times when they smiled at each other, and his heart caught, and other times he would look at her and she would just lower her eyes and fuss with Robbie. Was he making the same mistake he'd made with Jenna? Was he allowing his heart to open to her when perhaps he should not? *Oh Mary, give me a sign that you feel the same.* But if she did, what then? How could he take her back to England – she would undoubtedly go to prison for what she had done. The police may have dropped the case, but if Mary was to return with him as his wife, which if he was truthful that was what he would like, Marianne might wield some more mischief towards her.

*

It was Sunday, the 26th of September, three days before Gabriel and Robbie were to leave them and Mary was dreading it. Ruby had done all she could to welcome her, but her heart was sore at the thought of parting with both

Gabriel and Robbie. She was sure that Gabriel felt something for her, and many times she wondered if she should tell Gabriel how she felt, but to what end – she was a fugitive for want of a better word. She simply could not return – attempted suicide meant she would go to prison if she did. She couldn't expect Gabriel to stay here in Italy with her, he had his life in London as a sculptor and Robbie, as the son of a gentleman, needed to be educated in an English school. No, she must let them go, but oh goodness, it would break her heart a second time to lose them.

*

On Monday the 27th of September – two days before the ship docked bringing Jenna, Lyndon, Matthew, and Hillary home, a stranger walked into the Halzhephron Inn, Gunwalloe.

Richard Tredinnick the landlord was securing a beer barrel on the back of the bar when he heard footsteps behind him.

'We're not open until eleven,' he said, pouring a drop to taste.

'I'm looking for someone, actually.'

Richard turned and clasped his hand to his chest. 'Good god! I thought I was seeing a ghost for a moment. You don't have to tell me who you are, you're the image of James Blackwell.'

'A slightly older version perhaps.' The man laughed. 'Graham Blackwell, James's father. Please to meet you Mr….'

'Tredinnick, Richard,' he said reaching out his hand to shake.

'Jenna is away at the moment – I'm not sure where - but she won't be back until Wednesday I believe.'

'Yes, I know,' he lied, 'I've come down to start the house clearance – it's too big a job for the poor woman.'

'Jenna's leaving!' Richard said scratching his head.

'Yes, she finds it difficult to be here without James – hence the reason she has been away so long.'

'How strange. She never said anything to us about the fact that she was leaving.'

'It was a decision she made while away, and asked me, as James's closest relative, to assist her in the move – I don't think she can face it to tell you the truth,' he added in hushed tones.

Richard's face fell at the thought of the custom that he would lose if the usual set didn't come down to James's house anymore. 'Well, we will be sad to see her go, but I do understand.'

'I've been to the house, but the housekeeper is not in. Do you know where Mrs.... damn, I'm terrible with names; do you know where she is?'

'Celia Inman - she lives at Toy Cottage, the white house with the roses around it, just down the road.'

'Thank you, you have been very helpful.

*

With slight trepidation, Celia Inman let Graham Blackwell into Loe House and watched as he immediately walked to the mantlepiece to inspect objects of art there which James had collected, and which Celia knew to be valuable.

'I really can't believe that Jenna wouldn't have told me about this,' Celia said folding her arms.

He turned and narrowed his eyes. 'Perhaps she doesn't share all her private information with her housekeeper,' he said scathingly.

Celia felt her hackles rise. Something felt very wrong here, but she didn't know quite how to deal with it.

Graham turned. 'I won't be needing your assistance anymore. Except, is there anything to eat here?'

'No, I wasn't expecting anyone. You can eat at the Inn if you need to. Are you staying long?'

'No. I'm just here to sort things out and then I shall be gone. Where is the telephone?'

'In the hall.'

'Thank you, that will be all.'

Celia felt his large hand to the small of her back as he ushered her out of the house. As she walked back towards her house, she knew in her heart that something was not right here and she made a detour to the Halzhephron.

'We're not open until eleven,' Richard said wearily.

'It's me, Celia. I need Jake to take me to Helston and quick about it. I need to telephone Mrs Hemp the housekeeper in Jenna's London residence, because I have a strange feeling that Mr Blackwell is doing something very underhand.'

*

Christian Jacques was sitting in his lawyer's office sifting through some very worrying papers Graham Blackwell's solicitor had sent to the solicitor Christian had employed to oversee Blackwell's contest of James's will.

The cover letter read: - We believe that under (Section 5 (3)) "Gain" of the Sham marriage act, Jenna Blackwell née Trevone, did marry James Blackwell purely for financial gain and that there was no genuine relationship between the parties.

The evidence for this case has been collated from several different sources. Namely Marianne Enys of Mullion. Edna FitzSimmons of Hayle, formerly of Helston and Minnie Drago of Gweek. All three concur to damning evidence of Mrs Jenna Blackwell's character.

He was just deciding how to proceed when a telephone call came through.

'Mr Jacques, I have Mrs Hemp on the phone – Jenna Blackwell's housekeeper. She sounds rather worried.'

Christian listened with dismay. 'Leave it with me, Mrs Hemp. If anyone tries to gain entry to Bellevue Gardens, call the police immediately, do you understand? Will you be able to speak to Mrs Inman again?'

'Yes, she phoned from the Helston Post Office and is waiting there to see what to do.'

'Tell her I'll speak to the police here and they will deploy the constabulary down there. Mr Graham Blackwell has no jurisdiction to be in either of Jenna's properties – is that clear?'

'Yes, Mr Jacques, I'll make sure no one gains entry.'

As soon as she had rung off, he picked the receiver up again. 'Damn the man, he thinks he's won before it has even got to court,' he muttered, as he dialled the police to report attempted theft.

*

Once Celia had learned that her instincts had been correct, Jake drove her back to The Halzhephron Inn as fast as they could. There were several fisherman and farmers partaking in a drink that lunchtime and all listened with fury at the news that something untoward was going on.

'I've just come back from the cove with my catch,' Flaky Wilson the fisherman said, 'and there are two wagons and lots of men in and out of the house carrying furniture and the like, I wondered what was going on.'

'We have to stop them from taking things,' Celia shouted. 'The police are coming, but they could get away.'

'Not if I have anything to do with it,' Farmer Howes said, draining his drink. 'I'll put my wagon across the lane to the house – there is no other way out.

'I'm coming too,' Farmer Bray said.

Farmer Howes had only just got his wagon across the road when the first of the removal wagons trundled up the hill. Howes, Bray, and Richard had climbed aboard the wagon to brandish pitch forks.

'You're obstructing the highway,' the gaffer of the men said, angry that he wouldn't get paid if he didn't complete this job.

'And you are stealing goods from Mrs Blackwell's house,' Richard said.

'We have been employed by Mr Blackwell to clear this house ready for sale, now move aside or we'll move you with force – there are six of us you know.'

Richard turned and saw the police wagon pulling up behind him and smiled with relief when four police officers got out. He nudged the farmers and winked. 'Come on lads, there are too many for us to fight alone.'

They could hear the removal men laughing as the farmer began to move his wagon and then the laughter died when they were confronted with a row of police officers.

'Right lads, put it all back in that house,' the sergeant ordered.

'We have our orders from Mr Blackwell to clear this house,' the gaffer protested.

'And we have had notice that this is theft, and I shall arrest every one of you if you do not return those stolen goods back to the house immediately. Now, where is Mr Blackwell?'

'He's gone - drove off half an hour ago,' the gaffer grumbled, knowing full well they were not going to be paid now.

The police officer turned to the crowd that had accumulated. 'Anyone know who looks after this house when Mrs Blackwell is from home.'

'I do!' Celia Inman stepped forward. 'I'm afraid I let Mr Blackwell in, but his manner worried me that's why you were called.'

'Good work. Now, please come to the house and show these men where everything goes.'

'We'll put them back in the house, but we are not humping things up those bloody stairs again,' the gaffer protested.

'Officer Williams, arrest that man.'

'What? No!' The gaffer backed down. 'Come on men, get your backs behind it and get this lot back where it came from.'

It took an hour for them to put everything back and when it was done, the police searched the wagons one last time and took everyone's name and address before they sent them on their way.

'Is anything missing, Mrs Inman?' the sergeant asked.

'Yes. All the expensive antiquities James had brought back from his travels have gone. There were paintings, in each room – all missing, I know the Opie painting from the bedroom was extremely valuable. Mrs Blackwell's jewellery is missing too – she took some with her, but I know she left a few pieces behind locked in her dressing table. Look the lock has been broken. Her fine couture gowns have gone too,' she said opening the wardrobe.

'Well, I think we know where they are, don't we? Worry not we will recover them. Thank you, Mrs Inman, your prompt action has saved Mrs Blackwell a lot of heartache.'

'Will they come back when you've gone?' she asked, patting her heart anxiously.

'I shouldn't think so, we've marked their card now,' he said patting his nose. 'When will Mrs Blackwell return?'

'This Wednesday evening.'

'Then we will post a watch for now.'

When the officers had left, leaving one remaining outside the door, Celia phoned Mrs Hemp to tell her what had happened.

Ten minutes later, Christian phoned Loe House to commend Celia on her quick thinking, he also asked her to tell Jenna to phone him the moment she came home.

48

On Monday evening, Lyndon, Jenna, Matthew, and Hillary settled down to dinner on the ship.

'Well, this is our penultimate dinner on this ship. Twelve days afloat and Jenna is still with us.'

They all raised a glass to that.

'You say that, but I did feel a little queasy this morning.'

'Probably those prawns last night,' Hillary grimaced, 'I'm sure they weren't as fresh as they could have been.'

'So, Lyndon, you're to go to Devon when we get back for a month, might there be a wedding soon after you return?' Matthew asked.

Lyndon and Jenna glanced at each other and smiled.

'Perhaps a Christmas celebration might be on the cards,' Jenna said, 'It will have been six months since we lost James - hopefully, that will be long enough to stop James's father saying I married again too soon.'

'Damn that man!' Hillary grumbled. 'I know for a fact James would not have wanted you to wait this long. Life is short - one must make hay while the sun shines.'

The satisfied look, exchanged between Lyndon and Jenna, left no one in any doubt that they had made plenty of hay these last few weeks.

*

On Tuesday, it was Gabriel and Mary's last day together. They had walked down to the vineyard and sat amongst the vines where the air was cooler. Robbie was holding onto Mary as though his life depended on it, and Mary was doing her best to keep everything together – for if she cried that would be the ruin of them all.

'Mary,' Gabriel started.

She lifted her sad eyes hopefully to his. 'Yes?'

'Will you be all right here with Ruby and Justin?'

She bit her lip and nodded. 'They have made me very welcome.'

Gabriel moistened his lips, unsure of what to say to her. 'Robbie and I will miss you very much.'

Mary nodded again, and then it happened, her eyes filled with great fat tears, and she could not suppress the sob building in her throat. Her emotion set Robbie off and then there was no stopping the tears. When she looked at Gabriel, his eyes too had filled with sorrow. He reached for her hand and squeezed it tightly, sending shivers of need through her body.

'We will come back and see you - I promise,' he said.

Mary nodded but could not speak.

*

Ruby insisted that Mary accompany them when they took Gabriel and Robbie down to Florence to catch the train. It was a bit of a squeeze and suitcases had to be held on their laps, but Mary had been so relieved she was allowed to go with them to say their last farewell.

'Thank you for a lovely holiday, we will never forget it, will we Robbie?'

Robbie shook his head, though it was buried into Mary's chest as he was hugging her for dear life.

'It's been a pleasure to have you both,' Justin said shaking Gabriel's hand, 'please come back again soon.'

'We will, thank you.'

Gabriel turned to face Mary and her breath caught in her throat, knowing she would not be able to keep the tears in check. Stepping forward to gather her in his arms, Mary wound her arms tightly around Gabriel, inhaling the scent of him, storing this precious memory deep in her heart to pull on and remember when he had gone.

'Take care of yourself,' he whispered into her hair.

She squeezed him tighter, to try and stop her body trembling in his arms. 'And you take care of each other,' she said her voice breaking.

Justin and Ruby watched the long goodbye with sadness.

'Are you sure you haven't left anything behind now, Gabriel?' Ruby asked knowingly.

Gabriel released Mary from his arms and turned away from her – he was clearly distressed at the parting. 'If I have, please can you keep it safe until I come back?' he answered sadly.

Mary watched the train pull away through a veil of tears – she felt as though her heart had been ripped apart again - and this time she wouldn't have Gabriel to help mend it.

Ruby put her arm around Mary's shoulders, handed her a dry handkerchief and they climbed back into the car and made their way back up to the villa for Mary to start her new life there.

*

They made a sad pair on the train journey down to Naples. It felt like all the joy of life had been sucked out of them. It took a full twenty minutes for Robbie to stop crying. Then Gabriel's normally boisterous son, lent his head on his father's lap and laid in silence for the next hour.

At noon they walked to the dining carriage for a luncheon neither really wanted. After Robbie had finished his ice cream, he turned to the window, leant an elbow on the table, which Gabriel decided not to berate him for, rested his chin on his hand and watched the Italian countryside go by. Presently, Robbie said to the window, 'Why did we have to leave Mary?'

'We had to, Robbie, Mary needs to be here with Ruby, her friend – she has had a sad time and Ruby will care for her.'

'We have had a sad time too - I'm having a sad time now. Why can't we care for her – we are her friends,' he said tearfully. 'I love her!'

Gabriel took a huge breath. 'I know you do, son, and she loves you.'

Robbie turned from the window and his eyes turned serious. 'She loves you too, you know.'

Gabriel smiled sadly. 'I think she likes me.'

'No, she loves you, she said so in Italian.'

Gabriel took a sip of his wine and cleared his voice. 'When did she say that?'

'When you were putting our suitcases in the car. Mary was stood at the door watching and I heard her whisper, 'Ti amo, Gabriel. She didn't know I was behind her until I said, 'Ti amo, Mary, and she jumped and turned around - she nearly lost her balance.' He smiled for the first time they had got onto the train.

'And she definitely said those words?'

'Yes, Papa.' Robbie nodded and went back to looking out of the window.

'Mi scusi, a quale stazione ci fermiamo la prossima?' he asked the waiter.

'Roma,' he answered.

'Come on Robbie, we need to get our suitcases.'

'Are we in Naples. I thought we would be on the train for longer,' Robbie frowned.

'We need to get off here. I have something I must do.'

When they disembarked at Roma Termini. 'Telefono, per favore,' he asked the conductor, who directed him toward the Ufficio Postale in the city.

'I need to send a telegram,' he told the lady in the Ufficio Postale. 'I also need to make two telephone calls, one to the ticket office in Naples docks, this is the number and then a long-distance call to England on this number.'

*

At Bochym Manor, Joe picked up the telephone and waited for the operator to connect a long-distance phone call.

'Joe, is that you?' Gabriel said down the crackly line.
'Gabriel?'
'I urgently need to speak to Sarah. Is she in?'
'I'll just get her.'

A few moments later, Sarah asked anxiously, 'Gabriel, is everything all right,', 'Is Mary all right?'

'Yes, she's fine. Sarah, I need a huge favour. Can you somehow make Marianne go to the police and tell them that she was the one to cause mischief for Mary and none of it was true. I know it's not in your nature but threaten her with something if you must. We must clear Mary's name. We're extending our visit here by a week, so I'll phone again in a few days to see if you've been successful, and then I'll tell you why this is important.'

Sarah smiled knowingly. 'Leave it with me, Gabriel, I think I know exactly what to do.'

*

The bicycle bell heralded a telegram at Villa Casomi and as Justin was working in his studio, Ruby took it and paid the boy for his trouble.

'Justin,' she knocked on his studio door, 'sorry to bother you, but something has come that you need to see.'

Justin read the telegram and broke into a smile.

COMING BACK. 3P.M. DON'T TELL MARY.
GABRIEL.

'Where is Mary?' Justin asked.

'She's been weeping in her bedroom since we got back.'

He glanced at his watch. 'Well then, I shall have to go and fetch someone who will make her smile again.

*

At the train station, Gabriel stood on the platform looking sheepishly at Justin, when he came to pick them up.

'I'm so sorry, Justin, to impose on your fine hospitality again.'

'Nonsense, it's no imposition,' he said picking up one of the suitcases.

'I just hope I'm doing the right thing here,' Gabriel said settling Robbie in the back seat before climbing in the passenger seat.

'Believe me, you are definitely doing the right thing.' Justin turned to him and winked. 'Mary has been crying broken heartedly since you left - she has very nearly washed us away with her river of tears.'

'Is she crying for *me* though?'

'She is definitely crying for *you*, my friend.'

*

Mary was curled up on her bed, her pillow soaked with tears, for no matter how she tried to pull herself together she could not stop the tears from falling.

Ruby had been in to see her earlier and brought her a cool drink, and then gently sat beside her.

'Let it all go, Mary, it's better than bottling it in, you'll feel better soon,' she'd soothed, and then left her to her sorrow.

Mary's distress was such, she began to hear the voices of Gabriel and Robbie in her head – it was so clear it was almost as if they were outside. She lifted her weary head when she heard it again.

'Mary,' two voices called, 'Mary, where are you?'

Pulling herself up and off the bed, her hand shot to her aching head. Almost in a dream, she walked slowly down the hall towards the voices. With her hair and dress dishevelled, she stood at the front door, shading her eyes from the sun, and suddenly she could not believe what she was seeing. Gabriel and Robbie were standing there!

'You…you've come back,' she said her voice cracking with emotion.

'We forgot something,' Gabriel said stepping towards her.

'Did you? What?'

'You, Mary. We forgot you,' he said holding his arms out to her. As he folded her into his arms, he whispered, 'Ti amo, Mary.'

'Oh goodness,' she cried into his arms, 'Anch'io ti amo, Gabriel.'

'Well, thank goodness for that, because we have something to ask you.'

He released her from his arms and stepped back to stand with Robbie, then they both knelt on one knee and said in unison, 'Will you marry us, Mary?'

'Yes, oh yes,' she cried happy tears.

*

It had been a grey drizzly day when the ship docked in Southampton harbour earlier that morning and Lyndon, Jenna, Matthew, and Hillary disembarked. With a quick dash to the train station, they boarded the train to Cornwall and back to normality.

Jenna took this opportunity to tell Matthew and Hillary her plans for James's houses – if she was allowed to keep them - and that she and Lyndon would like to live on the Trevarno Estate, each paying their fair share of the rent.

Matthew smiled. 'Well, if that is what you both want, Namskerris cottage on the Estate is yours to rent – it has a good outhouse, Jenna, which you could convert to a studio as well.'

With their future sorted, they clasped hands, knowing that for now they must part again. Just before the train pulled into Helston train station, Matthew and Hillary went out into the corridor to give Lyndon and Jenna a moment to say their goodbyes.

'I wish I wasn't going to Devon – I've hardly had an episode all the time we've been away,' Lyndon said kissing her.

'Best to get it sorted though, once and for all,' she answered, holding him tightly, 'and when you return,' she smiled, 'we shall soon be together forever.'

After a tearful goodbye, they kissed one last time as the train came to a standstill.

*

In Tuscany, after the proposal, Ruby took Robbie inside to find a glass of lemonade for him while Gabriel took Mary off into the garden.

'I don't understand,' Mary said, 'Are you going to stay in Italy with me?'

'That is the plan. We'll be married here if we don't get your name cleared, yes.'

'But your work, your studio in London, your family, Robbie's schooling?'

Gabriel pulled her into his arms. 'Nothing matters more than us being with you. You have given me back something other than Robbie to live for. I love you, Mary, you have grown into my life until I cannot be without you anymore. I had no idea if you felt the same – you never indicated. It was only because Robbie told me you had whispered that you loved me.'

Lifting her eyes to his, she admitted, 'I dared not say out loud how I felt for you. You are a gentleman and I…well, I am an assistant cook.'

Gabriel grabbed her hands and brought them to his lips to kiss them. 'You are so much more than an assistant cook, Mary. You're the mother my boy needs, and the wife I want. To me, dearest, darling Mary, you are the sun that shines every day, the moon that lights my sky at night and the stars that twinkle in my universe. You are love, and there is nothing bigger nor better than love.

49

As arranged before she left for Italy, Jake Tredinnick was waiting at the station for Jenna in the car. Within minutes of her getting into the car, all joy from the holiday had faded into the far distance as she listened to Jake's account of what had happened.

Celia Inman was waiting at Loe House when she got home to inform her as to what valuables were missing, and to pass on Christian Jacques's urgent request for her to call him.

Jenna glanced at the clock which was no longer there but knew it was at least six o clock. 'It's late, I don't think he will be in his office in the evenings.

'Well, I'm just passing on what he told me to tell you, to phone as soon as you got in.'

Jenna nodded. 'I'll try him then.'

'I'm ever so sorry I let that man in to your home, Jenna,' Celia said anxiously. 'I've had the locksmith in, and they've changed all your locks, because that man took your keys.'

'Don't worry, Celia, I'm thankful of what you did to rescue the situation.'

'Do you mind me asking – why did he do it?'

'James's father is contesting James's will. He believes I married James for his money and that I didn't love him.'

'Fiddlesticks, I've never met a more frugal woman than you. Oh, I know you have fine clothes and all that, as James's wife you needed them, but you do not fritter money or spend on luxuries like James did. As for not loving him, well, I had my doubts at first, I admit, your marriage was all so sudden, but I saw you together, I saw you nurse him through that dreadful illness and if what you two shared was not love, well, I don't know what is!' she said dusting down her dress to finish the conversation.

'Thank you, Celia,' she said sincerely.

Jenna rang Christian, not expecting him to pick up but he did on the first ring.

'Jenna, thank goodness,' he said gravely. 'I've been waiting for your call.'

'It's all right. Celia has told me all that has happened. Have they recovered the items Graham Blackwell stole?'

'They have, they intercepted the rascal as he arrived at his home in Hertfordshire. Unfortunately, they will not return them, until after the hearing.'

'Hearing?' Jenna breathed.

'I'm sorry, Jenna, Graham Blackwell has brought charges against you under the Sham marriage act. He is claiming that you married James for money and that there was no genuine relationship between the parties. They have gathered damning evidence against your character.'

Jenna slumped down on the chair by the phone. 'What damning evidence? I'm not a bad person - this is ridiculous. And how do they know there was no genuine relationship between us?' she cried.

'Jenna, you must stay calm, but I need you to come to London and present yourself to the police here. When can you come?'

'I'll come up tomorrow, but it will be late when I get there.'

'Then I'll see you first thing on Friday morning. I have an excellent lawyer working for you who is building a case for you, and Jenna….'

'Yes,' she said tentatively.

'I'm so sorry this has happened to you - all because you wanted to help me and James.'

'Christian, I would do it again in a heartbeat. James and I may not have had a conventional marriage, but it was a marriage and I loved him, just as I love you. I'll see you on Friday.'

*

While Jenna was boarding the train to London on Thursday morning, Sarah Dunstan had galloped over to Mullion to catch Marianne before she went to work.

Marianne stopped short when she turned the corner to walk down the hill towards Poldhu and found the fine white horse and the Countess de Bochym waiting. For an instance she started to back track.

'Stop right there, Marianne,' Sarah ordered, as she dismounted.

Marianne felt her heart begin to race.

'I know it was you who wrote that falsehood about Mary and left it in the mushroom box in the grocery store for Mrs Jennings to find, and *don't* think you can deny it,' she said when Marianne opened her mouth to protest. 'We know it was you! You were the only person who was not staff in the kitchen the day Mary accidently ate a poisoned mushroom and fell terribly ill.'

Marianne tried to swallow the lump which had formed in her throat.

'Have you any idea what your false allegation could have led to? You could have put Mary in prison! The poor woman found she was unable to stay at the manor, she had to move far away from everyone she loved – people who had been her family for years! Why? Because your lies not only put her in peril if the police had believed them, but everyone in the Bochym household. What you did was downright wicked, to attack someone who had been widowed so brutally in the war – I hope you are truly ashamed of yourself.'

Marianne felt the tears prick behind her eyes and nodded, but as she tried to move away, Sarah stopped her again.

'Do not think you are getting away unpunished because you are not. You are going to the police, and you are going to tell them what you did and that what you wrote was a complete falsehood.'

Marianne's eyes widened as she shook her head.

'Yes, you are! I will give you twenty-four hours to put this right, or I shall first tell Ellie what you have done and insist she dismisses you. And as Gabriel has been kind enough to give his time to Mary to help her heal from the wounds of grief, only for you to do this to her, I shall be informing the Trelease's of what you did. I shall insist that your mother be dismissed from their employment – I should think they will not delay in doing so. They are kind, decent people, like Mary was.' She moved her horse to a stone to aid her to mount again. 'Twenty-four hours, Marianne, and if I don't get a favourable report from the police, expect me to do the worst.'

*

Marianne felt she was going to die of embarrassment as she walked up to the police station that evening to admit her misdemeanour. She had fretted all day about it and dropped a whole tray of crockery at the tearoom because her mind was elsewhere. Ellie was fast losing patience with her, she could tell.

P.C. Cole listened to her confession and shook his head in dismay, berating her, not only for telling fibs, but for wasting police time.

Marianne lifted her eyes dolefully. 'I'm terribly sorry, P.C. Cole. It was just a jest – I didn't think.'

'A poor jest. Do you now realise the consequences of your actions?'

'I do now, yes.'

'I am surprised at you, Marianne. You're meant to be an intelligent young woman.'

Marianne had to resist from narrowing her eyes at him. *She was intelligent! Obviously more so than this silly policeman if he believed her faux apology.*

'It's a good job Mary had moved away from here before you did what you did, or she would have been very upset.'

'Yes, I know but,' she raised her eyebrow, 'she would have seen the joke. We were always having banter up at the manor.'

'*Marianne*, stop calling this a joke – it was a very serious allegation. If we had believed your silly letter, Mary could have been arrested and put in prison for doing what you said she had done. I'm relieved it was my wife who picked that damning note out of the mushrooms in the grocery store. Now, go on, get out of my sight, you silly young woman and we'll say no more about this.'

Marianne flared her nostrils, as he once again berated her as though she was an imbecile.'

As she was shown the door, he added, 'I'll not tell your parents. They would be heartily ashamed of you, but *never* do anything like this again, you understand?'

'Yes, P.C. Cole,' she answered disingenuously.

*

The last couple of days flew by for Gabriel and Mary in Tuscany. Gabriel had been tentatively looking for a villa hereabouts to set up his studio and had made enquiries about where they could marry and how soon. Their love for each other shone out as they walked hand in hand everywhere, and then a telegram arrived on Friday morning from Bochym which settled everything.

EVERYTHING SORTED. MARY SAFE. BRING HER HOME.

'So, I can go back to Britain, safe in the knowledge I won't be going to prison?' Mary said reading the telegram.

'Yes, my love,' Gabriel said kissing her full on the lips. 'I can book the tickets for the voyage today and we can sail home next Wednesday together. We can be married in Cornwall three weeks after we arrive home, with all your friends from Bochym around you.'

Mary's eyes swam with happy tears. 'Thank you, Gabriel, for giving me something to live for too. It will be an honour to be your wife.'

'Well, you had to marry me – after all you spent the night with me, and Robbie told everyone about it.'

Mary laughed. 'There really is nothing that gets past that boy of ours.'

*

On Friday morning, Jenna sat in Christian's office with Mr Kingthorn QC and read the statements damning her character.

'What do you make of them?' he asked.

'This one, Edna FitzSimmons – though she is not meant to use that name, was Lyndon's wife. The part where I continued my love affair with Lyndon is true to a point. I wrote to him regularly while he was away at war because she did not bother, and I spent one night with him just before he went back to the front because,' she swallowed hard, 'we both believed he would not be coming back. I did not ruin their marriage, because they had no marriage to ruin. Edna never let Lyndon into her bed, though she claimed to have fallen pregnant by him when he was inebriated one night and then pretended to miscarry on their wedding day! Lyndon had a doctor examine her when he returned from the war, and she was found to be still a virgin – he had their marriage annulled for non-consummation.'

'I see.' Mr Kingthorn steepled his fingers.

'This from Marianne – is just mischief making, something at which she is rather good at. Marianne is a woman scorned you see. It seems she had fallen in love with Gabriel Trelease, mentioned here. I took tea with Gabriel, his parents and his little boy, Marianne must have read more in to it than there was. She sent a well-wisher's letter to Lyndon telling him that I was going to marry Gabriel and he should know about it. Somehow, she must have found out that Lyndon and I were connected – I know not how. She has also made an unfounded allegation about one of her friends trying to commit suicide – a friend she thought was getting too close to Gabriel.'

Mr Kingthorn raised his eyebrows. 'She sounds charming.'

Jenna tapped the statement from Minnie Drago. 'This one is the village busybody in Gweek. Her allegations of me leaving my first husband and feigning drowning are true, but I did not, as she says, run off with Lyndon – he was betrothed to Edna by then. What I did do was change my name slightly, to keep me safe from my violent husband and I lived in with Lyndon's father as his housekeeper. What I will say though, is that I have been in love with Lyndon since I was eighteen years old, so for seven years. When I married James, I believed Lyndon to be dead. He was found in a hospital with amnesia in May, a month after I married James. I did not tell James when I found out. I had married him, and I was happy with him. But James found out about us from a third party and knowing he was going to die, wrote to Lyndon on his deathbed and gave his blessing for us to be together. I knew nothing of it. For decency's sake though, we intend to wait six full months and then I will marry Lyndon. As for marrying James for financial gain, I earn more than enough with my art, if you have the time, I shall tell you my plans for both the houses James left me.'

'Ah, yes, Mr Jacques here has informed me of your splendid plans to house young women in need – I commend you on it.'

'It's the best solution. Lyndon is a proud man - he wants to provide a house for me and wants not a penny of James's money and that is how it will be when we marry. My wealth is my own to put to the best good possible use, which I intend to do so if I am allowed.'

'The other issue we must deal with is that Mr Blackwell has made claims that his son was a homosexual, and therefore there was no genuine relationship between you. He is claiming that Mr Jacques here had the more intimate relationship with him. Everything will be denied of course, and fortunately there has been no more evidence to further those claims, but it will be damning for my learned colleague here.' He glanced at Christian who in turn lifted his weary eyes to Jenna.

'Now, Mr Jacques, have you somewhere Mrs Blackwell and I can go in private so we can go through everything in more detail before she accompanies me to the police station. We shall put in our plea of not guilty.'

'If I plead not guilty it will go to trial, won't it?' Jenna asked.

'Invariably.'

'Can I not just give it all to Mr Blackwell, that way they cannot expose Christian, and he won't go to prison.'

Both Christian and Mr Kingthorn shook their heads.

'Your actions would then suggest that you were guilty of fraud, and you will go to prison, Jenna,' Christian answered.

Jenna closed her eyes and her shoulders drooped wearily. 'Then we will have to win.'

50

Back at Bellevue Gardens, Jenna tried to put her mind to painting. She had many wonderful sketches of the Tuscan landscape just waiting to be transferred onto canvas, but the impending hearing which was to be held on Tuesday 25th November was at the forefront of her mind.

Mr Kingthorn had been confident that the verdict would go her way because the witnesses speaking against her had a personal score to settle, but it was Christian that she worried about the most. He would be named as co-respondent in Graham Blackwell's claim that James was homosexual. The worry was making her feel sick as well, and no matter what Mrs Hemp tried to tempt her with, everything seemed to leave a sour taste in her mouth.

Ever hopeful for a good outcome at the hearing, Jenna put her suggestion about turning Bellevue Gardens into a refuge for young woman to Mrs Hemp, and how she would feel about running it. Mrs Hemp had clasped her hands together in joy at the suggestion and they had tentatively walked around the house, planning the whole thing out.

*

On Monday morning, Jenna had a meeting with Christian, and was shocked when she was shown into his office and saw him. He looked as though he had aged over the weekend and his skin, normally so fresh faced, looked grey and sallow.

'Christian, I'm so sorry for you,' Jenna wrapped her arms around him.

'I'm afraid it's the risk we take to love who we really want to love, Jenna. I'm going to have to tell my wife, Judith. She will divorce me of course to save face, but it is the loss of the children, Philip, and Celine, which is going to kill me - if prison does not. I'll never see them again, and never walk my lovely daughter Celine up the aisle.'

'Christian, this is so unfair on you. When will you tell her?'

'I think perhaps tonight,' he said sadly. 'Anyway, that is my problem. Please, take a seat and tell me about the holiday, was it a success?'

'It was wonderful. Lyndon and I hope to marry at Christmas – if all goes well at the hearing and I'm not imprisoned for fraud.'

'Don't worry. Mr Kingthorn is confident things will go your way, but he has suggested that I speak about something very important - something that he thinks you might need to know.'

'Oh?'

Christian gave an embarrassed cough. 'It may not be necessary, so forgive me for asking this first, but this is crucial. Were you ever intimate with James?'

Jenna frowned and then broke into a half smile. 'No, Christian, James loved only you!'

'I know, but he did say to me, that he might, you know, need to fulfil your needs.'

Jenna smiled sweetly. 'That was never on the agenda.' She tipped her head. 'Why was it necessary to ask?'

'At the hearing, you may be asked personal questions to verify your intimacy with James.

'Oh! *Oh!*'

'Therefore, I need to tell you things about him. Things that only someone who was... intimately involved with him would know.'

'I see,' she breathed.

Christian paused for a moment and then shook his head. 'Forgive me, Jenna, I am going to be very rude and turn my back on you while I tell you the things you need to know.'

Jenna felt her cheeks pink. 'I think I might turn my back on you too, while I listen, if you don't mind.'

They exchanged a quick embarrassed smile before they both swivelled their chairs around.

Christian cleared his throat. 'James had a large scar running from the very top of the inside of his left thigh to his knee, and another smaller one on the inside of his upper left arm, where he fell through a window as a child. He also had several, round, faded pink scars the size of halfpennies on his buttocks - he would not tell me how he got them – I think he had locked that memory away in a deep dark cavern of his mind. And last, but not least, as this is important, James was circumcised – not for any religious purposes, it was due to a medical problem as a child.'

When he finished speaking, they both turned slowly back to face each other.

'Phew! It has gone rather hot in here, don't you think?' Jenna fanned herself with her hand, trying to lighten the atmosphere.

'Forgive me, Jenna, I can't imagine how embarrassing that was to hear.'

'Or for you to say it!' She smiled. 'I'm sorry you lost the love of your life, Christian,' she said with heartfelt sympathy. 'The scars are a bit worrying, aren't they?'

'Yes. Something dreadful had happened to him, but I could never find the underlying cause of it. I do suspect that it had something to do with his father because he hated him.'

Jenna folded her arms. 'And now the man wants to take all his wealth.'

'Yes. That is why it is important to fight him for this. Oh, I forgot, there is one more thing you should know,' he added.

'Do I need to turn around again?' she joked.

He laughed and the atmosphere lightened considerably. 'No, I think I can tell you this without shying away. James dressed to the right.'

Jenna took a moment to understand this, but when she could not make sense of it, she frowned. 'Pardon?'

'James, he dressed to the right.'

'What on earth does that mean?' she asked incredulously.

'Oh, erm,' Christian raked his hands through his tidy hair, 'It means,' he struggled to search for the right word, 'it means his... manhood falls to the right when he is dressed.'

'Oh, right.' Jenna bit her lip to suppress a smile.

Christian nodded. 'They might ask, that's all.'

There was a marked silence between them for a moment before Christian added, 'I was going to ask you to lunch, but I'm not sure we can face each other now over the dining table.'

'Well, Christian Jacques, if you think you are doing me out of a good lunch at the Ritz after putting me through that ordeal, you are very much mistaken,' she grinned. 'I think you owe me it. Now is there somewhere we can splash some cold water on our faces before we go – we look like a couple of beetroots.'

*

Later that night, Christian had downed a couple of brandies after his wife had retired to bed, but they were just leaving a sour taste in his mouth. All evening he had wondered how he was going to tell Judith what he must tell her, and he could put it off no longer. He had lived this lie too long now, so he knocked on Judith's bedroom door and she beckoned him in.

'May I speak with you?'

Judith put her book down and smiled.' I wondered when you would finally decide to tell me what has been bothering you these past few weeks.'

Christian sighed and sat down on Judith's dressing table chair.

Judith tipped her head, waiting.

'I'm going to tell you something that will make you despise me, but I want to apologise before I say anything and tell you none of this is a fault of yours and I am truly sorry for you.'

Judith folded her arms.

'I still love you and the children – you have been a wonderful wife, but I am not the man you think I am. I loved someone else for ten years,' he paused to take a breath,' another man.'

'I know, Christian,' Judith said gently.

Christian opened his mouth to say more and then closed it again. 'You know?'

'I'm your wife; how could I not know?'

'Do you know who?' he asked tentatively.

'I suspect it was your good friend James Blackwell. You were devastated by his death, and still are if the truth be told. You even went down to Cornwall to see him before he died and stayed for his funeral. I wanted to say something to you at the time, but you were so lost to grief, I did not want to embarrass you.'

'Oh god, Judith.' He dropped his head in his hands.

She pushed the bedcovers back and went to stand beside him.

'Do you hate me?' he asked, lifting his eyes to hers.

'No, sweet man,' she gently touched his hair. 'Of course, I don't hate you. I have known for a long time – probably the duration of your relationship with James.'

'But our marriage?'

'Our marriage has worked for both of us. You provide for us. You gave me two beautiful children. I lead a life of luxury and I have a man on whom I can rely. I want for nothing more, Christian. I'm intrigued though, why tell me now?'

'Sit down and I'll explain,' he said, and told her about the upcoming hearing, all the while, wringing his hands as he spoke.

'Is there any real evidence, that Blackwell knows something happened between you and James.'

'I don't believe so, no, in fact I am certain he doesn't – we were very discreet.'

'And did Blackwell know his son was homosexual?'

'James told me that his father always suspected because of his gentle nature, but he would never admit it to him. He said he had tried to punish it out of him as a boy. James hated male dominated pursuits like boxing, wrestling, shooting and rugby, and to 'make a man of him,' his father made him do them. Of course, James did not excel at any of these pursuits and his father would punish him severely when he did not perform as well as he should. James hated his father and I have a suspicion that his father tortured him too – he had terrible marks on his body, but I do not know for sure, because James would not speak of it.

'So, if you were discreet, what makes Blackwell think you were lovers?'

'Blackwell had us watched at Bellevue Gardens in the spring of this year, and assumed we were indulging in an assignation. It was while we were all at the Knightsbridge Ball in February, when a newspaper reporter informed me that a story about my relationship with James would break the next day. Apparently, I had been implicated in the report as I was a frequent visitor to Bellevue Gardens. Jenna, bless her, stepped into the breach, told James to announce their forthcoming marriage to stop a story breaking in the newspaper. When questioned about my involvement with them, Jenna spun a yarn saying the reason I had been visiting Bellevue Gardens was because I was helping with the wedding arrangements as I had been chosen to give the bride away at the wedding. So, the story was dropped, and from what we gathered, they had no factual evidence on us, but of course if the story had run it would have been damning for all of us.'

'I see.' Judith nodded. 'Jenna Blackwell is a remarkable young woman then. I did wonder why you were so involved in that wedding, and happy to see James married.'

'She saved our lives that day, but it was in vain.' His shoulders drooped.

'No, Christian. Defeatism is not in your make up, so do not let it in. Tell me, did James have other lovers?'

'No, I was the only one.'

'Very well. I'm not the lawyer here, but I do not think they have a basis for a case, and I'm going to put in a letter of intent to sue Graham Blackwell for defamation of your character, and libel. I will defend you to the hilt, Christian. He will not expect that from me, your wife, and if he has no factual evidence, this will cost him dearly.'

'It's a risk.' Christian lifted his eyes to meet his wife. 'You would do that?'

'Of course, and as you say, Christian, we have a great deal to lose. We shall call Graham Blackwell's bluff.'

51

Jenna had a dinner date at Trevarno the following Friday and was to stay the night with Matthew and Hillary. For once she had no feelings of trepidation at going. Edna had gone, and so too had all the unpleasantness associated with her.

Because all the couture gowns she owned had been stolen by Graham Blackwell, Jenna only had her summer clothes to wear, and with the current cold and misty weather these clothes were not serviceable. In the end she wore the navy dress she'd had made for Charlie and Lizzy's wedding.

At Trevarno, she called first to see Michael and Gina and found to her delight that Michael had finally forgiven her for marrying James. Thankfully, Lyndon had had a long talk with them before setting off to Devon, leaving them in no doubt that he and Jenna would marry at Christmas.

At Holme Farm, a butler-come-valet whom Matthew and Hillary had employed, answered the door to her and led her to the drawing room.

'Darling.' Hillary kissed her, then frowned at her attire. 'How very provincial you are in your dress tonight!'

'Oh, Hillary, don't, it's a long story.' She took the drink offered to her and began to tell her about Graham Blackwell emptying Loe House.

Outraged Hillary said, 'You will get them back though?'

'If my hearing goes my way, yes. But there have been damning statements made against my character – one from Edna – not that I'm at all surprised.' She went on to tell them exactly what had been said in the statements.

'My god, Matthew, is there nothing we can do?' Hillary turned to him.

'Well, I can vouch that Jenna sought refuge here, and put the magistrate right as to the fact that Jenna lived with

Lyndon's father and not with Lyndon. If you give me the details of your solicitor, Jenna, I'll sort that out.'

'Thank you, Matthew that would help.'

'As for Edna, I shall give her family notice of eviction in the morning unless Edna retracts her statement.' Matthew paused from speaking while the dinner was served and then asked, 'Have you heard from Lyndon, Jenna?'

'Yes, we write to each other every week – it's a bit like when he was at war, except this time I know he's coming home to me – well, I hope I'm still here when he comes home.'

'What does he say about the hearing – will he come up to London for it?' Matthew asked.

Jenna shook her head. 'I haven't told him.'

Matthew held his fork aloft. 'Why?'

'I want him to stay in Devon and get better. London is not good for him – it may undo the good that has already been done.'

'But Jenna, if you go to prison, he'll be devastated, not only because of that, but the fact that he didn't spend your last days of freedom with him!'

Jenna blanched. 'Well, I shall just have to make sure I don't go to prison, won't I? I shall put my trust in the law that they will not condemn an innocent woman and *I* am innocent of their claims that I married James for gain.' She then promptly burst into tears.

Hillary glared at Matthew. 'Thank you, Matthew, please remember a closed mouth gathers no foot.'

'I was just pointing out how Lyndon would feel, that's all!'

'Well don't,' Hillary berated as she comforted Jenna.

Suitably admonished, Matthew said, 'I'm sorry, that *was* insensitive of me.'

'It's all right, Matthew. Hillary don't berate him,' Jenna said tearfully. 'It all just overwhelms me sometimes and the tears come.'

'Of course it does, here, have another drink,' Hillary pushed a glass of claret in front of her.

Jenna smiled at Hillary's unchanging belief that a drink was the only medicine one needed to make things better.

*

For the next week, Jenna put her mind to her work and produced a fantastic painting of the view from Villa Casomi. As she stood back to admire it – she did wonder if her art was going to be stripped from the walls of The Black Gallery if things went wrong for her. The hearing was creeping up on her – a week today she could be behind bars, the very thought made her feel unwell.

*

While Jenna was pondering her future, at Southampton, Gabriel, Mary, and Robbie disembarked onto a very chilly dockside. The first thing Gabriel needed to do was to find a post office and put a call through to Bochym where he had left his car. He needed his car brought to the station as they had somewhere they needed to go before he went home to his parents.

*

Later that day, Jenna heard a car pull up outside, for a split second a chill ran down her spine – she wasn't expecting anyone, but since Graham Blackwell had violated her home, she felt terribly nervous about being alone in the house. The idea that once again she was being intimidated by a man, angered her. She had hoped that she had left that feeling behind long ago. She tentatively glanced through the window to see who was there and could see the car but no occupants. Suddenly a face appeared and made her jump.

'Jenna,' Robbie yelled through the window as he jumped up to see if she was in. She heard Gabriel's' voice call, 'Robbie, come here, it's rude to look in windows.'

Jenna opened the door, but it seemed her smile had not masked the fear in her eyes because he stepped forward and touched her arm gently.

'Jenna, forgive us, did Robbie scare you?'

'No, no, it's all right – I'm just a little on edge. Strange things have been happening over the last few weeks. She hugged Robbie who had wrapped his arms around her legs. 'Anyway, hello, this is a surprise. Oh, and Mary too! That *is* a surprise, but a very welcome one,' she said embracing Mary.

'I've come to ask a favour,' Gabriel said seriously.

She smiled and teased, 'The last favour you asked me to do got me into trouble with Lyndon.'

Gabriel grimaced. 'Well, I'm glad all that is settled now. No, I wonder if you can accommodate Mary for three weeks, until our marriage banns have been heard.'

'How wonderful – you're getting married! I could not be happier for you, and in the normal scheme of things I would welcome you with open arms, Mary, but I must go to London on Monday, and if things don't turn out well, I may end up in prison and this house will be lost to me.'

'Goodness me,' Gabriel frowned, 'what scenario could make that happen?'

'Come in, sit down, I'll get you all some refreshments and I'll tell you, but first you must tell me how this wedding has come about. Is it not unsafe for you to come back here, Mary?'

Gabriel explained what had happened and how Sarah had made Marianne retract her lies.

'How very romantic of you, Gabriel.'

'And me, I was romantic too,' Robbie said munching on a sandwich Jenna had made for him.

'Bochym won't have room for Mary back in the staff quarters, and though I know Sarah would accommodate her in one of the guest rooms…'

'But I don't feel comfortable doing that for obvious reasons,' Mary interjected.

Jenna nodded that she understood.

'Also, I rather wanted to tell my parents of our impending marriage before Bochym hears about it,'

Gabriel explained, 'I thought I would bring Mary here to stay, while I tell my parents, and then present her to them tomorrow.'

'Well of course you can stay, Mary and if you want to travel up to London with me on Monday to stay at Bellevue Gardens you are very welcome. It's just that if things go the wrong way on Tuesday, I fear other accommodation must be found.'

'What on earth has happened, Jenna that you find yourself in this predicament? You must tell us now.'

So, she explained about Graham Blackwell and all that had happened and the impending hearing - only leaving out the part about James being a homosexual.

'This is why Lyndon and I kept our love a secret. I was trying to safeguard James's wealth and property from his father – whom I understand James hated.'

'He did indeed hate him and with good reason. Jenna, I know Graham Blackwell - I know what he is capable of. He is the worst of men. I think I told you when we first met that I knew James, well I knew him well. Our estate in Hertfordshire boarders Netherdale Hall the Blackwell's estate and James was a frequent visitor to our house especially after his dear mother had died. We played together as children and stayed friends even though he was sent to Rugby and I to Eton. During the holidays, James would often arrive at our house, crying in pain from a severe beating he had received from his father, once he was even bleeding profusely from cuts to his leg and arm after being thrown through a window. My father had a good friend - Doctor Carmichael - who was repeatedly called to our house to administer aid to James. When the doctor saw the extent of the injuries, it was the last straw. Doctor Carmichael stitched James's wounds, and then he and my father went to speak with Blackwell.' Gabriel shook his head. 'Blackwell sent them both packing and told Doctor Carmichael in no uncertain terms that he would have the doctor prosecuted and struck off for intervening with James's health needs when his services had not been sought by him. Blackwell was a rich and powerful man then, and Doctor Carmichael, an impoverished country physician, could not afford to let this happened to his career. The very next day, James limped over to see us, in deep distress. He could not sit down and when my father summoned the good doctor again – he found,' he paused glanced at Robbie who was down on the rug now reading, and lowered his voice, 'that James had four deep burns to his buttocks.'

Mary who had been listening intently, took a sharp intake of breath.

'Forgive me, Mary for speaking so bluntly, but I need to tell Jenna about this man. Though I suspect you have already seen the scars Jenna, and he may already have told you how they came about.'

Jenna cleared her throat. 'I do know about them yes,' she said - it wasn't a lie, it just wasn't the truth, 'but he never said how they had come about.'

Gabriel nodded. 'After the doctor tended his wounds again, James told me that his father had burnt him following the visit by my father and the doctor to his house. James said that his father had taken a drag of his cigar and pressed the end into his skin four times punctuating the burns with the words DO. NOT. TELL. TALES. James went back to Rugby the next week, and never came home again for the holidays. James wrote to me to say his stepmother did not want him at home anymore and that he was to board full time. We met up again at university and picked up where our friendship left off. I mentioned the incidents to him, but James just shook his head and said quite bluntly, "I don't want to remember that time." I was always amazed at how he turned out as a man – he must have been deeply traumatised with what had happened, though he kept it to himself. I don't think I have ever come across a kinder more gregarious person than James. I applaud him for it –

it would have destroyed a weaker man. The only thing he did speak of regarding his father was that he had heard he had serious money problems having made several bad investments. He said his stepmother had sued his father for divorce and that he would probably lose the Hertfordshire estate. He told me that his father had tried to make him marry some horse-mouth heiress to save the estate – which James refused point blank to do. We lost touch after university, though I followed James's career as a writer.'

'What a dreadful man – it makes me more determined to fight him over this.'

'And so you should! Jenna, would you mind if I share the details of the hearing with my parents?'

'Not at all – I've done nothing wrong.'

'It is just that they are still in contact with Doctor Carmichael who is retired now. Did you know James helped him to buy a small cottage on the Devon coast in return for his kindness to him as a young boy?'

'No, I didn't,' Jenna smiled, 'but it's a very James thing to do.'

'Yes, it is. Well, it was my parents who told me about it after I told them about you and that you were James's widow. They have often said how Doctor Carmichael regrets not being able to help James when he was younger. I believe he would now be willing to stand up in a court of law and tell them what a monster father Graham Blackwell was to his son.'

Jenna's heart lightened. 'Everything will help, I'm sure.'

Just at that moment, Robbie yawned loudly.

'I think I must take Robbie home. It has been a long day.'

Jenna left them alone to share a tender goodbye before parting, and then she welcomed Mary back in and showed her the room she could stay in for the time being.

'Would you like to come to London with me, Mary?'

'I would love to. I have never been, but I don't want to be away from Gabriel and Robbie.'

'Well let's see what happens over the weekend. Perhaps they will come too. Are you looking forward to meeting Gabriel's parents?'

'I'm terrified actually, I haven't told Gabriel of my fears, after all I'm only an assistant cook, what will they think of me?'

'You are not just an assistant cook. Anyway, there is nothing wrong with being a good cook, at least they know you will keep them well fed and besides, Gabriel's parents are perfectly charming. I believe all they want for Gabriel is someone who genuinely loves him and Robbie, and you surely do. They will love you - I promise.'

52

Gabriel reported that his parents had been delighted at his news, when he phoned Jenna the next morning to tell Mary he was going to come and take her to see them.

Jenna had lent Mary the navy dress she had made for Charlie and Lizzy's wedding to go to luncheon, until they could have some more clothes made for her.

'There, you look lovely. Anyone would be proud to have you as a daughter-in-law.'

'I'm shaking in my boots, Jenna.'

'Everything will be fine.'

When Gabriel came to fetch Mary, he was so happy he picked her up and swung her around. 'You look wonderful, my darling girl. My parents cannot wait to meet you. We shall take luncheon with them and then go to see the vicar to arrange a date for the wedding and have the banns read.'

Jenna smiled at them with delight. 'Mary tells me you have decided you would like to be married at St Winwaloe Church here at Gunwalloe.'

'Yes, it's such a lovely church – and very romantic to be married near the sea. Where will you and Lyndon marry?'

'Probably the same place. We just want a small wedding, but Hillary has other ideas. It all depends on the hearing of course – I may still go to prison for something I did not do if they believe Blackwell over me.'

'Ah, well now, I spoke to my parents last night about this and they are outraged. They rang Doctor Carmichael this morning and he is very eager to lend his voice to defame Blackwell in the eyes of the magistrate.'

Jenna put her hand to her chest, truly touched. 'He would do that for me?'

'And for James.' He kissed Jenna tenderly on the cheek. 'Now, Mary, come and meet your soon-to-be in-laws. I thought we could go to Bochym Manor after seeing the vicar to tell them our good news.'

*

Gabriel's parents welcomed Mary with open arms and were enamoured with her the moment they saw the love both Robbie and Gabriel had for her. Afterwards they went to see the vicar to set a wedding date for Wednesday the 10th of December, and then Gabriel drove Mary up to Bochym to tell them the good news.

Mary was nervous to enter the manor via the front door after having worked here these last twelve years, but this was her life now – she was to be married to a gentleman.

Joe opened the door to them with a happy smile. 'His Lordship sends his apologies, he is out on business, but Her Ladyship, is waiting in the Jacobean drawing room for you. I won't tell the others you are here yet, until you've seen her.'

Mary blushed to think His Lordship would be even bothered with her coming.

Sarah kissed Gabriel and gathered Mary into her arms. 'Welcome back, Mary.'

Mary could not find her voice she was so overcome with emotion.

'Gabriel telephoned us this morning to say you were coming and that you have wonderful news.'

Mary could do nothing but nod, so Gabriel stepped in. 'We are to be married on the 10th of December.'

'Splendid. Joe, could we have some tea please?'

'Yes, my lady.'

'This is all thanks to you, Sarah,' Gabriel said. 'I have no idea what you said to Marianne, but it worked.'

'I threatened her like you told me too. I said that if she didn't retract what she had said, I would tell Ellie who would dismiss her, I also told her I would tell your parents of what she had done, and they in turn would dismiss Marianne's mother – that was a bit mean, I know, and I probably wouldn't have done that, but my threat worked. P.C. Cole rang shortly after she had been to see him, to say that he was deeply sorry to have implicated Mary in any wrongdoing and the case was well and truly dropped.'

'Well, I'm going to tell Ellie anyway,' Gabriel said seriously. 'Marianne has done several things recently that have caused a great deal of heartache.' He went on to tell her about the well-wisher letter she had written to Lyndon and the statement she had given to a reporter damning Jenna Blackwell's character and reputation. 'Jenna is about to lose everything James left her because of what Marianne told the reporter.'

'Gracious me! Then she must be punished for her actions,' Sarah agreed.

Mary was fiddling nervously with her gloves as Gabriel had been talking and Sarah turned her attention to her. 'Are you happy, Mary?'

Finding her voice now she said, 'I truly am, my lady. Thank you for everything you did for me.'

'I think you can call me Sarah, now you are to be married to Gabriel!'

Mary was overcome with emotion. 'Thank you!'

After tea, Gabriel led Mary into the kitchen she never thought she would see again and as the day was cold and drizzly outside, all the staff were present around the kitchen table.

'Gabriel!' Dorothy squealed, 'Oh and Mary! Look everybody, Mary is here!'

Everyone made a great fuss of her and when Gabriel told them the news that they were to marry, there was a collective gasp amongst them.

'Oh, lordy me,' Mrs Blair declared on hearing the news. 'Are all our staff going to go off and marry gentlemen?'

'Gosh, I hope so!' Dorothy enthused.

'What with Ruby marrying Mr Justin, and Mary marrying Gabriel here, I don't know what the world is coming to,' Mrs Blair said.

'Don't forget that Jessie Blackthorn from Poldhu who used to work here, married Daniel Chandler – he is a gentleman too!' Dorothy reminded her.

'Yes, well,' Mrs Blair's mouth set hard, 'the least said about *that* the better,' she grumbled. 'Conducting an affair while you're still married is not my idea of how to get a gentleman husband.'

Joe, a long-time friend of Jessie, jumped to her defence. 'She was in an unhappy marriage remember, and she is expecting her third child with Daniel.'

Mrs Blair pursed her lips not convinced.

Dorothy flopped down at the table. 'Everyone is getting married, and I'm still left on the shelf! Gabriel, have you any gentleman friends who are looking for a vibrant young, reasonably pretty woman who is exceptionally good domestically?'

Gabriel laughed. 'I'll send them this way if I have, Dorothy, but,' noting David the footman, gazing longingly at Dorothy, he added, 'you never know though, the man of your dreams may be closer than you think.'

Dorothy's eyebrows lifted as she turned her head to see for herself the look David was giving her. 'Are you making cows eyes at me, David Harker?'

David cleared his throat, glanced at Gabriel who nodded to him, and said, 'I might be, yes.'

'Oh!' Dorothy said interested, turning her body towards him, 'I see.'

'Matchmaker,' Mary whispered to Gabriel.

'Well, I want everyone to be as happy as we are.' He lifted her hand to kiss it.

*

When Marianne arrived for work on Friday morning, she was fizzing with delight. Her mother had come home from work from the Trelease's the previous evening with news that Gabriel was home with plans to marry a local woman – though they had not disclosed who it was. *Well, it can only be me he has come back for*, Marianne thought, *for who else would he choose from the local girls around here?* So, she had put her favourite perfume on, much to Ellie's annoyance. Her mood was heightened when Ellie told Marianne that Gabriel Trelease had sent word that he wanted to speak with her in the tearoom after work that day. Marianne could not contain her excitement, and she didn't care a hoot if she was discourteous with the more difficult customers that day – she was going to be married to a gentleman!

*

Gabriel arrived with another gentleman shortly after they had closed. Ellie showed them to a seat inside and asked if they wanted any refreshments, but they refused and asked if both she and Marianne could take a seat with them.

Marianne practically danced to her chair and gave Gabriel her best smile, but he seemed preoccupied with some papers on the table.

'This is my lawyer, Marianne,' Gabriel said seriously. 'He is going to sit with you while you write a statement, retracting all the lies you have told that reporter regarding myself, and Mrs Blackwell.'

'What?' Ellie looked astonished.

'Marianne has told several untruths about Mrs Jenna Blackwell which has blemished her good reputation. This has gone to a hearing where a claimant - namely James's father, is trying to revoke Mrs Blackwell's right to the inheritance her late husband left her. Because of Marianne's actions, Mr Blackwell believes that Jenna only married James for money and has been conducting at least two affairs, one of which is allegedly with me!'

Marianne felt her stomach lurch as Ellie glared at her.

'I must also tell you, Ellie, that Marianne wrote a well-wisher letter to Lyndon FitzSimmons stating much the same story, which caused deep problems between Lyndon and myself, as we are great friends. Not only that, but Marianne wrote a damning note which was found by the police, about my soon-to-be wife, Mary Ellis.'

Marianne's mouth dropped. 'You're marrying *Mary!*' she said flabbergasted.

Ignoring her, Gabriel continued. 'Marianne claimed that Mary had done something criminal, which she had not. I had to take Mary away from Bochym for a while until we could put the record straight.'

Ellie turned to Marianne and folded her arms. 'I would never have believed you could be so nasty, Marianne, if I had not heard this from Gabriel's own mouth. I suggest you write this statement as Gabriel demands and then you can leave these premises forever. What you have done is unforgivable. I will not have you anywhere near my tearoom again. I will not give you a reference and if anyone hereabouts attempts to employ you, I shall speak to them immediately.'

*

On Monday morning, Graham Blackwell arrived at his solicitor's office for a last brief on the hearing the next day, but it was not the briefing he was expecting.

'I'm sorry, Mr Blackwell,' Mr Lennox said, 'it seems that we have been blocked on all sides here. We have a letter of intent from Mrs Judith Jacques to sue you for defamation of her husband's character, and to be honest, we do not have any real evidence to back our allegations - we were just relying on him crumbling in order to save his family.

Edna FitzSimmons has retracted her statement that Mrs Blackwell ruined her marriage – apparently it was annulled through non consummation. As to the allegation that Mrs Blackwell continued her affair during their marriage, Mrs Blackwell denies nothing about her love for Mr Lyndon FitzSimmons or the night she spent with him before he went back to fight in the war. As you know, during war time many such rules were broken, for good reason – and this one act of infidelity, with it being long before she met James, will probably be thrown out.

Marianne Ellis has retracted her statement – saying she was talking out of turn and what she told the reporter was lies. It seems the story that Mrs Blackwell was going to marry Gabriel Trelease was pure fabrication – Gabriel Trelease is set to marry Mary Ellis on the 10th of December. The only one we still have is from a village gossip, Minnie Drago, in Gweek where Mrs Blackwell used to live. As far as my learned friend, Mr Kingthorn tells me, Mrs Blackwell faking her death by drowning and her escape with Mr FitzSimmons was the truth in order for her to get away from her violent first husband. I have a statement of facts from Matthew Bickford, the owner of Trevarno Estate, saying that when Mrs Blackwell sought sanctuary there, she resided in Lyndon FitzSimmons father's house as his housekeeper, while Lyndon FitzSimmons slept in his wagon until he wed the aforementioned wife, Edna.

Graham Blackwell tapped his chin. 'So, if she admits she knew this FitzSimmons chap before she married my son, surely this is evidence that she married James, knowing he was ill, for financial gain - so they could comfortably set up together after his death?'

'I'm afraid not. When Mrs Blackwell married James, she believed FitzSimmons to be dead, and James was not diagnosed with a terminal illness until after the wedding. Also, there is even evidence that once James knew he was dying, and that Mrs Blackwell's first love had returned from the dead, James gave his blessing to them by writing to Mr FitzSimmons to say as much.'

'Do we have a copy of that letter?' Blackwell said gravely.

'No.'

'Ah, then he cannot prove that! It is all just a ploy. I know they have been conducting an affair almost since James died.'

'They have indeed seen each other, but have been watched constantly and though they have attended social events together – they always returned home to their respective houses. Therefore, we have no evidence of them conducting an affair.'

Blackwell was furious. 'But I have no doubt she intends to marry this man, and use the money I need, to set up their nest!'

'Which, I understand, was James's wish.' He handed over James's new novel. 'The fact that James wrote a dedication in his final novel, and I quote, *"Go forth, my darling girl, live life and write the next great love story for me,"* is evidence that he gave that blessing. I suspect hundreds of people will have read it by now. She will not be damned if she does marry FitzSimmons at some point.'

'Argh! I still think we should try,' he said stubbornly. 'Perhaps try to get at least one house and half the money that floozy is raking in. After all, Netherdale Hall was James's ancestral home – his money should go towards saving it and we could plead that. A good son would not want to see his poor father ruined now, would he?'

Mr Lennox shook his head. 'By all accounts you cut him out of *your* will.'

'We can alter that, surely, alter a few dates - write a new will.'

Mr Lennox shook his head again.

'What now?'

'We have another two signed affidavits from a retired Doctor Carmichael and Mr Grant Trelease whose estate bordered yours in Hertfordshire, and where James went to beg for help when you punished him.'

'Those interfering bastards, I warned Carmichael I'd have him struck off if he continued with his allegations.'

'Well, he is retired now and both he and Mr Trelease will both speak against you under oath to say that your punishment amounted to torture on some occasions and that Mr Trelease had to bring Doctor Carmichael several times to the boy's aid. You were hardly the loving father!'

Graham Blackwell slammed his hands on the desk, stood up and paced the room. 'And this is it – I have to give in and let her have everything?'

'I'm afraid so, the case is a nonstarter. There will be no hearing tomorrow.'

'I will be bankrupt at the end of the year if I do not secure that money. Is there no scenario that I could ever gain from my son's wealth?'

'Not unless Mrs Blackwell dies in the very near future, that is before she has a chance to make her own will, or remarries, because once she marries again, her wealth would automatically go to her spouse on her death. As Mrs Blackwell is a fit and healthy young woman – her demise is highly unlikely.'

Graham Blackwell's mouth turned into a cruel smile. *Highly unlikely is it?*

53

After taking the early train to London, Jenna, Gabriel, and Mary parted company - Gabriel to his own house in Kensington and the ladies to Bellevue Gardens.

A welcome hearty aroma of cooking beef greeted the women.

'Mr Jacques requests that you phone him as soon as you get in,' Mrs Hemp informed her. 'I'll show Mrs Ellis to her room.'

Jenna picked up the phone fearing the worst – had more people come forward with damning evidence?

'Jenna?' Christian's voice sounded unusually bright considering what was about to happen the next day.

'Hello, Christian,' she said resignedly.

'I have marvellous news! The case against you has been dropped and the hearing has been cancelled.'

'Pardon?' She flopped on the chair by the phone. 'Dropped completely?'

'Absolutely. I'm so sorry - I could not inform you before you set off to London. I didn't receive the news until midday.'

'But how - why?'

'Most of the people who gave statements have revoked them. Also, someone called Doctor Carmichael had told them he was prepared to give damning evidence to Blackwell's character, and…my wife, would you believe, has told them she would sue them for libel should they attempt to defame my good name.'

'Your wife!'

'Yes. It seems Judith knew all along. I must say, she has been rather marvellous about the whole thing.'

Jenna could hear his voice crack with emotion. 'Christian that is wonderful, I'm so happy and enormously relieved for both of us.'

'Judith would like to meet you for lunch - she says she shares a common bond in saving my life. Shall we say, tomorrow at one and we can celebrate.

*

With Gabriel taking Mary out for the day, Jenna had a rather lovely lunch with Christian and Judith Jacques. After celebrating their good fortune, Jenna decided to walk home, and her thoughts turned to more solid plans for Bellevue Gardens to help people like Emily. It was almost as if she had conjured Emily from thin air, because there she was, standing outside a newsagent, selling her artificial flowers. Jenna quickened her step, but before she could reach her, a kerfuffle broke out. The dreadful one-man-band musician, which had so frightened Lyndon that day, was quarrelling with Emily. He had taken her basket from her, and as she tried to retrieve it, he'd grasped her around her waist and was molesting her breasts.

Furious, Jenna was at her side in an instant. 'Unhand that girl at once,' she demanded.

He bared his teeth at Jenna. 'I'll do what I want with her - she belongs to me.'

'No, I don't!' Emily screamed furiously.

'Unhand her at once!' Jenna bent to retrieve Emily's basket from where he had kicked it, before stepping forward to confront the man. Keeping hold of his captive, his repulsive face, lit with malice, and for a split second, Jenna was reminded of her violent husband Blewett. Shuddering with revulsion, she gave the man a hard slap on his face. The shock made him reel and let Emily go.

Emily staggered backwards, frantically trying to wipe away the disgusting touch of his hands from her breasts.

'Come here, Emily,' Jenna beckoned.

Alerted by the commotion, a policeman arrived on the scene. 'Can I be of any assistance, Madam?'

'You must arrest that man for harassment.' Jenna pointed to the man who had taken off in great haste, clanking and banging in his wake.

'Worry not. He'll be easy enough to locate,' the policeman mused, 'did he harm you in any way, Madam?'

'I'm fine. It's Emily here who has been violated - he stole her basket of work and molested her when she tried to retrieve it.'

The policeman gave Emily a derisory glance. 'She looks fine to me,' he said dismissively.

'Well, she isn't!' Jenna snapped, but the policeman had lost interest, and an incident further down the street had caught his attention – someone had collapsed on the pavement.

'It seems someone is in greater need of my help, so I'll bid you good day, Madam.' He turned to walk away.

'Well, really!' Jenna stamped her foot. 'Are you all right, Emily?'

Emily nodded tearfully.

'Has this happened before?'

She nodded again. 'This is my patch, I sell here, and the fashionable ladies know it, but 'orrible Mr Gifford has started his racket here and has taken my work three times now. That's why I was hiding down the alleyway that day your friend had that funny turn.'

'Oh, bless you, Emily, I'm so sorry for you. Look, why don't you come back with me? I would like to speak with you about an idea I have had.'

'I aint clean, missus. I'll mucky your lovely house and make it smelly if I come back with you.'

'Don't worry, you're very welcome to use my facilities.'

'Oh, ta,' then Emily frowned, 'what's a facility?'

Jenna laughed. 'I'll show you.'

Mrs Hemp gave a welcome smile. 'Emily, you're back!'

'I'm going to show her the bathroom and find her some clothes, Mrs Hemp. I wonder if you could make Emily a sandwich?'

'My pleasure, Mrs Blackwell.'

After running a hot bath, Jenna left Emily to strip and bathe.

'Wash your hair as well,' Jenna said, 'we'll light a fire in the bedroom you slept in last time, so you can dry it. There are towels there for you and a house coat. Leave your clothes in the bathroom and I'll find some clea...' she paused to correct herself, 'some nice things for you to wear.'

As Jenna collected fresh clothes for Emily, she smiled at the joyous noises coming from the bathroom. There were splashes and sighs, giggles, and squeaks of pleasure. When she emerged, Emily's face was glowing pink.

'There was a rare good scum in that bath, but it cleaned off with that sponge you had in there.'

'Thank you, Emily.' Jenna made a mental note to dispose of the sponge later. 'I've laid clothes on the bed for you. Once your hair has dried, come down to the parlour for tea and sandwiches.'

Emily stood with the towel clutched to her neck, suddenly her face constricted, and she burst into tears.

'Oh, Emily, don't cry.'

'Aint nobody ever been so kind to me before,' she sobbed.

'Well, all that will change from now on.'

Jenna closed the door to the bedroom and smiled. It wasn't so long ago when Hillary had done the self-same thing to Jenna when she arrived at James's house in an impoverished state. Hillary had been her rock throughout the good and the bad days. Always one to make her smile, she could not have managed this life without her.

*

When Emily finally came down to the parlour, Jenna's smiled at the transformation.

'Come and sit down.'

'Thank you, missus.'

'Emily, we're friends now, please call me Jenna.'

Emily's eyes sparkled with joy.

'Where are your parents?'

'They are dead - died last year. Father came home on leave from the war, but then the flu got him, Mother nursed him, but he died, and then she caught it and died - both gone in a fortnight.'

'I'm terribly sorry to hear that. What did your Mother do for a living?'

'She worked downstairs in a haberdashery as a seamstress. I worked there too, but one of the other girls I worked with caught the flu and died and the others blamed me for bringing the sickness to them from home. Mrs Winman, the shop owner had to let me go. So I lost my parents, home, and job in the space of three weeks.'

'So, if you lost your home, where do you live?'

Emily sniffed and shrugged. 'Nowhere, everywhere - anywhere I can.'

'You're terribly thin.'

'I don't get enough to eat, see. Especially since 'orrible Mr Gifford came to my patch with his racket and keeps stealing my flowers.'

'How do you afford to make the flowers?'

'I don't steal the stuff, you know?' she said emphatically, 'I make 'em from the money I get, I keep a penny for a bun and buy my stuff from Mrs Winman at the haberdashery - off cuts and the like. Mr Goodman from the iron mongers lets me have the wire cheap as well. He fought with my dad in the war you see!'

Jenna nodded. 'Emily, do you know who I am?'

'No, missus, I mean Jenna.'

'I'm an artist. I have just had a successful exhibition – that was where I was going when I first encountered you.'

Emily listened intently, not knowing if she had to comment or not.

'I've been fortunate to marry well, although I'm widowed now, but I'm a successful artist.'

'Might you want to buy some more of me flowers then?' Emily asked hopefully.

'I'd like to do more than that.'

'You want to paint me?'

Jenna smiled. 'Possibly, but what I actually have in mind is to take you under my wing.'

Emily pursed her lips. 'What like, adopt me?'

Jenna laughed openly. 'I think perhaps you're a little old to be adopted. How old are you?'

'Seventeen, just gone.'

'I want to help you, Emily.'

'Why?'

'Because you helped me, and I want to return the favour.'

Emily bit her lip for a moment. 'How you gonna help me?'

Jenna began to tell her about her plans for Bellevue Gardens. 'I take it you will know other young women who could benefit from my help?'

'I do, yes.' Emily could hardly contain her excitement.

'You will all be given new clothes to wear. I shall employ someone to teach the girls to read and write if they need help. You will all learn how to keep house, how to cook and sew and hopefully we can get everyone into gainful employment.'

'It sounds lovely,' Emily said glassy eyed.

Well then, I need to go back to Cornwall on Thursday, but if you want to help Mrs Hemp and myself set things up, I'm sure we can get things sorted before then. I'll pay you to help Mrs Hemp. You won't need to sleep or work on the streets ever again.'

*

On Friday the 28th of November, Lyndon was on the train home to Cornwall and looking forward to sleeping in his own bed at last – something he had not done for nigh on three months. The time away in Devon had worked - he was sure of it. Arthur Hurst had put him through many tests, and even had him shoot a gun without him turning into a gibbering wreck. Hopefully, his life could get back to some sort of normality now. He and Jenna had exchanged letters every week he had been away, but Lyndon had a strange feeling that Jenna was holding something back from him. Her letters felt different to the upbeat letters she wrote to him when he was at the front. Would he be coming home to arrange his wedding to her or was there going to be something else to keep them apart? He would know soon enough.

At Helston station, he stepped off the train and onto the platform. The steam from the train billowed out, obscuring his view, so he stood for a moment waiting for it to clear, and when it did, he saw something that made his heart sing. Jenna was waiting, and she was smiling.

In full view of everyone, she ran to him, put her arms around him and kissed him full on the mouth. 'Are you cured?' she asked.

'Time will tell,' he said dropping his bag and wrapping his arms around her. 'Goodness, but it's good to see you. Are we all right to be seen in public?'

She nodded. 'I have a long story to tell you, but first I'm taking you somewhere. Come,' she beckoned.

'Trevarno, I hope?' he said wearily.

'No, not yet. I need you to come somewhere with me first.'

Half an hour later, Jenna drove them into Gweek. She parked the car outside Barleyfield Farm and reached for his hand. They walked up the meadow – the ground now shorn and resting for winter - and came to the centre of the field where Lyndon had first met Jenna. It had rained during the night, so the ground was soft and wet underfoot, but the November sun held a little warmth and lit the valley of Gweek in a pale-yellow hue.

'It was here on Wednesday 7th of August 1912, that I lay in the sunshine amongst cornflowers and long grass and opened my eyes to see you for the first time, Lyndon.'

'It is a date imprinted on my memory too. It was the day I fell hopelessly in love with the most beautiful woman I had ever seen.' His eyes twinkled.

'Well, seven years, three months and twenty-two days have passed since then – not that I am counting or anything,' she laughed gently. 'We have been through many heartaches and separations, but our love has stood the test of time. So, please will you ask me again the question you asked at the harvest dance all those years ago?'

Lyndon gave a half smile, scratched the stubble on his chin and said, 'Well, now, let me think, what was that question?'

'Ah, well if you can't remember,' she teased as she began to skip away from him.

He caught her hand and pulled her back. 'Oh no, you're not getting away this time.' He knelt on one knee, feeling the damp seep through his trousers. 'Jenna Trevone, love of my life, woman of my dreams, will you please marry me now?'

'I will,' she leant forward, cupped his handsome face, and kissed him passionately. 'But you missed something out when you were describing me!' He tipped his head, and she took his hands and placed them on her tummy. 'You need to include 'mother of your child,' so we need to look sharp and set a date – we have a baby FitzSimmons on the way.'

Getting up off his knee, he wrapped her in his arms. 'Oh, Jen! Can this be true?'

She nodded happily and they laughed together as he picked her up to swing her around.

54

On the 10th of December, Gabriel and Mary married at St Winwaloe Church, Church Cove Gunwalloe. It was a fine affair despite the stormy weather. As the wind howled and the roof tiles chattered, they exchanged vows, while little Robbie, never one to miss an opportunity to be centre of attention, stood between them dressed in his smart pageboy suit. Their wedding breakfast, to their delight, was held in the French drawing room at Bochym Manor. Sarah and Peter thought it would be fitting to hold it there as Gabriel had brought the room back to its former glory. It also meant that Mrs Blair could produce the cake and a wonderful buffet for her long-time assistant, and all her friends amongst the staff at Bochym could join in the celebration. Once the happy couple had exchanged a kiss, they rushed out of the church hand in hand, towards the wedding car, laughing as they were buffeted by the wind and rain.

*

Watching the long cortege of wedding vehicles begin to make their way up the lane through Poldhu golf course and onto Bochym Manor, was Marianne Enys. Drenched in rain and self-pity, the only reason she had hauled her sorry self over to Church Cove was that she'd heard Jake Treen was attending Mary and Gabriel's wedding.

Ousted from her job, ostracised from friends and everyone she worked with, coupled with little chance now of finding a gentleman to take her on – she supposed Jake would have to do. People might like her again if she chose a local lad to settle down with, especially as he had an excellent reputation for being a genuinely nice man and a very good thatcher. He hadn't appeared yet from the church, but Guy Blackthorn's wagon was parked outside the church gates so it would only be a matter of time.

When she saw him appear and open the door to the wagon, she stepped forward.

'Hello, Jake.' Giving him her most brilliant smile. 'I wondered if perhaps you would still like to walk out with me one day?'

'No, Marianne.' Jake stared at her in astonishment. 'That is the very last thing in the world that I would want to do.' He turned as Agnes Blackthorn ran out of the church shielding under her coat from the rain, laughing as she made for the open wagon door. Once Agnes was settled in the wagon seat, he closed the door and gave one last chilling look at Marianne. He was about to get into the driver's seat when he stopped and walked over to her.

Marianne's heart lifted – she'd done it – she'd won him over, she knew he would not be able to resist her, but when he got to her, he said, 'You can easily judge the character of a person by how they treat those who can do nothing for them. I was not good enough for you once, and you, Marianne, are certainly not good enough for me now. Everyone who knows you, knows what you have done. I suggest you move a long, long way from here and start again. Only this time, learn how to become a decent human being.' He turned on his heel and left her in the rain.

*

After everyone raised their glasses to toast Mary and Gabriel's health and future happiness, Hillary turned to Lyndon and Jenna.

'In fourteen days, on Christmas Eve, we will be doing the same for you two,' she said raising her glass again. 'I'm so looking forward to organising your wedding breakfast at Trevarno, now you have decided to hold it there.'

'Thank you, Hillary,' Jenna said. 'We had thought at first it would be just a small wedding and buffet back at Loe House, but as all James's usual Christmas visitors want to come down for the wedding, which is nice that they are giving us their blessing, they have asked if they can stay at Loe House for the festive season. We're grateful for your offer, and we are so looking forward to spending our wedding night in our new home, Namskerris Cottage on the estate.'

Hillary clasped her hands together in glee. 'I am so happy we are going to be neighbours. Without Glen by my side down here, you are the next best 'partner in crime'. We are going to have so much fun.'

Lyndon and Matthew exchanged nervous glances.

'Oh, stop it you two,' Hillary slapped them both playfully. 'I'm only kidding,' she said, winking surreptitiously at Jenna.

It was growing dark outside, and the weather was worsening, so everyone decided to set off home before trees came down to block the roads. After a flurry of kisses and goodbyes, Lyndon got into Matthew and Hillary's car, and Jenna into her own to drive to their respective homes.

*

At Bochym Manor, only the Trelease family were left to say goodbye to their hosts. Gabriel and Mary were to spend their wedding night at the manor, and Grant and Catherine Trelease were to take a very disgruntled Robbie home with them.

As Mary and Gabriel waved them goodbye and watched the car lights disappear, Mary took a sudden intake of breath.

'Whatever is the matter, Mary?' Gabriel asked anxiously.

'My bag, with my clothes – they are still in Jenna's car, and she's gone home. I put them in the boot when we set off to church.'

'Don't worry, I'll go and fetch them in the morning.' Gabriel smiled

'But I need things out of it now! The medication I take to heal the lining of my stomach is in the bag - if I don't take it before bedtime, I get terrible stomach gripes,' she cried.

'It's all right, sweetheart, I'll follow Jenna and get it for you. I shall return shortly.' He smiled and kissed her tenderly.

*

Jenna was glad when the drive was over as she pulled up outside Loe House - she had been buffeted quite violently on the road and had a few hair-raising episodes when branches of trees fell on the car roof. After enjoying Mary's company for nigh on four weeks, she did not relish entering the empty house. Still, it wouldn't be for much longer. Collecting her bag, she slammed the car door shut, dashed to the door, and fumbled with her keys, suddenly, despite the howling wind whipping around her, she had the distinct impression that she was not alone. With the key in the lock, she turned and listened, but there was no one in sight. Opening the door, she tried the light switch, but the electricity was off with the storm. Fiddling in the dark for the oil lamp, which was kept in the hall for such occasions, she lit the wick, held the lamp high and stepped into the lounge. A sudden movement behind her set every fibre of her body on edge and then a searing pain to the back of her head propelled her forwards. Vomit rose in her throat as she fell to the ground, staying conscious long enough to see the oil lamp smash and the curtains ignite – and then everything went black!

*

Rather than go down the rutted, muddy track past the Poldhu golf course, which had been almost unpassable earlier that day, Gabriel took the longer main road to Gunwalloe fishing cove. As he turned into the lane towards Loe House, a figure appeared before him and then ran towards the sea. Gabriel's breath caught – was he seeing a ghost? It was then he noticed the flames licking up the inside of the windows of Jenna's house.

*

Graham Blackwell ran like the wind, cursing himself for being seen, but confident that no one would recognise him, anyway, he would be away from here just as soon as he could get back to his car which was parked on the Penrose road a mile down the coast. He would have taken the coast path, which was easier underfoot, but decided the shingle beach would hide his footprints better. What he hadn't banked on, was that it was like walking in treacle. He seemed to take one step forwards only to slip two back. He moved closer to the water's edge where the shingle seemed to be more stable, but he'd not walked twenty yards before a wave rushed up and took him off his feet. The icy cold sea took his breath away as he felt the gravel beneath him move alarmingly. He scrambled back to his feet, soaked and freezing, only to be knocked down again and pulled further into the wave. Gaining no purchase now with his hands or his feet, sheer panic set in as the next wave pulled him back into the surf and began to tumble him over and over. Coughing and spluttering for breath he shouted for help. His arms splayed and grasped for some sort of hold, as another wave engulfed him filling his mouth with choking sea water and Graham Blackwell disappeared into the inky black ocean.

*

Gabriel ran to Jenna's front door and found it locked. With all his strength he put his shoulder to it, but still, it would not budge. Running to the window he could see the fire inside was well alight, so he picked up a garden chair and threw it at the window, shattering it. Behind him, people from the village who had seen the flames were arriving with buckets.

'I can't get in, the door is locked, and Jenna is inside,' he yelled at the crowd. 'Someone, help me through this window.'

Two burly men lifted him up and passed him through the broken window. Scrambling around by the light of the flames, Gabriel found Jenna unconscious on the floor by the door. Her clothes were alight, so taking his coat off, Gabriel threw it over her to dampen the flames down.

A fearful battering at the front door made it suddenly give way, splintering in its wake, as the first of many people with buckets of water entered to douse the fire. Carefully Gabriel picked Jenna's seemingly lifeless body up and stepped over the splintered shards of glass and wood to carry her outside.

Celia Inman had arrived in her dressing gown. 'Oh, good god! What's happened?' she cried.

'I think somebody did this deliberately. I saw someone running away.'

'But who would do such a thing.'

'I think it was Graham Blackwell – James's father! I'm taking her to hospital in Helston. I'm afraid this doesn't look good.'

*

Mary had said her goodnights to everyone in the kitchen and had gone up to her room but hadn't taken her wedding dress off because her nightgown was in her bag. It had been over an hour since Gabriel had left to get her bag, and with the storm howling outside, a curl of unease settled in her tummy that something awful had happened to him. It was another half hour before the telephone rang at the manor and she ran down the stairs, knowing it was something to do with Gabriel. Mary slowed her pace and feared the worst, when she heard the Countess gasp and say, 'Oh good god, no!'

*

Gabriel paced the hospital corridor. He had made two phone calls, one to put Mary's mind at ease and the second to Matthew which in turn he knew would send the fear of god through Lyndon. It took Matthew no more than a quarter of an hour to drive Lyndon to the hospital, where he burst through the doors shouting her name.

'Gabriel,' Lyndon said, his face stricken, 'where's Jenna, where is she?'

'Please, sir, lower your voice,' a nurse tried to calm him, 'there are people very poorly in here. Now, the doctor is expecting you, could you follow me,' she said gravely.

*

Leaving Lyndon and Matthew at the hospital, Gabriel set off to Loe House to collect the bag from Jenna's car for Mary. The police and fire brigade were there now. The fire was out, and fortunately, the damage seemed to be contained to the front room. After giving a quick statement to the police, Gabriel set off back to Bochym Manor and Mary. He felt terrible - his clothes were ruined, he had burns to his hands and a choking cough that no amount of brandy could ease.

'You're a hero, Gabriel,' Mary soothed as she gently tended his wounds. 'You always seemed to be there at the right time to save someone.'

He lifted his stricken face. 'I'm not sure I was there in time today though.'

55
Christmas Eve

The churchyard at St Winwaloe, Gunwalloe, was covered in a thin crust of frost, penetrating the boots of the many people who stood, snuffling from emotion, as well as the cold, around the newly erected flower strewn headstone. A lone robin sang from the bare branches of the great oak tree, and a restless sea crashed against the shore two hundred yards away.

'For goodness' sake you lot, pull yourself together,' Hillary chided, 'this is meant to be a celebration of life!' Everyone shifted uncomfortably as they sniffed back tears. Hillary thumped her fists into her sides. 'James would not want his friends to be in tears. Now, pull yourself together, and as for you two,' she turned to Lyndon and Jenna, 'the vicar is waiting to marry you. The sooner it is done, the better, and we can all go back to Trevarno for the fantastic wedding breakfast we have laid on.'

While James's friends peeled away from the gravestone, Jenna pulled a red rose from her bouquet and placed it on the mound.

'Thank you for everything you've done for me, James. Your memory will never die as long as I walk this earth.' She kissed her fingers and pressed them to his name.

'Yes. Rest in peace, my friend.' Lyndon put his arm around Jenna. 'I promise I'll look after Jenna for you,' he said, safe in the knowledge that Graham Blackwell could no longer harm her, as his body had washed up in Dollar Cove five days after the fire.

It could have all been so different. Lyndon had kept vigil by Jenna's hospital bed for four days as she lay in a coma. He'd seen the worried look on the doctor's face who feared she would not wake up, but love prevailed, and his care and devotion brought her through. She had sustained burns to her right hand and arm, and if not for

Gabriel's quick thinking in smothering the flames before they engulfed her body, she might not have survived.

Lyndon smiled with love at his bride to be. Dressed in a cream gown with silk embroidered bracken *fronds* to the bodice, the matching cloak, its hood trimmed with cream marabou feathers, framed Jenna's happy face. Though he knew she still suffered terrible headaches from the blow to her head, only the bandaged hand showed evidence of the burns she had sustained that terrible night in the fire before Gabriel Trelease so dramatically rescued her.

'Come, my love.' Lyndon's fingers curled gently around Jenna's hand. 'It's time to write that next great love story for James.'

BOCHYM MANOR

Please note, Bochym Manor is a private family home, and the house is not open to the public.

⁓ ⁓

Please, if you can, share your love of this book by writing a short review on Amazon.
Thank you. Ann x

⁓ ⁓

Printed in Great Britain
by Amazon